MASTER!
MASTER, HAVE A CARE!
IT COMES!

The words were cut off with a shriek and the stench of death and waiting death mingled in Dammon's head. He howled a battle cry that he did not recognize, and his feet pounded forward across punishingly hard rock. Hot wind plastered his hair against his brow, and pain slashed suddenly across his back. He staggered with the impact and lashed out behind. But it was already too late. The beast was on him, the dragon powered by blood lust and the need to destroy the hated enemy—man...

Also by Esther M. Friesner

Harlot's Ruse

Published by
POPULAR LIBRARY

THE SILVER MOUNTAIN

ESTHER M. FRIESNER

POPULAR LIBRARY

An Imprint of Warner Books, Inc.

A Warner Communications Company

For Jake and Jerry Stutzman, with thanks and love.

PROLOGUE

In Mar-Halira

The princess Devra waited, the silver looking-glass in her hand. Waves of raven hair cloaked her shoulders and shimmered with blue highlights where the soft luster of the candles fell. She smiled as she looked into the mirror, but it was not her face she saw.

A clatter of servants shod in wooden pattens sounded in the corridor outside her bedchamber door. Shadows danced in sarabands of smoke above the golden candles. A sound of hushed voices from the bedchamber's inner room disturbed her thoughts. Impatiently, she clapped her hands and the whispering ceased. She returned to the thoughts of the mirror.

"It must be begun soon," she murmured. "Soon. If he does not come tonight, if he has failed..." She bit her lip to stop the sudden flow of fearful thoughts. Already she felt the chill of prison walls, the shivery scuttling of creatures not hers to command. Where was Lord Maldonar? Surely he had had time enough to perform his task. What reason could he have for dawdling, for keeping her waiting?

"He grows arrogant," she said fiercely to the empty room.

"And will grow more arrogant still," said a voice of air.

The princess Devra whirled around, holding the silver mirror high. "Who calls?" she demanded.

"Your servant," returned the voice, but there was mockery beneath the humble tone.

"Then you forget yourself! You speak when I call you. Who gave you the right to interrupt my meditations? You shall be punished for this!"

"Alas..." The voice came as a drifting sigh. "I only meant to serve you, my mistress, with a warning."

"To warn me of Lord Maldonar? I know he is arrogant. I am on my guard. But I need him. You know I need him."

"For the present." The voice was fading away into the higher darkness of the room. "For a time."

A heavy tread, strong legs cased in leather riding boots, sounded like approaching thunder on the stairs to Devra's chamber. She heard his voice ordering the guards aside, saw the door swing wide to admit him, smelled the reek of blood still clinging to his clothes.

"Is it done?"

Lord Maldonar grinned. "Done." The oak door swung shut behind him, moved as if by the wind. The faint creak of the black iron hinges made him start. "I shall never grow used to your ways, my dear," he said, shaking his head.

The princess Devra laughed deep in her throat and came across the floor toward him. Carpets of exquisite workmanship, red silken weaves embroidered with gold thread, caressed her naked feet. Her thick black hair covered her body like a cloak of shadows, her only ornament a small amethyst teardrop on a silver chain, violet fire between her breasts.

"You have done well," she said, twining her arms around his neck.

Lord Maldonar inhaled deeply the honeyed scent that rose from her hair, her flesh, and his head began to spin.

"More of your magics," he muttered. "Nothing human distilled the perfume you wear." Old tales of enchantresses filled his brain. For a moment he was a boy again, playing at lordship in his father's castle and hearing the old men tell their tales of sorcery, of fair women who vanished on dark roads, of changeling children, of evil spirits that took appealing form to work their black doings. Lord Maldonar shuddered and tried to draw away from the princess, but a snare of fragrance stole across his senses and made him burn for her. She smiled at the force of his kisses, the urgency of his hands, the frantic haste with which he swept her up and carried her to the inner chamber, where the bed of starlight waited.

Later, when the golden candles were hollow, smoking waxy stubs in their sockets, she turned toward the sleeping Lord Maldonar and studied his features by the watery moonlight. She had chosen him for many reasons—his strength, his ambition, his weak, malleable nature. Now she realized that she had been weak herself. His looks, too, had made her choose him. Hair nearly as black as her own curled thickly on his head. His skin was the tanned bronze of a fighting man, but if he tarried indoors too long, it would become as milky as hers. Beneath his dark-fringed eyelids his eyes glowed icy blue.

"A memento," she said to herself. "And why not? They say the dead can live again." A flicker of uneasiness struck her as she lay there gazing at him. He said he had done the thing, but what proof did he have? Bloody clothes? Easily gotten. What proof? She needed proof.

Naked as a sword, she rose from the bed and went swiftly from the room. In the outer chamber a tapestry of fat, silly sprites at play hung before hidden door. She passed through it and up the winding stairway it concealed. The upper room held nothing but a shining mahogany table with something draped in black on it. Her fingers plucked the ebon veil away and a shining filled the chamber.

"Aglora!" she called, laying two fingers on the table. There was a rushing noise and a pair of green eyes floated in the midst of the brilliant light.

"My mistress would have?"

"Proof," she said urgently. "Lord Maldonar says he has done it, but I must know. I must *know*!"

"If he has done it," the eyes answered in a drowsy drone, "then you will know. And if he has not done it, then you will also know, for your brother will return."

"I must know *now*. Have I brought you here to ask me riddles? If Dammon has escaped, if he lives, then you and yours will suffer for it as well as I. Do you think your masters will be pleased with you if you do not help me?"

The green eyes blinked once. "I serve you to the best of my abilities, my lady. I can do no more. You forget that we are of the air, and our strengths fade the closer we come to earth. Those are the boundaries of my powers. I can only see so far."

"I swear," said the princess, a terrible fierceness in her voice. "I swear by blood and bone, by air and summoning, that one day I will build for you and your people a bridge that will span from earth to air but will be free of all earth-taint. And by that bridge your powers—and mine—will never again know any limitation."

"Limits are set by other powers." The eyes floated as if dreaming. "Other powers not of earth or air."

"Do not presume to lecture me. I have the old books, and I can read. But I stand by the oath I have given. A bridge, Aglora! A bridge such as neither the air nor the earth has ever seen!"

The eyes closed slowly, opened gracefully, a gesture of silent acquiescence.

"Now . . . tell me what you see."

"I see caverns," said the eyes. "They are faint, for they lie far beneath the surface. I see men and monsters. I see death."

"Men?" Devra leaned forward eagerly. "How many men? How many dead men?"

"More than one death. One man walks away."

"That will be Lord Maldonar. Go on."

"Now I see one who is close kin to men yet not a man. The dwellers beneath, the children of the stone. He comes to see what has happened. He crouches over the dead men. He takes a stone flask from his belt and touches their faces with some drops from it, but they do not move. He scrambles away."

"Enough!" cried the princess. The silver glow outlined the exultation on her face. "Enough, by the horns! You have done very well for me, Aglora. You have shown me all I wished to know. If not even a Gryagi could revive them, the dead are dead indeed. You have leave to go."

"I serve you," purred the eyes, and vanished.

The princess Devra returned to the bed of starlight and took her place beside Lord Maldonar again. He slept undisturbed, like a tired dog. Before she too closed her eyes, she stroked his cheek once, in gratitude. He had not lied to her, and she owed him all that she was, or would be. In her mood of thanks, she removed the slender dagger from beneath her pillow and placed it back in its sheath in the ropes supporting the down-filled mattress. She would not kill him yet. Those who serve well should be saved.

"Besides," she told herself in the moment before sleep. "The child should know its father." Although it was too early, she thought she felt it move once in her belly. A baby's laughter came out of the darkness.

PART I

In Neb-Halira

He thought he had awakened to death.

Gray light that was not light surrounded him and the air was cold. Gray and cold, that was how the land of the dead was spoken of by the bards, the land of sorrow, Hori-Halira.

In his mind he repeated the name the poets had given to the awful land of shadow. *Hori-Halira, Hori-Halira* . . . the sound was like weird music, such a fair sound for such a dismal place. They were strange men, the poets.

Then he felt the pain. It struck him like a burning arrow and spread scarlet fingers across his chest. The right side of his head throbbed and ached horribly. The gray light shivered to crimson while points of yellow brilliance flashed before his eyes like dying stars.

This is not death, he thought. How could I feel pain if I were dead? And yet something is pressing me down, like the weight of grave-earth. I can see nothing but shadows. What has happened to me?

His mind reached out in the darkness. The pain gave him new hope. Slowly, like a cat stretching in the sun, he urged the farthest limits of his brain to touch the dreaming borders of his body. If he could move at all, if he could make the smallest voluntary motion, then perhaps there was a chance.

A chance for what?

The question blinked across his brain. *Can the dead move? Not on the earth, but in their own land, who is to say that the dead cannot walk and talk and feel pain? What man ever entered Hori-Halira and returned to tell us what the dead do? For all your efforts, you may still be dead.*

His eyes grew accustomed to the dim light. The pain in his side dwindled to a sudden throbbing to match the rhythmic pulsing in his head. His thoughts were too disturbing to follow down. If he were dead, he had no desire to know it. He would try getting to his feet.

He felt his right hand move obediently at the brain's summons. It tightened to a fist and closed around an icy, hard rounded object. The hilt of a sword, said his brain. It is the hilt of your sword. His hand found its well-loved and remembered grip around the mighty hilt. He tried to raise the blade.

The weight still pressed across his chest, pinning his right arm as well. His left hand was free and reached for the thing that kept him down. He felt a bulk like the trunk of a young tree, except that no bark ever felt like that. It too was cold, like the sword hilt. His neck hairs bristled with involuntary fear at the touch.

Blindly, he exerted himself, shoved at the thing. To his surprise, it rolled limply off him and fell to one side with a muffled thud. He was free. He knelt, his swordblade scraping the stone, and tried to see what had held him.

The smell of the dead dragon came to him before his eyes could focus at the immense, lifeless body. In the darkness of that place, the massive scaly back looked like a range of mountains. The creature's tail had pinioned him, but now it was powerless. He stood up and trod carefully around the monster's corpse, still dazed, compelled to see its face.

You have slain a dragon, said his inner voice. *There are few such creatures left, fewer men brave enough to fight them. Fewer still survive.*

Pride swelled his chest as he gazed at the dead green eyes, the lolling forked tongue, the yellowed fangs that still gleamed like sickle moons. Behind the pride there surged a second emotion, and it rushed over him, irresistible as a thunderstorm, driving out all thoughts of glory. The beast he saw was dead.

Its blood gleamed dark on his swordblade. This was death, death he had dealt, and only the living could kill. Another's death proved his life. He was alive.

Alive! He savored the word. I have killed a dragon, and I am alive. When I return with the proof of it, men will praise me. Women will tell their children tales of me. I shall sit with heroes, and they shall speak of—of—

His thoughts froze. A pod of blackness burst in his belly. A sailor whose small, doomed ship teeters at the apex of a wave before plunging down into the hungry trough of the sea would know that hollow, horrible feeling; overwhelming; chill; inexorable. Cold-panic sweat starred his brow. He clutched his sword with both hands and raised it high, for a second kill, but the terrible thing that menaced him had no heart to pierce, no head to sever. It was the final emptiness, the last horror: to be so alone. He was alone in darkness with the dead. That was all he knew; no more.

Nothing more!

He did not even know his own name.

He looked around with desperate eyes, vainly trying to wrest clues from the shadows. Was he the only human creature here? Had he come with other men? Were they alive, dead, fled? Would they return? How had he come, on horseback? What man faces dragons without warhorse and lance and battle spear? He held the sword close to his eyes, conning it for some hint of his identity. Was there a name scratched on the blade? A heraldic crest set in the pommel?

Then he saw the dead. They lay on the far side of the monster, sprawled like rag dolls. One was no more than a boy— a page, perhaps— who had come away from his mother's irritating, solicitous fussings to be slashed open, neck to groin, with a clawstroke. He lay on his side, one leg pulled up as if settling for sleep, arms outflung. *Be careful, son. Please be careful.* The words hung in the cavern air. *Oh, Mother! I'm not your baby anymore!* No; not anymore.

The other was a man. He lay face upward. There was no blood on his body beyond a wide dried brown smear at the corner of his mouth. No breath, no heartbeat; the ribs were crushed. A tangle of black curls made the dead man look like an overgrown child. His pale skin was as fine as any lady's, and he wore rich clothes. The moment of death had left him wide-eyed. As a final service to the dead man, the living one lowered the lids over those horribly staring eyes, so blue, so very blue.

There was nothing about the dead to tell the living man his name. His sword was only a plain sword. He might have stolen it. For all he knew, it was the dead man's sword. There was an empty scabbard at the corpse's side, but who knew how the dragon had fallen, whether there was another sword hidden beneath that huge body? Or two? Or none? He examined his clothing for a clue. Not much was left of it after the battle. He and the dead man wore similar attire: plain leather sandals, a short tunic of the softest blue wool, unadorned black hose, all of the highest quality. Through the rents in his tunic, he saw and felt the fine metal mesh of light mail. So he had come to this place expecting trouble. It was not much to know.

Well, he told himself, first I must find my way out of this cavern. First I must take the trophy, then find my way out.

He took a hunting dagger from his belt and knelt beside the dragon. With the swift skill of one who had done the same thing many times, he sliced the monster's rubbery flesh and extracted the four talons of the right forepaw. They were tipped black. Maybe this was the same claw that had killed the boy. The thought of exacting even so small a vengeance comforted him. A thin, shiny trim of blue satin hung in a tattered loop from his sleeve. He tore it free and strung the talons, then tied them around his neck. The dragon's claws clattered together like gibbet bones in the wind.

Trophy taken, he cast his eyes around the rocky chamber and tried to recall how he had come there. Three passageways yawned at the far end of the cave, all equally dark, all equally possible. The wanderer peered down each, and each became the mirror of his mind—empty, unfamiliar. A small voice in his head laughed bitterly.

He studied the cavern floor. There was not even the faintest trace of the dragon's tracks on the flat stone. Should he look for flakes of shed scales? What signs would a dragon leave?

At least I know that I am no master huntsman, he said to himself. They can follow any quarry over bare rock and find a trail.

His eyes gave him no clues for choosing the right way, so he stood at the mouth of each passage and listened, then sniffed the air. All reeked of the cold, reptilian stench that was dragon spoor. The dead beast had frequented all the tunnels in that underground warren. It might have had many dens or many hidden rooms of dragon's gold, but no wise beast—a beast with not a single natural enemy—would keep a lair with more than one entrance. One entrance was easiest to guard. Rabbits had several routes out of their burrows, and field mice too, but a dragon had no need for emergency escapes. Only one door led to the surface. He had to find the one.

As he stood there, he felt a gentle touch on his cheek as if a feather brushed it, or the ghost of a feather. He held his breath and waited, willing it to come again. A second touch confirmed the first. A breeze, and coming from the middle passageway.

Moving air means fresh air, he thought. And fresh air means freedom. I'll follow it.

The small voice laughed again.

The chosen path descended, then climbed. It ended in a cavern larger than the one where he had left the dragon's corpse to rot. (*And the others? The others?* More harsh laughter.) Frozen waterfalls of stone plunged green-golden into stone basins from the tops of stony cliffs. White pillars like dancing goddesses reared themselves, rank after rank, balancing the vaulted ceiling on their heads as they whirled, motionless, a mystery. From somewhere came the slow sound of water dripping, echoing in the silence.

The breeze was lost in the vast rocky hall. Now he chose the patient, plopping sound of living water as his guide. A golden half light radiated from the ribby walls, an impossible light such as men see in dreams. He ran through it, tracing the sound of water, while the pillared goddesses seemed to bend their rigid bodies to see him run. A tunnel opened in front of him and he plunged into it. The steady drop, drop, drop sounded louder in his ears.

The water was illusion. He never found it. The siren song of falling droplets led him on, from one cavern to the next, up chimneyways of black stone and down ramps of yellow rock. Once he paused and pressed his parched mouth against the thin, shining trickle of moisture seeping down stone walls rosy red as blood. He did little more than wet his lips. His throat burned and thirsted.

Time changed from minutes to steps, from steps to stones. A wall of glassy quartz reflected one cavern into a hundred copies of itself. He stopped and saw his own face in the murky natural mirror and shuddered. A thick white scar ran from the bushy red hair above his right temple all the way down to his chin. It was not a handsome face or a wise one. Above all, he felt a coldly certain sensation in his belly that it was not the face of a well-born man. Cloudy memories of similar faces came to him; peasant faces, all with the same hard features, coarse skin, eyes the color of earth.

The face of the dead man flashed across his eyes. It made him feel a plaintive longing for so much beauty, now lost. He must have been my master, he told himself. Now my master is dead. May his spirit find peace.

He no longer ran through the halls of rock. He was too tired, and his old hurts were sharper with every step. Time could not penetrate underground. He lost all sense that time had ever existed. With no sun to set, no stars to rise over the rim of the world, how could there be hours or days or years for the counting? He began to wish that he had died.

Habit—and the fear that if he stopped, he would not be able to start walking again—made him go on. He passed beneath an arch of stone like the gaping maw of a sea monster and followed a winding tunnel in utter blackness, using his hands to guide him. The half light of the caverns flickered just ahead of him, and he emerged into yet another wide stone chamber.

He sank down, panting. This was smaller than the other caverns and plainer. It had the look of a room hewn out by hands, not by water. The side walls had been cut into a series of niches, and in each one his fatigue-blurred eyes glimpsed the rough shapes of vaguely human images.

A temple, he thought. How many ages since the world was born until men began to build homes for their gods? How many ages since this one was raised here, far from the light of day, used, abandoned? Who were those statues? What gods did they represent, with what powers?

Exhaustion made him giddy. He had gone too long without the sound of a human voice. Now he spoke aloud, calling on the spirits of the place in desperation.

"Gods!" The echoes brought back the word a score of times, rebounding from every crevice in the rock. "You guardians of this place, hear me! If you were once my gods, if I have forgotten you, but as you are the gods of some person somewhere, hear me! Accept my worship and my prayers. This gray realm is yours; I am a wanderer through it. Save me, set me free of it, send me back to the daylight! Or if I must die, let death come soon." The gods gave no sign. They were waiting for something; he could guess what. He held out his sword. "Take this in sacrifice." To say that made him ache more deeply than any wound. "Let me go." It was a child's soft, tentative plea.

He could not rise. No strength was left in his limbs. He brandished the blade overhead one last time, then stretched it out toward the images he could not reach. The cave floor tipped and tilted beneath him and the sword went clattering across the stone as he collapsed forward, unconcious.

A final echo of the fallen sword died on the subterranean air. All was quiet in the temple chamber. The nameless man lay still, even when he found himself awake once more. This time it was worse than coming to with the dragon's tail holding him down. This time his own body pinned him, helpless, to the ground; weariness itself. The enemy was in his bones.

I shall die here, he thought. Now I shall die.

Hands touched his shoulder. A harsh gabble of voices filled his head. He let himself be turned over, like a newborn baby, and gazed up into the ashy face of one of the stone images. But it was not stone. The thin, crusty lips moved and spoke, the obsidian eyes flashed and sparkled. Making an effort to turn his head, he saw that he was surrounded by the living images. Their hands were on him, poking, prodding. One of them held his sword.

An argument was in progress. It came to him that he was the cause. They plucked at his clothing, pointed their long, thin fingers in his face. Their voices rose and got louder. Through lowered lashes, he watched the weird ballet of the stone people as all but two drew away from him; one of the two remaining clutched the sword. The other was the largest and spoke in a voice ringing with authority. The sword bearer sounded young, his voice shrill and excited. As the nameless man watched, the young gray creature made a gesture with the blade. Its meaning was clear, universal; he demanded death.

The older one said no.

Something in the nameless man burned with sudden, indignant flame. Would they decide his fate and he lie like an ox, awaiting its master's pleasure? *By the Seed, no!* Battle armor and a sea of lances spread themselves across the warped eye of his memory. He heard war cries and the clash of swords. Above his head, the graveyard birds screamed delight for the slain. A battle! He had known a battle. A man who has passed the test of blood does not lie still to wait for death.

He summoned strength to his arms and threw himself forward. He meant to follow through, to leap to his feet and confront these creatures, but his body failed him. His legs crumpled. Shrieks of surprise rose from a dozen gray throats. As he collapsed, they leaped between him and the light, pummeling him with their knotty fists. In the haze, he saw the shining blade of the sword descending, felt a chill blow just above his eyes, then knew nothing.

"Are you awake? Can you drink? It may make you sick. Drink slowly, or you will get no good from it."

He moaned and tried to open his eyes. A wet cloth was on his brow, trickles of water running down his face. He removed the cloth, wincing as each movement revealed some new ache. He blinked away the water and was looking into the depths of a homely wooden bowl filled with thin, fragrant brew the color of new grass. Gray hands held the bowl.

"Drink it," the voice urged. "It will take away the pain."

The nameless man stared at the speaker and wondered if he were part of a fever madness. Often a wound would not heal and the sufferer raved on and on, speaking to folk who were not there, acting as if he were thousands of miles away, in the arms of his loved ones. Then he died. This could be such a madness. For all he knew, he was still lying under a dragon's tail in a distant, rocky chamber, waiting to die.

"Do you think it's poisoned?" Snapping black eyes with

only the thinnest line of white around the inky centers looked
at him with wry good humor. This creature looked remarkably
like the moving stone images, but much younger. His gray
skin was lined like theirs, but the lines were fewer. A shock
of chalky hair fell over his forehead, the coarse ends brushing
all the way down his neck, partly concealing his ears. He
squatted comfortably beside the nameless man, long toes gripping the rock like a falcon gripping its perch. Around his middle
was a length of rough cloth the color of mud.

"Who are you?"

"I am Mrygo," the gray one replied. "Does knowing my
name let you trust me?"

"I—yes. Yes, it does." He took the beechwood bowl from
Mrygo's hands and drank it down. The green broth had a
sickeningly sour tang, but he forced himself to keep it down.
His stomach shuddered with the foul dose, then subsided as a
wonderfully soothing sensation began to spread its branches
outward, stealing the pain from his body and the bleak depres-
sion from his mind.

"Amazing," breathed Mrygo. "You have outdone yourself,
slave. Not even the old one himself ever kept down a full dose
of my brewing. A sip would have been enough to make you
well. With all that inside you, we shall have to be careful that
you don't smash the caverns around us."

"We are still underground?" He uttered the question in the
voice of a plaintive child.

"Ha! So they were right about you. Yes, we are still here,
where life is. You are from the other place, but you bring a
mystery. You act as if you know nothing about us. When you
trespassed on our guard post, they wanted to kill you. No man
of aboveground comes deliberately among the Gryagi unless
he is bent on mischief. Aboveground, everyone knows enough
to leave us alone if they want to live. But Vrygi argued that
you could be a madman. You behaved like a madman, attacking
the guards. Srugo tried to kill you with your own sword, but
he missed when you fell. You only got a blow with the flat of
the blade. They do say madmen are lucky. Are you mad? I
have brews that will cure madness."

He heard out Mrygo, then tossed back his head and laughed
until he felt his cheeks grow wet. Mrygo crouched patiently

beside him until the fit was done. At last he said, "If I were mad, I think I'd be grateful. But I'm nothing. I don't know where I am or who you and your people are or my own name. All I know is that I can use a sword."

Mrygo bent closer, interested. "Not know your own name? How strange! A Gryagi can't forget his name, not even in death. So you are surely aboveground to your bones. Vrygi's brother thought perhaps one of the other tribes—the ones who dwell nearer to aboveground—had found the earth-magic for shape-change and had disguised one of their own to spy on us. Vrygi's brother said—"

"Vrygi's brother is a young fool!" A strong, clear voice interrupted Mrygo's tale.

The nameless man strained to see from where the voice came. Behind Myrgo stood a sort of palisade, a wall of logs set firmly into stone sockets. The voice came from behind the wall. Looking around, he saw that he was lying on a pallet in a large niche whose mouth was closed off by the palisade. And what was it Mrygo had called him?

"It seems you have a visitor, slave." Mrygo smiled. "A curiosity seeker. Shall we let her in? We'd better. It sounds like Larya, and she'll hang there like a bat until we give her what she wants." He went to open the narrow gateway in the palisade.

Slave, the nameless one thought. So that is what I have become. That is why they spared me. His heart fell, and he hardly noticed the tall, slim, pale girl who slipped through the gate and knelt to study him.

"This is the one? How could Vrygi's brother be so stupid? No shape-change spell lasts so long or wears so well. And see, Mrygo! The scar, the red hair—they stand out too much. A spy should be inconspicuous. No, you're no spy. Who are you?"

Mrygo gently tapped Larya's shoulder and murmured, "He doesn't know. He has forgotten. Maybe it's just as well. In time they all forget."

"In time?" Larya's face showed puzzlement, which grad-ually changed to realization and, finally, anger. "No! You can't mean that! It's been years since this tribe took aboveground slaves! Will you become like the Surin Gryagi? The Old One took an oath—"

"Time changes things." Mrygo seemed saddened. "We must do as the other tribes do."

"Even the Surin." She mouthed the name like something sour. "One day the tribes will find they've cut their own throats."

"Hush." Myrgo indicated the nameless one, who sat with knees drawn up, head cradled in his folded arms. "I think he sleeps. We will disturb him. Come." The nameless one heard their soft, retreating footfalls, the gate opening, closing, a bolt shot home.

It did not take him long to recover from his hurts or for his captors to see that he was healed and ready to be put to work. Aside from Myrgo and the girl Larya, he never heard a familiar word spoken to him. The Gryagi who took him from his cell to the place he was to labor spoke their own tongue. By signs, they showed him he was to join a host of their own kind who worked with pick and shovel in a wide pit. One of them pointed to a tray where ill-sorted pebbles were heaped up. Closer inspection showed the "pebbles" to be gemstones. So he was to be a miner.

They never asked him his name. They never asked him anything. They took his clothes from him and gave him the brown loincloth most Gryagi wore. Those who toiled beside him in the pit were all hard-faced, with a criminal look about them. Their time in the mine was punishment; his was to be his life.

Mrygo came to see him once or twice a span. He learned the Gryagi way of keeping time from bits of information gleaned from the convict miners. Their sentences were calculated by spans; forty stints of mining equalled a span. He looked forward to seeing Mrygo. No one asked his name, but Mrygo was the only one who cared that it was lost.

One day he surprised Mrygo by addressing him in the Gryagi tongue. "Why do you come to see me?"

"Where did you learn that?"

"A word here, a word there. I learned curses first. Other words followed. Answer me. Why do you come?"

They faced each other Gryagi-fashion now. The nameless

one had had to assume the squatting posture many times in the mines. Rock dust covered his skin with a gray film, whitening his red hair, until he looked like a Gryagi himself. Only his eyes betrayed him.

Mrygo shifted his weight uneasily. "I come to look after your health. I am the tribe's best healer."

The nameless one barked laughter and let loose a string of the foulest oaths his convict companions had taught him unwittingly. "Tell that tale elsewhere. I can count. You're too young to be more than a true healer's apprentice. They sent you to me in the first place because it was wasteful to send a full-fledged healer to treat a slave. Once I was cured, you vanished. Suddenly you returned, then you came to see me regularly. Why? Speak the truth or save your breath."

Mrygo shook his head. "Why should I lie? It's too late now. Plans, always plans, and none of them will help her. Or me. Or you." His manner hardened and he shot a question at the nameless one like the bolt from a crossbow. "Why should a sword be the answer?"

"What? What sword? They took my sword away. I don't understand you."

There was much bitterness in Mrygo's voice. "She said she needed you because you can wield a sword. She has The Old One's favor. He indulges her in everything. She was at his side when the guards brought you in. I was there too, in the presence chamber. When they showed The Old One your sword, I thought her eyes were going to set fire to the rocks. You could see her soul hovering on her lips while they debated what to do with you. When The Old One decreed that you should be a slave and your life spared, I was amazed that her sigh didn't dislodge the hanging stones. She asked The Old One to have me tend you, and he granted it. She has her way with him, and she knows she can have her way with me. The Old One and I are the stepping stones to bring her to you, and once she reaches you—"

"She! Who is this she you're talking about?"

"She is Larya," said Mrygo. "You saw her. Larya was with me on the first day. Do you remember her?"

He thought back. Many spans had passed. He recalled a slim, white figure with long, silvery hair, and eyes . . . the eyes bothered him. Blue eyes, eyes like mountain water, eyes like his own. Aboveground eyes. Larya's eyes.

"A woman from aboveground! By the Seed, how did she come here? Is she a slave too?"

Mrygo's face was expressionless. "No slaves may come into The Old One's presence. Larya is free. Free and not free, now."

"You're speaking in riddles."

"And you show too much spirit for a slave. I do you a favor by speaking to you at all. I do it for her sake, not yours. Hold your tongue and listen."

Mrygo's casual disdain for the slave made him yearn to beat some respect into that gray hide. Instead, he fought back his rage and listened. As he listened to Mrygo's tale, the ghost of an old woman flickered into being in his mind. Ghost, or memory from the time when he still knew who he was? She sat by the fireside, robed in red, and stirred a pot of savory stew while she spun her stories.

She told of how the Gryagi who live beneath the surface of the world will sometimes leave their caverns by night to steal away fair-haired children. In the gray lands of the gray ones there can be no sunlight. They steal the little ones for their sun-gold hair and raise them underground. But mortal children cannot live long hidden from the sun. When the small ones grow sick, the Gryagi return them to the surface world, always by night. Never will they give the children back to the families that lost them, but they scatter them among strangers to begin new lives.

Mrygo's voice grew stronger and dissolved the dream of the old woman. "But Larya was different," he said. "She thrived among us, and the color of her hair never darkened or faded. The Old One took her into his household as his petted darling, and he taught her all his ways. Yet by teaching her, he made a grave error. She learned too much. She learned that she was not Gryagi. She learned she belonged aboveground. Since that time, her wish and her dream have been to return to the upper world. But The Old One cannot bear to let her go. He puts her off with promises."

"Well, if she hopes to use me to get her back to the upper world, she's a dreamer," said the nameless one. "If I could have found my way out of these cursed caves, would I have blundered into your guard post?"

"I only know what Larya tells me." Mrygo sighed. "She wants your help, that's all I know about it." ·

"Small help I'll be to her with no sword."

Before the slave could react, Mrygo seized his necklace. The four dragon claws clacked together in the Gryagi's fist. He had no name, but he still had that much. His sword and his clothes had been taken from him, but no one had removed the silk-tied claws. Many times in the mines he had noticed the way the convict miners would point at the necklace and mutter under their breath. They played cruel jokes on one another in the pits, just to relieve the monotony, but never on him. Now he understood.

"This is proof enough for her." Mrygo let the claws slip through his fingers. He seemed unawed by the talisman. "She wants your courage more than your sword."

The nameless one chuckled. "She does? And what am I going to get out of it?"

"Passage to the upper world. Your world." Mrygo was grim. "Don't tell me you enjoy a slave's life that much."

"Here at least I know who—or what—I am. I know a lot, and I've learned more. What if she does know the way back to the surface? Suppose we're followed. Suppose they catch us. This Old One of yours. I take it he's some kind of king over you and she's his favorite. What's to stop her from claiming I stole her away, forced her to lead me to the upper world? The Old One will believe her. No thanks, Mrygo. I want more time before I make a move, for myself or for Larya."

Mrygo stood up and appeared to consider the slave's words. "You could wait a lifetime for what you want. Larya doesn't have a lifetime. Did you also take your time to ponder things when you faced the dragon? Heroes act. Can it be that you carried a sword and wear a charm that were never rightly yours?"

His face grew hot under Mrygo's scornful glance. "Are you calling me a coward? Or a thief?" His own voice sounded unfamiliar to his ears.

"I call you what you are. I call you slave; slave, and unworthy of her. But I owe you thanks. I too wanted time before

I'd do anything to help Larya. I thought I was being so wise, thinking things over like that. You've shown me the true name for what I thought was wisdom. You've shamed me out of it. Stay here and think until your bones know the rocks. I'll help Larya if you won't." He turned to go.

Muscles grow hard in the mines. The darkness itself is a weight to be moved, heavier than pick or shovel or gem sifter. Muscles grow strong, tempered like the finest sword steel, but tempers grow short.

He leaped on Mrygo's back and threw the Gryagi youth to the floor. His toil-hardened hands closed around the slim gray neck. Mrygo shouted while he could.

Guards poured through the palisade door. There were too many for him to fight. They seized him, pulled him off Mrygo. He flung himself back and forth, trying to break from their grip. It took three blows from a stout club to tame him. He was alone when he regained his senses; alone, and they had taken his food and water bowls with them.

They gave him nothing for two days of mining, then half rations for three days more. He counted out a span, but Mrygo never came back. For half a span after the attack, he was marched back and forth from the pit under double guard, then things went back to normal. He forgot most of what Mrygo had told him, but he continued to learn more of the Gryagi tongue. His studies brought no comfort; neither guards nor fellow miners answered when he spoke to them. He was a slave. It was shame for a Gryagi, even a convict, to speak to a slave. He overheard their whispers and knew.

The world folded itself inward around him, like a flower closing its petals against the cold night. He stopped counting days and spans. He stopped caring if he ever found his lost name. He stopped trying to communicate with the guards or the other miners. He was the slave. He called himself Slave for a name. He amused himself by pretending there were other slaves in the cell with him and he was their respected leader.

Sometimes he wondered if he was going mad. When he awoke from sleep and saw the face of another human being next to his, he feared that the madness had finally come. It was the face of a woman.

"Say nothing." She laid her hand across his lips. "If they knew I'm here, I'd be—"

"Are you . . . Larya?" He whispered the words against her hand and felt her own breath warm him. Words came slowly, uncertainly, after so much disuse.

"Mrygo told you about me, didn't he?" Her smile was gentle and wonderful. "So you know we are both strangers here in Neb-Halira."

He looked puzzled. "I thought the Gryagi lived in the land of the dead."

"You are a man of the upper lands, truly you are. You still believe old nursewife tales. We are a long way from the land of the dead here, my friend. It's taken me longer than I'd like to divert your guards, so let's not waste a moment. Mrygo told me you were a coward. I don't believe him. Here, take this." She pushed a cumbersome bundle of brown rags into his hands. He felt something long and hard at the core. Tearing the rags away, he looked again at his sword.

"How did you get this?"

"I asked for it. The Old One gave it to me." Her sharp face twisted into a mischievous smile. "It was a wedding present."

His head buzzed with questions. Each begged to be asked, to be answered. Then one thought as clean and strong as the swordblade cut them all aside. Their eyes met and he knew she shared the thought: escape.

"You know the way to the upper lands. Lead me," he said. "I'll fight for you if we must fight."

She nodded, not surprised. "This way." She flitted from him through the open gate and glided quickly into a maze of shadows.

He recognized parts of the many roads they took, knowing them from his daily marches to and from the mines. Here was the Gryagi marketplace; there was the adit leading to the vast dormitory caverns where the tribal families lived all together, one generation with another. That way lay the road to the pit, beyond the pit stood the entrance to The Old One's council chamber, and further still beyond that there lay the guard post that he had blundered into on that lost day.

The pathways were deserted. It was the time for rest. The guards on duty were the only Gryagi awake and about at that hour, and for the most part they were at their assigned posts, immovable until rest ended and a new shift came on—or a carefully calculated distraction. Despite that, Larya hugged the walls and made him do likewise. They came to places he did not know. Larya conducted him in and out between stone pillars like huge teeth, clamped tight in a fantastic grin. She slithered between sheets of rock as lithely as a salamander, and he was forced to follow. She took him down passageways where the dark was so complete that even Gryagi eyes would wish for a torch.

She was like a silvery plume of water in the dark, her frost-gilt hair flickering with a secret fire. As he went after her, never taking his eyes from her, he began to understand why Mrygo had spoken so bitterly when he voiced the possibility of Larya's leaving, and leaving Mrygo behind. It must be a hard thing, he mused, to wear those invisible shackles and to know that the woman you love thinks only of escaping your world. If Mrygo had not slipped some subtle poison into that first bowl of green broth, it spoke highly of his character. What was the nameless one to him, after all, but a potential rival? A dangerous rival, because he was of Larya's own kind.

He remembered the wooden bowl, the way the green liquid had lapped against its nut-brown sides. Now it seemed as if the bowl took shape from his memory and harnessed the earth-magic to make itself grow and grow to unthinkable proportions before setting itself at his feet. The last of the tunnels stood behind them. They had emerged onto a small outcropping of brown stone and were looking down across an emerald expanse of waves.

"The boundary lake," said Larya. "I never hoped we'd find it this easily. I've never come this far from home before, and I only had the descriptions of the road here that our rangers gave to go on. We're in luck that they were accurate. If we can cross the water before they discover we're gone, we'll be safe."

In the undergound light, the waters of the lake gave off their own eerie radiance. "Is there a boat?" he asked her.

"There." She pointed. "My cockleshell. I had Mrygo bring it here for me from The Old One's pleasure lake."

"Mrygo knows you're escaping—with me?"

She scrambled down the rocks to the lakeshore without answering, retrieving the flimsy craft from its hiding place, launching it and handing him a paddle. He thought she might not have heard his question the first time, so he repeated it. She slammed her own paddle down across her knees and glowered at him.

"What do you care about Mrygo? You tried to kill him! Why should you care what he knows or doesn't know? What I do concerns only me! Remember that!" She tossed her head and struck the water so hard with her paddle that the shallow, bowl-shaped boat spun like a top, going nowhere.

He snatched her paddle away. She gasped with anger, her eyes wild as a fox's. He saw the muscles tense beneath her milky skin and knew that she longed to strike him but was too wise to start a fight in such an easily capsized craft. Why had his question angered her so deeply? He didn't know, and he remembered too little about human souls to guess.

"My lady." He let each word drop carefully into the anger between them. "My lady, you're setting me free. I owe you a debt for that; not insolence. I've asked my last question. I swear it by the Seed."

She relaxed gradually, like a cat growing accustomed to a strange house, and took back the paddle from his hands. Together, they propelled the cockleshell away from the near shore. Water lapped against the tiny boat as it bobbed across the lake. Above their heads, the roof of the cavern soared in a mighty arc that seemed to have no apex.

On the other side, they beached the cockleshell. Larya lay down on the slate shore, and he took his cue from her, stretching out at ease. "Now we're safe," she said. "Beyond the boundary lake, all the caverns lead to the upper lands, and they're fairly short—the rangers say so. We can rest here a bit before the last leg of our journey." She rolled onto her belly and traced invisible pictures on the stone.

He stared, not believing that he saw the solid rock melting away under her fingertip. Her drawings—apart from how she was making them—were unremarkable: rough and simple things, crude outlines of animals, stick figures of men and women and houses, whorls and swirls and jagged lines in between. She felt his astonished breath over her shoulder and gave him a taunting look.

"An oath is an oath with you, I see," she said. "You swore to ask no questions, but you've got a mouthful of them dying to be asked."

"I keep promises."

"Why? Mrygo said you remember nothing, not even your own name. So how can you remember if you were a man whose word meant anything?"

"I don't. I might never have kept an oath in my life before now. But I don't remember any other life. In this one, I keep my promises."

"Well, that's a good beginning. And do you recall nothing of the upper world?"

He shrugged. "Houses, fire, flowers, the way people dress, battles, music; generalities. You—drew a house. I thought you were a baby when the Gryagi took you. How can you remember what houses look like?"

"The Old One often said that the mind is its own lord." Larya sat up tailor-fashion. "I think I'll free you from that oath of yours. Yes, I will. We haven't much farther to go together, you and I. Let's part friends. Friends need no boundaries set between them." She offered him her hand.

He reached for it blindly, grasped it so hard that it seemed he would never let it go. They would part friends. Which meant they would part, and that was a thought he hadn't been expecting. Larya acted as if separation were only natural. *Impossible! Impossible!* something inside him protested, and shuddered away from the idea that they would step into the sunlight of the upper lands together and she would take a different road than his. He might never see her again.

Which road could he possibly take? What did he have with which to build a life for himself? Only a handful of memories—scraps of memories—and the long spans spent beneath the earth among the Gryagi. She was his last link to that buried life, and she would leave him. It was like being dropped into the heart of the sea, being saved by a passing ship, then without warning being thrown back into the icy salt water.

"What's wrong?" Her voice was gentle. "You look frightened."

"Me? You said we're safe now. Why should I be afraid after danger's past?" He managed a laugh that did not quite drown out the pounding of his heart. He was afraid; afraid to be left alone, nameless, in the upper lands.

The pounding sound grew louder. Larya dropped his hand and scrambled to her feet, poised like a deer before flight, scenting the air. The lake cupped the pulsing, swelling sound and amplified it. Closer it came, louder. Mixed with the marching tread there also came the frightful sounds of wailing, weeping, sobbing, and cries for mercy or for help in the now-familiar tongue of the Gryagi.

They burst from the mouth of the passage across the lake, captives and conquerors. Larya peered in disbelief as she recognized face after face among the huddled mass flinching and cowering under the whips of their herdsmen. Face after gray face looked back at her across the heaving surface of the boundary lake, but terror stole their sight. She might have been invisible. She called their names, softly at first, then clearly, when she realized that their captors were too preoccupied to pay any mind to two solitary humans on the far shore. They had other business.

A young Gryagi woman with a baby in her arms heard Larya call her name. Wildly, she flung herself toward the sound, calling to Larya, holding the whimpering baby over the waters as if to pass it to safety. A bored guard struck her between the shoulder blades with the butt of his whip and she stumbled, slipping into the lake. Larya screamed as mother and child dipped beneath the green waves and disappeared.

"What is it? What's happening?" The nameless one drew his sword, shaded his eyes, tried to see the faces of the conquerors. "But—but they're Gryagi too!"

"Surin Gryagi." Larya's voice came strangely flat and dead. "The dwellers near the surface world. Our tribe has little to do with them. We scorned them for aping the ways of the upper lands." Her eyes were bitter as she added, "That was why I mocked The Old One for taking you as his slave. Slave labor is a custom of the Surin Gryagi, learned from the surface folk. Now it seems they've learned another lesson from your people."

He wanted to say, *They are your people, too. You are as*

much of the surface world as I. He wanted to praise the land of sunlight, of rain, of drifting clouds and snow and springtime. That was what he remembered, the beauty of his lost life, not slavery.

A broad-shouldered Surin Gryagi male waded through the crowd of captives and raised his hand. Immediately, the guards administered cuffs, slaps, blows of the whip to quiet the wretched. When there was silence, the big one gave an order. He spoke too low for them to hear him on the far side of the lake, but what happened next showed his meaning.

The whips were cast down. Short stone knives flashed in the green twilight. Within moments, the mute herd of captives turned to a writhing, shrieking, futilely thrashing mass of bodies as the guards set to their task of winnowing living grain. They killed all the unfit males, even the babies. They threw the bodies into the lake. They murdered the old, the infirm, the ill-favored. They spared all young females of the tribe, maid and matron, shoving them aside into the keeping of a small whip-squad, tearing them from the arms of father, brother, and son.

Sometimes a girl would hurl herself back into the slaughter and be killed by mistake. Sometimes a young mother, her arms abruptly empty, would attack the guards with nails and teeth, then cast herself into waters and drown. Sometimes a female would only stare and stare at the carnage and die where she stood, with something snapped inside her. The green water swirled red.

A young whip-squad guard with a brass collar around his neck as a mark of rank looked idly toward the far side of the lake and saw the humans. It was plain that he thought nothing of their presence, but casually mentioned it to the leader. The big Surin Gryagi's face convulsed when he saw what his underling pointed out. This time the orders he gave were loud enough to reach the far shore. Standing beside Larya, nearly as paralyzed with horror, the nameless one heard, and he saw a contingent of Surin Gryagi guards sent scuttling around the lake's narrow border.

He grabbed Larya's arm. "They're after us. We can't do anything to save your tribe. We have to get to the surface. Lead me."

Her arm felt clammy under his fingers. She gave no response. He shook her violently until she snapped out of her daze, then barked, "Lead me!" Dumbly, she nodded and stumbled into the midnight tunnels.

He did not know how fast Gryagi could scramble over rocks, even the slippery, lichen-grown lip of the boundary lake. The dreaded pounding sound echoed behind them as they trotted through the gloom, the cadenced tread of their pursuers beating down the distance separating them.

If they catch us here in the dark, he thought, I'm a dead man. I've seen how they use those stone knives. This long sword against them in a tunnel will be more of a handicap than a weapon. Only let me get to open ground, and we'll have a chance!

Over the sound of tramping feet he thought he heard their breath. It was hungry and heavy, and it was always coming nearer.

Sunlight startled him, making him raise his arms to shield his eyes. It was a single shaft of sunshine no broader than a sword, striking sparks of mica from the stones. Beyond it, he saw a second beam of light, and a third. Larya fled from one ray to the next like a moth flirting with candles. In the shadows at his back, he heard grunts of bewilderment and the start of a dispute. The hunters' footsteps paused. A wide circle of light beckoned, and in that suspended moment the two humans leaped from the mouth of the caverns and into the light of day.

Instead of the relief he expected daylight to bring him, the nameless one felt a sudden dread. He thought, If they follow us now, it's bad. I can hardly see. I'm a mole, an owl, a bat. I've lived underground with the Gryagi too long. How long will I stay this blind? What if Gryagi eyes adjust faster than mine? They could take us now, drag us back under the earth, and I'd be swinging my sword at phantoms. Just one clear sight of them! Just one sight of those murderers, that's all I ask. By the Seed, if Surin Gryagi blood doesn't wet my sword, I deserve to die without a name.

Larya's voice reached him at the same moment he regained tearful use of his eyes. "We're out of it. They won't come for us here. I heard one tell the others that we're only the slaves of my tribe. They don't want to risk their skins going after slaves of slaves."

She was sitting with her back against the bark of a titan oak that grew a hundred paces from the cave mouth. He cast one last look back into the shadows before he joined her. The shade cast by its great branches bathed his eyes in comfort. He looked at Larya. Her face was expressionless, without tears, without sorrow.

"Larya . . ."

"They were my people. I was wrong to leave them. Their fate should have been mine. I was wrong." Her eyes closed, and she slumped against him, unconscious.

Farmer Rycote thought he had been on the road under the blazing sun too long. Greed to get to the cattle market and eagerness to get back home with his earnings had made him try to make the entire journey there and back without taking shelter by the roadside from time to time. His wife had cautioned him about it, and now he saw that she was right. He was seeing things, sunstruck.

Plain as a black cow in a snowfield he saw them, and he made the gesture to ward off evil: a tall man, red-haired, with the sign of the sword crossing his face, but covered head to foot in grave dust. In his powerful arms he held a slender woman with star-fall hair, and both of them nigh naked. Farmer Rycote rubbed his eyes and pinched his wrist. It was his old man's remedy for seeing demons, infallible. Only this time it didn't work.

"Bottle-born demons, that's what it'll chase," he growled to himself. "It's no good on the real kind. Oh Rycote, you half-witted ninny, broad daylight's the wrong time to be seeing haunts. You've gone mad."

Well, if madness called, Farmer Rycote was not the kind of man to run sniveling away. He would make the best of it, just as he'd made the best of his tumbledown farm. Just as he'd made the best of his shrew of a wife, for that matter, he told himself. If madness was to keep him company from now on, he'd better be on good terms with it. He greeted the hallucination like a brother.

"Halloo, friend," he said, reining in his oxen and descending from the cart. "How goes it, eh? Hard at work frightening decent people, are you? Never mind, never mind," he added hastily, seeing the red-haired fiend frown. "I meant it as a compliment. But tell me. Is that one—the one you're toting there—also a bad sprite, or only a captive for you? Just asking."

"Old man, are you out of your mind?" the nameless one roared. "Have we come out in a land of lunatics?"

"Come out . . ." The graybeard farmer looked past the roadside apparition to where the cave mouth gaped black and secret against the hill. Stories told in the marketplace by wandering entertainers came to mind. Farmer Rycote chewed his lip and the answer came.

"Humans," he breathed. "I've heard tell that they—the ones who live beneath—sometimes snatch humans. Oh my dear fellow, praise the gods! You've come back among your own at last! And the poor, sweet lady . . . what's wrong with her? Ah!" Farmer Rycote stroked Larya's brow and gasped. It was burning. "No, this is not good. Come, you can ride with me to my house. My wife'll take care of her. I'll give her a taste of birch if she doesn't do a proper job of it, mark me. Come, come lay her in the cart, lad. All will be well. Tell me, who are you? Where do you come from? Who is this poor lady?"

The nameless one placed Larya tenderly among the sacks of meal and flour in the back of Farmer Rycote's oxcart, covering her with an empty sack before replying. "She is Larya," he said. "And I—I am Ophar."

It was a name of his own choosing. It was the Gryagi word for sword.

PART II

In Kor-Halira

"What shall the story be?" asked the conjure-man.

The throng of giggling children nudged and poked one another, but no one dared to request a specific tale. The conjure-man sat on a bench of split ashwood, casting a frail shadow against the white plastered outer wall of Bellman's Tavern. The children stood at a respectful distance, their elders behind them. The grown-up folk were seated, some puffing on short clay pipes in the early summer evening, some making a great show of transacting business. The truth of it was that they were all waiting for the conjure-man to begin his story. If possible, they were more eager for it than the children.

Farmer Rycote's man saw the gathering in front of Bellman's Tavern and hesitated. He'd had a good day at market, a very good day. By rights he should be out of the town and well on the road for home. He scratched his red head with one hand, jingling the coins he'd garnered at market with the other.

"I will just have a word with young Springer," he said, half aloud. "I have to ask him about those brown heifers of his anyway. I think I see him with the others near Bellman's, and who knows when Rycote'll send me this way again? I'll speak to him now, quickly." With his excuse in mind, he ambled toward the crowd and took a place by the tavern wall just as the conjure-man began his story.

"I will tell you a tale of the days of the mountains," he said. His voice was as soft as a woman's, deep as the heart of a tree. The children composed themselves to silence. The elders assumed a look of respectful expectation.

The conjure-man's beard was short and bristly, streaked like the back of a badger. When he spoke, it quivered. His voice rose and fell in the fragrant evening air, twining itself through the smoke rings of a dozen pipes, hanging motionless as a dragonfly on a child's bated breath.

"What lies beyond the forest?" asked the conjure-man. "What lies beyond the trees? If a man packs his gear and takes the old roadways, he will come from farmland to river, from river to meadow, from meadow to city to royal house, and yet always he will return to the forest that rings our lands. But what lies beyond?

"They tell that in the lost times, before the death of heroes, there were men brave enough to enter the forest. They went where the road went, they made new roads, and then they went past the point where all roads ended. They conquered the forests and came back again to tell those who waited for them that beyond the forests were the mountains. In any direction, in all directions, beyond the trees the mountains rose in majesty.

"So the people followed those first bold ones through the forests to the mountains. And there the holy ones—the brave—remained, at the mountains' feet. 'There is power here,' they said. 'There is strong magic in the heart of the mountains. Let us stay here and walk with the gods.'

"They stayed there, the holy ones, and the people came to worship on the high places. They found great powers there, in the realm of stone. There they found the secrets of the earth-magic and the air-magic and the magic from beyond the stars. They called on the gods in the holy places on the mountains. Then the race of great sorcerers and great heroes was born."

The elders puffed their pipes and crossed their legs. The mothers with babies at the breast hushed them, and the children gazed at the old conjure-man as he spread his tapering fingers to trace paths of fire on the air.

"Salamar!" A fistful of flaming blue burst from the conjure-man's hands at mention of that famous sorceress, long dead. "Mellora! Kundobasch the Wise! Prince Velior!" Tame lightnings criss-crossed in a golden latticework around him. Sparkling serpents, red and green and gold, cut whirligigs in the dust at the doorway of Bellman's Tavern. One of the children began to sob and ran for home, followed by his harried mother.

The conjure-man grinned, yellow teeth showing under his grizzled moustache. His voice fell to a whisper. "But the last," he purred, "and the greatest of these . . . was Dammon."

The people sighed, expectations fulfilled. To mention Dammon's name was to evoke a subject forever dear to the townsfolk's hearts. The conjure-man was only one of a number of itinerant singers and tellers of old tales who visited Bellman's Tavern on market days. Like his canny fellows, he knew there was no hero whose exploits were so consistently popular with the people as Dammon's.

The minstrels sang songs of Dammon in the villages. The harpers called up the wraith of Dammon in the courtyards of great castles. The smallest child present who could walk could also recite a baby rhyme about Dammon that had lulled him to sleep many times. Even Ophar—so new to the ways of the surface world—already knew Dammon's whole life history. He reasoned that he had probably known it before his loss of memory, too. It had sounded familiar to him the first time he'd heard it, more like an old memory regained than a new thing discovered.

The Dammon story that the conjure-man told was one of the rarer ones. In it, the teller praised the young hero who defied and conquered the flame-witch of Nel. She had been an evil hag adept in the air-magic who sought to call down fire from the sky to destroy all those who would not serve her. Rare or not, the conjure-man's listeners all knew the plot of the tale. Therefore the teller was free to devote his skills to embellishing the bare bones with pretty images and long descriptions of what Dammon wore, what Dammon ate, how Dammon held his sword and shield. In the end, the flame-witch of Nel died horribly and satisfactorily. The conjure-man tied up the ends of his tale, saying, "That was why evil never walked with us long while Dammon lived. But now the world

is old and there are no more heroes. No heroes, nor shall there
be any until Dammon's return. May our eyes see his sword!"

"May our eyes see his sword," intoned children and grown-
ups together. It was the ceremonial ending proper to any song
or story mentioning Dammon.

The crowd dispersed, children running home ahead of their
parents, men pausing to exchange a word or two, wives cal-
culating what to serve for a cold market-day supper. Dogs
barked from alleyways. There was the smell of rain.

Ophar leaned against the tavern wall, watching the people
go their way. The conjure-man waited also. Just the two of
them were left by Bellman's Tavern before the conjure-man
got up and stretched his thin arms high overhead and yawned
like a tomcat. A considerable heap of small coins lay on the
bench near him. Ophar dug deep into his pouch and added his
offering.

"Thank you," said the conjure-man. "I am glad the story
pleased you. It was intended for children."

Ophar hunched his shoulders and muttered a bland reply
under his breath. The conjure-man's eyes were on him, very
green-gold.

"Really?" remarked the conjure-man, just as if he had heard
what Ophar had said. "Then you must have a drink with me.
I insist."

"I can't," said Ophar, taking a step backward.

"Why not?"

"I'm late. I have to go home now." Shame stabbed him.
He towered over the conjure-man and could have hefted the
scrawny body in one hand. The strength he'd won in the mines
had not faded. Hard work on Farmer Rycote's land had hardened him more.

"You ought to be home by now, in fact." The conjure-man
smiled. "I know that's so. But you stayed to hear my story.
You can share a cup of wine with me in less time than you
wasted against this tavern wall. Come. I like company."

The conjure-man's gentle insistence made Ophar feel edgy
as a horse before a thunderstorm. "The road—the road will
be dark."

"Which road do you take, friend?" Ophar pointed out his
route. "Ah! Isn't that fine for us both! It happens that my own

humble home lies that way. We shall walk together. I can give you some excellent helgras wine, better than anything they'd serve us in there." He jerked his thumb at the tavern door.

Ophar saw no way out of a bad situation. He could always claim he'd been mistaken about which was his homeward road, he supposed. But that would sound patently stupid, and then he would have to take a roundabout way back to the farm to avoid the conjure-man. It would make him late, and he didn't like coming home late. He couldn't risk it, especially not to-night. The sun was going down and the bloated curve of a yellow moon showed itself on the horizon. The dreams were always worse at the full moon. He had to get home to help.

Help. The word nudged him. Hadn't they spoken many times at home of getting someone to help her? This invitation to drink with the conjure-man was no accident. Ophar had brought it about himself, deliberately, although he'd been going through a charade of self-deception to make it happen. He had told himself lies in order to stop at Bellman's Tavern and see what sort of hedgerow magic the fellow would display. He had done it on purpose, recalling how Farmer Rycote's wife once said that even the worst of the wandering illusion-jugglers were often competent herbalists.

Why lie? Why not go up to the conjure-man directly and tell him what was wrong? He had been on the point of doing just that, offering the wanderer a little money and the promise of a warm bed, payment enough for his aid. Then he had seen the fires leaping from the older man's palms, and he knew that there was more than sleight-of-hand behind such a show. There was power. It frightened him. This conjure-man had too much true magic at his command to be wasted on market-day idlers or to be bought with a farmer's coin and a straw pallet. Then why had he come to show miracles to such a raw-boned crowd? Ophar didn't know. Perhaps with power came the freedom to do things just because they were new or unthinkable or they amused you.

What if the conjure-man refused the thing Ophar had to ask? No; he had suffered too many disappointments already, even in his short new lifespan. He would not court another one. Rather, he would play out the charade, waiting for the chance to make his plea.

And if that chance never came?...

Ophar swallowed his fear and awe of the conjure-man. His voice was steady as he said, "I have never drunk helgras. I accept with pleasure." The conjure-man laughed and bowed, then swung off down the road without a word more, setting a brisk pace. Ophar fell in beside him.

They passed scattered houses where smoke rose blue from stone chimneys and the clatter of wooden plates and spoons told of dinner being eaten at the long table. The oiled paper windows shone with a serene glow, calm candles in the night. The conjure-man snapped a sprig of lilac from a bush growing at the road end of a homely kitchen garden and took a deep breath of the fragrant plant.

"Isn't it odd on what small things they build their lives?" he asked in a way that forbade an answer. "A roof, a wife, a child or two, a dog, a plot of earth. Then they ask for tales of heroes."

The moon stood free of the trees as they went on. The road was deserted but for them. Once they heard a gallop of horses and stepped prudently into the ditch to let a squad of mounted men stream by, capes of purple and scarlet flapping in the wind, moonlight reflected in bright shards on a dozen helmets.

"They go south," remarked the conjure-man. "They wear the royal insignia."

"Good," said Ophar. "The farther south, the better. Far away from here, I hope. No good ever comes of horsemen."

The conjure-man stared. "So you've learned that much already. I didn't think you would absorb their comfortable, meaningless sayings so soon. One would almost take you for a farmer's lout born and bred. I may even be mistaken. Well, the price of a cup of helgras is small enough to pay for finding out a mistake. My house lies there, away from the road." He gestured over the rolling grasslands to where a low hill rose like a burial mound out of the summer night.

Ophar tensed in his tracks. The cave mouth yawned, blacker than the surrounding blackness. The great oak raised leaf-thick branches to snare the stars. The pounding of pursuing footsteps haunted the spot, and from under the stone arch the cries of murdered ghosts called to him in the tongue of the Gryagi.

The conjure-man appeared to notice nothing unusual in

Ophar's behavior. He went striding through the tall grass, skirting the oak and the cave mouth. Ophar forced himself to go after him. The conjure-man circled the hillock until he came to the slope facing away from the road. There, hidden from the eyes of passersby, stood a little stone hut, round as a pudding, with a hole in the side for a door and a hole in the roof for a chimney. He ducked his head to enter and Ophar did likewise.

In the conjure-man's hut there was a thick smell of oil, wax, herbs, and dried flowers. A circle of granite chunks made a sunken fireplace over which a tripod stood on iron legs, with a brazen kettle slung above the embers. Three black wood chests clung to the walls, two of them flanking a tattered pallet. Ophar thought it looked like a poorer place to sleep than his own shabby mattress in Farmer Rycote's house, but what a contrast were the silk cushions and heavily embroidered coverlet piled beside it!

"You may call me Kor," said the conjure-man. He indicated that Ophar was to seat himself on a three-legged stool with a leather sling-saddle. He rummaged in one of the black chests and took out two wine cups while his guest made himself as comfortable as possible. Handing the cups to Ophar, he knelt beside the curving stone wall and began to dig, just like the badger his hair suggested. He unearthed a bottle of wine.

"Helgras," he said, holding it high. The embers in the hearth leaped into flame. "The best. From the old days. Worthy of heroes," he added with a touch of irony. Ophar felt ill at ease. If this helgras was a hero's drink, it had fallen onto bad times, being wasted on a farmer's lad and an eccentric storyteller.

Kor unstoppered the bottle and poured the rose-red wine into Ophar's cup, then served himself before taking a seat on the ground at Ophar's feet. The young man raised the drink gingerly to his lips. It smelled of the earth and long burial. He tasted it, found it pleasant, then remembered his manners. It would not do to drink a man's wine without returning his introduction.

"I am Ophar."

"That's what you call yourself," said Kor. "Is it hard, finding a name?"

The helgras's pungent bouquet filled his head and made

what Kor said seem matter-of-fact. *He's a conjure-man, isn't he? He can do sleight-of-hand and juggle fire. Why shouldn't he be able to read your mind?* asked Ophar's little voice.

"Very hard," Ophar replied. "But you grow used to many hard things in life."

Kor spat into the fire. "Another piece of farmer's philosophy. Did he fill your head with it, or is there still room for something worthwhile?"

"Like what?" Ophar chuckled. The wine was good, with a welcome tendency to make him light-headed after only one cup. It was a relief to be free from thinking, especially thinking of the consequences for talking back so brazenly to a conjure-man. Who could tell what powers Kor was keeping back to himself? Farmer Rycote had told him the tale of what one of that black brood had done to Kelmor's cow. "What's worthwhile to you, Kor? Spinning tales of heroes, all dead? And while they were alive they needed bread, just like the rest of us. Don't scorn the farmer, my friend. If he didn't raise the wheat, the hero couldn't raise his sword." Ophar's tipsy laughter filled the room.

There was no laughter. It cut away clean, leaving Ophar's mouth agape. From the heart of the hearthfire a woman's face formed itself of smoke. Rivers of hair like frozen waterfalls parted to reveal a heart-shaped face and luminous eyes. The face floated back into the distance and vanished. Where it had hovered there were now two small yellow eyes, the pupils like black stars. The eyes wafted higher above the crackling wood like bits of thistledown and came level with Ophar's face before they melted into a vision: a vision of death, and four curved claws rattling on a silken cord.

"Tell me what the farmer would have done against the dragon," Kor's mocking voice hissed in his ear. "Tell me."

The seeing in the fire was gone. Ophar gulped once and tossed off what was left of his wine, only a few droplets. Kor blandly filled the cup a second time, but the young man put it down and drank no more.

"You wanted to ask me a question," said Kor. "Let us pretend that that is all that happened here tonight. But you will come back to this hut to see me again another day. We have further business, you and I." Ophar opened his mouth to object. Kor silenced him with a look. "Your question?"

And suddenly neither the mysterious, all-knowing smile of the conjure-man nor the seeings of the fire nor the oddly reminiscent taste of the helgras wine on his tongue mattered. "I have come to ask you to help my sister. She's very ill."

The conjure-man sniffed. "Indeed? And don't you farmers have a host of recipes to cure yourselves? Like dogs who know which weed to gnaw when they're sick? A good dose of spring tonic will be all the girl needs, I'm sure."

If not for his need—and hers—Ophar would have struck the conjure-man then. Instead, he held back his rage and said, "She is not sick in body." He told Kor all he could about Larya: his captivity, their flight, the slaughter of the Gryagi they had witnessed by the lakeside. The conjure-man listened thoughtfully, toying with his silver ring.

Farmer Rycote's wife propped her elbows on the windowsill as she watched the full moon rise. "Another bad night," she commented indifferently. "And Ophar's not home yet."

Farmer Rycote pushed his chair away from the dinner table and patted his stomach. Things on the farm had always gone fairly well, but never so well as since the day he'd brought that Ophar and his queer, fair-haired sister home to live with them. The girl was even now clearing away the dishes and dumping them into a wide wooden bucket filled with sudsy water. She'd have them clean in no time, dried and back in the cupboard. What nonsense his wife preached, and Ophar with her, about how bad the girl got taken when the full moon came up. If she had evil dreams, what of it? Everyone closed a dark eye now and then.

"You're talking her into it," Farmer Rycote grumped. "Maybe if you and Ophar didn't act like you expected her to be took with the horrors, she'd forget all about it. Larya my dear, come to me."

Larya dropped the last load of dishes in the washtub and came obediently to Farmer Rycote's side. He sat her on his lap and bounced her on his knee like a little girl.

"Larya, love, you know you mustn't listen to the old woman all the time. If I'd do that, I'd be mad. You had one or two bad dreams and she's making them into a curse that's on you, no less! Here's our chance to show the old woman she's wrong, childie. Now you go up to your bed and you sleep with pretty dreams for me. Will you do that? We'll break the demons down and toss them away on the wind, won't we?"

Larya smiled and gave Farmer Rycote a hug before going back to her chores. "I will do my best to please you," she said.

"Well, no one's asking for anything more. Here now, woman, you finish up the dishes. Let the girl get to sleep early. That's what's bringing on the bad dreams, too much work and worry. And where's that blamed brother of hers? I'd have nightmares too if I didn't know what'd become of my kin."

Farmer Rycote's wife came away from the window to take over the dishwashing. "I saw something coming down the road," she said. "It must be Ophar. No need fretting for him. He'll be here directly."

"Must've been a good day at market," said Farmer Rycote between teeth clenched around the stem of his pipe. "Those geese he drove to sale were nice and fat. Wonder what he's brought back." His wondering was answered when the cottage door opened to admit Ophar and the conjure-man Kor.

"By everything under the mountains, what's this?" Farmer Rycote shouted and leaped out of his comfortable chair. Kor gave a tight-lipped smile and bowed in reply. "Ophar, you give me an explanation!"

Farmer Rycote's wife was there, tugging at his elbow with soapy hands. He cocked his head toward her as she whispered frantically in his ear. His whole expression changed. He calmed down and lowered his eyes.

"I beg your pardon, sir," he said gruffly to Kor. "We—we didn't mean any insult to you, you know. It's an honor for us, having one of your brotherhood in our house. Can we offer you food? Drink? You see, my eyes aren't so good, and my wife just now tells me—"

Kor assumed a look of innocence that sat ill on his swarthy features. "Brotherhood?" he echoed. "Then you are familiar with the people of the road in these parts. Yes, I suppose you might say that there is a bond between all wanderers, but I have resigned it. I've left the road and built myself a small house of stones in the neighborhood. My bones are too old to venture onto the highway when winter comes. Not like in the old days. My thanks for your hospitality."

Farmer Rycote looked from Kor's calm eyes to his wife's fearful ones and cleared his throat. "Sir, I don't know what your scheme may be. Keep it to yourself if you like. But don't deny what you are when you're under my roof. I'm a simple man, as my old dad before me was, but he never took kindly to dissemblers and no more do I, no matter what powers they've got. You've got the sign on you, the mountain look. My wife here saw it, so don't play mealy-mouth with us if you please. You've gotten our lad Ophar to bring you here for your own reasons, and I'd be much obliged if you'd tell 'em."

Kor shook his head as if pitying the farmer. "I see your hospitality wears many faces, friend," he said. "Accusation among them. I will leave you—"

"Don't!" The farmer's wife shrieked and flung herself on her knees before the conjure-man, her hands fluttering up to her face like frightened sparrows. "By the holy mountain, don't! Don't go! Ah, by the ones who sleep and the ones who wake, bad luck will come to us all if we turn one of the brotherhood from our door. Stay, please stay. I pray of you, stay!"

The four people faced each other in the small cottage. Ophar could hear the floorboards creak, the dying fire crackle among its embers. Farmer Rycote was fiddling with his pipe, at a loss for what do, while his wife still clung, weeping, to the conjure-man's sleeve. Only Kor bided in perfect silence, waiting.

Ophar spoke up. "He must stay. He's come here to—to see my sister, Larya. I asked him to help her, he's agreed, and he's not leaving until he's cured her. That's all."

The dark conjure-man raised one eyebrow in a mocking glance at Ophar, who had moved to block the door with his broad-shouldered body. Even in the humble garb of a farmer's boy, his strength was plain. "You're right," said Kor lightly. "I'd disgrace my calling if I left a place without doing what I'd come for. What ails the girl?"

The little clay pipe snapped in Farmer Rycote's hands as the flush of anger mounted to his face. "Nothing! I say nothing ails her! Is this what you've brought this ragtag herbman here for, boy? To frighten your poor mam and set the house on end?

There's nothing wrong with Larya but living under the same roof with you!"

The house began to shake. It was the veriest tremor at first, a vague shiver running up the walls on mouse feet. The clay vessels on the shelf gave a thin rumble, and the iron pots and pokers by the fireplace thrummed in answer. Then the walls moaned and leaned this way and that, in unison, like branches in a storm. Bony cracks seamed the plaster and the beaten earth floor, sending bowls and goblets dancing, crashing down.

Farmer Rycote's wife screamed, "Nothing wrong! Nothing wrong with her! Yes, and all *this* comes of ordinary dreams!" She would have said more. She was not the sort of woman to speak her piece and let it be. But a gap in the floor beside her groaned open then. A hideous gray apparition filtered up, a creature made of blood and filmy darkness that arose like silt from the bottom of a long-stagnant pond. The poor country-woman's shrill voice choked off into dry sobs of terror. She covered her face with her apron and her arms.

They were all around, the ghosts out of the earth. With eyeless sockets and faces unlike anything alive, they came at the bidding of an unseen master and leered the secrets of Hori-Halira with their melting mouths. Farmer Rycote lurched away from one that plucked at the pieces of his pipe with dripping fingers. Ophar held his ground, trying to stare them down, but he was very white in the face, hands clenched tightly on his thighs as if to guarantee that he would not bolt and run. Only Kor remained unshaken by the hungry phantoms. Only Kor did they avoid.

Light arced above Ophar's red head. A shriek from fleshless throats split the little cottage from rooftree to foundations. The conjure-man leaped to the center of the room, holding dawn-light in his dusky hands, sending bolts of brightness flying to pierce the ghosts to the heart and sink them back into the avid depths of Hori-Halira. The last of the phantoms seeped away. The house sighed and settled, the web of cracks closing without a trace. Smashed crockery and a broken clay pipe remained.

Ophar knelt to comfort Farmer Rycote's wife where she lay huddled, her thin body trembling. He gently drew back the apron from her face and cradled her in his arms. She clutched at him while her sobs became senseless laughter and finally subsided. He hugged her closer, whispering.

Farmer Rycote refused to meet Kor's inquiring look. He turned glumly away to stare into the fire. The conjure-man took a rush-bottomed chair and sat down, waiting for thanks that did not come.

At last, he said, "Tell me about Larya. If she's your blood-daughter, I'd be surprised."

"She's not," Rycote muttered. "Took her in, her and the lad. No children of our own. She was sick when she came, but she got well, and Ophar helps me a lot in the field, with the animals, at market. The girl's a comfort to my wife, you know. We didn't know how we got on without them. When Larya first came here, sick, she couldn't tell us much about herself, and the lad didn't want to. Once she was well, we got used to them being here and figured the less questions, the better. Never thought we'd need to ask them questions. Look at him, look at Ophar there now." He pointed a shaking hand at him, still holding Rycote's wife so tenderly. "What blood-born son ever showed more love, eh? And we love 'em too."

"Bring me the girl," said Kor.

"No." Farmer Rycote's wife had regained her composure. Her refusal was calm and determined. "Let her sleep. It's over for tonight. The full moon makes them bad. Ordinary times, we just have the house shift a bit. It's full-moon time, the only time when—those ones—come. And they always go away, sooner or later. You leave Larya alone."

"It's all right, Mother." Larya was standing in the doorway that led to the sleeping loft. Her silvery-gold hair was tousled. A damp curl clung to her cheek. In her white homespun sleep-shift, she looked very small and delicate. Every curve of her body was visible, and in a way she looked more naked now than when she had lived underground, with only the wisp of Gryagi weave clothing her. Ophar tried not to stare.

"This was the worst yet," she said, stepping from the doorway with a sleepwalker's tread. "They are growing worse and worse, the dreams. Who knows when they'll stop, or where?" She took Kor's brown hand with a gesture of reverence. "You are a stranger here, sir. Did you see what happened when I dreamed? My family will never tell me how bad the dreams are for them. I trust you not to lie."

The old conjure-man smoothed the tangled waves of hair away from Larya's cheeks. "Something happened that I have only seen done by the masters of the earth-magic. It was the riving of the earth itself, a terrible skill when used in battle. But not even the masters I knew could call forth the spirits of Hori-Halira. You did. And you did so in your sleep. I expected this farmer's adopted daughter to have a gray face, a Gryagi face. Is this pretty mask a disguise? Shall I call up a spell of showing to break your spell of seeming?"

Larya bowed her head. "As you wish, master. I recognize your powers, and submit."

"Gryagi speech!" Kor exclaimed. "Just the ceremonious way in which a Gryagi shaman would address a brother adept. How do you come to speak like the children of stone? Why do you have such powers over the earth-magic? Tell me. I also trust you to tell me the truth."

"*Trust her?*" roared Farmer Rycote. "Do I have to listen to a two-penny witcher call my girl a liar in my own house?"

"Peace, peace," said his wife, trying to soothe him. It was in vain.

"No, I won't have it! Calling my dearie hard names. Children of stone, indeed! With a face like his, the color of winter mud, he dares to insult my girlie!"

"*Hush!*" His wife was on her feet and gave his hand a vicious tweak. "Can't anything penetrate your hollow skull? He is one of the last, one of the true seers! Look there." She pointed to the palm of Kor's hand, where Larya still held it. It was stained a rosy red and pricked with a black design of a winged lion. "The mountain sign," she hissed. "He comes from the lost halls of stone."

Farmer Rycote understood his crops and and his animals. He had never pretended to understand his wife. A tale-teller outside Bellman's Tavern would never seize his attention. He— not Ophar—would have come home smartly and left the story of Dammon behind without regret. His life had no room in it for high doings, and he disliked having a mystery seated by his hearthside.

"Blither-blather. Any charlatan could ape that mark if he

had the courage to endure the needle. But if you'll just leave off speaking ill of our Larya and see if you can brew up a little something that'll help her sleep sound, you'll have a reasonable reward for your troubles, friend conjure-man."

Kor flashed a smile. "Done. I will set a reasonable price on my services. Let the girl be left alone with me."

Farmer Rycote got a stubborn look on his scrawny face, a look that Ophar and his wife knew well. Much as Ophar silently agreed with Rycote, much as he too did not want to leave Larya alone with the conjure-man, he realized that it would have to be. Larya had to be cured of the living dreams.

Ophar laid his hand on Farmer Rycote's back. "It's a warm night. It won't hurt us to wait outside," he said.

"I'm not going to leave her with him." The farmer lowered his head just like a recalcitrant billy goat.

"Listen, haven't you always preached compromise to us, from the first day we came here? Getting along, making do with how things are, bending with the way it blows. We'll be right outside the cottage. If anything foxy's going on, I'll be inside before you can blink. You think I'd let him hurt Larya?"

Mumbling vague threats, Farmer Rycote allowed Ophar to persuade him to leave. His wife linked her arm in his to make sure he got out the door. The three of them stood huddled together under the stars and waited.

"How long has it been?" asked Farmer Rycote. His wife made no answer, resting her graying head on his shoulder. "How long will he stay in there with her?"

"It doesn't matter," said Ophar. "Time never matters when you're waiting. Let it be. We'll be called in when he's done."

"Waiting." Farmer Rycote gave a cold laugh. "What do you know about waiting, boy? Waiting's for women. Waiting's for dreamers who think things will change tomorrow. Well, they won't. The fields will still need a hand to guide the plow, and the mill will still need a hand to grind the corn. My father was a farmer, and his old dad before, and you'll be farmer here after me if you're smart. They've had their wars and they've had their sorceries—those who fancy themselves the great 'uns—but they always needed a hunk of bread in between. We've endured. We've seen them all at their games and we're still here. Always will be, too. We've seen it all."

"Seen what?" Ophar asked suddenly. "Have you seen heroes? Wizards? Dragons? What could you possibly see, buried out here in the fields?" The four claws around his neck clacked together with witch's mirth. He felt their coldness against his chest and saw the handsome face of the dead man beside the dragon's corpse. "By the Seed, I've seen more in the little life I can remember than you've seen in all your years on this forsaken scrap of ground!"

The cottage door opened. Kor's smooth words barred Farmer Rycote's enraged would-be reply. "You may enter. She is well." The worn brown hood of his cloak shaded his face from their sight.

They filed in as if entering a stranger's house and they unwelcome visitors. Larya sat on a stool by the fire that leaped and crackled around a fat new log. Her starry hair lay smooth on her back; her looks were serene. The plain white of her sleeping shift seemed transformed into a high-born lady's gown. Farmer Rycote and his wife regarded her dubiously, even when she smiled at them in her familiar way.

"I was right," said Kor. "Right in my suspicions. A Gryagi had a hand in the shaping of this one's dreams. She is their changeling—though by the polar star, I never yet heard of one they kept with them for so long. Treasure her, farmer. She holds the secrets of the earth-magic in the palm of her hand. I would take her with me if I could, back to the mountains. The time will come when we may need to call upon her knowledge. I could train her against that day. Ah, that day!"

A tongue of flame erupted from the center of the log and split the wood in two.

"Get out!" shouted Farmer Rycote. He seized the iron poker and waved it clumsily in the conjure-man's face. "Get out of my house, black one! Take your evil doings with you! If that's your price, taking my Larya, you won't have it without you kill me first. Get away from her!"

Kor's eyes glittered with green sparks under the shadow of his hood. "Hospitality." The word was a whisper. "Gratitude. Precaution. I would learn their meanings, farmer. The girl was never intended to be my price. All that I'd have asked was . . . companionship. No, not hers! Put down that poker before you hurt yourself with it. I dwell nearby, or did. I am old and have no children. My own son is dead. A brief visit from your boy—not long, but daily—was all I'd have asked. I would have taught him much. Who knows? It might have helped you someday. But let the road unwind itself to the path determined from the beginning. Good night."

A wind sparkling with grains of ice blossomed in the snug cottage, closing its snowy fist over the conjure-man's head. It whirled around him, melted to a blue light, and left the keen tang of winter behind. Larya stared into the fire, the only one to smile.

The round house of stones was never seen again. Ophar went with the dawn to find it and to apologize to Kor. The family had passed a bad night after the conjure-man's departure. Farmer Rycote's wife wailed and cried, calling on the ancestors of her family to witness what a blockhead she had married who dared insult a man like Kor, a man who was obviously among the last of the holy ones who had gone to the mountains in the time of heroes. Rycote snorted and scoffed nervously, and he ended the evening by threatening her with a beating if she would not be still. She knew he wouldn't dare lift a finger against her—he never had—but she kept quiet.

Ophar came back to the cottage with a great confusion in his mind. Not so much as a pebble remained to show where the conjure-man's stone hut had stood, not a single mark on the ground. All around the hillside, the grass grew thick and springy under foot, fresh as on the morning of creation. Rycote, seeing Ophar coming so late to join him at their field work, guessed where he had gone.

"No use running after the conjure-man, boy," he chuckled. "That house of his probably wasn't there to begin with. All tale-tellers can hypnotize a man when they like. He built the place out of air, then took advantage of the darkness to bollix your eyes and make you believe you saw it."

Ophar shook his head. "No. We all saw his power last night. That was real enough." The taste of helgras wine lingered on his tongue like a half-remembered song.

"You'd have gone away with the mage." Farmer Rycote's manner turned sober as the truth came to him. "You'd have gone after him if he'd beckoned and left us behind. Even Larya.

All of my words mean nothing to you. All of our—" He was about to say *love*, but held it back. Ophar's eyes were on him, but the young man's thoughts were elsewhere.

As they stood knee-deep in the young corn, a score of armored horsemen galloped across the brow of a hill within sight to the south. A black-and-silver pennant whipped in the wind from the tip of their leader's lance.

Farmer Rycote saw the way Ophar's eyes followed the riders. "So that's the life you'd have," he said thoughtfully. "Think the conjure-man would groom you for a hero? Well if you'd be a hero, you'd better know that it takes more than just the brawn to lift a sword. Any fool with muscles in his arms can do that. If you'd ever seen a hero—a *real* hero—you'd know how far you are from stepping into those shoes."

"Have *you* ever seen one?" Ophar was testy and snappish. He had been feeling irritable all morning, more so since he'd found the conjure-man gone. Even out in the open fields, far from any man-made walls, he felt closed in, trapped, miserable.

Farmer Rycote shrugged, a sly gleam in his eyes. "Oh, I suppose I have. If you count Lord Dammon among the heroes, I suppose I've seen one."

"Lord Dammon? But isn't he—?"

"Now don't confuse the man with the myths they spin over his grave. Lord Dammon's dead, poor man, and all the silly sing-songs about him coming back to save us all, the old brown cow included, won't put breath back under his ribs. But it wasn't so many years ago that he died. Here, hoe that row and I'll tell you about it."

Ophar did as he was told. He knew the songs and stories of Dammon, and here was Farmer Rycote, who made fun of them all, saying that he'd actually laid eyes on the great one. Ophar hacked at the weeds and listened while Farmer Rycote made him wise.

"Those men you saw go by, they're queen's men. I don't have much use for knowing how the land's ruled beyond paying homage to our local lord when it's needful. It doesn't concern us who he pays his respects to, in his turn. But seeing as we're talking of Lord Dammon, you might as well know that Lord Dammon himself was once the ruler of all the lands from here to the western forest. The lady who rules now in Mar-Halira, she was Lord Dammon's sister. Now, our good lord, he never called himself king, but lately it's become the fashion to call her Queen Devra. Ah, it doesn't make any difference to me what we call her. If it pleases her to be called lady or queen or empress, that won't sprout the wheat any sooner, will it?

"But back when she was only called Princess Devra, she and Lord Dammon ruled Mar-Halira together. It couldn't have been over ten years ago, now I think of it. He was a fine man to see, boy. A handsome man, just the way they paint him in the stories, with raven hair and sky-blue eyes. And he never held himself too proud or too good for ordinary folk. You could take your grievances to him if the local lord didn't clear 'em up for you, and he'd listen. You respected him. It was natural to respect him. He revered the spirits on all sides: earth-magic, air-magic, fire-magic. He made pilgrimages to the sacred places in the mountains, too. That was when it was safe for a woman to go alone through the land and the forests, in Lord Dammon's day. My wife—the reason she took on so when she thought that old fraud of a conjure-man was one of the mountain brotherhood was because she'd gone up the peaks with her family to worship when she was a girl."

Ophar took a rest, leaning on his hoe. "I wonder what I believed in when I knew who I was," he said. "Earth-magic? Air-magic? For all Larya's nightmares, I might be an adept as well as she. Why else would the old conjure-man have asked me to visit him?"

Farmer Rycote was complacent. "You were a farmer's lad like everyone else, judging by the way you swing that hoe. Our Larya's powers showed themselves even when she tried to forget she had 'em. Come in her sleep, they did. If you were something more than a man of the land, it'd have shown itself by now. Be content."

"I think I was a servant," said Ophar, getting back after the weeds.

"Oh, palace notions." Rycote dismissed the matter with a well-aimed spit between Ophar's feet. "Every lout wanting to better himself has palace notions."

"I was a servant," Ophar maintained stubbornly. "My first recollection was—was my master's death. He was a fine-looking man, my master. Almost as handsome as Lord Dammon. Same black hair and blue eyes."

"Pah, that's common enough looks to find among the high born. Our own Lord Maldonar looks most like Lord Dammon. It was him I saw in Lord Dammon's company that time I saw them ride through here. They dismounted at our door and asked for water. My wife brought them beer she'd brewed herself. Lord Maldonar turned up his nose at it and sulked because we had no wine. Wine! Where are country folk to store wine, just for the nobles' pleasure? But Lord Dammon, he drank down the beer and praised it, and he gave my woman a silver coin with his likeness on it. Now *that's* how you tell a hero, lad. He doesn't need a thousand bits of false ceremony surrounding him, because he knows he's worthy without 'em."

They spoke no more that day. There was a lot of tilling to be done, and Farmer Rycote had missed Ophar's help the day before, when the tall redhead had taken the geese to market. The lad's thoughts could wander where they liked, thought the old man, so long as he didn't slice off a toe with the hoe in an absent-minded moment. He was too valuable to the farm. Besides, it wouldn't be the same without him now.

Ophar bent over the land, smelling the warmth of the turned earth. He tried to recall whether that smell was as familiar to him as so many other, stranger things seemed to be. He felt a stirring in his heart when he saw the first green shoots in springtime, but that was all. He thought with longing of Lord Dammon, content to drink beer brewed by a farmer's wife, while Ophar dreamed of helgras wine. He imagined Lord Dammon coming back, as the songs promised, and stopping at Farmer Rycote's door again because the beer had been so good. He saw himself kneeling at the hero's feet and offering him the use of his sword and strength to stand against his enemies.

The daydream floated away under the summer sun, riding the wings of dragonflies. It had been too many months since Ophar had lifted his sword. There was no call for it on the farm. And besides, when Lord Dammon came again, he would have no enemies. They would line the roads to welcome him home, with little children holding up nosegays of field poppies and maidens tossing roses after him and the streets all paved with gold and silver coins. Meantime, there was still another acre of land to tend and cows to be milked before nightfall.

"He will return by another road," Ophar mumbled, chopping down the weeds. "Why should he pass by *this* door twice? He's sure to return by another road."

In the distance, a second company of the queen's horsemen raced past on the road leading to the market village. Ophar and Farmer Rycote did not see them go, and when they galloped away from the village, they took another road too.

"Look there," said the old man. Ophar shouldered his hoe and stared. The glow of burning houses and the rising smoke of desolation blended with the clouds of sunset.

PART III

In Seti-Halira

Farmer Rycote's wife sighed. "If another band of beggars comes, then may the holy ones aid us. There is nothing more we can spare."

Larya came up softly behind her where she sat, woebegone, on a joggedy stool by the fire. "You'll find something for them. You'd make soup out of air if it would feed a hungry mouth."

"There are so many of them." The old woman shrugged her shoulders helplessly. "There is no end to them. They never stop coming. I don't know what's worse, the men or the women and children."

"The men are doing themselves the worse service." Larya went back to the washtub to scour the few platters left to the family. "They try to get food by fear, and all they get is a beating. Then we bar the door and their women and children go hungry. If they asked—"

"They get nothing by merely asking. Not at other doors than ours, at any rate. How should they know that we're any better-hearted? They learn that threats work, an excellent way to force charity." The weak, mewling cry of a baby reached the two women. It came from the sleeping loft and was joined by a host of drowsy complaints in high, childish voices.

"The sick one again," said Larya, wiping her hands on her

apron. "He keeps waking the others. I sent Ophar out to gather herbs for the posset an hour ago. Where is he?"

"Why bother about him?" The old woman got up to start making their supper. Lately it seemed that all she had to work with was well-water and potatoes spiced with the wild greens that Larya found in the meadows. "He can look out for himself. He's got the only sword for miles, and Rycote needs him to stand guard while he tills the fields."

"I can't believe the beggars would steal standing grain," said Larya, one foot on the ladder to the sleeping loft. The thin sound of the baby's crying faltered as the grumblings of the other children grew louder.

"Believe what you like. They've done it. This is what comes of a curse, Larya. We've left too much undone. We've forgotten the holy places, and this is what comes of it."

Larya paused midway up the ladder. "This is what comes of something closer to the earth than curses or slighted gods." She spoke more sharply than Rycote's wife had ever heard her. "This comes from men and war and the wranglings of great lords. And it ends with the children."

She disappeared into the dark of the loft and so did not hear Farmer Rycote's wife say, "We have nothing to do with the great ones, Larya." As with all of her husband's sayings, she parroted it poorly, lacking his faith.

Larya reappeared on the ladder carrying a small, swaddled bundle in her arms.

"The child has fever. Some of the others have it too. I hope Ophar brings back enough herbs. Otherwise I'll have to gather them by moonlight."

"You're not going out that door!" The old woman's voice was shrill. "Not by night, and never alone!"

Larya carefully plucked back a flap of the baby's blanket to show Rycote's wife the sick child's sallow, wrinkled face. "If I must, I'll gather the posset herbs at the gates of the Dark Ones themselves."

Farmer Rycote's wife made the sign against evil. "Don't speak of them! Isn't that what I've said? We forget the holy places and the Dark Ones come. They will descend on the land from the black places between the stars if we don't remember the old ways in time. They will take Kor-Halira and destroy it. Ah! If I were as young as you, I'd gather together as many maidens as I could and make the pilgrimage to the mountains. I'd take the flower offerings and the cake offerings and the offerings of bird-flight. But when the Dark Ones come, there will only be offerings of blood."

The baby squirmed in Larya's arms and sucked on his fist. She held him close and began to chant over him, a lilting sing-song spell. Farmer Rycote's wife saw that Larya had decided to ignore her, concentrating all her attention on the child. Perhaps that was good. Ever since that terrible night when the conjure-man came, Larya had taken to showing her powers. They were good powers, strong, the powers of the earth-magic. Once she had asked the girl to teach her one of the spells, the one for sleep.

"There is no spell to teach," Larya had said. "The earth-magic is not the air-magic. The Old One taught me that from the first. The spells of the air-magic are constant and unchanging but weak. The spells of the earth-magic are strong but forever changing, as the earth changes with the seasons. Before you can work the earth-magic, you must learn to listen."

"I can listen," the farmer's wife had replied.

"No, not listen to me; there's more. You must listen to the earth itself. The words you need will come to you from the earth. You listen, and you cull each word of the spell from what the earth tells you. It takes a long time before you can learn how to listen, but I can teach you if—"

Rycote's wife had declined. She was in too much of a hurry. She had hoped for a catchpenny spell like the ones Baba Dran had cast at fairs in her town when she was a girl. Now she wished she had taken the time to learn earth-listening.

News of Larya's skills with healing traveled fast. That was what most of the earth-magic was, so near as the farmer's wife could see—healing. At first not many folk outside the Rycote's little circle of relations came to Larya. But that had been before the bad times came and the healers, like everyone else, put their lives on their backs and took to the road.

The cottage door opened to admit Ophar, a hefty burlap sack in one hand, his sword in the other. Farmer Rycote straggled in behind him. His beard was matted and his face was bruised.

"Save us all, what happened to you?" cried his wife.

"Save us all except him," snarled the old farmer. "While he went about stuffing that sack full of grass, I was set upon by four men. They broke the handle of my hoe and tried to steal my seed corn."

"I came back in time," Ophar piped up, sounding like a shamefaced child. "They had to drop the seed corn and run."

"The handle of the hoe is still broken!" Farmer Rycote flung the words back at him. "And I'm still hurt."

"I'll buy you another hoe, and Larya will heal you." Ophar wasn't sheepish anymore, but he still sounded like a child— a sulky one. Larya had handed the ailing baby to the farmer's wife and was rummaging through the herb sack. Ophar's tetchy tone made her stop and stare at him. She'd heard Farmer Rycote dress him down in harsher terms many times, with only a polite, submissive response from Ophar. Now there was resentment, plain to hear. Ophar had changed.

Holding a sword does it, she thought. Since it's been needful for him to clean and hone that blade, he's been different. There's a very thin thread binding him to this land. It will take less than a sword blade to sever it. But when?

"Buy me a new hoe, will you?" Farmer Rycote rubbed his cheek tenderly where a large patch of black-and-blue was already showing itself. "Where? It's no longer a day's stroll to market these days. The market's not held anymore. The town itself's gone. Those precious horsemen you gawked after burned it to the ground. Not even Bellman's Tavern was left standing when they were through, just husks for the wind."

Ophar laid his sword on the mantel over the fire. Larya saw how his eyes lingered on the blade before he turned to give her a hand pouring the boiled water over the herbs she'd crushed into a copper pot. Fragrant steam filled the small cottage. The baby whined, twisting and wriggling like a beached salmon.

"They had a good reason for what they did." Ophar spoke without looking at the old man. "The town was on Lord Fergan's land, and he was a traitor to his overlord. If every man followed Lord Fergan's example and he went unpunished, we'd be in a bad way. There is order in the world. We have to obey it."

Larya took two wooden bowls and emptied a dipperful of

the herb brew into one. Back and forth, back and forth she poured the hot liquid from bowl to bowl until it was cool, then sat the baby on her knee and spooned the infusion into his dainty mouth. The little one kicked and turned his head away, but Larya coaxed him from one sip to another until the bowl was empty. The baby sucked his fist and went to sleep.

"Who taught you to toss the names of lords around so quickly?" Farmer Rycote sneered. "You'd think you knew what you're talking about! Their doings don't concern us, do you hear?"

"Don't concern us? When you're afraid to till your own field?" Ophar's shout made Farmer Rycote take a step back, surprised at the young man's passion. "How can they not concern us when we see what happens to a traitor lord's people? The same will happen to us if Lord Maldonar ever betrays his trust. Lord Fergan's folk are turned off their land, poor wretches, and have to quit the boundaries of the old lord's domain. Where would we go if Lord Maldonar ever played the traitor's part?"

"Lord Maldonar will never do that, " said Rycote's wife. She seemed serenely sure of what she said. "He is favored by our dear lady, may she live blessed."

Farmer Rycote took his cue from his wife. "Yes, that's so. Lord Maldonar's no fool, not like Lord Fergan. He knows enough to obey, and he's got the queen's ear. What she takes from the traitor lords she'll give to him. And he'll pass it on to us, his faithful people. Why, I've half a mind to send you to Mar-Halira to ask him for a land grant. Lord Maldonar's got his eyes open for likely young men he can entrust his new lands to. Then you'd have your portion, and Larya could have all my holdings as dower-lands when she marries, or—"

"Larya, please come!" A small, urgent voice called from the foot of the ladder. A little girl with tousled brown hair and arms showing too thin under the sleeves of her sleeping gown stood rubbing her eyes and calling. "Please, Larya. It's my brother, Bar. He's awfully cold. I touched his forehead and it was like ice. I'm afraid."

The baby was laid in the old, old cradle that Farmer Rycote's wife had dug out of a dim corner of the storage loft. Larya clambered up the ladder while the little girl remained below, too tired to follow. She returned with a bird-boned little boy in her arms, his head swinging slowly back and forth over the crook of her arm.

"Bar is dead." Larya carried him to the stool by the fire. She gazed into the flames and would not look at the dead child or his sister or anyone there in the room with her. When she spoke, no one knew whom she addressed or what she meant when she said, "Lord Fergan is not the only traitor."

Farmer Rycote and Ophar were working in the fields together as the autumn came in. There was not much to harvest, but there was hope for next year. The bad times were over. Everyone said so. There were legitimate travelers on the roads again and scarcely a beggar to be seen. Men rode horses without fear of being pulled from their mounts, the beasts to be torn apart and devoured raw by roving bands of human wolves.

"We can thank our good queen for it," said Farmer Rycote as he enjoyed his first pipeful of tobacco in months. "You see? I was right. It was the rotten apples she had to be rid of. Now that they're gone, we'll have us a golden age. I wish I was young as you, Ophar. I'd have that many more years to enjoy it."

Ophar's scythe whirled in a silver arc and the wheat stalks fell. He thought it was oddly appropriate for Farmer Rycote to speak of rotten apples. Lord Fergan had not been the only lord to defy his queen. Now his severed head kept company with those of eleven other insurgent lords. They sat in a line on the battlements of Lord Maldonar's fortress, exactly like a row of rotten apples.

"Oh, I grant you there's still one or two outlaws to be weeded out," Farmer Rycote went on, "but our good Queen Devra will see to it. And honest folk will do their part to help her. You remember that, lad. If you see some stranger skulking around here, you take that misbegotten sword of yours and you lay him by the heels. There'll be something good in it for you if you bring an outlaw before the queen's justice. Land, I shouldn't doubt."

Ophar worked on in silence. He stretched once to straighten his kinked back, then slashed at the wheat with new vigor. It was easy to give himself entirely up to bone-wearying work. He knew it was easier to break his back in the fields than it would be to confront Farmer Rycote with the decision he'd made. When would he tell him? He didn't know, but his mind was made up: He was going to go away.

He broke the news to them all that night. The women were chatting happily about Larya's betrothal when he made his announcement. His unexpected declaration cracked Farmer Rycote's pretty dreams about the magnificent match Larya had made. With one of the queen's own men, by the gods! Not every farmer thereabouts got to call one of Queen Devra's knights son-in-law.

They had been talking about flowers and feasts and a gown of pale green for Larya and new shoes for her mam. Farmer Rycote was to have a brand new tunic of sea blue as a present from his new son also. Then they began to consider what Ophar would wear at the ceremonies and celebrations.

"Let him wear something green as well," said Farmer Rycote's wife, ruffling Ophar's thick, foxy hair. "But we must be careful as to the tint. He'll look like a juniper bush if we choose the shade wrongly."

"No," said Ophar. "That won't be necessary. I won't be here for the wedding. I'm going away."

The words were so simple when he said them aloud. He wondered why he'd hesitated so long before making his announcement. Nobody spoke. They transfixed him with their eyes. When he read the shock and sorrow there, he understood the nameless thing that had bridled his tongue. Not one of them moved. Then Larya sprang up from her place at the supper table and ran outside, her white hair streaming out like a unicorn's tail behind her.

He was after her at once. She was hard to find in the early autumn dusk. His heart led him before his eyes could spy her. It guided him to the modest rose garden that Farmer Rycote had planted so lately for the ladies' pleasure, as a kind of private celebration of the newly established peace.

The roses were all dead in the cold autumn air, their thorny stems scraping the dwindling light from the sky. A rounded white boulder had been set at the end of the garden and there sat Larya. Ophar came closer. She was not crying, just staring up into the leafless branches of the willow tree that sheltered the white stone seat.

"Are you mad at me?" She gave him no response. "It was only a matter of time, you know. You were the one who said we'd take our separate roads once we reached the surface world. That was years ago."

"So you run away now. You pick up your sword and run away. You're like the rest of them, Ophar, a coward hiding his fear with armor."

"I'm not running anywhere!" His anger flashed at her, but she ignored it. "Don't you understand? I'm no closer to my real life now than I was as a slave in the land of the Gryagi. All I know is that I won't find it on a farm. It was nice for a while, staying here, letting life just happen to me, and you were too sick to be left alone, and then you had those nightmares, and then the bad times came. I couldn't abandon you or the Rycotes. I owed you all a debt. Now you're marrying a queen's knight. The Rycotes can live secure under his protection. Everything's settled. *You're* settled; it's my turn to find my place in the world."

Larya's balled fists gradually unclenched in her lap. "I'm sorry, Ophar. I didn't know you felt that way. If you don't believe you belong on a farm, where do you think you'll go?"

Her face drew his eyes. Absurdly, he thought of ships lost at sea, pulled inexorably to a white beacon seen at midnight. If he could only reach it, touch the light, he would be safe. Words rose in his throat, but these were even harder to utter than his declaration of farewell, and so he let them remain unvoiced. He told himself that it was too late for such words. Earlier, maybe, but now the time for saying them was lost. The knight's name was Sir Raimon; Larya's knight. He was fresh-faced and handsome, a warrior newly blooded in the recent bad times. He had killed his man in battle and received a reward from the hands of Lord Maldonar himself. He would make Larya happy.

Ophar looked away from her. "I'll know the place when I see it, the place where I belong. If I have to travel every road in this land and cross the forests to the mountains, I'll find it."

"I wish you good fortune." Larya's voice sounded even more musical in the dark. "I'll cast a spell of safety over you before you go. It will shield you while your feet touch the ground."

He grinned. "I'd prefer taking my chances without a shielding spell. It might shield me from the very person I want to find."

She said nothing for a time. Then, like a dart, she flung the question: "Are you after the conjure-man?"

She had seen through him. She generally did. He thought it was her hold on the earth-magic that gave her such insight. "Yes. Yes, that's my real need for going. I have to find him, Larya. I think—I think he knows something about who I am. Or suspects something. I'd be glad to have even a suspicion to go on. That night in his stone hut, he told me that I'd be back to see him again. So I must."

"He is more than a conjure-man." Larya studied her hands as if they held a mirror of far-seeing. "That night—the night when he made me take back my powers—he also told me who he was. He made me see that the horror we witnessed by the boundary lake would haunt me forever unless I found the strength and the spells to defy it. We talked about strength. Conjure-men are strong, but the men of the mountains are stronger. The silver wizards are strongest of all." Her hands seized Ophar's. "Or so they were, until the Dark Ones tried to take our lands. Then the silver wizards rose up and fought them, defeated them. But many of their brotherhood died. The Dark Ones only retreated. There were hiding places prepared for them. Kor is the last of the silver wizards. You're right, Ophar; for your sake and for ours, you must find him." She thought a moment, then added, "But why won't you wait until after my wedding? It will be soon. A few days more or less won't matter since you've waited so long already."

Ophar shook his head. He felt the hurt going deep into his belly. Why should unsaid words cause such keen pain? They were only air. "I said I was going. If I linger now, it'll be worse. Rycote will think I've changed my mind. It'll hurt him more when I finally do leave after all."

"Then go!" Larya stood and struck his chest with her fists. "Go now, if you're in such a hurry! Get out of here! Don't let me see your—your ugly face again!" He tried to seize her wrists, but she jumped back. Perched on tiptoe, she ran a finger down the length of the white scar on his face. "Find your conjure-man! Find your lost life! But I wager when you do, you'll learn that you were never any woman's lover!" Her

brittle, taunting laughter rang out in the garden as she raced
back to the cottage.

Alone among the dead roses, Ophar followed with his hand
the path her finger had traced. The scar tissue was thick and
raised, livid by sunlight and sometimes even visible in the
dark. It was a terrible scar. Then he touched the hilt of his
sword. In its own way, the presence of the blade comforted
him. He hadn't retired it to its wrappings when the bad times
ended, no matter how much Farmer Rycote objected.

A rustling in the thorns made his hand tighten on the hilt.
His heart exulted, all Larya's words momentarily forgotten.
Something was moving, a lighter shadow against the sharp
black lines of the barren rosebushes. It hunched low to the
ground like a turtle and tried to hug the prickly barricade for
protection. Ophar's arms were covered by a thick wool tunic.
Beneath the cloth, they were tanned tough as leather by the
sun. A few scratches from a withered rose were unimportant.
He plunged his free hand into the thorns and hauled out the
intruder.

He got him by the scruff of the neck. Actually, it was the
back of a hooded robe. Ophar had seen robes of that design
many times on the persons of hoaxers and quacks seeking to
pass themselves off as healers. The deeply belled hood gave
anonymity. Ophar shook his catch roughly and the hood fell
back, showing a remembered face the color of lead.

"Mrygo!" The name was a gasp. Ophar's hand unclenched
from his sword. The Gryagi's all-black eyes were emotionless.
"I—we thought you were dead."

"Your thoughts mean nothing. Where is Larya?"

All the joy Ophar felt at seeing a survivor of the lakeside
massacre was erased by suspicion. "Why? What do you want
with her?"

"With her, nothing. My business is with you."

"With me?" Ophar felt like a bumpkin, repeating Mrygo's
words witlessly. "Why do you—"

"Where is Larya? Near?"

"She's in the house." Ophar motioned toward the comfortable golden lights of the farmstead. The Gryagi nodded, silently
gauging the distance with his eyes.

"Out of earshot. Good. I have a horror of spies." He laughed dryly. There was no merriment in the sound. A bewildered, curious Ophar allowed himself to be led from the nighted garden into a nearby stand of evergreens. The small, thick grove had been planted as windbreak long ago and was old when the first Rycote came to till those acres.

The darkness took on a different nature among the ancient trees. Shadows wrapped themselves around the man and the Gryagi, seemed to close a door behind them that shut out the farm, the moon, everything but the night and the children of night. Ophar shuddered, watching furtive stars dance across Mrygo's black eyes.

"What's your business with me?" He sounded gruff. He wanted to be gone.

Mrygo's hand on his arm was the dry, firm touch of a skilled Gryagi herbman. "I have a message for you. An old debt's come due. You're called to render payment, Ophar, and I'm to take you there. When can we go?"

"Go? Go where? What debts are you talking about and in whose name?"

"Names." The Gryagi shrugged. "Names are the least of it. Names don't matter. You've been called, that's all, and your debt demands that you follow me."

"Mrygo, you're talking madness." Ophar turned away. His eyes looked back to where he knew Farmer Rycote's house stood, but only a spearpoint of starlight pierced the interlacing of black-green branches. "Come back to the farmhouse with me. I don't know where you've sprung from or how you found us, but I do know something's wrong with you. You're talking dreams—" unconsciously, he parroted one of Farmer Rycote's favorite phrases—"talking dreams and babbling conjure-man's tales. Come inside."

"And see Larya?" Even in the darkness of the windbreak, Ophar could see how small and bitter was Mrygo's smile. "No thank you."

"Why not? She thinks you're dead. It would make her so happy to see you again, to hear—"

"To hear a ghost speak? You are naïve, Ophar. It's been a long time since she resigned herself to the death of our people. She doesn't need a reminder. Once a wound has healed, leave it alone. Don't open it up again."

"Yes . . . yes, she had some bad times. There were dreams . . ."

"The wounds I mean weren't only Larya's." He met Ophar's inquiring glance with a tight flash of teeth. "I thought you knew, worldling. She was everything to me. All of those times I came to see you were because she'd asked it. I'd never have done it for anyone else, not even for The Old One himself."

"I remember." Again he was the slave, the nameless one who worked in the eternal subterranean night. He squatted nearly naked behind his prison palisade and heard Mrygo ask for help, in Larya's name. "You loved her. You still love her."

"We waste time." Mrygo's voice was harsh. "What difference does it make to you? Or to me, for that matter? She'll be happier not seeing me, and I'll sleep as well as I can for not seeing her. I'll give you time enough to make your farewells. Say goodbye to her and to any others you like, but we must leave before dawn."

"Leave, by the Seed! Leave to go where, you lump?" Ophar knotted Mrygo's cowl with one fist. "I go nowhere for riddles!"

"Ophar?" Larya's voice drifted through the pines, sweet and fragile as a springtime breeze. "Ophar, are you there?"

"Go to her, then, if you won't come with me." Mrygo hissed and wriggled like a snake in Ophar's grip. "It won't be the first debt you've left unpaid. Go! Your pretty bride's calling you."

Numbness spread from Ophar's fingertips and touched his heart. His grip on Mrygo's robes relaxed slowly, and he released the Gryagi. "No bride of mine. She's another man's."

"Is that so?" Mrygo's brows went up swiftly, like the black wings of a startled bird. "So bravery and a good sword arm weren't enough for her after all. Our little Larya found other things to tempt and please her once she regained the surface world. What is he like, the lucky one?"

"A knight. One of Queen Devra's men, if that name means anything to you in your caverns."

"Is that all? Is that how you give the sum of a man here?"

Ophar shot the Gryagi a look of loathing. "That would be enough for any creature who didn't spend his life tunneling through the earth like a blindworm. I said he was a knight, didn't I? But that means nothing to you. Your ignorance—"

"Let's just say that it means nothing. What do I care for

your knights or you for my ignorance? If he hadn't sent me to find you and bring you back, heavenfires couldn't have made me come looking for you. I thought I'd seen the last of you beside the lake. Even if it meant dying, I was glad. Death offered me something sweet if it meant never having to see your ugly face again, slave."

Larya's last taunt echoed in Mrygo's words. Without thinking, Ophar swung back his hand and struck the Gryagi a staggering blow across the face. Mrygo lurched under the impact but did not fall. A grinding growl escaped his thin gray lips. He crouched into a ball of darkness and sprang at Ophar, clawlike hands reaching for his throat.

Ophar sidestepped, stiff-arming Mrygo's attack aside. Before he could return the assault, the Gryagi had landed, crouched, and flung himself against his foe a second time. His attack was so swift, so fierce, so full of hatred that their skirmish became little more than all crude assault on one side, all hasty defense on the other. Ophar's sword never came into play. He could not bring himself to draw it against the child of stone, and he had no time to wonder why.

One of Mrygo's leaps caught Ophar off guard. His heels snagged in the roots of a towering pine and he tumbled backward among mossy rocks and orange toadstools. Mrygo gave him no chance to regain his feet. He could only raise his arms as a shield against the Gryagi's next leap. Ophar drew in his legs, lashed out at Mrygo. Lithe as a shadow, the Gryagi danced out of range, too quick for Ophar's clumsy kicks to touch him, quick enough to be able to rip at the prone man with taloned hands. Ophar cried out as Mrygo rent the shoulder of his tunic and warm blood began to flow in a thin, sluggish trail. The Gryagi's laughter sounded like the chittering of little brown bats.

"Ophar! Ophar, plague take you and me besides, where are you? You be coming back now, you hear me? Leave your sulk, you great lout! Larya's unhappy. Get yourself in now!"

Farmer Rycote's voice carried from the cottage door, across the dead and dreaming garden, and through the lacy shadows of the pinewood. Mrygo heard it and tensed beneath his roughspun robes. Rycote's heavy feet came breaking through the sere stalks of vanished flowers, crunching the narrow gravel path, trampling down the yellowed grass.

"Ophar! Answer me, you worthless chunk! *Now*, I say!" In an angry murmur, he added, "Making my sweet girl cry. I'll skin you for it, see if I don't. Making her cry so bitterly, curse you."

Ophar pushed himself on one arm and opened his mouth to call out. In the dark, Mrygo plucked a stone from its wormy bed and brought it down on Ophar's head with all his might. The night around him exploded into a hundred different kinds of blackness. Ophar slumped down without a moan.

When he came back to his senses, he was first conscious of how badly the thin ribbon of light seeping through his half-closed lids hurt his eyes. He squeezed them shut, but that hurt worse. Trying to roll away from the light or to raise his arms across his face was agony. He heard a mewling like a kitten's and to his shame realized it was his own voice, feeble and desperate with pain.

Cool hands touched his brow gently. He tried to squirm away, but they were firm and the pain inside his head was their ally. He was pushed back into the softness of a thickly mattressed bed. He fought the pain and the hands because something outside his brain made him fight, but soon enough he realized that their touch meant him no harm. Their strokings eased him. He sighed gratefully and gave himself up to the hands until the hot light in his skull cooled from red to amber. He slept, lulled by their patient touch.

The second time he awoke was abrupter. The pain returned sharply too. Ophar's eyes flew wide and he jerked upright, staring about in the cold-sweat panic that follows nightmares. "Larya! Larya!" The hoarse cry caught in his throat, sounded bestial.

"Calm yourself. She's not here."

Ophar blinked, his eyes still fogged and out of focus. When his sight cleared, he saw that he was stretched out near a middling campfire. What he'd taken for a fancy bed was only a pile of pine boughs covered with a toss of soft cloth. The damp smell of old leaves and chill sap said *forest* even before he was able to pick out the obscure bulks of trees. The voice came from the other side of the flames, mocking.

"I should be flattered. You mistook me for her more than once. It was almost a shame to have you wake up. If it were entirely up to me, I'd have let you follow the dark road down and good riddance. But"—Mrygo yawned and stretched into view—"none of this is up to me."

Ophar's head still throbbed miserably. He groped cautiously for the spot where Mrygo's stone had hit him and encountered a plump pad secured to his skull by a strip of linen. Even the lightest probing sent fire needles shooting behind his eyes. He forced himself to keep a rigid expression. He'd be damned if he'd let Mrygo see that he was hurting. "You meant to kill me."

The Gryagi chuckled. "So I did. That rock started out to smash your thick skull, crawler. But about halfway there, I checked it a bit. Not that I wanted to; as I said, it's not all up to me. Still, a stone was a good means of silencing you before that furrowing farmer could surprise us. In a manner of speaking "—his grin was yellow in the firelight—"I killed two birds with one stone."

"Kill you if I get the chance," muttered Ophar. He tried to get up, but his limbs refused to obey. His body had turned into one giant ache. The little Gryagi only had to spring lightly over the licking flames and give Ophar the gentlest shove to send him sprawling back. The big man groaned in spite of himself.

"Rest easy. You're going nowhere for a while. Sit up if you like. I've a stew on the simmer in the coals. We'll eat presently."

He turned his back on Ophar as if the man were now beneath notice. He had discarded his hooded hoaxer's robe and squatted near the fire wearing only the rag of colorless cloth all Gryagi males kept twisted around their loins. With a long, cleanly peeled branch, he poked and stirred at something in the embers. Ophar watched. His mouth began to water as the strong, captivating smells of an expert herbman's stew reached his nostrils. Before long, he was cupping a rough-carved wooden bowl in his hands and greedily downing the fragrant mixture.

"Just like the old days, eh?" Mrygo's black eyes flickered with malice. "We used to steal close to your pen at feeding times just to see how you gulped your slops. We'd hold our young ones up to look through gaps in the palisade so they could learn good manners from watching bad ones." Casually, he dipped his long gray fingers into his own bowl and conveyed a morsel to his mouth. "You haven't changed." The utterance brimmed with contempt.

Ophar chose to ignore the barbs. He finished his stew and wiped his lips with an edge of the cloth covering his pine mattress. Then he tried to stand up. Mrygo observed him out of the corner of his eye, pretending disinterest. The Gryagi's muscles tightened slightly, ready to spring at Ophar's first hostile move. The big man was able to get to his feet and stood there, swaying a bit, until he felt steadier. It was plain enough that he wasn't going to attack anyone for some time yet. All he did was edge himself around the fire and help himself to a second bowlful of stew. He ate this standing over the pot, then returned to his place and stretched out full length, his back to the campfire.

Sleep took him. The stew warmed his insides pleasantly, conjuring away much of his pain. He did not open his eyes again until sunshine bathed his face.

"Good morning." Mrygo sat tailor-wise, greeting him from across the ashes of their dead fire. He was back in the hooded robe, with something long and bright balanced on his knees. Ophar's sword glittered like frozen water in the crisp autumn sunlight. Mrygo's small gray hands held the hilt inexpertly. It took a visible effort for him to raise and brandish the blade. Ophar's simple leather scabbard rested within arm's reach. Mrygo sheathed the sword after some fumbling and then, with a loud grunt, heaved the weapon through the air. It landed beside Ophar.

"Polished it for you." He showed his teeth briefly. Ophar found the Gryagi's no-smile unnerving. "Did a good job, or so I hope. You'll have no complaints about me as your squire." He stood and brushed ashes from his robe. "Well, come on. Buckle it on and follow me. We lost too much traveling time last night and we've far to go."

Mutely, Ophar did as he was told. His head hurt less this morning, but he still felt wobbly in the knees. Straightening, he took a steady searching look all around their campsite clearing. Ancient hardwoods surrounded them, and one lone pine, efficiently stripped of its lower branches to make Ophar's bed. Here and there a waxy torch of mistletoe peeped from between the knobbed leaves of an oak. Nothing tainted the forest smells, no scent that might have indicated a farm nearby or any human presence but their own. Sunlight dappled down, making golden splashes on the forest floor. However hard Ophar strained his eyes or strengthened them with hope, the forest went on forever.

"We're far from Rycote's farm. How did you get me here?"

"That's my secret. I didn't drag you, or your bones would tell you so. No, don't lose sleep over it. Pick up the cloth you slept on."

Ophar did, and saw the long poles of a travois sticking out under the piled pine branches. Their twin ruts ran back into the forest and for one mad moment he thought he would backtrack them to Farmer Rycote's cottage. Mrygo laughed his hollow laugh, reading Ophar's thoughts. "I've some of the earth-magic, crawler. Enough to hide a trail so well that you'd lose it before you went ten yards into the forest. Fold up the cloth. We can use it again, but we won't need the litter."

Seeing Ophar hesitate, Mrygo made a sound of disgust and did it for him, stuffing the folded cloth into the stewpot he'd used last night. He slipped it onto his left forearm like a maiden's berry basket. "Ready, slave?" he asked lightly. "Oh, but I beg your pardon. Those days are gone, long dead. Let's leave them so. You're no one's slave now. You'd prefer a more *honorable* title, wouldn't you? Shall I call you master? Would that please your ears?"

"My sword." Ophar spoke dully, as if stunned. "You gave me back my sword."

"If I did, so what? Clumsy thing. But it's been well cared for."

"Aren't you afraid I'll—" He hesitated, the palm of his right hand lovingly cradling the hilt. For some reason the touch of a sword's hilt sent deep thrills through and through him in a way nothing else ever had done. Farmer Rycote claimed similar pleasure every time his hands closed on the guide bars of the plow. When Ophar plowed, he felt only smooth wood.

"Afraid you'll kill me with it? With *that*?" Mrygo seemed amused. "I took your measure . . . master. I took your fighting measure out in the pines near Larya's house. I've faced opponents who were better armed than you and better trained. I'm still here; they've gone to the waters."

"Trained? You were an herbman—"

"Get moving. We want to make some distance." Mrygo glanced up at the sun boldly. Ophar always expected a Gryagi to cower from its light. With his head tilted back, a thick weal showed itself momentarily at Mrygo's collarbone. Under the weal, Ophar spied a round red boss. It might have been a pendant jewel worthy of a prince, but no chain held it. The red mark bulged obscenely, like a toad's eye, and pulsed clearly in the daylight.

"Root and Seed, Mrygo, what is that thing?"

The Gryagi's arm darted out to deal Ophar a cuff for an answer. It froze in midair and dropped slowly, reluctantly, to Mrygo's side without touching Ophar. All Mrygo said was, "That way lies the west." He took the path with a pilgrim's stride, leaving Ophar to follow.

Ophar's mind spun with questions, one piled on another. If he went docilely after Mrygo, it was half out of curiosity, half out of lacking anything else to do. The questions tapped and scratched at his mind the way the wandering beggars had assailed the cottage windows in the bad times.

He knew Mrygo hated him and had always hated him; that much was clear. Larya's face blinked across his thoughts like the ghost of a white butterfly. At least there was some reason for Mrygo to hate him so much. He had taken Larya away—and never mind that their escape had saved her from the Surin Gryagi raid. But what had happened to Mrygo? Their fight in the piney wood was a world away from their first clash in his slave pen under the earth. How quickly he'd overpowered the Gryagi herbman then! How close he'd come to forfeiting his life this time.

Yes, but he took me by surprise. The voice inside him seemed ready to make excuses. *I was distracted. He only won because he hit me with a rock when I wasn't looking.*

Did it matter how Mrygo had won that fight? The fact remained that Ophar's enemy—his anything but secret foe—could have killed him but instead had spared him. More, he had tended Ophar's wounds, even rearmed him, and now he was walking ahead without any patent fear that the selfsame swordblade he'd cleaned and honed might be thrust between his shoulders by the man he'd dared to call slave. You had to be a hard-trained fighter to go so casually, unarmed, with danger at your back. It made no sense. Ophar felt as lost and helpless as the day he'd awakened pinned under a dragon's tail.

The strange companions marched in silence. The forest path ran straight as an arrow, something else Ophar found peculiarly disturbing. The trees did not shoulder each other too closely alongside the trail. There was only scrappy undergrowth and a hands'-count of skinny saplings anywhere near the path. Three men could walk the path abreast without touching each other or brushing the sidegrowth. That wasn't normal in a forest so old. Ophar thought he felt something smoother and firmer than tramped earth underfoot, but leaves and other woodland debris cheated his eyes.

Mrygo stopped suddenly, at random, without a word of warning. A rough twitch of his elbow caught Ophar in the ribs as the big man walked heedlessly on. "The hour's late. You'd better rest. Night comes sooner the nearer we get. We haven't run into any danger yet, but I'd feel better if we had the fire going before the sun goes down. You *can* tell green wood from dry?" he added with a sour look.

Ophar set to gathering branches. Mrygo joined him, and before long they had a good fire kindled in the shelter of a huge oak a bowshot from the path. Wood for feeding the blaze through the night stood stacked and ready.

"You're hungry." Like most of Mrygo's speech with Ophar, the statement was flat and cold, totally uncaring. "I have some bread left in my pouch, but we can scour for small game if you want meat."

"I am hungry." Mrygo's stew was a faint memory. They hadn't eaten all day. It didn't seem to bother the Gryagi, but Ophar's stomach rumbled for more food. He eyed the woods speculatively. "What sort of hunt-luck can we expect in these parts?"

"You? Not much, if you hunt as well as you fight. But you might dig up a mole or two. There's also a stream over beyond those hornbeams where the mud turtles aren't especially ferocious. If you like—"

"Enough!" Ophar's shout silenced Mrygo. "I'm sick of your jabs. You've got me here—wherever here is—and heading who knows where. I don't know what you meant by a debt due, and you don't seem likely to answer my questions. I don't even care about your answers. They'd probably be half daft anyhow. But let's at least travel in silence if we can't go in friendship."

Mrygo's thin lips twisted. "Friendship . . . " he said slowly. "It's a precious thing, isn't it? Something to be savored and nurtured. Only time can prove it. Did you enjoy many friendships, master, while you were the farmer's man? Were you a man who attracted friends easily, so that now you expect some pretty words to make an enemy a friend, just like that?"

"Stay my enemy, then." He walked into the woods beyond the oak, vowing privately to bring back a good bag of game for the fire or spend the night trying. An old hurt without a face or a name swelled in his chest. *I'll show them. I'll teach them who I am.* He didn't know who *they* were, but he somehow understood that on the day he'd uttered those long-ago words, he'd given up all chance at friendship. Instead, he had given all his strength to proving . . . what? That he could not remember. What he did remember was nagging emptiness.

But there was one! . . . One who treated me as if we were friends. And that was impossible. I was alone . . . alone. . . . The ghost of remembrance faded into dull pain. He put it from his mind.

The sun was an arm's length from the western horizon when Ophar entered the forest. The overhanging trees were still heavy with foliage. Even in the fading light, their crimson and gold torches flamed with heart-stopping glory. But their thick crowns also hastened the darkness on. Ophar had the good luck to catch a hen pheasant before too long, although nightfall was already lapping close around the mighty trees.

The bird was a fine, fat one. He'd taken her with a fast slash of his sword across the throat as she rose from cover. It was a quick, tricky stroke and he was proud of himself. The limp, feathered body hung by the heels in the crook of his arm as he turned to pick out the distant glow of the campfire. Golden fingers of flame arched and beckoned. He picked his way back with his sword still in his hand.

Ophar stepped into range of the firelight and tossed the carcass down. He enjoyed the triumph of announcing, "My hunting's not so bad after all, Mrygo. And as for my fighting—"

He stopped. The small figure hunched beside the fire raised its head and regarded him calmly. The coarse robe with its deeply belled hood was the same but not the face within. Ophar felt as if someone had rammed his chest with a hammer.

She was a child; only a child. Even robes small enough for a Gryagi hung loosely on her. The hood tumbled back, showing a face of such perfection and delicacy that she might have been an artist's god-dream, but not a mortal girl. Her eyes were thick with smoky lashes, the deep brown of savory honey. Her skin blushed faint rose beneath flawless white, making a striking contrast against her raven's-wing hair.

"Who are you?" Ophar knelt. His voice sounded like Rycote's wife when she spoke of the holy places. "Where have you come from? Are you lost, child? Can I help you?"

The little girl's gaze was cool and steady. "I'm not lost." Apparently, the remark was meant to dismiss him, for she looked away, back at the leaping flames. The hood fell over her face, concealing everything but a stray black curl.

"But—how did you come here? Where are your people?" He got no response. He wondered whether he'd blundered into another encampment. Shading his eyes from the girl's fire, he tried to make out the gleam of his own. Perhaps Mrygo would help him with this remarkable child. Her hands were just visible under the drooping cuffs of the robe. They were soft, small, pampered things. This was some lord's child, a little one castle-raised, certainly not the kind of little maid a man expected to find in the wildwood.

No second dot of light showed itself. Darkness was absolute beyond the wavering light of the girl's campfire. She juggled the burning branches with a stick and fed the blaze from a neatly stacked pile of wood close by. The brilliance flared. By its light, Ophar recognized the vernerable oak that loomed above them. Mrygo's little cookpot lay on its side near the roots, the folded cloth still stuffed inside. He had found his own campfire after all.

His voice failed him. "Who are you?" he whispered. All the winter's tales Farmer Rycote yarned of ghosts and wood-sprites crowded into the clearing. "Who are you?"

The little girl's eyes flashed up at him. She laughed, a sound iced and silvery as the pole star. "I am Lilla. Naughty Lilla who loves to play tricks. Oh yes, I do. Mama scolds me for it. But she only scolds me when she knows what I've been up to, when she finds out. You won't tell her, will you? *Will you?*"

Ophar shook his head. He felt half paralyzed with her depth-less eyes on him. "I won't tell."

She clapped her tiny hands. "Oh good! I knew I could trust you. So strong, so very strong, but you are kind. Are all ugly people kind? I think they must be. No one else would like them at all if they weren't. When you're beautiful, you can behave any way you like." She looked for invisible spies in the empty clearing before adding, "My mama is very beauti-ful."

A flurry of black and green darted from the oak's branches and landed squawking on Lilla's wrist. It tightened its taloned grip and flapped leathery wings until it was comfortably settled. Baleful green eyes glared at Ophar. He felt a stab of cold and nausea in his stomach. Bird or beast, he'd never seen anything like that abominable liveling. Apart from its ebony wings, it was all frosty green eyes and gaping red maw. It had no head. The eyes and mouth were wide, horrible gashes on a squat body huddled between monstrous wings. The girl Lilla teased and petted it as happily as if it were a kitten.

"I must go now." It was a matter of fact the way she said it. "Gira says it's time, before Mama sends the others after me." She stood, the foul thing still swaying on her wrist, ready to go hawking down in Hori-Halira. By her height, Ophar judged her to be some nine years old, if that. She raised her free hand to him with a court lady's practiced air.

"You may kiss it," she said. "I allow it." He complied for the same reason he had followed Mrygo: He did not know what else to do. She giggled her delight while the thing on her wrist flapped its wings wide and gave a raspy shriek. The cry still echoed under the oak leaves when the pair vanished.

"Sorcery." Mrygo's robe lay in a brown pool at Ophar's feet.

He wasted an uncounted time staring at the empty robe while Lilla's face faded from his eyes. "Where is he?" He picked up the robe. "Where is Mrygo?" The robe was warm and scented.

Ophar called the Gryagi's name aloud several times. The forest swallowed the sound and gave nothing back. Night noises teased him; the fire died down. The dead golden eye of the pheasant regarded him and his fears dispassionately.

He couldn't let the fire go out. He got down to feed the glowing ashes, and as he did so, a sound distinct from the other woodland sounds came to his ears. It was weak, but he knew what it was. He didn't wait for a second summons. He only paused long enough to thrust a thick branch into the fire, a crude torch to light his steps.

He found Mrygo's body sprawled face down across the gnarled roots of a beech tree. His torch cast weird shadows but gave enough light to show how close the Gryagi lay to death. Mrygo was naked, stripped even of his loincloth. His gray skin looked like dried potter's clay about to flake and crumble into nothingness.

Ophar jammed his torch between the roots of the tree. Gently, he turned Mrygo over onto his back. Blood smeared his fingers. It came from a deep wound in the Gryagi's throat, still oozing more blood with every pulse of Mrygo's heart. Ophar tore loose the dressing binding his head and wadded the cloth tying-strips on top of the pad. He pressed it down as firmly as he dared, in such a delicate spot, to staunch the dark red flow. The Gryagi opened his lips, but any sound he made now was too weak to be heard. He had used all the strength left him in the cry that had fetched Ophar. Ophar's free hand rested on Mrygo's chest. He could scarcely feel it rise and fall. All around the pair, the night drew in closer. Jeering eyes like frozen stars watched from among the leaves.

"Master, the trail lies that way!"

The alien voice came from the direction of their abandoned campfire. It was high and hoarse, like nothing Ophar had ever heard before. In the darkness, with Mrygo dying in his arms, Ophar interpreted anything as a warning of approaching enemies. He tensed, drawing his sword. His body leaned forward over Mrygo's almost automatically, as if he meant to shield the dying Gryagi with his own flesh.

And for what? asked the thin voice inside him. *Why, for an enemy?*

"There, master, there! An easy trail." A thrilling chuckle rippled the darkness. The luminous eyes in the trees vanished, unnoticed. "Too easy a trail for my likings. There's a torch a-burning there. This way, master."

Then a second voice sounded, and its sound lifted Ophar out of fears, out of the living forest, to take him back to before the bad times and the beggars and Larya about to be wed. He was in a snug round stone hut—a hut like a clean, dry cave that smelled of mysterious flowers—drinking a wine he more than half remembered from the days when he'd known his own name. One more sip and the mysteries would all come clear ... one more ...

A raggedy being like a fat brown spider scuttled from the trees. Behind it came the low, melodious voice of the conjure-man.

"So this is how you pay your old debts, I see." He stepped into the single torch's light. His mountebank's robes were gone. His tall frame shimmered in white and silver and gold. The little spider-thing loosed a wild shriek, bright eyes fixed on Mrygo's body.

"Killed him!" it wailed. "He's killed him, master! Killed Mrygo, who was always so kind to me! Oh, the blood, the blood!" Its skeletal fingers clawed the empty air.

"I didn't harm him." Ophar searched Kor's eyes for a glimmer of belief. "I was hunting, and when I came back to our camp—"

The conjure-man stopped him with a flick of his hand.

"There is no time to hear your explanations now. We must save Mrygo."

"Can you, Master Kor? Can you?" The spider-thing seized the shining robes in hands so filthy looking that Ophar winced, expecting to see long smears left behind. The creature clung to Kor's clothes with toes as well as fingers, like a squirrel.

"I can try, Pryun. We'll all try. You, Ophar, can make your excuses later, in the sanctuary."

The wizened brown one flung itself deeper into the trailing

skirts of the conjure-man's robes and whimpered. "You're not taking him there, master? Not there, surely? Foul! He's foul past telling with blood, blood, blood! Blood in the sanctuary!"

The conjure-man's shadowed eyes looked down kindly at the tiny, cowering being. "It will not be the first time, Pryun. Or the last. Can you carry Mrygo, Ophar?"

In answer, Ophar resheathed his sword and gathered up Mrygo's body carefully, repositioning the pad over his wound. He held him with awkward tenderness against his broad chest. The Gryagi's head hung at a crazy angle over the crook of his arm. Madness made Ophar recall the hen-pheasant he'd killed, its dead golden eye, and the lovely child, Lilla.

The conjure-man gently shooed Pryun out of his robes. He came nearer to Ophar and removed the pad, laying his weathered hands on the terrible gash. His touch did not heal it completely or immediately. It hardly seemed to have any effect at all. Yet when Ophar looked again, he could swear that the blood no longer welled up so eagerly to leave the body.

"He will live until we reach the sanctuary, but we must be swift. Keep pace with us, Ophar. We may have to walk the winds. That can be a frightening experience. You must carry Mrygo, and you daren't be afraid."

"I won't."

"Never walked the winds before," tittered Pryun. "They all say they won't be afraid. They all say that until they've really done it."

"Hush. Ophar isn't the sort of man who promises bravery and then panics." Kor smiled and rested one hand on Ophar's shoulder. "We are old friends."

"Blood isn't much to you, then, is it, master? Very well, I'll lead him wherever you command. Come on." The spider-thing led the way. He clutched Ophar's torch, which he'd retrieved from between the tree roots. His irregular gait made it a bobbing light. Ophar followed with Mrygo in his arms, and Kor came after. As he walked, Ophar was ever aware of the conjure-man's presence behind him. He sensed it the way children feel a nameless evil thing behind them on the road that passes dark places. But there was only strength emanating from Kor, a silver and golden cloud of strength, a power without name. In spite of this, something inside Ophar turned cold and childishly afraid of stealing a backward glance over his shoulder for fear of seeing no conjure-man there, but a creature from the nightmares of his lost memories.

A wind began to blow. It was a wind out of winter, with the whisper of ice and snow on its breath. At first, Ophar ignored it, but the wind blew stronger. He had to lean into it, and as he did so, he fought to keep his eyes on Pryun's dipping torch. His tears smarted for a moment, forming crystal drops on his lashes. Pryun danced and gamboled through a rainbow. Mrygo's small body seemed to become heavier, sheathed in the ice the wind carried. Ophar's feet slipped and skidded underneath him. He looked down to mark his footing, up to mind Pryun's erratic path. For a moment he thought he saw the spider-thing cavorting on air. When he looked down again to check himself against stumbling, he saw nothing at all under his feet but night.

They were walking the winds.

Ophar's terror swallowed him. Not even the hope of seeing how high up they were, not even that! *This is the conjure-man's revenge!* whispered his little voice. *Make your excuses later? When will later come? In his eyes you murdered Mrygo, and he'll take your life for it. How high will he raise you before his magic lets you fall? Of all the debts you ever made, the worst was with the conjure-man!*

He knew he was going to scream. He was too frightened not to. His lungs filled with the cutting cold of the heights, his chest swelled with the desire to shriek like a birthing woman. And yet, with the scream at the back of his throat trying to claw its way free, he knew he would have to fight it back, to hold it inside him until he died. If he let his fears loose here, where the stars were black and the earth another lost memory, they would take their true forms and tear him apart in their midst.

I must think of Mrygo, he told himself. His fingers tightened on the Gryagi's thin arms and thighs. He thought he felt Mrygo move. "It's all right," he whispered. "We're taking you to safety. Kor will heal you there. It will be fine." He forced the scream out in endless, meaningless words of comfort. When he took breath for more, he inhaled the fragrance of evergreens.

He stubbed his foot on a rock and nearly fell, but blessed the pain. They were down. They were back among trees.

The trees thinned and soon were gone altogether. The night air was colder, but not so cold as while he had walked the winds. Overhead, the stars were pinpricks of ice.

Beyond the trees the mountains rose in majesty. Kor's old storytelling words came back. Now Ophar knew where they were going: to the holy places, the high places, the last hold of wizardry in the mountains. Hadn't Kor spoken of a sanctuary? Yes, the mountains . . . Ophar felt the mountain grow with each step he took, the slope getting steeper, the air thinner and biting. Pryun's will-o'-the-wisp torchlight was pathetic against the overwhelming night. Soon Ophar lost sight of it, following only the patter of gravel dislodging by the spider-thing's scrambling gait. Mrygo's body felt ominously heavy in his arms.

At first he thought it was a sheer wall of snow rising up out of the mountain's heart. Smooth, featureless, shining with a blue brilliance, it filled his eyes. The beauty of it drew him toward it, unconscious of everything else, uncaring. If his arms had been free, he would have run to it with them flung wide, trying to embrace so much glory. As it was, he trudged on, straight for it. Only one small back corner of his mind protested that it was solid and immovable. He would walk headfirst into unyielding ice.

Then the marvel of it surrounded him, returning his wished embrace, enfolding him in warm blue light sweet and heady as the first spring sky. Too soon the wonder faded. He had passed through. Ophar found himself standing in the middle of a sea-tiled courtyard, conjure-man and spider-thing at his sides, boxed in by topless sheets of azure marble. These were pierced with lancet archways that gave only flashes of distant, white light to hint at what lay beyond them.

"Welcome to sanctuary, Ophar," said the conjure-man. His long arms gently took charge of Mrygo's body. Ophar hardly noticed.

"I never thought it would be . . ." He found himself searching for words. His skin still tingled all over. His memories were just on the other side of a thin veil, but the veil was made of something stronger than cloth or skin. He could not quite break through.

Kor was already striding through the archway on the right, Pryun scampering after him. Ophar paused only long enough to look back through the archway behind him, expecting to see the snowy slope of the mountain trailing down into the woods. A fountain of striped green stone filled most of a courtyard, where three small girls and one little boy knelt over a gameboard. They looked up with fawns' eyes when they became aware of Ophar staring at them. The tallest of the girls recovered her calmness first and raised her hands with the fingers spread into stars. Small flashes of light exploded across the archway, filling it, dazzling Ophar's eyes. He rubbed away the red and yellow afterimages and looked a second time. Now the archway framed an empty courtyard, where the fountain still played.

He shook his head and went under the right-hand archway. Kor and Pryun had a good head start. If all the doors in this place were as capricious as the gate by which they'd entered, he despaired of finding his companions again. This one led into an echoing loggia, the pillars on his left all carved like golden lily flowers. Between the stone effigies, he saw a garden where real lilies bloomed, pink and white, green and flame. Other flowers were painted on the loggia wall, a sea of them so real that he imagined a breeze would make them sway. Only one door led out of the loggia and the lily garden. There was Pryun, waiting for him.

"Master Kor has taken Mrygo to be healed," he said. "He'll live. You be happy for that. I saw your sword!"

"I didn't use it against Mrygo, I swear. I met a child—"

"Oh, you kill children with that sword, is that it?" A grotesque bulge of flesh between Pryun's shoulder blades made it difficult for him to tilt his head back too far. He pressed it to the limit trying to throw it back in hard laughter. His seamy throat worked desperately under the strain until he looked as if he were drowning on dry land instead of enjoying himself.

"No, no. Never mind me," he said when he stopped the awful gulping sounds. "They let me tease and torment because that is what jesters do. And every royal court needs a jester. If he is malformed, that's all the better to conjure laughter, isn't it? So I guess that makes me a conjure-man as well. But am I able to match my spells against Master Kor's? Dear me, we must see."

"I don't understand. I thought the mountains were only places of worship, not royal courts. Is Kor a king?"

"He'd like to think so. He'd rule a realm so wide . . . he would if he could. But he can't. But soon he shall—perhaps. I can't read futures. I'm not a very good conjure-man after all. But I can read pasts very well. What's your name?"

"I'm Ophar. I heard Kor call you Pryun."

Pryun's long, lipless mouth spread itself even wider in a grin. His eyes were bulbous and unevenly made, but their deep brown color was absolute, without a trace of white to circle it. "Pryun *sed* Byuric. Let's not forget my due. So little is! We Gryagi set great value on our ancestry. My father was unique among his people. They must speak of Byuric sed Lyum to this very day."

"Why?"

Pryun tried to ape a human shrug. The gesture cost him his balance and set him stumbling sideways. He caught himself and looked eagerly at Ophar. "You're not laughing. My best trick, the drunken taxman, and you didn't laugh."

Ophar persisted. "Why was your father unique, Pryun?"

"Pryun *sed Byuric*! Son of Byuric sed Lyum! And Lyum was a famous shaman among the Surin Gryagi of his tribe. Oh, no one ever walked away forever whole after Lyum sent his curse after him. But Byuric wasn't afraid of his father's curses. When he packed up and said he was going to the mountains to follow the holy men, Lyum threatened him with this plague and that undoing. And do you know what my father said?"

Ophar shook his head. A great passion was building up inside the tiny creature, making his twisted limbs tremble.

"He said: *No curse can touch belief. Belief is all.*" Pryun paused. "Well? Is it any wonder I make such a fine jester, with a father like that?"

"I still don't—"

Pryun made a clucking sound. "The time! I must take you to the master's study. You can worship my father in person there. And Kor. We mustn't forget to worship Master Kor. This way, *this* way."

More archways went past, more courtyards. Once they entered a huge hall lined with dusty tables and benches. Even the sunlight that entered from the high, golden windows above looked gray and cobwebbed. They climbed three stairways, each narrower than the last, and ended by corkscrewing up a winding tread that left them outside a perfectly square scarlet door.

"We don't knock. Just go in. My place is *after*." Seeing Ophar falter, Pryun added, "You're expected," and gave way to more of his pain-filled laughter.

Not knowing what else to do, feeling more and more ill at ease in Pryun's company, Ophar did as he was told. He pushed on the scarlet door, his hand flat to the wood. It had no latch or handle to show him which side of the door he had to push or even whether it was meant to pull open instead. There was a soft sound, like the outrushing tide, and the door swung inward from a central pivot. Ophar's hand felt sticky—the red-stained wood seemed to cling to it—and he had to hunch over in order to squeeze his way into the room beyond. He heard Pryun's shrill giggles behind him.

The light within was warm and yellow. It felt full of the gentle weight of dreams after the clean blue and white sword-light illuminating the rest of the mountain sanctuary. It came from a ring of bronze wall sconces, each holding a three-branched candelabrum. The honey-colored beeswax tapers burned without smoke and cast a mellow golden ring. By that soft light, Ophar found it impossible to measure the dimensions of the tower room with his eyes. Shadows deceived him. At first he thought he saw Master Kor sitting there alone, then realized that there was another chair, another person in the room.

The red door whispered at his back. He turned and saw that it had closed. Pryun had not come in with him. He went closer to the two seated forms and knelt so that his forehead brushed Master Kor's knees.

The conjure-man's laughter was kind, quick, and so were his hands as he raised Ophar from the floor.

"My boy, what's this? Did I frighten you so badly? I hoped

you had more backbone than to be scared by my little perfor-
mance when we found you and Mrygo in the wood. It was
necessary, you understand."

"Necessary?" He could still feel the accusation burning in
Kor's eyes, the look that said, more than words, *You are a
murderer, and you will have a reckoning to pay.* Now the
conjure-man's eyes were crinkled with goodwill, smiling broadly
at him. For some reason he felt less able to trust Kor's benev-
olence than his wrath.

"Well, of course. We did not meet alone. A witness alters
many circumstances. I know you, Ophar. I know you better
than you know yourself. You can kill a man, and more than a
man, but you never raised your sword against Mrygo."

"How can you be so sure of that? Magic?" Ophar felt a
reasonless urge to dare Kor, to try provoking him back to rage.
Every fiber in his body was pulled taut, humming with a warning of something horrible hiding behind the conjure-man's smile.
If he could obliterate that smile, he would be safe. If not, a
gate was about to open and pull him through into a place he
half knew and fully dreaded.

Master Kor chuckled. The sound chilled Ophar's bones.
"Magic forms very little of my life here. Knowing you for
what you are takes very little sorcery. Knowing *who* you are
cost me more effort, I admit that."

Cold swirled around Ophar. He felt his limbs go stiff. "What
do you mean?" He had to force out the words. "What do you
mean, knowing *who* I am? I am Ophar."

"You are now called Ophar," said Kor. "There is a difference." He saw Ophar's mouth begin to form a question, but
Kor held it off for just a while. His dark hand rose to pluck it
away from Ophar's lips. "I know what you'll ask me, Ophar.
And I will answer you, I swear it. But it's a question I would
rather not answer alone. Here sits my brother, waiting to meet
you again after so long. He knows you as well as I do, or
nearly so. And like me, Byuric sed Lyum is one of the silver."

"Bid you welcome." The voice from the other chair was
rough and trembling with age. A twist of white satin parted as
a dusky brown Gryagi hand slowly emerged. Ophar extended
his own, not without a momentary hesitation. The brown hand
darted upward suddenly and tightened around the muscles of

the swordsman's upper arm, squeezing and testing what it found there before dropping away.

"Strong, Brother Kor." A second hand came up to pull back the gold-trimmed hood of Byuric's robes of wizardry. His face was creased and wizened as a dried apple. "The time lost has not been badly lost. I think he is even more powerful than before, in body at least."

"We can thank chance for that. He worked the mining tunnels of Mrygo's tribe for many years, but when he came back to the surface world, he fell in with a farmer. Hard work to make him ready for harder. He might have gone soft if he'd landed in a townsman's household."

Ophar's face turned from wizard to wizard. They were discussing him as if he were not present, speaking about his past in the calm, proprietary manner that suggested they could likewise set out his future for him and he would have to accept it. Anger began to take the place of fear.

Kor noticed, and it made his grin twist into a wry smile. "Good. We've pricked him, but he won't say anything ... yet. That is the man I knew, and know. As careful with his rage as a miser with his gold, but when he looses it—ah! The farmer kept him strong for us, Brother Byuric, but I had my doubts as to the wisdom of leaving him there."

"Whyever so?"

"Because that farmer—Rycote was his name—also fed our friend a steady diet of cling-close caution. Caution that might have grown into fear of every shadow not cast by a cow or a wheat field. Goodman Rycote came near to weakening him past help or use even while he was keeping him strong." Kor sat back down in his armchair. His fingers patted the carved griffin-heads. "Of course we could not allow that to happen. I sent Mrygo to fetch him just in time."

Ophar wheeled and walked grimly toward the door. He yearned to wipe away Kor's knowing looks. He wanted to run down the mountainside, leaving the sinister beauties of the wizards' sanctuary behind him. He heard Byuric's small cry of protest. When the scarlet door refused to turn for him, he was hardly surprised.

His voice sounded weary when he faced Kor again and said, "How much longer?" The conjure-man gave him a look of innocent puzzlement. "You can keep me in this room as long as it pleases you. I'm not fool enough to turn my sword against magic, so I suppose I must stay here until you tire of talking about me." He glanced around the room. "Is there no other chair? If I must put up with your games, I'd appreciate a place to sit and rest."

Kor and Byuric exchanged a look. "By all means." A third chair, of the same meticulously sculpted black wood as the others, appeared between the two silver wizards. Its arms ended in dragons' heads, not griffins'. Ophar settled himself, doing his best not to look at either Kor or Byuric. But the armrests of the three chairs were touching; his fingers could not avoid slight, disturbing contact with theirs. When he tried to draw his hands into his lap, as if on a silent signal the wizards seized them and pressed them fast against the sharp edges of the carved dragons' scaly crests.

"Shall we play one last game with him, Brother Byuric?"

"Oh yes! We must. And this time let him play too, for he must." Byuric leaned across Ophar. The red-haired swordsman was unable to move. He saw how long the Gryagi mage's fingernails were, how like amber claws. The tips were very white, and with one Byuric etched the outline of Ophar's scar.

At his touch, Ophar gave a loud cry that was a confusion of pain and protest. His face twitched as burning followed the trail of Byuric's claw. Answering pain erupted from his chest, four claws of pain raking upward from heart to throat. A silken noose tightened around Ophar's neck. The dragon claws, still threaded on their cord, leaped out of his shirt to clatter and dance before his eyes. Four black sickle moons dipped and soared against a searing blueness that dimmed his vision to a fog. Red streaked behind them, ripping apart the blue, bleeding away into new vision.

Maldonar! I should have suspected—don't run, coward! You won't outdistance—

Master! Master, have a care! It comes!

The words were cut off into a shriek. A swordblade halved the darkness. The stench of death and waiting death mingled in his head. He was howling a battle cry that he did not recognize. His feet pounded forward across rock so hard that every stride jarred up through his bones until he had to clench his

teeth or else they would shatter in his jaw. Another sword
darted out beside him. Blood was trickling down the side of
a huge, nameless shape. Hot wind plastered his hair against
his brow. Pain slashed suddenly across his back. He staggered
with the impact of a treacherous swordstroke and lashed out
weakly behind him. A tall man in rich garments jeered at him
and ran. He could not follow. The beast was on him. There
was his blood mingling with the monster's, and his clothing
was in tatters. The black claws whistled through the under-air
of nightmares. They searched for a way to end what the traitor's
sword had begun. Another shriek sounded, not human, just as
a heavy weight struck him down into unconsciousness.

He remembered that death. He remembered it as well as
any memory, because it was the first memory left to him after
he awoke, pinned beneath the dragon's tail. Therefore, his mind
objected violently, silently, when that treasured first remembrance was now torn from his keeping. He could do nothing
but watch while it happened.

He was no longer a part of the scene but a witness. His
perceptions hovered in the indefinite regions above the cave
floor where three human bodies and a dragon's corpse strewed
the stone. One was a boy, one a red-haired man he recognized
as himself, one a man with hair black enough to hold a blue
light.

But it was impossible. The red-haired man was dead, and
it was the other who was held down by the dragon's tail.

A huddled figure came creeping out of the shadows. It stole
from one body to the next, a stone bottle in its hand. Ophar's
face became wet, as if he'd been sleeping in Farmer Rycote's
fields all night and the morning dew had surprised him. Even
floating so high above his body, he felt that phantom moisture
and saw Byuric's face blink in and out of sight. Without his
icy robes, the silver wizard looked like any other Gryagi. Ophar
watched Byuric from above and below at once, lost in the
miracle of redoubled seeing.

Two slips of green light blazed against the twilight of the
cavern. They were there only a moment, but their presence
filled him with a harsh panic. He felt the green fires watching
him, and their cold vigil filled him with the desire to escape,
to give up all-seeing flight for safety, abandoning air for earth,

plummeting back down into the familiar shelter of his body. Even if it no longer lived, his flesh would protect him from the things he glimpsed in the emptiness beyond the watching fires' emerald glow.

Still air parted to let him fall, but when he tried to force his way into the body of the red-haired man, he was barred. Again and again, he tried. It was like pummeling his hands against the flank of a mountain. His spirit flickered its fear and desperation. *Let me in! Let me in!*

Then his terror broke. It was too strong a passion for his spirit to sustain. Inexplicably, a warm calm embraced him. It made him cease his fruitless efforts to enter that vacant shell. He would never be able to return to that body, he knew it for a certainty now, and knowing that there was nothing he could do about it worked an oddly tranquilizing effect on him. He was once more the detached witness, waiting to see.

Why should you want to return? Was your face so fine, your body so beautiful that the world will mourn the loss? The little voice that was always with him buzzed more faintly now that he had no skull to close it in. Its words lost most of their hard impact when unconfined by mortal flesh. He answered it from a place past words:

No one will mourn.

The voice persisted, as if peeved by his unaccustomed indifference to its taunts. *Not even Larya. And she mourned for the Gryagi, whose looks were less than human! Recall! Recall! She turned from you because you were ugly. She found a handsome man to suit her heart instead. You are dead, Ophar, and Larya's children will play in the dust of your bones.*

The high, thin sound dwindled on the air. Ophar felt the voice depart, abandoning him with the dead. It tugged by a thread as it went away, and the thread snapped easily. He was free of it.

Another thread tugged at him, drawing his sight back to the dead men. In a way impossible for human eyes, he saw the two widely separate bodies at once, and as he watched, the cavern where they lay began to fill with the thrum of waking magic.

It seeped from the rocks like water. It oozed and welled up around the bodies, softening everything it touched, laving them with change. Facial features rippled in the currents of power, skin and hair paled to the color of fresh canvas waiting for the artist's brush. New colors spread themselves through every strand, every pore, and when the spell had done its work and trickled back into the heart of the world, the living man had given his face to the dead.

Ophar's spirit shimmered with astonishment at the transformation he had seen. He did not have long to wonder. Something stronger than a thread pulled at him, drew him across the cavern floor, and dragged him down into the flesh of the man who lay beneath the dragon's tail. He fought it at first, instinctively. The cavern around him spun into a chaos of echoing sounds, phantom battles, whirling sights. Mortality closed over him like a wave, but in the final moment he knew that he was where he was meant to be, where he had always belonged. Four black half-moon ships sailed across his sight and he hailed them joyfully. He reached out to grasp the first one by the prow and haul himself out of the deep waters. A man in white loomed above him and gave him his hands.

Now it is safe for your return, my lord.

Brown hands touched his cheeks. They were wet. The vision was gone. He was seated in the dragon-head chair, his face cradled in Byuric's hands. The Gryagi mage's shallow breath was warm enough to dry the moisture still clinging to his face.

"Now you know," said Byuric.

"Now you may see," said Kor. He held a round mirror like a shield.

Ophar looked. He had last seen that face on a corpse. Black hair, blue-black, fair skin and the fine bones of a nobleman, blue eyes . . . so very blue . . .

"Welcome back, my lord Prince Dammon."

PART IV

Khana

His bed was gray ironwood traced with silver, the hangings white with silver threads. A silver eye, the mirror, sent the first sunlight rocketing across the room from the open terrace to wake him as soon as dawn light came.

And every dawn for twelve days he repeated, as soon as the light opened his eyes, "My name is Dammon."

On the thirteenth day, his lips began to form the now-familiar words and instead paused, trembled, and burst into a broad smile.

"Of *course* I'm Dammon. And the Seed keep Master Kor from knowing what a fool I've become." He rose from his bed and walked over to the mirror, an unframed circle of bright metal set flush with the wall so that it appeared to have seeped up out of the solid blue stone. He considered the face he saw reflected there, and for the first time he knew he'd lost all sense of wonderment at its perfection. It was simply his face, just as Dammon—Prince Dammon—was simply his name. Neither one was a miracle anymore.

It had taken him twelve days to come home again to his own skin.

He put on the saffron robe his page always left neatly folded for him at the foot of his bed and tied the sash securely. The morning sun was now a solid wash of light pouring across the tiled floor from the terrace. He could just see the thin, rippling line of magic that allowed the light to enter while it kept the purifying mountain cold at bay. It would be wonderful to throw off his robe and night-tunic, to part the invisible veil with his hands, and take the full blast of the morning winds on his naked skin.

But Master Kor would frown. Master Byuric sed Lyum would shake his aged head slowly, in a way that said without words how much of the hero Dammon had been lost while he wore the disguise of the farmer's clod Ophar.

It was a stupid impulse, worthy of someone as thick-headed and slow as Ophar. But he was almost fully free of Ophar's ugly ghost now. He knew who he was at last. He was the hero of the songs, the legend, the prince who had come again to lead his people . . .

His people . . .

On the first morning after his return to proper shape, he had clung to the shelter of his royal bed, ignoring the summons of the little page-boy the silver wizards had sent to serve him. The child was one of the four he had seen in the fountain court on the day of his arrival—the only boy. Still, Ophar's brain would refuse to identify the dutiful child-servant with the boy he'd first glimpsed in that weirdly lovely place until two more days went by. Ophar buried his head in the pillows and would not budge, afraid to look at a child. He knew he had gone mad.

Kor had come to him then. Dammon shuddered with embarassment now to recall how he had whined and begged the dark man to finish the joke and send him home again. He swore he would not abandon Farmer Rycote and his wife. He promised he would give Larya's marriage his blessing, as if anything so small could possibly matter.

"What does my lord prince fear?" asked Kor. His voice was warm and gentle, hiding a strong current of healing magic. He laid his long fingers against Dammon's arm, four swarthy streaks against skin the color of rose gold. "This? There was no easier way to restore you. If you can't take back a skin, how will you take back a kingdom?"

"I have no kingdom." His voice had dwindled to a miserable

whisper. He'd heard the beggars speak with such a beaten tone when the bad times first began, before they turned into animals and took what they could with a snarl when they learned that pleas did nothing.

"Not now. But you did, and you shall." He lowered his eyes and smiled slyly. "Didn't an old conjure-man once sing about how Prince Dammon would return? Will you make a lie out of my best marketplace story?" The smile slipped away. "Oh my lord, my lord, you were a king in everything but name, and while you reigned, this land was whole. I used to call you the Horseman King, did you know that? . . . No, how could you? You and I were strangers."

"Were we? Why—?"

"Why should I leave this palace? Why would I want to, so long as I was left in peace to study, to teach, to reach out and draw in the secrets of the outer magics? Earth and air, fire and water, and yet there are greater than these to be touched. And there were the pilgrims still, sometimes, who came to us to ask for the old blessings and to make the old sacrifices."

Ophar—he could not yet call himself Dammon without going cold—sat up straighter in bed, listening just as raptly as he had on the distant evening when Kor had come to set Larya's ghosts to rest and disturb Ophar's dreams.

"In those times, there were more souls sheltered here than a handful of children and a brace of old men." Master Kor's eyes sought the past and filled with longing for what was lost. "Master Byuric sed Lyum and I were Silver Wizards then as well as now, but that is all that remains the same. Where have the fair young maidens gone who made a sacrifice of song to the Powers of Air? Where are the strong young men who trained captive birds to soar in sweeps of beauty, a sacrifice of flight, evanescent as any flame, to please the Powers of Fire? They married—the fair, the strong—and their children came to scatter flowers from the mountaintop, a sacrifice to delight the Powers of Earth."

The old man's voice dropped. He had crept back into the past, lured by his own words into the shadowy pathways.

"And . . . the other?" asked Ophar. Master Kor stayed silent. "The other?" he asked, leaning nearer, speaking with some of his old force.

The conjure-man blinked, awaking. "What other, my lord?"

"Was no sacrifice made to the Powers of Water, too?"

That made the conjure-man laugh, casting off the seductive chains of memory. "Oh, sometimes we sprinkled a few drops of dew into the mountain lakes, I suppose, but this isn't a river realm. The forests go on forever, remember? And beyond the forests lie the mountains. Who knows what lies beyond the mountains, my lord? Who has had the leisure to wonder? They say the broad stream that flows south and east from Mar-Halira leads to a greater water, but—"

"Mar-Halira." Ophar repeated the name as if hearing it for the first time. Impossible, of course; Farmer Rycote had mentioned the distant glories of the queen's stronghold many times while ice hung in diamond strands from the eaves of the little farmhouse and a hare-and-hounds wind raced around the outer walls.

"Castle-land. The hub and heart of your kingdom, my lord. It *is* a kingdom, though you were always too modest to claim a king's crown. Long ago, longer past than before the time the Silver Wizards arose in the mountains, this land was a true principality. The lords of the realm paid homage to a distant king and did not dare to call themselves more than princes. But all things change. Kingdoms fall. The embassies sent out with the yearly vows of homage and the taxes and tributes did not return. It is written that a lone man who claimed to be the prince's chief ambassador straggled back to his lord's castle. He was ragged, filthy, half-mad with the burden of having witnessed terrible things."

"What had happened, Master Kor? What had he seen?"

The conjure-man studied his hands, dark, made for cupping secrets. "The man died, babbling horrors. The distant lord who ruled our princes had toppled from his throne, all his house had been slain, his flesh torn from his bones, his wives from their towers, his children . . . In the end, no one was able to ascertain whether that ragged man truly was the lost ambassador or only a wandering madman. None of the true ambassador's family claimed to recognize him, but the wise know the power terror has to tear one mask from a man and substitute another. Whatever he was, his words contained some seeds of truth: The world beyond the mountains was torn by a war that cut through all other realities, neat and cool as an executioner's blade."

Kor sighed. "It was a sword that cut us off from that ravaged outer land, too. The ruling prince decreed that no further embassies would be sent to the king until the full truth of things could be learned. If his lord the king wanted our tribute, let him send for it and guarantee its safe-conduct. Until then, let the mountains hide us, the forests shelter us, the land feed us, and the far-off king call when it suited him."

"He never did," said Ophar. Inwardly, he marveled how close in kin that ancient prince was to Farmer Rycote, forbidding adventure when the price of it was security.

"Never. That was many years past. Your ancestors could have called themselves kings in their own right, if only by virtue of how wide their holdings were, but tradition is a strange thing. They remained princes. And you, who deserved to be called king for reasons greater than wealth or influence, you followed their example."

Ophar gazed out the window. He saw mountains, and a dream of what lay beyond. At last he said, "You called me the Horseman King. I mean—you said that's what you called Prince Dammon." The slip set his teeth grating, but the cold was not so bad.

"*You* are Dammon, my lord." Kor's hand was dry and hot, a husk of heat against Ophar's new flesh. "In time, you will know it as well as I. I have seen many men afraid to acknowledge their true self, and they never had to step from skin to skin." His eyes shone with affectionate humor. "But some tales must be told by time alone. For now, I'll sing the song of Lord Prince Dammon, also called the Horseman King. It was one of the first songs of Dammon I made when I first started out from Khana in search of you."

The vanished summer evening returned, the drifting spirits of men and children slipped from the warm, dusky shadows. They had died in the bad times, many of them, and those who had survived had changed. Yet here they came and here they stood in the lee of a ghostly Bellman's Tavern to hear the song the wandering conjure-man sang of their hero, whose name at least could never die.

"The horses that lived within the mountains' circle were a

small breed, fat in the barrel, jolly, plodding, peasants at heart, every one of them. They would carry a fine lady with the same dignified air they assumed when transporting a bushel of pumpkins. As for the noble lords who served the princes of Mar-Halira, they adored their tiny steeds when they were boys and too proud to admit they feared to mount a taller steed. But when they grew in size and shank and pride, when they swung into the saddle and their feet dragged in the dust..." The conjure-man spread his hands to ask what-would-you, and the phantoms laughed.

Ophar laughed too. The ironwood bed lost much of the illusion of prison bars, the elfin richness of the room no longer frightened him, and the silver mirror's unblinking eye did not make his neck hairs stand upright every time he caught a glimpse of his new face in its flawless surface. That was how the change began, with laughter.

"And what did the Horseman King do about it?" Ophar asked. He had meant to ask: *What did Dammon do?* He had nearly asked: *What did I do?* Compromise was more comfortable and came naturally to his lips.

"Well, what you'd expect. He rode beyond the mountains and after many perils brought back horses fit for men to ride; tall-shouldered steeds bred by the Powers of Air and the Powers of Fire together at Lord Dammon's command. Only he could bring those two great magics together. Every child knows that war exists forever between fire and air, every flame that drives back the dark a sword in that ageless conflict, every cold breeze that flickers the candles a lance. But for this one time, to make such magnificent horses, to obey Lord Prince Dammon's will, the warring powers met in peace."

"That's a nursery tale, isn't it?" Ophar's smile was small but peaceful. "Made out of whole cloth. No one's gone beyond the mountains for ages, as you just told me. Not even Lord Prince Dammon."

"No, my lord, not even you." Master Kor's hand fluttered once in the air, and a tiny bronze statue of a running stallion appeared perched on his fingertips. He passed the trinket to Ophar. "A keepsake, my lord. They sing the songs of how Prince Dammon went beyond the mountains to fetch the magic horses just as sincerely as they sing about the closing of the mountains to the outer world. One is history, and one . . . merely song. There were tall horses in the land before you were ever born, but when you were gone, your people ascribed many great deeds to you. The bringing of the tall horses is only one of them."

"Lies."

"No, my lord. Love. A wise man learns the worth of a legend. It can be more precious than any sword, more powerful than any army. Think of how much your people love you if they sacrifice the truth to your memory. Not even the Powers receive such a sacrifice."

That had been thirteen days ago. The terrors had ebbed a little farther away with each day, but the nights brought too many of Ophar's memories back to let him come into Dammon's skin any sooner. At last, however, the change was complete. The memories held in Ophar's name belonged to life on the other side of a dream.

Prince Dammon walked from his room and found the narrow corridors of the palace empty. Somewhere, meat was frying, bread was being baked. Dammon might have summoned his page and ordered breakfast brought to him, but this day was special. This day was as new as his reconquered self. He intercepted the boy farther down the corridor and touched his sun-bright hair for luck.

"My lord, I will bring—"

"No, lad. Just tell me where you have your morning meal, then lead me there. I've been a rock-rabbit, huddled in my hole till now. That's done. I'd like to learn the limits of this place and the best starting point is always the kitchen; especially when you're as hungry as I am."

The boy grinned and took him down through winding ways, twisting staircases, and smoothly sloping ramps that seemed to feed into the roots of the mountain.

When they reached the palace kitchen, Dammon had a disquieting sensation. The room was cavernous, the size and shape of one of the endless vaults he'd wandered through underground before the Gryagi found him. He inhaled deeply, filling his head with the reassuring smells of bread and meat and warming milk to dispatch the ghosts of damp stone and clinging lichen.

There were five children in the kitchen besides his page. The oldest was a fair-haired boy who appeared to serve as the palace cook, with all the godlike privileges of temperament and prestige most good cooks enjoy.

"Another for breakfast, Telli!" called Dammon's page.

"Another?" Angry words died on the boy-cook's lips when he saw who the latecomer was. "My lord!" He sank to one knee, and the other children did the same.

Prince Dammon saw the small bowed heads, and his throat grew thick with an alien feeling. *My people* . . . "Please, don't. I want breakfast more than ceremony. Telli, won't you?"

The boy-cook rose, giving his prince a sidelong look of mistrust. A kindly tone when stern authority was expected put him off. "My lord? What would you have?"

Dammon strode forward until he could seize the youth by his shoulders and hold him stiff as a guardsman for inspection. Happiness burst over him, and he couldn't explain it. Somehow, the way in which they'd knelt before him as naturally as breathing made him want to embrace them all, these strange, white-robed children of the holy mountain.

"What I'd *have*, Telli, is a plate and a cup and a smile when you tell me where I can get whatever the rest of you are having to eat this morning. Lots of it! I've been eating your cooking for twelve days, remember? Not a day passed without my wishing to find the kitchens, just to sneak away a bite more."

A little dark-haired girl giggled. It was the first time Dammon saw one of the palace children without the mask of a sober-sided adult in miniature. "You wouldn't be happy if you tried sneaking extras! Telli tries to whack us with his ladle when he catches us filching snacks."

Telli glared at her, which only made the other children titter too, a conspiracy. His face went crimson, and he pretended they did not exist and addressed Dammon alone. "My lord, I—pleased you?"

"Someone who makes raisin-honey cakes like the ones I tasted yesterday? 'Please' is too mild a word! If any are left, I'll have them now, only . . . put your ladle out of reach for a while." Telli had to smile. Before long, they were all seated at the breakfast table while Telli doled out the leftover cakes, and each child from eldest to youngest doing his best to make Prince Dammon pay attention to him.

That was how Pryun found him.

The children froze in place as soon as they became aware of his presence. A shell formed around each one, and every note of frivolity faded in mid-air.

"Good morning, my lord." Pryun hobbled toward Dammon, taking a weaving route that made him stumble into as many of the children as possible. They did not move, but Dammon saw the nearly imperceptible way they flinched when he touched them. Pryun's wide mouth twisted.

"Don't worry, my little frost doves. My bones won't warp yours by touch. Anyway, Lord Prince Dammon's presence is proof against all kinds of monsters. You're safe from me. I've only come to fetch away your hero for a time, at the request of someone special." He dipped one shoulder in a bow. "Will it please you to come, my lord?"

"Whose children are those?" asked Dammon as Pryun led him up out of the kitchens by a different path than the one he'd come by.

The self-styled jester stopped to lean against a railing carved of steel-blue stone, the eyes of winged lions staring out over the fog-hung slope below. Pryun's chosen route clung to open walkways high on the outer wall of the palace, and was cold.

"Those children? Why? You've plenty of time to get an heir of your own after you retake your land, my lord. Still, I suppose it never hurts to be prepared. Lord Prince Dammon's successor, the chosen one! A boy as tall and straight as a spear, a fighting daughter lithe and lovely as a willow! There'd be a sorrowful song for the bards to sing, the tale of how your only child broke head and heart against the wall of his father's legend! For what child of yours could hope to outdo your exploits and make his own fame in the world? So perhaps it would be more merciful to adopt your heir. That way he'd always have the excuse of tainted blood to keep him from equaling your glory. But a child of your own begetting? Ah, no; no excuses there." Pryun shook his head as well as he could. "It's cruel to cast a child into shadow."

He was off again without another word, hurrying from the railing, setting his own peculiarly swift, scrambling pace.

Dammon was taken by surprise and never had the chance to repeat his question about the children until his eccentric guide ducked back inside the palace and stopped at a door like many others.

"Here we are, my lord." He whisked himself from sight, leaving Dammon gaping.

"Impertinent," he mumbled to himself, then chuckled because a prince who took umbrage at a jester's tricks was a prince who didn't trust his own claims to royalty. He tried the door and was mildly surprised when it opened easily. It would have been Pryun's bitter style to carry him through the maze of halls and passages only to leave him fighting a locked door at the end.

"Welcome, my lord. Kind of you to come at last."

Sunshine dazzled on the white of sickbed linens. Mrygo's face looked even gaunter and more gray against the snowy pillows. The trim wrap of bandages at his throat and the fat, billowy coverlet concealing the rest of his body made him look like one of those prophesying severed heads that evil magicians forever consult in crone-tales.

Dammon closed the door softly before crossing the room to sit in the chair at Mrygo's bedside. Black eyes took his measure. "We have made many crossings these past few weeks, my lord, for a pair of inexperienced travelers. I saw the outlands of a realm darker than my old caverns, and I didn't care for what I saw, so I came back. But you've made your crossing and it looks as if you're going to stay."

"Mrygo." He laid his hand on the coverlet and felt the underlying hump of the Gryagi's hand. "Master Kor said he sent you to fetch me here from Farmer Rycote's house. Why didn't you tell me your true purpose that night in the garden?"

"Instead of cracking your skull? That was easier. Come now, my lord, even after the silver wizards gave you back your proper face and form, did you believe them? Did you believe you were Prince Dammon right away?"

The prince's blue eyes turned inward, recalling the paralyzing fear of the twelve days after his return. "You did, what you had to. I see. I'm only glad I got a new skull in the bargain."

"My lord, I promise to use less forceful means of persuasion with you from now on. Will that satisfy you?"

"It will; if you will make me another promise to go with it, it will."

The Gryagi healer turned on his side toward Dammon. The coverlet fell away. Now the bulbous red scar at the base of his neck was again visible, more horrible than the bound-up throat wound above it. "You are our ruler, the hope of my people as well as your own. I've taken an oath to serve and support you, the same oath that every other fighting man in this palace took from the silver wizards the moment the gates were opened to him. What's one more promise compared to that? Name it."

The prince's lips were dry. *I am Dammon.* "I am Dammon, Mrygo. Call me by my name. Not 'lord prince', not 'my lord,' nothing that sounds like a title. Call me Dammon the way you once called me slave."

"Slave." Mrygo lay back and watched the watery reflected light of sun on snow dapple the ceiling. "I never changed skins the way you did, my—Dammon—but I've had my share of different lives in spite of that. One of them was a slave's life, although . . ." His exposed skin trembled.

"Are you cold?" Dammon made a move to readjust the coverlet.

"Leave that off. It smothers me, but the healer they've got here is fussy as a wet cat, and jealous of me besides. He'll never be raised to ranks of the silver, and he knows it. He also knows I'd only have to hint that I was interested in studying the ways of the Powers and Master Kor would take me under his private tutelage immediately. He gets even by smothering me with little attentions twenty times a day. There's few crueler ways to kill a man than nittering him to death. Pillow fluffings! Cover tuckings! Syrupy doses and bowls of meatless broth . . . blah!"

"You were pretty ready with the broth bowl yourself, Mrygo. When do you think your rival will give up on it and pick up a good, solid rock instead?" The Gryagi's face folded into a scowl until he saw that Dammon was jesting. Still, he did not smile.

"When you were a slave, I took care of you because Larya asked me to."

"So you said." Her name stirred memories, but they were Ophar's memories. He tried to banish them with words. "You loved her."

Mrygo's smile was barely there, the feelings behind it unreadable. "You speak as if I no longer love her. Well, since we're talking about past things we've shared, I've heard that *you* helped *me*, once upon a time. You were the one who brought me here, walking the winds with Master Kor. I wanted to thank you for that. I would have died if we'd come here by a slower route, but not many men would dare take the path of a silver wizard without knowing what to expect up there."

"It was frightening." Dammon allowed this part of Ophar's memories to come back without shame. The farmer's lout had shown courage. It was a part of his exile that the prince could acknowledge proudly. "But it had to be."

"Not every man would agree with you. I was your enemy, Dammon. I was your rival, whether or not you were mine. I hated you and I would have killed you for what you did— taking Larya from us—if too many other things hadn't intervened. Now I have had time to think about the past. If you hadn't been there to steal her away, she would have shared a fate . . ."

Dammon quickly touched the Gryagi's shoulder. His heart ached for the remembered agony reflected in Mrygo's eyes. Larya wasn't the only one dream-haunted by what had happened at the boundary lake. "Don't. That's all in the past, as you said. Larya's in the past too—for me, anyway—with the man you called slave. Mrygo . . . we can't lose the past completely, no matter how much we'd like that. But we can use it for better things than bitter memories."

"Bitter." Mrygo tasted the word. "Like Pryun. You're right, Dammon. I've taken the oath to serve you and help you win back your lands, but I'll add something more. We can't deny that we knew each other in the past, but I'll forget everything about that time except the fact that you saved my life."

"And I'll remember that you saved mine."

"Saved yours? You weren't near death when I poured my brews down your throat—in a bad way, but not dying."

"There's more to it than medicine. You spoke to me. When I was all alone, without even knowing who I was, you spoke to me. No one else did except Larya, and she came to me later than you. If your brews healed my body, what good would that be if I'd gone mad in solitude?"

Mrygo considered what Dammon said. "Then we're even."

Dammon's teeth flashed in a broad grin. "Yes, we're even. No debts and no grudges, but we're not total strangers, either. And if we aren't friends . . ." He gave Mrygo a hopeful look, but the Gryagi's face was stone-cool.

"We aren't enemies," was all he said. Dammon had to be satisfied with that.

The prince stood up and offered Mrygo his hand. "I'm going to find Master Kor now, but I'll be back."

Mrygo nodded, making no move to offer his own hand in return. "Pryun can bring you to me whenever you like; or the boy they've got serving you, but he'll have his lessons to attend. Still, if you could manage to have the boy be your guide instead of Pryun . . ."

Dammon paused in the doorway. "Before today's over, I mean to make sure that I never need to rely on a guide again." Mrygo's brows rose in silent question. "I'm going to learn my own way around this palace. I'm tired of mysteries, Mrygo. I doubt I ever had much patience with them, even when I was Ophar. Remember how enraged I got when you wouldn't tell me why you'd come for me?"

This time Mrygo's smile was fuller and truer. "Don't take that tack with Master Kor. He needs no rocks to shatter skulls."

It was Dammon's turn to look somber. "I have no magic in me; that much I know. Farmer Rycote's wife used to shudder at the thought of all the power a silver wizard could control, but . . . I'm not afraid of offending Master Kor or Master Byuric sed Lyum. Does that sound strange to you? Either one of them could destroy me in a blink, but I'm not afraid."

"Of course you're not afraid. You're Dammon, remember?" There was something wickedly appealing in the Gryagi's gentle taunt. Dammon realized it was the first time he'd heard Mrygo chaff him without putting a hurtful edge to the words. "If you've come again with the golden age hot on your heels, you can't sour the legend straight off by hiding in a cupboard from an old conjure-man."

"I don't even know if this castle's got cupboards. I'll let you know if any of them are your size."

Mrygo's smile remained, and Dammon's answered it. The healer even waved and wished Dammon luck in his explorations of the mountain sanctuary. Once he'd closed Mrygo's door behind him, the prince did not run off at once, but leaned his weight against the facing wall and slowly subsided to a weary crouch, arms hugging his knees.

By the Seed, how to take him? He looked at Mrygo's door for a moment, then hid his head in his arms. *How to take any of them! It's like paying court to a half-dozen coy ladies at once, and if I ever knew how to do that, it's gone the other side of Ophar. No, the legends don't paint Prince Dammon as a ladies' man. Slaying monsters is a more straightforward business than the niceties of a courtship dance. I don't know which way to tread with Mrygo, or Pryun, or the silver wizards, or even with the older children like Telli. They all expect something. But what? At least Farmer Rycote wasn't shy about coming out and saying he expected me to grow into a farmer like him, and no excuses.*

The prince's mouth turned up on one side as he thought of the older man's tirades against fool dreams of swords and adventures. The only truth he valued was bread. Dammon unfolded himself and stretched. It was time to put a name to Master Kor's truth.

He took his time seeking out the tower where he'd last met with the swarthy conjure-man. He was determined to make up for the thirteen days he'd lost thanks to his own weakness. Those lost days rankled badly. He would prove to Master Kor that they were gone for good. He was no longer afraid of where he was and who he was. He would learn every secret byway and niche of the wizards' hold, conquering this palace of mysteries the only way he could.

Only then he would go to Master Kor and learn all that it meant to be Dammon.

He did not find Master Kor in his study. It was Master Byuric sed Lyum who found him first as he was wandering through a small inner courtyard where flowers with gold-dust heads made a rippling carpet around a marble basin whose water was too blue to be so shallow. Dammon sat in the midst of the flowers and seemed to be watching for something.

"You aren't dreaming," said the fragile wizard. He leaned on a staff made of the metal that named his rank. It was as thick around as Dammon's wrist and it ended in a starburst that topped his head. "You did see them; once. That's their favorite game, to try to make men believe that their eyes are false. We call them birras. Would you like to see one . . . again?"

Without waiting for Dammon's response, Master Byuric began a soft whistling call deep in his chest. The bushy heads of the yellow blossoms rippled in answer, except for those immediately around the prince's feet. Master Byuric called louder, adding a purling undertone to the whistle. The waves of motion began to flow into one another until the Gryagi image was encircled, a pebble tossed into a pool of flowers.

Abruptly, he cut off the call, then uttered a shrill, sharp, rapid chitter. The undulations in the flowers stopped as if on signal, and the courtyard was still. Only then Master Byuric stooped down. When he pulled himself upright, he held a tiny winged ball of golden down in his hand. Bright red eyes like ripe berries regarded him bravely. White paws the size of a hummingbird's feather held each other across the creature's flossy breast.

The wizard raised the creature to a level with his eyes. "What's the meaning of this, little friend? Playing your games with the children is one thing, but now you must know who *this* is." He extended his arm so that the birra could see Dammon. Its eyes appeared to glow as it cocked its head to take in a new face from every possible angle. The silken wings belled once on a breeze before the small animal folded them in against its sides. "We play no games with princes."

Dammon made a platform of his palm. The birra sniffed his fingertips, chirred once, and leaped. It was like catching a sun-warmed puff of milkweed. Up close, Dammon could see that the birra was not at all birdlike, but closer kin to the clever field mice who were Farmer Rycote's bane.

"I've never seen anything like this before, Master Byuric sed Lyum." He stroked the birra's minute head with a finger. It closed its eyes and made the purling sound, wings quivering with pleasure.

"You won't, anywhere else. Oh, they exist elsewhere, but you've seen how they are. They dwell in fields of flowers that match their coloring exactly and only leave their covert when they must, to feed by night. They are so quick and wise that no man sees them unless they want him to." The wizard made a wry face. "When they allow a man to glimpse them by daylight, it's just to tease him. Men who see their bobbing flight by moonlight claim they've seen wood-sprites, and everyone believes them; but if a man would claim he'd seen a *birra* ... well, everyone knows there's no such thing!"

The birra in Dammon's hand tired of the prince's attention and took flight, climbing the air like a windblown seed before diving back into the flowers. "Beautiful."

"Yes, they are wondrous little creatures." Master Byuric nodded, adjusting his grasp on the silver staff. "Give me your arm, my lord. I would like to speak with you, but I must rest."

"There's a bench in the courtyard through there, Master Byuric sed Lyum." Dammon took the old man's elbow and jerked his head at an archway of copper-spattered stone. The hidden birras made the flowery carpet part before them as they left the golden garden. There were several benches in the neighboring courtyard, as Dammon had said, and the crouched shapes of seven winter-dreaming apple trees.

"Strange," said Dammon when the two of them were seated. "The grass here is dead, and the trees are barren."

"What would you expect, my lord? Winter comes earlier in the mountains."

"But back there, where the birras are, the flowers bloom as thickly as in high summer."

"Oh. Well, that is magic." The Gryagi mage's eyes twinkled. "You look puzzled, my lord. We use much magic here, being silver wizards."

"I know. In my own room—"

"In many rooms."

"But ... why not *here*?"

Master Byuric sed Lyum leaned his staff against the rough-hewn granite of the bench. Metal scraped on stone. "To know the powers means to serve them if you would have them serve you. The willingness to honor this truth marks the difference between true wizard and dark sorcerer. Any man can use tools—

we are made to use them—but only a wise man knows what to do with the tools he is not presently using. Your tool is the sword, my lord prince. When you must fight, it is a fearsome thing in your hands, but it would kill for another man as well as for you. The difference lies in the fact that you know how to care for the blade when you let it rest—well cleaned, properly sheathed, carefully honed. It will serve as well the hundredth time as the first. That is how magic must be treated, too."

Dammon regarded the twisted black branches of the apple trees. He knew how little effort it would take for Master Byuric sed Lyum to touch them with his staff and summon pink and white blossoms or even fully ripened fruit. "You let the Powers of Earth rest when they must so that when you truly need to call on them, they'll answer."

The old wizard nodded. "Just so. Magic tugs at the edges of things. Tug too long or too hard or too insistently, and things tear." He reached toward the nearest tree, the one whose branches cast a smoky arch over their heads. The tree creaked as it obediently bent to meet the wizard's hand. A touch, and the warped trunk and branches shot up straight and tall as a poplar.

"Wonderful," said Prince Dammon, staring at the miraculously transformed tree.

"Wonderful? When the spring comes and decks this tree with blossoms, the first strong wind will shake them from the topmost branches, leaving a ridiculous-looking half-bare skeleton behind. The few blooms that may survive the winds will die useless, the bees too tired to climb so far to turn flower to fruit. And how will the apples ripen, up so high, held on such fragile branches? The earth calls, with a pull stronger than any magic. They will fall too early, and the ones that do ripen well will hang out of reach of the earthbound pickers' hands."

The wizard touched the stiffened apple tree again, restoring it to its proper shape, gnarled and twisted, but beautiful. Byuric sed Lyum sought Dammon's eyes and held them. "You have met my son."

Dammon stood to run his hands along one crooked gray limb. He could already see the juicy green start of budding at the tips of the twigs. "You made this tree grow straight, Master Byuric sed Lyum. Your son . . ."

"My son blames magic, curses it, envies it . . . and will never understand it. Neither do you, my lord, but I see that in you which tells me you are willing to learn. Perhaps too willing." He hoisted himself upright, using his staff for a lever. "Let us speak with Master Kor now."

They left the courtyards and entered the inner labyrinth of the palace. Dammon set himself the task of walking always several strides ahead of the Gryagi wizard, peering through each archway they passed, familiarizing himself with their path, trying to guess every turn the old one would take before he took it.

Once Master Byuric sed Lyum said. "You seem to know where we're going," and pride warmed Dammon.

In the tower study, beyond the red door, the dreamlight of his first visit was gone. The bronze candelabra showed empty sockets. Instead, a window had appeared to let in icy daylight and the breath of the mountains. Master Kor leaned on the sill, throwing wheat from a glazed brown bowl to a cloud of birds. They stooped and wheeled in flight to catch the tumbling grains in mid-air, and not one morsel fell past their sweep of sky.

When the bowl was empty, Master Kor attended to his callers. "My lord, I'm happy to see you. We have much to discuss. Or has my brother already—?"

"We spoke of many things, Brother Kor, but nothing vital," said the Gryagi wizard. "The lord prince has been showing a commendable desire to learn the lay of the land, even when the land's limited to this castle."

Master Kor's eyes narrowed. "My lord Prince Dammon, that *is* commendable. You have initiative, though the songs men have made about you give it many other, more high-sounding names: boldness, brashness, courage, heart-strength. However, legends live outside of time; we don't. Now that you're prepared to accept yourself, there are many other labors ahead of you and little time."

"I know; the recapture of my lands—"

"That will come. That will come last of all, for if you neglect to accomplish the tasks we now set for you, the retaking of your realm will never come at all."

"He's willing to learn, my brother," said the Gryagi.

"What will I have to do?" asked Dammon.

"Just what Brother Byuric said." The conjure-man patted Dammon's shoulder. "You must learn."

That day and for twenty days after, Prince Dammon's life was bounded by books. Mornings had no space for long, pleasant breakfasts with the castle children or idle hours in the birras' garden. No saffron robe was left at the foot of his bed, but a student's rough tunic, the cloth coarse enough to keep a man irritable but alert through the thickest volume.

Dammon studied in a narrow, comfortless room whose sole window overlooked the sea of mountains lying west of Khana—the holy place of the silver wizards. The snow-capped crags had no end, and the view soon lost its ability to distract Dammon from his texts. His only interruptions were for meals and other necessities.

Living with few distractions made Dammon value every one he got. A week into his studies, someone scratched at the door.

"Come in, come in." Dammon tried to sound very busy with his reading and unwilling to be disturbed, but he was a poor actor. The door opened just wide enough for Pryun's crook-backed body to sidle through.

"So this is where they keep you, my lord?" A rolling walk took him past Dammon's desk to the window. He vaulted onto the sill and hugged the stone with toes and fingers, leaning out against the skeins of enchantment that kept a high winter storm at bay. Granular snow clung to the Gryagi's cragged features until he tired of his perch and did a somersault backward over Dammon's head to land on the floor behind the prince's lectern. The magic netting held the shape of Pryun's snow-covered face—a deathbed mask of white—before it recovered its former flatness.

"What a shame," said the jester, watching the mask crumble and fly away on the wind. "I thought it was a marvelous likeness. I am not like you, my lord, who'll have his features struck in gold someday. But then again, it's your face the marshwives will bite in the marketplace, not mine."

"What are you going on about? Who'll bite me?"

Pryun clicked his tongue and balanced himself on the rungs of Dammon's stool to have a better look at the huge book open on the lectern, clinging to the prince's shoulders. "So many pages you've read and you can't riddle me *that*? What's the use of education? I speak of *coins*, my lord; the coin of the realm that will have your face, that honest men will bless and evil men will clip and marshwives, with their creels of snared waterfowl, will test between their teeth to know the true value of a prince's noble looks."

Dammon slapped his knees and laughed, nearly casting Pryun off his back. "There's something to look forward to, having my face gnawed! In one sentence you manage to put kingship in perspective better than a stack of these books."

"Kingship . . ." The Gryagi gave a low whistle. "So you'll keep that much of your sister's—reforms?"

The mention of Devra was enough to end all laughter. "My sister has called herself a queen without the right to do so. She plays the all-powerful monarch, but I have no intention of aping her; not in that, not in anything. If I said kingship, Pryun, I should have spoken of governing."

"Don't let it bother you, my lord. You're not the only one in this palace who says one thing and means another." Pryun swayed at Dammon's back, still stealing peeks at the open book over one shoulder and the other. "A book of maps! Limned by my father's own hand, or I'm a turtle. All I remember of my childhood was a quilt spread in a corner, a wooden ball, and my father's back turned on me while he picked out invisible borders with his pen. If the ball rolled out of my reach, I'd call him to bring it back. That was one way of seeing his face, but a way I soon abandoned."

"Why, Pryun?"

"Silly reasons. A sigh. The oh-so-patient way he'd shake his head. All that pity in his eyes every time he was forced to look at me. I learned to curl my body into a ball and roll myself across the floor when I wanted to retrieve my plaything rather than draw Master Byuric sed Lyum away from his more important callings. In time I learned to walk as tall and gracefully as any lordling, of course, but until then, what were a few bruises to a child whose father could heal any hurt, any hurt at all."

The jester jumped flatfooted to the floor, landing with a loud slap. His mouth pulled to its widest when Dammon turned to look at him.

"Is that *more* pity for little Pryun I see, my lord? No thank you, my father's will do. Save it for those who'll have use for it! Save it for your people. Have the silver wizards told you how things go in your stolen lands these days? But"—a look of exaggerated perplexity made Pryun's face even more grotesque—"what *are* these days, my lord? They claim men lose all track of time in Khana. Have you been here a week? A month? A year? How old is Master Kor, really? Why do the children here have so much knowledge in their eyes? A pleasant thing, to live outside of time. A pity on your people, who don't share your good fortune."

"I know what my people have suffered. I lived through the bad times with them, even if I did it with another face and name."

Pryun's mouth looked ready to shear his head in two. "All the better reason to bide your time with books. Read *slowly*, my lord. Finish, and the silver wizards might decide that it's time you left this sweet sanctuary. Though I wouldn't worry about that too much. What are years to them? They hold the fourfold powers the way a houndmaster holds his pack in leads, but how many years did they let you wait inside a skin that wasn't your own?"

Dammon slammed shut the book of maps, his hands bunched to white-boned fists on the leather cover. Pryun tittered as he swept past, his mind dulled by unreasoning rage. He charged into the hallway, the jester at his tail, but he went only a half-dozen strides before his path was blocked by another of the Children of Stone.

"Get out of my way, Mrygo."

The Gryagi healer carried a stack of five hefty books in his arms. He stared at Dammon, then deliberately let them drop. They scattered over the narrow hallway in an irregular barricade. Dammon could either kick them aside, try leaping over them, or stand where he was.

He stood, not believing what he'd witnessed. "By the Seed, Mrygo, have you gone out of your mind?" He knelt to stack the volumns, picking them up one by one, wincing at the many hurts he saw. One had had its spine cracked in the fall, another had its pages crumpled, a third was so old that a page had torn out merely from impact.

"Light a fire to stop a fire," said the healer. "That's what my master taught me about sweating out fevers. You looked like you were burning up from the inside out. I just lowered the flame for you. Where did you think to go in that state?"

"We were going to find the wizards and—"

"We?"

Dammon looked back over his shoulder. No one was there.

"Pryun's handiwork is always signed with a flourish," said Mrygo. He squatted to help Dammon with the books. "He used to spend his time stirring up quarrels among the children and the garrison, but they all got his measure and wouldn't take the bait as often. You're fresh fish to him."

They made two smaller piles of the books and carried them into Dammon's study before giving the damage a second examination. The torn page and the cracked spine were the worst of it. Just looking at them gave Dammon a twinge of almost physical pain.

"Oh, don't worry, Dammon," said Mrygo. "It's nothing that can't be fixed." He smoothed the crumpled pages of the third book with his rough gray hands, then eyed the printed words. "This is about the Gryagi. Why have they got you reading about my folk?"

Dammon shrugged. He felt more than tired, and his eyes were suddenly heavy with a week of books weighing down the lids. "That I don't know. Maybe there's some connection between my folk and yours that I forgot; the powers know I've forgotten more than that. Mrygo, did your people ever trade with mine? Did we ever cross paths on purpose?"

"The surface dwellers and the Gryagi? *My* tribe? Never; not for lack of your people trying. You know how deep in the earth we lived, and you saw first-hand the gems our miners uncovered. Star-daughters and sky-tears and the scarlet birra's-eye ... why should we part with them? What could your people ever offer us that would be a worthy exchange?" Mrygo's mouth grew grim. "The Surin Gryagi had other ideas. They took to your trade goods ... and your ways."

"Master Byuric sed Lyum is Surin Gryagi," said Dammon. "So is his son. Ever since I've come here, I've seen how people edge away from Pryun, the children especially. At first I thought it was because of his looks."

Mrygo ran his fingers along the book with the broken spine.

"To surface eyes, all of the Children of Stone are monstrous. Tell me if that's a lie." Dammon did not deny it. "Living in the light, your folk place a great value on what their eyes tell them. Living on the world's outer skin, you prize the visible surfaces of things."

"Now *that's* not so."

Mrygo's rough fingers coaxed a rasping music from the cracked leather spine. Almost inaudibly, the healer asked, "Is Larya promised to an ugly man?"

He thought he had sent all the old thoughts of her away, all the old pain. Her name, coming at him so suddenly, showed him what a poor liar he was to himself.

"Sir Raimon is a queen's man—one of Devra's personal guard. She chooses them for their skill with sword and lance, but"—Mrygo raised one eyebrow—"also for their fine looks. They must make a handsome showing when they ride behind their queen."

"So. Larya's betrothed is not ugly after all. I thought not. Surface blood will tell, no matter how long you dwell in our caverns. But here in the mountains, the silver wizards have cast away the prejudice of sight. Even the smallest children learn to look below the surface of things to where the essence lies. If they fear Pryun, it's not for his looks. They don't fear his father or me."

"Yes, but Master Byuric sed Lyum and you—your limbs are straight, your bodies—"

"Look." Mrygo wore a linen tunic, its drawstring neck pulled tight and high to cover him almost to the chin. With one hand he untied the string, with the other pulled the tunic open wide. Dammon thought the healer wanted him to see the wound he'd taken that night in the forest, but he was wrong; not even a scar was left to speak of Mrygo's ordeal.

That did not mean that the Gryagi was entirely whole.

A raw, red circle pulsed like an evil third eye at the base of his throat. Webs of small blue lines stood out against the fiery mark, and as he stared, Dammon thought he saw fresh blood swirl up within the globe to dew its bulging surface. Mrygo touched the mark and let Dammon see the bright red smear on his fingers. There was also a ghostly brown stain on the inner side of his tunic.

"The sight of this makes the children cry. It's ugly, and it will never heal. A true Gryagi goes in his skin, and mountain cold is nothing next to the chill regions I've known underground, but I wear the surface garb I hate, just to spare the children. Blood frightens them, and this will always bleed—a few drops a day, but it doesn't take much to scare a child. Or an adult. You look green, Dammon."

In truth, Dammon felt a deep nausea that clenched his stomach and made his legs go watery. "What is that thing, Mrygo? Why can't—why can't the silver wizards heal it? Why can't they heal Pryun's bones?"

"They can," said Mrygo simply.

"Then why won't they?"

"Why won't Master Byuric sed Lyum heal himself?" the Gryagi countered. "He is dying, Dammon. The children know it. They fear death even more than they fear seeing this." He touched the mark once more, then retied his drawstring. Dammon felt his muscles unknot themselves as soon as the swollen red eye was safely hidden. "They fear his coming death and my deformity, but they love us. They only fear Pryun, and that won't change no matter how straight his bones become."

Dammon fitted the torn page back into its place. That book was another history that mentioned the Children of Stone. It was an old book and very thin. Not even the silver wizard who had written it in the better times of Khana knew much about that reclusive people.

"If Pryun's looks have nothing to do with how the children act toward him, then why—? I thought it might be because he's Surin Gryagi. Do the children know what the Surin did to your tribe? Is that the reason..."

"Pryun's father is Surin Gryagi too, and they love him."

Dammon exhaled a long breath and shaded his eyes. "Too many mysteries."

He was surprised to feel Mrygo's hard hand on his back. "Too many for one man alone. I confess, Dammon, that like you, I've found too many black corners in this castle for my liking, and I've been here longer than you. I've been thinking about many things since the day you came to visit my bedside.

Do you know what I've decided? We're each the only past the other's got left, and we need the past."

"Yes." A nameless man awoke in an unknown cavern. He was hungry and thirsty, bruised and weary, but he wanted one thing more than food, drink, or rest. Without knowing who he was, without knowing what he'd been—even if learning the answer would unearth the deepest shame—above all things, he craved the past; his past.

Mrygo placed his hand where Dammon could see it, palm upward. "I am your past, Dammon, as you are mine. Now let me also be your friend."

Dammon accepted Mrygo's hand. In the warmth of that handclasp, Dammon felt ghosts lift from his body and fly out into the storm.

Thirteen days more made up the sum of twenty, and Mrygo contrived to come back to Dammon's study on every one of them. Although the prince had no way of knowing it for a fact, he suspected that the Gryagi healer had also done something to ensure that Pryun was kept occupied elsewhere. What else would keep the embittered jester away from his "fresh fish" when he might have been prodding up discontent and enjoying the results?

The thirteen days went more swiftly than the first seven, mostly thanks to Mrygo. He was the one who gave Dammon what he needed to make the tedious studies pass better: the reason behind the labor.

"The silver wizards assume too much," said Mrygo, sitting cross-legged on the windowsill. "They never thought to *tell* you why you have to slog through all these books. They just took it for granted that you knew."

"And you just . . . asked them for a reason?"

"Why not? It was such a simple question and such a simple answer that they were embarrassed they'd forgotten to tell you and I was embarrassed to have to ask in the first place. You see, my friend, you've come back into your own skin like a man who comes back to his own house and finds that thieves have robbed it clean to the walls. They've done such a thorough job that he can't even remember everything that's missing. You're that man. What the wizards have you doing now"—he thumbed through the book he balanced on his knees—"is re-furnishing."

"At least I remember how to use a sword." Dammon leaned his cheek on his palm and gave the pages in front of him the lightest of skims. "Think where we'd be if they had to retrain me for battle as well as reeducate me to my old level."

"Ah, but the examination that Master Kor will give you in history and courtly manners and textbook strategies will be something you can take again if you fail the first time. When it comes to testing how much you recall of swords, it will be in battle against your sister's forces—and we won't get a second try."

"Glad to hear you say we."

The Gryagi closed his book. "I don't mean just me, Dammon." He slipped from the windowsill and shut the prince's book too. "Leave that and come with me."

"But Master Kor said that there's not many days left before we have to—"

"That book's a traveler's tale of how a man can journey underground through your land as well as above. Apart from the maps, you could have written an account like that—or a better one—yourself. Let it go. Master Kor didn't expect you to absorb so much so quickly. He's giving you any book he can lay hands on now to hold you busy. He thought it would take you longer to conquer the necessary texts, but your speed surprised him, and he's not yet ready to take the next step with you."

Dammon pushed himself away from the lectern. "I suppose you know what that step is."

"The sword is honed by the smith who makes it," said the Gryagi. "Meanwhile, the boy who'll use it practices with a sword of wood and cane. If the sword is ready before the boy or the boy before the sword, one or the other has to wait. Nothing can be done until both are equally ready to come together."

"I take it that I'm the boy you mean. As for the sword, I've kept my old blade in proper shape. There's no need for waiting on that account."

Mrygo looked bemused, but only for an instant. "You take things by the letter. That's funny. One of your songs has you trading the subtlest riddles with a witch until she burst into a thousand pieces out of frustration. She should've asked for a rematch today."

"There's probably a song about me claiming I gave birth to fire. Forget the songs and say what you mean."

"I mean that a prince's sword isn't just the one he carries at his side. Come along and I'll show you yours . . . a trifle early."

Despite the endless hours Dammon had spent locked up with his books, he'd made it a point to pass a part of each day exploring the wizards' palace. Days spent learning maps of the land and floorplans of the distant castle that were his birthright sharpened Dammon's desire to *know* the place that sheltered him now. Yet no matter how many rooms and halls, corridors, and courtyards he added to his knowledge, the way Mrygo now took him was completely strange.

"Is it impossible, or do Master Kor and Master Byuric sed Lyum shift the shape of Khana from one day to the next?" They were skittering down a corkscrew staircase whose outer wall was wrought-iron vines and air.

Mrygo was outdistancing Dammon, scrambling down the steep treads crab-wise almost on his rump, using hands as well as feet to propel himself. From far below, he answered, "That's one more thing they *could* do but *won't*. Khana has grown out of the mountains from the days of the first wanderers, the founders of all wizardry in these lands. They made it grow in the usual way—with the help of architects and masons and gardeners and so on—but never magic. They wouldn't use magic to change its shape either."

Dammon doubled his pace and slipped, bouncing and sliding down the spiral stairs until he tumbled into Mrygo, who grabbed onto the webwork outer wall to keep the pair of them from falling any farther.

"Patience," said Mrygo. "Let's get where we're going in one piece."

Dammon got back on his feet and flinched as he felt out his new bruises. "Sorry. Are you all right?"

"Stone doesn't mind a few bumps." He touched Dammon's arms and legs with the practiced hands of a healer. "Nothing to fuss over, but we'll stop racing. What we're after won't run away, and we're nearly there."

They took the last few turns of the stair at a more sober pace, then entered a child-size niche at the foot of the flight that appeared to lead nowhere but into a storage room. Wooden chests and barrels and crates stacked in neat ranks lined the walls. Mrygo slithered between two rows of barrels and showed Dammon a narrow door without bolt or bar.

"Through this, and we're there. Now no more talk. We aren't expected."

"A lot of roundabouting just to see a sword. Is the blade enchanted? Or guarded by a sleeping monster?"

Mrygo smiled and held a finger to his lipless mouth. He pushed so that the door opened silently by degrees.

After the murk of the storeroom, mountain sunlight had a sharper edge. Following Mrygo's lead, Dammon crept out into the daylight on his belly. Eyes squinted against the glare, he could just see the broad slabs of blue stone they crawled over and a wall of the same substance rearing up ahead of them. At the wall, Mrygo imitated a basking lizard, pressing his body flat against the stones and inching up until only his eyes cleared the top of it. Dammon did the same.

"Ahhhh . . ."

Mrygo poked him, made the sign for silence again, but Dammon didn't care. He had to do something to express the wonder that exploded inside him when he saw what lay beyond the wall. Wall? It would have been no more than a waist-high parapet on their side if they'd approached it in the ordinary way. On the far side, however, it dropped three stories down to a wide, grassy plain. This was no jewellike castle courtyard, but a full mountain meadow—the entire top of a peak somehow slashed off as flat and even as if by a giant's knife.

And covering most of that broad vista were the tents and steeds and banners of an armed host. Helmets and shields flashed lozenges of sunlight. Riders galloped their mounts through the ranks of striped tents or challenged each other in mock battles. A strip of land nearest the castle walls was churned muddy by horses' hooves and scattered with the remnants of splintered cane lances. A square patch of ground nearby was a cloud of gray dust as foot soldiers tested their sword arts against their comrades.

Mrygo stroked Dammon's skin with one finger, to get his attention. Dammon turned reluctantly from the spectacle below and saw the Gryagi form words without sound.

Ophar.

Ophar; the sword. A prince's sword of men.

"What're you two doing here?" A cane spear can be sharp enough to make a man jump when there's nothing between his ribs and the fire-hardened point but a student's tunic. Dammon leaped like a spring trout. Mrygo was more circumspect as he got to his feet, but the guardsman glowered at both of them with equal venom.

"I'm sick and tired of shooing you fry off this perch. You two look old enough to know better." He was grouchy as a winter-roused bear, and the resemblance went on from there. Dammon didn't think a man could be so hairy without a couple of animal pelts to help, but the thick black hair he saw under the guardsman's boiled leather shirt was all his own. One black eyebrow made an angry V above the man's small eyes, and under his nose was an inverted V of hair to match that bushed and bristled when he spoke.

"How'd you come up here anyhow? Who taught you the way? Was it that little devil-get Telli? I'll break my spear on his back for it."

Dammon couldn't keep from blurting, "Devil-get? The *cook*? He never—"

"Never anymore." The guard looked smug. "Used to be he was as bad as Master Byuric sed Lyum's get when it came to stirring things up, making trouble for others. *I* beat it out of him. Or I thought I did." The angry V was back. "The waiting's been tiresome enough for a trooper, and us with training every day, but all the boy's got is cookpots to keep him out of mischief. He could've forgot his lesson by now, and back to his old ways. Might be it's time I refreshed his memory."

"Telli didn't send us," said Dammon, eager to turn the burly guard's mind from his peculiar idea of *lessons*. "We found our way here ourselves."

The black V folded into an M that was fearsome. "That so? All right, you've sewn yourselves into a tight sack with your own needle. I'm bringing you to the captain's tent and see if he doesn't summon the Silver for this! They take us in and give us all we need with a free hand, but they tell us to keep to the place they want us. Your friend looks like he wouldn't do too poorly if they toss him out—Child of Stone can usually take care of himself. But you! Skin white and soft as that? A grown man with a face that fine? It's a long road from Khana to Mar-Halira, and that's the only place in these cursed lands they'd welcome looks like yours."

The guard finished his tirade and poked Dammon and Mrygo by turns with his spear, herding them along the parapet. He didn't address another word to them until they had descended to the plain by a series of shallow steps cut into the facade of the palace. These were scarcely more than toeholds and required tight-lipped concentration to negotiate. By the time they were on flat ground, Dammon felt no wish to do more than catch his breath and slow his heartbeat.

The captain's tent was the one nearest the swordplay ground but was no grander or finer than any of the others. The captain himself sat on a wooden stool before his tent and received reports from a series of men and women clad and armed in similar style to the bearish guardsman. Dammon and Mrygo waited in line with their keeper until the captain could attend to them.

"What is it this time, Turgan? Scooping up fledgling rock-falcons again?" The captain's curly red head was bowed over a scroll held on his knees. He seemed able to recognize the big guard from his boots alone, for he didn't bother looking up to greet him.

"You'd do better to have a look at these, sir," the guard replied. He was clearly miffed by his superior's casual attitude toward his catches. "They're full-grown birds this time. Well, one is, anyhow. The other's Gryagi, and telling *their* age . . ." He shrugged off the impossible task.

The captain raised his head. "Hello, Mrygo." The Gryagi healer nodded acknowledgment. "Now, don't you know better than to come nosing around Turgan's prowlway when you want to pay us a call? Up so high . . ."

"My people don't live underground because we're afraid of heights, sir."

"What kept you from coming to see me by the readier way, out the north gate?" He rolled up his scroll and gestured at the gate in question, a vast, towering portal situated at a few spearcasts' distance directly behind them. It was the first thing close to a conventional way for entering and leaving Khana that Dammon had seen since his arrival.

There are probably other gates besides; ordinary ones, he told himself. *The number of spells the silver wizards refuse to work outstrips the few they use. Bringing me into this castle through a solid wall is one thing, but moving so many fighters in and out the same way—!*

The captain and Mrygo were now deep in private conversation, speaking in voices low enough to make a wall between themselves and the others. Turgan and Dammon were left shuffling their feet and passing what-now looks.

At last the big guard snorted. "Well, that's the thanks I get for doing my job. Still . . . no better man than Captain Iskander to command *me*." He glanced at the captain, still oblivious to them, and rubbed his temple until he reached a decision. "Right. No sense standing here like field-frights, lad. He'll call us when he wants. Come one, then. Into this tent."

Turgan led the prince to a nearby shelter and held the flap open with his spear so that Dammon could enter first. Inside, the tent was comfortless but clean: a low rope-work bed, a stool, a flat-lidded chest, and that was all. A wet-weather cloak hung from a nail driven into the central pole, and an empty wineskin lay on the tramped-earth floor near the bed.

Turgan motioned Dammon to take the stool while he sprawled on the bed, mock-spear cradled in the crook of one arm. He pointed at the discarded wineskin with the toe of his boot.

"I'd offer you something to dull what's coming to you, but I'm facing the week without a friend myself. Let that be a lesson to you, lad: Pace it. Measure it out, whether it's wine or a fight or a woman, else you'll gulp it all down at a go and have nothing put by."

Dammon chuckled. Turgan's animated eyebrows described an impossible contortion, making it quite clear that he didn't see the joke. "I didn't mean any disrespect, Turgan, but just then you sounded like—like someone I haven't seen in a long time." He conjured up Farmer Rycote's face in his mind's eye, and for a while he forgot where he was.

A growl from his keeper recalled him. "Whoever he was, you didn't learn manners from him. I'm *Decad* Turgan to anyone but Captain Iskander."

"I'm sorry. *Decad* Turgan. Ten men under you?"

"Ten *spearmen*, pup." Turgan lay back on his bed, one arm folded behind his head, looking pleased with himself. "When you're ready to join the troopers, you'll still have a long ways to go until you're fit to be a spearman. *If* you're ever fit for more than looking pretty. We've got just two full decads of spearmen, but they're each worth three of swords."

"Only two—"

"When the word comes down, that's when we'll give a certain lady a surprise she won't relish." He swung his legs off the bed and shook his spear at the invisible foe. "Only cane now, but the silver wizards are making us spears of magic for this war! That's what takes time. That's why we wait here when we'd rather march. And when we *do* march, we'll march the bad times into the ground along with Queen Devra's ill-doings."

Slowly, the cane spear came down. Turgan sighed and leaned his bristled cheek against the knobby wood. "If we ever do march. It's the waiting that tells; it tells on us all."

"How long have you been here, Decad Turgan?"

Turgan took off his leather helmet and set it on the bed. The one spot on his body not covered with the thick black pelt was a circle of shining brown skin at the very crown of his head. "Longer than most, not as long as some. Captain Iskander, for one. *She* sharped up her claws on his father for practice, before she turned her minions loose on the other lords who wouldn't dance her tune. One day he was one of the council—named to it by Lord Prince Dammon himself!—and the next he was food for birds. She'd've served the son the same as the father, but Iskander wasn't where she looked for him."

"How did he know to come here?"

"How did you know? How did I, wandering the roads with a baby brother to mind and our land ashes? How did any of the lucky ones here today know where to go for safety? They were chosen, chosen by the silver wizards themselves! Plucked off the hungry roads, saved from Devra's dungeons, hid from her dog-guards, and brought here, every last one of us." Turgan threw his arms wide to embrace his unprepossessing canvas home. "Not much, is it? But more than I had for a long time. And my brother given the chance to grow up with no fear. Chief cook of Khana already, and him a brat! Where we'd be today if not for Master Kor—I don't like thinking of it. None of us do, except maybe that Gryagi friend of yours."

"Mrygo? He and your captain seem like old friends, but he's no fighter."

Turgan's dark eyes goggled. "No fighter?" he repeated. "Mrygo no fighter? What are you, blind in those big blue eyes? Didn't you see the crest-mark?" When his question only drew a puzzled stare, Turgan explained. "Here." He tapped the base of his neck, the same place where Mrygo's skin bore the bulbous red horror. Dammon shuddered involuntarily. The guardsman nodded, satisfied. "Then you've seen it."

"I wish I hadn't. What is that thing? A brand of some kind. I know that Mrygo's people were enslaved—"

"—by the Surin Gryagi; yes. And how much do you know about them, lad, beyond a bow to our good Master Byuric sed Lyum? Or his son." It was difficult to read Turgan's opinion of Pryun from his stolid face.

Piles of books in a narrow study ranked themselves through Dammon's mind. "The Surin Gryagi are the tribe that dwell nearest to the surface. They even emerge near dawn and dusklight to trade with us. They've adopted surface ways, customs, clothing, and in exchange for certain concessions on the part of the reigning princes—"

Turgan spat eloquently at Dammon's feet. "Leave that off. You don't impress me, even if they did cull you for the wizardly training. Books! Teach you everything and nothing. Think you'll ever learn just *what* surface ways the Surin Gryagi love best? Sport, lad; sport and wagers and all that means besides. And their favorite sport is pitting fighters against each other to the death; collared fighters that they train to the killing games. Someday, when you don't go all squeamish just thinking about the crest-mark Mrygo bears, I'll show you the collar that made it. I was one of the men that Master Kor sent down below, into the Surin holds, to free him. We lost twelve men..."

"Twelve men to free one Gryagi?"

"Twelve men to free a band of thirty!" Turgan's roar filled the tent. "Thirty souls, and we'd have saved more if our own number'd been greater. But we couldn't risk it, and of the thirty we freed, twenty died."

Dammon listened stunned as the burly guard recounted the ancient raid. The men under Captain Iskander had come into the Surin holds by a secret route that the old books of maps described. They came in the hours of rest, the span before a match of games was scheduled to be played. The picked fighters were always left penned up together near the match-ground for two spans before the games, letting death-fear work on them—*We share food and sleep today; will you kill me tomorrow?*

Captain Iskander had learned the underground ways of the deep-dwelling Gryagi. Surprise and ruthlessness were the strengths of the Surin Gryagi, but stealth was the strength of Mrygo's people. The troop from Khana learned silence from their captain. They had the captives out of the pens and free of their collars without a whisper of alarm reaching the surrounding Surin holds.

Then the madness struck.

"You should've seen them, lad." Turgan looked back into the past with a grimace of disbelief. "A chance to come quietly with us, to get safely away, to reach the mountains—they ran mad. No sooner we got their collars off than they let out a yowl and charged barehanded for the Surin holds. Roused every living thing, brought 'em down on us with their weapons drawn, and died shrieking on the points of a score of swords. We'd've all died with them, too, if it wasn't for the fact that our captain's a wizard in his own way. Turned our little handful of troopers and freed slaves into an army, fought a way out for us, and took two damn Surin hides for every one of our men that died."

Dammon searched his own past to find the feelings of a slave, newly freed. Escape—that had been foremost in his mind; escape and distance put between himself and his captors. Even the need to bring Larya back to the surface world was only a sliver of the deep need to get away. To turn back—to alert the sleeping masters and to die for it—that was an unaccountable madness.

"But . . . why did they—"

"Ah, there he is, Mrygo." Captain Iskander ducked his red head into Turgan's tent. The decad sprang to instant attention, but his commander waved him to relax. If Turgan did relax, it was not to any degree Dammon could see.

"Sir! Will you be wanting the lad for judgment now, sir?"

"Lad?" Captain Iskander cocked his head at Dammon, who stood up from his stool and made a polite bow. "Everyone's a lad to you, Turgan, if he's not a trooper. This man's older than a lot of your spearmen."

"Yes, sir."

"Bring him outside. Someone's waiting for him."

Turgan obeyed. All the easy camaraderie of their conversation inside the tent was gone. The bear was back, growls and grouches redoubled. He even feinted at Dammon with the cane spear again, just to show he meant business. But when they stepped out into the sunshine and Decad Turgan saw who was waiting for them with Captain Iskander and Mrygo, awe and wonderment made him drop his spearpoint.

Master Kor took a step toward Dammon. Turgan backed away. The prince would have bowed to the silver wizard, but Master Kor's hands darted out to frame his face. The wizard's breath smelled of spices when he spoke.

"Once I was the one to reawaken you, my lord. Now it's been your turn to awaken me. You open my eyes to the fact that your time of study is done. Brother Byuric knows too and agrees. As soon as word reached us that you were no longer with your books, we knew." The dark hands released him and withdrew into the silken shelter of Master Kor's robe.

Dammon began to form words of apology, then thought better of it. Instead, he said, "I've learned more in the past few minutes, talking with Decad Turgan, than from all the books you gave me to read about the Gryagi. If you think I must learn more before I'm ready to—"

The silver wizard's dark hand flashed from his sleeve. "Learning has no end. I forgot that. If we have endless time, it becomes too easy to squander it. My lord"— Turgan's eyes grew wider when he heard the wizard address his prisoner by that title a second time— "I think you must learn from harder things than books now."

The conjure-man's fiery eyes swept the vast encampment once, a scythe of flame. From the rows between the tents, from the sword-ground and the horse-ground, from the depths of the castle as well, the people came. They ranged themselves in ring after ring of faces around the space before Iskander's tent. Pale-faced children clung to the parapets of Khana, looking down, brought there by a silent summons. Kor's eyes scanned them after they were all assembled, making cuts on an invisible tally-stick, and he seemed content.

"The waiting is done." Without shouting, his voice filled the sky.

A murmur from the people answered, "*Done*."

Their breath come together into a gust that battered Dammon where he stood and blew his student's tunic to tatters. He felt a rush of sun-warmed air, then the caress of silk against his skin. There was a heavy weight in his right hand, and the joints of his left-hand fingers were pressed apart by three thick rings. Sunlight glared, dazing him. The sun itself was balanced on the tip of the gilt-traced sword that raised his right hand by its own power. Blue silk flapped and flared behind him, a monstrous wing in the wind, and when the dazzle was out of his eyes, he saw that he and Master Kor stood on the bronzed skull of a dragon's bones that towered over castle and plain.

Four black claws leaped against their silken tether. Dammon felt them prick his chest, bulge against the white shirt that had replaced his student's tunic. The shining skeleton of the monster trickled away from under his feet, a cascade of bone, and the people of castle and encampment were shouting something, a roar like a mountain river, a thunder of words that shook him to the core of his soul.

"*MAY OUR EYES SEE HIS SWORD!*"
"*MAY OUR EYES SEE HIS SWORD!*"
"*MAY OUR EYES SEE HIS SWORD!*"

He held it high for all of them to see. He turned on the empty-socketed summit of the dragon's bones and let them know his face. Their voices surged over him, filling him with every dream that they thought had died in the bad times. He never noticed it when Master Kor was not beside him anymore. He held both arms high and seized what was his: the legends, the songs, the dreams.

"I am Dammon!" he shouted from the height, and the people cheered. *"I am Dammon, and I have returned!"*

"MAY OUR EYES SEE HIS SWORD!"

Suddenly, the wind turned wet and cold, colder than blood could bear. Prince Dammon's sword dropped to his side. The acclamations of the crowd ebbed into silence. Master Kor was with him atop the skull again, but his presence gave no comfort.

"What is it?" he asked the wizard. "What's happening?"

"What was certain to happen soon."

The silver wizard gestured for Dammon to look overhead. The roar of the people's voices still hung on the air in waves of power, silent but there, like a promise. The mountain sky had grown milky gray with holding it, curded clouds skimming in from the west, engulfing the sun. The crowd below huddled together; the children on the parapets fled back into the castle. A thin keening came, but if it was the cloud-thick wind or a human cry, it made no difference in what happened.

Master Kor's hand sparkled with ice-lights, a dance of shining motes that he cast onto the swelling wind. Dammon traced the flight of that luminous dust as it scattered over the upturned faces below.

One particle touched each person, each face. On some it only flared to a point of blue fire that drew a smile and sigh of pleasure. But when the twinkling dust touched most of the people who had cried their prince's name, the mote spread, washed over them in rippling yellow transparency from brow to feet.

When the waves of golden light touched the ground, the magic sank in like water and drank down the people with it.

Dammon's mouth hung open in horror. The broad mountain-top meadow was gone, and of all the army so lately there, eight of every ten fighters had vanished, taking tents and horses and weapons with them. The remnant of troops fit easily into the large, fully enclosed court that the meadow had become. The dragon's bronze bones subsided gently into the cracks between the courtyard flagstones, leaving Dammon gaping in Captain Iskander's face.

The red-haired captain fell to one knee, head bowed before his returned prince. All the fighters left did the same, but Dammon was in no state to acknowledge their homage.

"Where have they gone? In the name of all the powers, Master Kor, is this my sister's work?"

The silver wizard denied it. "Devra serves the powers of air, but Khana is carved of a mountain, most powerful source of the powers of earth. The nearer to the living earth they are, the weaker your sister's minions become. That was why we let you hide beneath the earth for so long, my lord; to keep you safe from them. They could see you there, but faintly, and never pierce the spells disguising you."

"Then if Devra hasn't stolen my troops—"

"His troops." That was Mrygo. The Gryagi wasn't kneeling with the rest. "If you can seize your lands from Devra as quickly as you take over Captain Iskander's command, we're in for a short war."

Head still bowed, Captain Iskander said, "Mrygo, you know they're his. Before we even dreamed that we'd be alive to see him come back, they were Lord Prince Dammon's. We serve him in all things." His chin lifted, and Dammon saw how brightly joy shone from the young commander's eyes. "We serve him gladly."

Captain Iskander unbuckled his sword and proffered it to his lord.

Dammon sheathed his own weapon and closed both hands on Iskander's blade. The red-haired captain was younger than the prince in years—much younger, if his father had served on Dammon's council in the distant times. Youth was still there in his face, but only in the eyes. Trial, sorrow, and the long-suppressed desire for revenge had marked and hardened Iskander in face and body. Seeing them as they were now, face to face, most people would pick Iskander as the older man.

"Rise, Captain. I won't take your sword or your men. I've heard too much about your military skills to replace you. I'm no fool."

"My lord, your own powers of command are legendary!"

"Most of what you've heard about me is legendary." Dammon smiled and tugged on the sword until Iskander got to his feet. The fighters rose with him, exchanging uneasy smiles, waiting to see what their next order would be and who would give it.

"But, my lord, these are your troops! If we can't fight in Lord Prince Dammon's name—"

"Fight in my name, then, Captain Iskander, but fight for yourselves. Fight for what we've all lost, and I'll fight at your side." He patted the hilt of his sword. "You've had years of waiting, years of practice in all the military arts we'll need. I know how to fight, but not how to direct my men in battle. That is something I've forgotten, and you've waited long enough. I don't want you waiting any longer while I relearn the tactics of war."

"Especially how to get the most out of the fewest." Dammon turned his head sharply and caught Mrygo's mischievous smile. "I said I'd show you your sword, Dammon. I didn't expect it to dwindle to a dagger while we watched. Master Kor, I never stop admiring your arts. I've come to spy on the troops many times, and even walked among them when I came openly to visit my friend Iskander. No matter when I came, secretly or openly, I always saw the same mob of them, the meadow, and not a hint that so many of them were phantoms; phantoms of your conjuring, if I'm right."

"Phantoms." Master Kor's eyes misted over. "Not of my conjuring, but phantoms. *The surface dwellers put their faith in their eyes,* he used to say. *Let our prince see a mighty army waiting for him. Let them acclaim him as their lord and it will fill him with strength and hope and courage. Then, when the time comes for him to learn the true numbers of his army, he will still have the memory of that glorious moment when a multitude cheered his name. He will fight harder to regain that moment than for all his lost land.*"

Quicksilver tears ran down the wizard's cheeks. "They were my Brother Byuric's phantoms, held here all these years by the power of his soul. In time, they bound him as strongly as he bound them. It was my task to cut the bonds today."

"He is dead?" Dammon's voice was hushed. More than a wind had raced away over Khana that day.

"My lord . . . he is free."

PART V

In Hori-Halira

Prince Dammon stood with hands linked behind his back and watched the rain pelt down. "Wet spring in the mountains, bounty in the valleys. Farmer Rycote must be happy. I wonder how he is."

"My lord, if you would rejoin us..." Captain Iskander's gentle suggestion spoke for all four of the people gathered at the long table, a rough sketch-map covering the pitted oak.

Dammon shook the cobwebbed memories out of his head. "Sorry. It's the first heavy rain I've seen since I've been here. When I was Ophar, I used to go out into our fields and stand in the first rain of the season, cold or not, just letting it bathe me. It was worth more to me than all the tonics Rycote's good wife used to pour down my throat. I wished I could find something bigger than a frog pond to soak in ... agh, there I go again. Forgive me, my friends."

He left the window and the spell of rainfall to take his place at the head of the table. "We're all agreed that there's nothing to be gained by waiting any longer to make our move. If anything, our troops are *over*ready to fight. Today, we make the final decision, and no more back-and-forth about it. I take it you've discussed my plan?"

Iskander sat at Dammon's left hand, Mrygo one place farther

126

down. Opposite the Gryagi, a tall, raw-boned woman in deer-skin shirt and trousers frowned and made mouths to herself. It was Beliza's way to chew over her words many times before she uttered them. She commanded the mounted troops, and it was a standing joke in the cavalry that three horses had died of old age under her while she pondered whether to feed them herself or order her lieutenants to do it. Fortunately, the woman showed no such tendency to mull over the orders she gave in battle. Those came quickly and were always apt.

Now Beliza tossed her yellow braid back over her shoulder and said, "My lord, a prince commands and we obey."

"But..." Dammon prompted. Beliza wasn't the sort to accept rote obedience as the natural order of things.

"But your ideas—" She groped for the proper words, lost hope, and retreated into silence.

"Captain Beliza's trying to say she doesn't know where you intend to put her horsemen for this maneuver," Mrygo said. "They don't do well down holes, do they?" His grin was answered by a glower from the cavalrywoman.

"What *I* am trying to say—and you keep out of this, moss-grubber!—is I don't know why you want to strike underground first. My lord," she added.

Dammon ran his fingers over the edge of the table. At his right hand, the last of the silver wizards pretended fascination with a smooth, translucent droplet of smoky stone. Master Kor had not volunteered one word of question or advice at any of the war-councils Dammon had called. Now he avoided the prince's eyes, leaving all explanation—or refusal to explain—to him.

"I know it's a sudden change from the plans we've been laying so far, Captain Beliza." He spoke slowly and distinctly. The scheme was new and might be unpopular. He wanted his small council to understand that his choice came from solid reason, not a prince's whim.

He could always present it to his subordinates as a royal imperative, leaving them to pass it on to the troops. That would be the simplest way. For that very reason, he fled from it. Somehow he knew that if he once succumbed to the seductive ease of issuing mandates instead of reviewing matters with his advisers, he would do it again and again.

If they're so glad to have me back among the living, why should I have to justify my decisions to them? Let them have the pleasure of making my desires palatable to the common fighters! That arrogant voice could become his, and the chance of it made him afraid.

Prince Dammon explained his wishes. "My sister holds her land by fear and force of arms. Fighter for fighter, her troops outnumber ours, even beyond the point where Captain Iskander's excellent strategies could help."

"When the people see it's you at the head of our troops, my lord, they'll swell our ranks to bursting!" Beliza slapped her palm on the parchment sketch-map, flattening a village. "*See* you? Why, they've only to hear the rumor that Lord Prince Dammon's come again and they tear Mar-Halira stone from stone to drag your sister from her lair!"

Dammon chuckled. "You overestimate our people, Captain, or you underestimate my castle, and my sister."

"Our people will rally to the prince's flag, but not as swiftly as you'd like, my lady," Iskander said. Beliza's scornful snort sounded like one of her own battle-prime stallions. "Your own folk hail from the eastern foothills, where the great gap lies, and it's all horse country. You made your livings from raising steeds, not crops, like most folk in this realm."

"Does that make my words worthless? Where I *come* from?" Her lips tightened, and she looked ready to murder the red-haired captain.

"All I'm saying is that you don't know farmers."

"I do," said Dammon.

"Then you know what I mean, my lord. They're not the kind of folk who'll fling down their hoes and go searching for swords just like that."

"They wouldn't even know where to find swords or what to do with them once they got them." Dammon pictured himself returning to Farmer Rycote's door, proclaiming himself as Lord Prince Dammon returned, the fulfillment of every legend and every dream.

And Farmer Rycote would nod and say how fine it all sounded. He would kneel to his prince and cheer for the golden age and pledge his heart to Dammon's cause. Then he would say he was sorry to rush off, but there was hay to be turned and chickens to be fed and half a field to be plowed for barley yet before sunset.

"If we're to take the land, we must take the castle of Mar-Halira; and if we must take that castle, we must have enough fighters. Captain Iskander has made a full report to me on our troop strength. As our numbers stand now, we can't hope to take it. Any common folk who did leave their farms to join us wouldn't help. They're not trained fighters. They'd only be spear meat."

Dammon rested his knuckles on the table and stood. "That is why I say we must first free Mrygo's people before we free our own."

The table broke up into a buzz of conferrals. Besides the four making up Prince Dammon's council, there were eight troopers ranged in twos behind each chair, two riders behind Captain Beliza's, two spearmen behind Dammon's. They were chosen at random before each meeting, at the prince's insistence.

("My troopers will fight for their captains and for me. They may die. Let them know the reasons behind the command that sends them into battle. Let them learn it from a man of their own rank, a fellow fighter they can question freely, without awe or fear.")

There was one exception—one trooper who was not picked at random for council duty but was always there: Decad Turgan. At first, the bearish spearman had feared the prince's summons. Visions of punishment for having poked the royal flesh with a cane spearpoint made him sweat until Dammon himself welcomed him. "Welcome as long as you swear to speak honestly."

"My lord, I'd never lie to you!"

"There are ways of not lying that are also not honest speech. Decad Turgan, when we first met, you saw a young man—palace pretty?—who'd benefit from a veteran's advice."

"My lord, I never—"

Dammon held Turgan's shoulders. "Give me that advice, now as then—openly. Now I truly need it. I want you with me always."

The prince's favor had made Turgan swagger a bit when with his fellows, but he still stood in awe of Dammon and never yet had uttered a single word in council beyond a mumbled agreement with his lord's decrees and suggestions. Now, however, he spoke up.

"Free the Children of Stone? All the powers hear you, my lord! Do that and you'll have what no king before you did: the loyalty of the land right down to its roots!"

"Listen to him," sneered Beliza, jerking her thumb at Turgan. "Easy for you to come out in favor of any scheme, with only a decad under you. What about me? How do I explain to my people that we're to leave the beasts aboveground and go slithering through the Surin tunnels like a twist of spotty worms? A rider fights best mounted, and from what we learned the last time someone went into Hori-Halira, the captive Gryagi don't fight at all; they throw themselves on swords and die!"

There was a deep hush. Master Kor still fondled his smoky stone, but every other eye in the room turned to Mrygo. The Gryagi spoke softly, obsidian eyes holding a still, steady flame.

"Captain Beliza, if you don't retract your words, it will be my pleasure to show you just how well a Gryagi can fight."

"Ohhh . . ." The cavalrywoman made a gesture of exasperation. "Damnit, Mrygo, I know what they did to your folk, forcing them to the games and all. But what's the good of getting my men slaughtered if all that your tribe'll do is kill themselves as soon as they're freed?"

"Those who died when Captain Iskander freed them were different from those of us who escaped with him."

"I'll say they were!"

The Gryagi's thin mouth twisted. "You do better when you think a week before speaking, Captain. This council isn't the place to educate you." He retreated into silence.

Beliza tried to retort, but once more she was unable to find the words for what she wanted to say. In any case, Mrygo's face told her that it would take some mighty carefully chosen phrases to get a reply out of him now. She clicked her tongue and gave it all up as a bad deal.

Instead, it was Dammon who spoke. "Captain Beliza, I share your concern. The Seed knows, we're a smaller band than I thought, and we have to husband our numbers. I see the liberation of the Surin Gryagi's slaves as a way to add to our forces, but the mission might also lose us much without gaining us anything. Therefore, I propose that your horsemen remain aboveground while I take only Captain Iskander's foot troops into the Surin holds. If we succeed, we'll have a substantial force to field against my sister's troops. If we fail—"

Beliza jumped from her chair and slammed both fists on the table. "*Damn*it! Leave my troops behind? *If* you succeed! *If* you fail! Yes, let's talk *ifs*. Iskander's men won't ever let mine forget it if they come back victorious; call us cowards at the least. And what if you fail, my lord? What if you don't live to see the sun again—may the powers prevent it! The songs they'll make then . . . I won't have my name tagged with your death, no. If you enter the land of death, you'll do it with me and mine at your side."

The riders behind her chair shouted their agreement with their captain, rattling the slim silver chains adorning the dress-lances they bore. The other troopers in the room countered with bawled reminders that Dammon himself had made the decision and no horse-reeker had the right to overrule a prince. Turgan threw himself into the uproar, banging his spear butt on the floor and bellowing for order. Mrygo remained obstinately mute and was no help at all. Dammon exchanged a helpless look with Iskander and sat down to wait it out.

In the midst of the dispute, Master Kor cupped his hands over the glassy gray pebble and flung them open with a burst of light. A golden birra flew meeping around the heads of the startled debaters until it lit on Captain Beliza's shoulder and began to groom her braid with busy paws. Taken aback, the cavalrywoman gave a surprisingly tender laugh. Her rein-hardened fingers stroked the creature's down.

"That's better." The dark wizard smiled indulgently as the council regained a measure of calm. "Beliza, no songs will ever be made to your shame if Lord Prince Dammon's plans fail. For if they fail, no songs will ever be made again."

Beliza brushed the birra's flossy fur with her lips. Dammon was amazed by its tame submission to the caress. "All the more reason for him to take my troops down into the hole with him, then. Once he's got enough fighters backing him, it shouldn't take much to polish off those Surin. Everyone knows they're cowards."

Mrygo's steely shell cracked. "The captain is free with that word when she speaks of the Children of Stone. Again I say, she may learn otherwise. But I agree with her this much: The Surin Gryagi are numerous, and they've been dealing with Devra's people long enough to have acquired more weapons and ruthlessness than they'd have gotten on their own. If we free the slaves, we must free them all, and there will be no way to do that stealthily. If we attack, we need every fighter we can get."

"Leave no reserves to guard Khana?" Iskander found the notion unthinkable.

"Isn't Master Kor reserve enough?" Mrygo countered.

"Ordinarily, yes. But once we attack Hori-Halira, how long before Devra learns who we are, who leads us, and who sent us? While we're fighting underground, she could besiege Khana."

"Master Kor could hold her off!" cried one guard.

"Not with what she's got backing her!" another replied.

"What about the children? You don't leave a garrison of babies behind!" The room broke up into renewed confusion.

Dammon leaned over to get the silver wizard's ear. "Another birra?" he suggested archly.

"Just for you." Red eyes winked at the prince from the shadow of Master Kor's left sleeve, but this time the tiny creature scuttled into sight and up Dammon's arm with no fanfare or fireworks. The others went on arguing until the wizard held up his hands.

"My friends, your words all have sense behind them— which is very fine, but still leaves us hanging fire. When I came to this council meeting, it was to bring some vital news to your attention, waiting only for the proper moment. It would seem the moment is now." He turned to the guard on his left. "A man is waiting in the corridor, on my orders. Have him come in."

Dammon's eyes grew wide. He had the odd sensation of being invisible, watching without danger of being seen. He knew the man who entered the council chamber—tall, proud, his hair a crown of dark gold and his face still painfully handsome beneath its weary mask. One of Decad Turgan's despised palace-pretty men, sure. Dammon knew him well. He had seen him often, too often before: lingering in the homely herb garden, bringing trinkets, ingratiating himself with Rycote's wife, pretending to listen attentively when Rycote rambled on about good times and bad times and farmers enduring always. He was Sir Raimon, the queen's man.

He was Larya's chosen husband.

Bitter memories overtook Dammon. He was no longer prince or leader or legend. He was Ophar, pastless, nameless, destined forever to plod behind Farmer Rycote's plow as surely as the yoked oxen were destined to plod before it. But even without past or name, he possessed one precious thing, one treasure without price or parallel. In the darkness of the Gryagi holds, in the silence of stone, he had seen a star. Scarred, ugly, unworthy, all he could do was gaze and dream. Then Sir Raimon had come, and in the arrogance of beauty he had reached out and plucked Ophar's star from the sky and tucked it into his pouch without a thought.

He didn't look so arrogant now. His skin was waxen, and dark smears showed under his moss-green eyes. Dammon heard with only half an ear as Master Kor presented Sir Raimon to the seated council, idly wondering what had brought the golden queen's-man so far, in such condition. He noted that Master Kor did not introduce the council members to Sir Raimon— a neat way of holding back his own presence. If Dammon knew the silver wizard, he'd choose a suitably dramatic moment to tell the knight he spoke in the presence of a prophecy fulfilled.

"Sir Raimon and his party set out from Mar-Halira more than a month ago," the silver wizard said. "Their progress was slowed by the need to keep their defection secret. Fortunately, Queen Devra's eyes are elsewhere lately."

"All her eyes?" Mrygo leaned forward.

Sir Raimon shot the Gryagi a probing look. "You know of the queen's familiars?"

"I've been told."

"Then it's time you were told more, Mrygo," Master Kor said. To Sir Raimon, he added. "It's no secret that your queen and my brotherhood are enemies, but there are as many sorts of enemies as friends. Devra serves the powers of air—the greedy, volatile, most capricious of the powers. I serve no power above another, but strive to understand and harmonize them all."

"Just like Master Byuric sed Lyum, while he lived," murmured Dammon.

"May he dwell beyond all mysteries." Master Kor bowed his head.

"While he lived, did you say?" Sir Raimon's haggard face tautened. "Master, how many of your brotherhood are still alive?"

Kor spread his hands in an eloquent gesture. "The brotherhood of the silver wizards sought harmony. What can be more harmonious than one brotherhood in one skin? Don't look aghast, Sir Raimon. Were you hoping to find an army of wizards to help you? The holy mountain is no garrison of magic. It is a sanctuary of study and praise. Khana was never even intended to shelter more than a small force of men-at-arms, as this man here can tell you." He nodded at Dammon.

"Sir Raimon, you're a fighting man." Captain Iskander spoke up, eager to defend the ways of Khana with words as well as blades. "You know that a weakness can often be a hidden strength. Khana is shielded by magic, but no spell is perfect. Only recently, Master Kor felt the need to erect several interweaving shields, no matter how much they drain him. Before these shields went up, your queen might have stolen many peeks into our stronghold, for all we know. She sent her spies, but never her soldiers, and left us in peace. Tell me, Sir Raimon, why a person might choose not to attack his known foe?"

Captain Beliza didn't give the fugitive queen's-man a chance to answer. "You don't waste time, men, or effort on quashing minor threats, not when you've got more than plenty of big ones to handle. Don't tell me Devra's been having a flowerpath time, balancing that stolen crown on her head."

"What threat is one old man, silver wizard or not?" Master Kor shrugged. "The conquest of Khana has not been worth Devra's while, because she chose to measure our potential threat by numbers alone. Don't share her mistake, Sir Raimon. One is a powerful number."

Sir Raimon took a long, quavering breath. "By all I love, I hope you're right, master."

"We'll learn that together. Now be seated and tell the council what you told me."

Dammon himself stood, ceding his chair to his unsuspecting

rival. The queen's man thanked him before beginning. All present watched Sir Raimon while he told his tale, none seeing the changes rippling across Dammon's face each time Sir Raimon mentioned Larya's name.

"I was a queen's man, like many of the men I've brought here with me. I served her well and loyally because that was what I'd expect of any man serving me: loyalty."

"Those who accompanied you here are proof of that, Sir Raimon," said Master Kor. As the council members all raised questioning eyes, he elaborated: "At this moment there is nearly a full queen's company being settled in the old wing of Khana, and every available member of our household busy procuring all the supplies we'll need to feed and accommodate our new brethren."

Beliza whistled softly. "Spur me over that one, Master Kor! I'm impressed." To Sir Raimon, she said, "You don't look like much, but you must be all right. Steal a whole queen's company out from under Devra's snotty little nose? How'd you do it?"

"They were my men, most of them, and those who weren't had plenty of cause to join with us." The young knight gazed over the unrolled map on the council table and pointed out the heartland of the realm, the royal castle called Mar-Halira.

"We queen's men were recruited from garrisons in all the strongholds loyal to Devra from the first. There weren't that many; not before the bad times came. Lord Maldonar rallied the few vassal lords who stood for Devra, and they brought their soldiers into it. Somehow the queen knew which of the common fighters were the best, and messages came from Mar-Halira naming us queen's men. When she had us, she put us to work rooting out the nobles who wouldn't pay her homage. That was when the bad times came."

Captain Iskander's voice sounded brittle as overstretched steel. "You speak as if you stood on a battlement and watched other men destroy our land. But you were there. Your sword was busy enough."

Sir Raimon's breath rasped in his throat as he forced himself to face the red-haired captain. "I was there. I did what I was told to do. The lords we brought down were called traitors, and traitors must be destroyed. How could we know that our lady and Lord Maldonar lied?"

"Let him speak, Iskander." Kor slipped behind his chair to press his hands on the captain's shoulders. "Hear him out. If your father hadn't been true to our lost lord, if he'd told you to serve Queen Devra instead, would you have had the wisdom to know you served wrongly?"

"At first her words were sensible, her desires always for peace, and the harmony of the kingdom." Sir Raimon was staring at the map again. "Internal divisions would weaken us. We battled her enemies because they were the enemies of unity."

"You waged war in the name of peace?" Beliza laughed. "No wonder I'd rather spend my time with horses! When they slash and bite, it's honest mayhem anyway."

An agonized look from Sir Raimon silenced her. None of the others present spoke again until much later. Each knew how difficult it was for a once-proud man to make a confession of shame and ignorance. For Sir Raimon this was doubly hard, a second round of admitting his guilt, for he had already recounted everything to Master Kor.

"Peace came. We all rejoiced and started to look for the age of gold. I was ready to settle down. I found a girl to marry— a wonderful girl named Larya. My comrades twitted me about marrying a farmer's lass when I could've had one of the queen's own ladies, but my heart knew. She was beautiful—hair white as the north star that gave her a name—yet my heart told me to look farther than beauty. It read her worth, and something about her that was almost magical..."

A sharp bark of bitter laughter tore from his chest. "Magical! By the flamesword, Queen Devra soon gave us all a bellyful of magic!"

His voice dropped and shrank into a whisper, dwelling again incredulous on what he had witnessed with his own eyes. "One day not long past, our queen decreed a festival to be celebrated in all parts of her kingdom in honor of the Princess Lilla's birthday. Honor guards of queen's men were dispatched to the manor-towns in order to oversee that the event was sufficiently feted. The exact nature of the festivities was left to the discretion of local officials, but one thing the queen did ask: a dance of maidens to honor her daughter; a flower-dance, in the old style. It was such a small favor. No one wanted to disappoint the queen, but whether it was out of loyalty or out of fear . . .

"My men and I were sent to a manor-town far in the east, near the foothills of the mountains. We arrived to find that Lord Prisan, one of Maldonar's oldest liegemen, had outdone himself to satisfy Devra. He had sent his men to scour all his territory and bring back every maiden within his borders for the dance. The night before the festival, a royal courier arrived with sealed orders from Mar-Halira. I was conferring with Lord Prisan when they arrived, and I would have left him as he read, but he detained me. He said that the orders involved my company. He let me read them."

Sir Raimon's head dropped into his hands. "The orders were plain. On the following day, when the maidens assembled for the flower-dance, my men and Lord Prisan's troops were to surround them, drive them like sheep, and force them into wagons that Lord Prisan was to have ready. If anyone attempted to interfere, we were to kill him.

"I was a soldier. I served my queen without question. I bloodied my sword in her name, never asking why, but this time I did ask. If Lord Prisan had been a wise man, he might have put me off with a plausible excuse, but that wasn't like him. He turned ugly. He demanded obedience without questions, and no exceptions. He snarled, snapped, threatened, and swore he'd call his guards to take me if I gave him any trouble over the queen's orders. Before, when I served her, at least they gave us reasons for our raids and battles, even if they were false. Now she and her followers no longer gave reasons, only orders. Even I knew how wrong that was."

Master Kor made an almost imperceptible gesture. The chamber door opened before white-robed children bearing trays of garnet wine and golden cakes. The silver wizard served Sir Raimon with his own hands. The former queen's man ate nothing, but took a few sips of wine.

"I killed Lord Prisan and took the queen's orders. I killed the guards outside his chamber too, quickly, and hid the bodies. Then I ran to find my company. I showed my men the scroll with Devra's own signature and seal, and they stood by me. That night, we crept from bed to bed in the manor-house like assassins. We were assassins. We slew every man we knew to be loyal to Lord Prisan, who might follow us when we fled. We rode out of the foothills and left a trail of blood behind, but the queen never bothered to track it. She had other business to attend.

"We rode away as fast as we could. At first all I thought about was escape, but the farther we rode that night, the more the questions nagged at me: *Why?* Why did the queen want those girls? Only in that one town? It was a good two days' hard riding from the next manor-town, and when we reached it, we got our answer. I sent in a scout, a man on foot to see how the previous day's festival had gone. He found sorrow and desolation. The queen's orders had been the same there as in Lord Prisan's domain, only here they'd been carried out. The maidens had been loaded into the wagons as directed."

"You overtook them on the road? A good horse is an easy match for an ox-cart," Beliza said confidently.

"Nothing could match what pulled those wagons. The people who weren't weeping for their lost daughters or sisters or intended brides all thought they'd been struck mad. Soon as the last girl was aboard, a shriek of wind swept out of the sky and whipped them all away."

"A wind?"

"A wind . . ." Master Kor spoke half to himself. "A voice of the powers of air."

"It was all the same tale throughout the land; in every manor-town, the same: the flower-dancers taken in wagons pulled by unseen hands, taken far away, maybe forever. Then, as we drew nearer to Mar-Halira, the story changed. We came through towns where half the people mourned and half rejoiced, but softly, out of respect for their neighbors' sorrow. The maidens had returned; not all, but most. It was from those who'd come back that we had the last, worst, part of it. The part that stole my Larya from me . . . my silver star . . . my love . . . my Larya."

Master Kor read his pain and spoke. "I will finish for you, if you will permit me." Sir Raimon nodded heavily. The queen's man's head was bent, but keen eyes saw tears. "What the girls who came back said was this: The wagons borne away by the Powers of Air came to rest in a meadow in the southernmost part of the realm. Too frightened to move, they clung to the sidebars of the carts until Queen Devra's soldiers drove them out, one by one. They were marched in the presence of the queen herself. She sat on an icy throne made of sheer brilliance, frozen light. Behind her was air poured into a misty curtain that hid something immense from view. How could clear air hide anything? The girls didn't know; only that it was so.

"Devra had them pass before her, and for each one she gave a certain signal. Most were guided back to their carts again and dispatched home. Many others stayed behind."

"His girl, too, I'm guessing." Captain Beliza jerked her thumb at Sir Raimon. "This sounds like the spring winnowing of the herds. We cut out the finest horses from the upland meadows, see which are fit for draft and which for battle. But what's horses got to do with women?"

Master Kor's mouth twitched up at one corner. "Queen Devra sees all her subjects as stock-beasts. Whether she's the only one with that view . . ." The half smile vanished. "When it's the beast who's brought for sacrifice, there's no more time left to laugh about it."

The word slipped from his lips almost casually, but every soul there caught it and took it up in an agitated whisper. *Sacrifice? What's this talk of sacrifice? What sacrifice does Master Kor? . . . Sacrifice?*

The two birras flew up from Beliza's shoulder and Dammon's arm to loop and soar through the rising murmurs. They chittered madly, gnashing sharp teeth, red eyes agog, tiny handfuls of panic, until Master Kor extended his hands and they took refuge curled up in his palms.

He closed his fingers around their warmth for a moment, speaking soft, unintelligible words. Then, without warning, the small winged ones were cast out of their warm haven, flung upward by the silver wizard. A veil of seeing trailed from their golden bodies, a shimmering sheet of vision that told its own tale.

"Behold the travesty," said Master Kor as darkness touched everything except the seeing itself.

The slopes of Khana, the holy mountain, glowed with the rich green of growth and life clinging almost to the summit where the silver wizards dwelled. Pilgrims came with willing tread, weaving up the paths, rejoicing in all the beauties of life that surrounded them and made their way lovely, preparing their hearts for worship. Sunlight found them, and the sweet waters of the moon. Nothing was hidden. At the summit, they gave their prayers of thanks with singing hearts and made the old sacrifices of bird-flight, golden cakes, song, and flowers.

Green eyes hovered above the mountain. Green eyes, once seen high in the cold places of a buried cavern, made Dammon shudder and long to run away. Green eyes, too cold to be human, blinked; eyes that blotted out the soft green slopes of Khana. They burned and grew, one alone sufficient to hold all the holy mountian captive between invisible lids.

Inside the demon eye, Khana changed.

Color fled, and the earth tore open. Sheets of shining metal crept upward out of the ground, dragged by the busy hands of Surin Gryagi workers. Gashes scored the mountain's flank, terraces where the earth lay raw until the slowly advancing silver skin covered it, sealed it, locked away all that could ever give life. Life was sealed into a silver tomb, and all the voices of the powers of earth faded to distant echoes.

A woman stood on the first terrace and surveyed the silvery skirt lapping up the mountainside. Her hair was blue-black, her eyes fiery blue, and the icy diamonds in her gold crown glittered. She nodded, content with what she saw, then turned and gestured.

Two armed men brought the girl forward. She was very young, very beautiful. A raw peasant girl, that was evident, but decked out in finery—an heirloom dress, perhaps, the work of many loving needles; a dress for a mother to give her child and sigh for all the memories embroidered there.

No child would have this dress again. The crowned woman raised her hand.

"Aglora! Avana! Acova!"

Three dark shapes swirled out of the sky, green eyes bright. They whipped in a ring around the lady's upraised hand, then soared against the bright dome of heaven. The lady's hand suddenly held a knife of rippling air.

In spite of their strength and size, the armed men had to fight to hold the terrified girl fast. Once she broke away from them, tried to reach the terrace edge, was caught by the sash at her waist, dragged back, shrieking. Her screams were lost in the whirling wind. The dark shapes feasted on her terror.

Then the knife of air fell, and all screams stopped. The dark shapes came to feed in earnest now.

Master Kor let the vision go.

The birras descended lightly from the ceiling. Both perched on Dammon's shoulders and whirred their clover-sweet breath in his ears, trying to take away evil dreams. He tickled their downy bodies with his fingertips and listened to the silver wizard speak.

"She calls it Lar-Khana: the Silver Mountain. Earth lies at its roots, but earth gives life. Even the hardest stone may fall into grains of sand, take power from honest deaths, and yield new life some day. Metal, never. Metal is of the earth, but never of the powers of earth, who love life and all its changes."

"Does she only build this thing to mock Khana, Master Kor?" Captain Iskander asked.

Mrygo answered instead. "Devra prefers stronger jokes. If that precious child of hers is any gauge, she's got a very thirsty sense of humor." He touched his throat reminiscently. The scars Lilla's familiar had left were fading, but the marks of another small mouth never would.

"Then why?"

Dammon finally came from behind his chair. "She serves the powers of air, doesn't she? I've heard that enough times since I've come here to know it off by heart. And I also know something of the limits put on each of the great powers. A river is bounded by its banks. Even when it trickles off into the marshes, there's still a place where water ends and earth begins."

"The powers allow bridges to be built between them." Master Kor nodded approval of Dammon's words. "In their way, they have always sought the harmony we silver wizards seek. When the borders and the balances are broken, that's when evil comes. Devra builds a bridge."

Mrygo gave a half smile. "Clever lady."

"I'm glad you understand, stone-face," Beliza growled. "Maybe you'd like telling me?"

"A pleasure . . . meat-face. The powers of air lose strength the nearer they come to the powers of earth. When they touch our land, they lose much of their malevolence and threat. Though the peaks of ordinary mountains trespass in their realm,

the creatures of air weaken near them. Even a barren mountaintop is capable of sustaining life someday. What Devra's
done is build them a stair that'll bring them closer to the earth
without stealing any of their strength. Their powers will flow
undiluted through the flanks of the Silver Mountain, and their
human agents can draw unrivaled forces from it."

"Agents like Devra." Beliza comprehended.

"She builds her bridge of silver and binds it with blood.
She offers potent sacrifices to the greedy powers of air as each
terrace of Lar-Khana is completed." Master Kor rested his chin
on steepled fingers. "Sir Raimon brings us this news. He also
brings us the seed of an army."

"We march!" shouted Captain Iskander.

"We ride!" Captain Beliza sprang to her feet.

The armed guards snatched their commanders' cries from
the air and redoubled them, stamping spear butts on the floor.
Sir Raimon's dark-circled eyes flitted from soul to soul, alter-
nately reflecting fear and hope.

"Free the land! Free the land!"

Dammon raised his hands. The cheers and chanting fell into
silence. His voice was pitched low, but every word filled the
council room.

"Yes, we'll free our land. We can't wait any longer. Tomorrow we march, we ride, with your men beside us, Sir
Raimon. At this point"— he touched the parchment map—
"there is an adit to the Surin Gryagi holds. The foot soldiers
will follow me down to release the captives, the horse will
ride on to begin the attack on Mar-Halira. We rejoin forces at
the royal stronghold, and after it's secure, we go on to destroy
Lar-Khana. Will your men be ready for another march tomorrow, Sir Raimon?"

"Who are you to take over my men like this?" The weariness
was gone, burnt to ashes. The queen's man glared at the dark-
haired upstart who had said so little until now, who had meekly
given up his chair to Sir Raimon.

"I command here." The words were still soft, yet they left
no room for argument. "If you want to undo my sister's works
in time, you'd better accept it."

"Your . . . sister?"

Realization came, and disbelief with it. Again Sir Raimon's

eyes searched the council table. All that he saw confirmed the impossible. There was solemn affirmation in every face: Kor's, Beliza's, Iskander's. Even the common soldiers' leathery faces softened as they looked with love and reverence at their lost prince returned. Only the Gryagi looked amused. Sir Raimon's amazement tickled him.

"Careful, queen's man. You've been raising your voice to a legend."

Sir Raimon pushed himself away from the table and knelt at his lord's feet. Somewhere in the dark places of memory, an ugly farmer's lad named Ophar let the queen's man remain kneeling for longer than truly necessary.

Word ran through Khana in eager whispers and harried shouts. The fighters were marching! The waiting was done! Children stripped off their ceremonial robes for the convenience of scullions' tunics and raced up and down the corridors on a thousand errands. The kitchen was a riot of field-cooks and provision-masters, all clamoring at once. Telli was in his glory, swinging the ladle like a mace, a baton, a shepherd's crook, as the occasion demanded.

Dammon sat in Mrygo's tower room and listened to the sounds of pandemonium waft up from below.

"You know how to start something," said the Gryagi. He tallied up the contents of his healer's kit one final time before closing the leather box.

"I hope I can finish it."

"Oh, ends come easily. It's beginnings that look so formidable." He threaded his belt through the loops on the box and tried how the heavy kit felt riding on left hip, right, and at the small of his back. "There, that feels comfortable enough for a long march. It might even save my innards from a backstabber's thrust one night." His looks sobered suddenly. "I didn't thank you."

"Thank me for what?"

"For your decision to free my folk first. It wasn't the most popular decision you might have made."

Dammon shrugged it off. "I was only being practical. We can use more fighters, even with Sir Raimon's men added to ours. I'm not Beliza; I know what you Gryagi can do."

"All you know is the story of what happened the last time they tried to free us."

Dammon shrugged again. "This time it's going to be different."

"Because you decided so?"

"Of course." Dammon grinned widely. "All of my decisions are right because they're mine. Or don't you remember the songs?"

"Can't say they're my favorite hums. And there was that fuzz-brained episode where you decided it was a wonderfully good idea to follow a dragon into his lair."

The prince's hand strayed to touch the claws still hanging at his throat. A small boy's death dangled from one, the stolen face of a loyal squire from the second, the lost years in Ophar's skin from the third, and the fourth hooked itself into places in Dammon's brain that were darker than any dragon's cavern.

"I guess you can't believe all the songs." He left Mrygo without further excuse.

In the birras' garden, the golden flowers still swayed and rustled as if hiding nothing but wind under their thick green leaves and yellow cups. Dammon perched on the rim of the marble pool and waited, but the birras remained out of sight.

"Hungry?" A hunk of cheese in one hand, a loaf of crusty bread tucked under his arm, Pryun came hobbling into the garden. He plopped himself down beside Dammon and passed him the cheese. "Hold that for me a second." Cunning fingers tore the bread apart, a shower of crumbs falling into the flowers. Dammon heard faint chirrings that grew louder when Pryun tossed a handful of crumbled crust to the invisible creatures.

Pryun took the cheese back and began slicing pieces from it with a whittling knife as if farmer's lunch with a prince was no great thing. "Haven't seen you in a while. All those council meetings, and always plenty of guards to make sure I keep *out*. Now whose order was that, do you suppose? Yours?"

"We had important things to discuss—"

"And no need for a jester? Councillors like to make their own jokes. Or would my looks offend one of your august colleagues? The gentle lady Beliza, perhaps? I can just see her swooning away at the sight of me."

The thought of Beliza swooning away made Dammon laugh.

"So! I'm still good for something after all? Have some more cheese. That took some dancing to get, believe me, my lord. If young Telli suspected I lifted this bit of bread, he'd skin me; if I'd let him. Other men can offer you their swords as proof of how worthy they are to serve you—whole companies of swords! But what good's a sword without something to give the swordsman strength?"

Dammon flicked raindrops from the flowers. "You sound like someone I knew."

"Do I, now?" The Surin jester heaved an exaggerated sigh. "Nothing original about me but my bones. I understand that there was never such a specimen as myself born when my father's kin stayed underground, where we belonged. This mountain air . . . it's not so healthful as they'd tell you."

The prince looked up. One peak of the great mountain chain fencing Mar-Halira from the outer world was so tall that on sunny days you could see a flash of light in the sky; a reflection of sun on its snowcap. Even in the enclosed courts and gardens this was visible, a reminder that Khana was not the final boundary of the world.

"The mountains are beautiful." Dammon chose a bland response. He had enough on his mind without setting Pryun off again on the whys and wherefores of his twisted bones.

"So are the Gryagi holds. Or so I've heard, my lord. Now you—you're in a position to know for sure." Pryun chuckled. "Don't gawp at me. It's not princely. Did you think it's a secret, where you spent all those years? Our Master Kor has been busy. Our troops march tomorrow, but other fighters have already gone forth. They've been on the road for weeks, armed to the teeth with song."

"What are you talking about?"

Pryun shoved another hunk of bread at Dammon's lips. The prince batted it away impatiently. "Tsk. Temper, my lord. Your sister has a fearsome one, I've heard. I hear much by keeping to the shadows. Do you mean to tell me that Master Kor hasn't informed you of what he's done? Made new songs about you, that's what! Made 'em and sent 'em to be learned by heart by a corps of child minstrels. Haven't you noticed any of the young ones missing? Hmm, but they're harder to keep track of than mice, and they are merely children. What's two decads of them missing, more or less? He's given them each a pack and a staff and a song. They go the hard roads, singing of Dammon's penance."

"Penance," Dammon repeated dumbly.

"Oh yes! You see, when you descended into the caverns to slay the monster, you remained below of your own free will. Some sort of mystic trance . . . I never did get the words to that verse tidy. Anyhow, you tarried there below slaying monsters and repenting for all the evils you'd seen in the world. Not you *own* wickedness, of course; you've got none. Now tell me, my lord, what better way to ensure that the common farming folk will welcome you, flock to you, die for you, than by paving your way back with a song of how you bought off the powers' anger for all your people?"

Pryun sliced a tidbit of cheese and popped it into his own lipless mouth. "It'd be most impolite not to die willingly for such a prince."

"You're a liar!" Dammon flung away his food. There was a scuffling in the flowers where it fell, a convergence of ripples, and a quiet chirring.

Pryun's bright eyes were on him. "I am a jester and an outcast, my lord, but not a liar. I haven't had the training. Since my father died, I doubt I'll ever have it. The silver wizards speak much of harmony, but truth strikes a single note and refuses to blend. You can put your ears about to learn whether I've lied to you or not about the child singers and the new song. I'll even strike a wager with you on it. If I lie, lock me out of sight. But if I've brought you the truth, then let me ride with you tomorrow."

"You can't ride with the army."

"I can sit a horse better than most of the foot soldiers and make better time afoot besides, though not in any sort of trim march-time. My gait's not pretty, but it's fast and it gets me where I want to go."

"Pryun . . . there'll be fighting." Dammon looked at the spidery body with pity, picturing it swept away, helpless, in the midst of battle.

"This is war, my lord. Fighting's a part of it, or do you still think my brain's as crippled as my body? I may not be the warrior, but I am a handy ear for the prince to lay against closed doors and come back with the truth. Many battles have been won not by the lord with more men in the field, but by the one who knew more of how things stood before the battle."

Dammon considered the jester's words. "All right. I'll see whether you've been lying to me. If not, you can come with us."

Pryun smiled.

There was some consternation in the leading ranks when they heard that Lord Prince Dammon wanted to take his jester with him on the great march. Oddly enough, the one soul from whom Dammon imagined he'd hear the most objections instead remained indifferent.

"You don't mind?" he asked Mrygo for perhaps the fifth time. They stood side by side in the stableyard, learning to curry their borrowed mounts. The prince's immediate entourage would ride in fitting style until they reached the entrance to the Surin Gryagi holds.

"My good Dammon, you're the prince after all, the leader. Whether I mind or not shouldn't matter to you."

"But it does. The others—Beliza, Iskander, even Master Kor—they've been at me to reconsider, to justify my decision. I think the only thing that keeps them from overruling me is how bad it'd look before the fighting men."

Mrygo stroked his horse's quivering flank. "You're learning about one of your best weapons: appearances. Laughter's another potent one. Why not take a jester along?"

Dammon gave his horse several long, strong passes with the brush. "A jester . . . but Pryun? That's what's annoying the others, I think; Pryun. I don't think they trust him."

"And you?"

"He's a bitter soul, but he told me the truth. All those children out on the roads for weeks, and I—I never even noticed they were gone from Khana. Mrygo, I *knew* most of them. I knew their names and their faces, but I lost track of them and never gave it a second thought. What kind of a leader am I? What kind of a prince?"

Mrygo's horse shied nervously. The Gryagi gave it another whiff of his hand to reassure it and smoothed the velvet muzzle. "What kind of prince? My experience with the breed is limited." He dropped his jesting air and spoke more seriously. "Dammon, what do you expect of yourself? No prince or hero was ever more than human. You can't be everywhere and know everything. You can't blame yourself for what you don't know."

"If I only knew more about *myself*!..." Dammon threw down the curry comb and took up a rough cloth, wiping the horse's black pelt hard enough to make it whinny and skitter sideways. "Hold still, damn you!" He yanked at the bridle.

Mrygo left his steed to wander at will in the stableyard. Quickly, firmly he took the horse's bridle from Dammon's grasp and breathed into the spooked creature's nostrils. The horse rolled its eyes and champed its huge teeth in pain until the Gryagi healer's soft attentions eased it.

"It's not the horse's fault, Dammon."

Dammon breathed in deeply and slowly, then let the air out in a sigh. "I'm sorry." He tried to pat the beast's rump, but the big black horse turned skittish, matching the prince's scent to a too-recent hurt.

"There, there." Myrgo had his hands full trying to soothe two unhappy creatures at once. "Don't worry, Dammon. By the time we're ready to ride tomorrow, he'll have forgotten all about this."

"It's easy for a beast to forget. They keep nothing in their memories to pain themselves, and they never waste time worrying about the blanks. It's all *now* for them. I wish it could be like that for me. I wish I'd truly been born the moment Master Kor and Master Byuric sed Lyum gave me back my first face and name. Or else...I wish they'd left me alone as Ophar. I'd built myself a new life on top of nothing, and they took that away from me."

"But you had a life before that. You're our lord, our prince—"

"A prince who remembers nothing of castles. A prince, the son of another prince, who can't recall whether his mother had dark hair or fair or even if she lived to see me grow up. You remember the seeing Master Kor gave us of Devra's Silver Mountain? That was the first time I saw what she looked like. My own sister!" His words were full of misery. "I never knew she was so beautiful. Not even Larya was..."

"Larya may be dead by now." Mrygo's words cut through

Dammon's self-pity like knives. "Dead, thanks to your beautiful sister. If Devra's the finest thing in the life you can't remember, maybe it's better forgotten."

Dammon offered the black horse his hand. The huge animal whiffed at the smell with his square muzzle and accepted him as friend, all previous offenses gone.

"Maybe it is better."

The healer read Dammon's eyes and knew the prince for a poor liar.

In all the lost times of the faithful pilgrimages, there was never such a grand procession of riders leaving Khana. The men of Sir Raimon's company were divided up to mingle with the other soldiers—mostly Beliza's cavalry, since the majority of queen's men fought best when mounted. A decad of Sir Raimon's oldest and most trusted fighters remained under his direct control and rode in double rank behind him and the rest of the commanders.

Two and two the troops rode, with Lord Prince Dammon himself at their head, Master Kor directly behind him. Sir Raimon's men had bawled themselves hoarse when they saw him and learned who he was. There had been no need for Master Kor to enhance his presentation to those fighters with apparitions of dead dragons: They were more than ready to believe.

The prince's plan to enter the Surin holds with his foot soldiers was acclaimed by the troops more readily than by their leaders. They saw the military genius behind the choice, the utter rightness of an underground attack first, then siege of Mar-Halira before riding on to raze the Silver Mountain. Could a choice made by Lord Prince Dammon be anything less than brilliant, fated, right?

"Crazy bastards." More than once Captain Beliza had had to bully some of her original troopers—hill-country horsemen like herself—when she made a doubtful decision and they balked before obeying. Dammon's instant success pricked her. "They'd march into the Great River if he said so. They're drunk on him."

Captain Iskander rode at her side and shared her feelings of resentment as automatically as he shared her bed. "Our prince is still too much of a legend and not enough of a man. Raimon's men never had to enter Gryagi holds. They don't know what's waiting for them. I just hope enough of us will survive to do Devra some real harm."

"Aye. She won't see us as a joke after we attack her blind-worm friends in force. Ah, Fire-sender! And there I'll be with my men, ringing in Dev's pet castle and waiting for the rest of you to show! She'll have us for breakfast."

A bony brown hand tugged at Beliza's deerskin trousers. Pryun loped along beside the cavalrywoman's roan stallion.

"My lady, you'd be the queen's lunch, I think. If she learns her dear brother lives and leads an assault against the Surin holds, she'll give that battle her attention first, just to take up old family ties. Your horsemen will come to her notice later."

Beliza tightened her knees around her mount's unsaddled barrel. A hidden touch of her hand in his mane made him dart his long head down at the jester and snap with broad teeth.

"Ill omens take you, and a quick death! Go listen at someone else's keyhole, toad!" Pryun squealed and fell back.

"A jest! A jest!" Pryun humbled himself, crumpling into a ball of contrition by the roadside. Beliza tossed her head and urged her stallion to double his pace. Iskander matched her, leaving Sir Raimon and Mrygo to exchange confused glances before digging their heels into their own mounts and speeding up the entire column.

The prince's army made good progress for its size. Less than a week after leaving Khana's great gate, they were camped a strategic distance from the entrance to the Surin Gryagi holds. Their own scouts reported that the Surin Gryagi did not post sentries aboveground, in this matter remaining true to the ways of the other Gryagi tribes.

"They don't station sentries at the tunnel mouths either," said Captain Iskander over the campfire. All of Dammon's staff were there for one last council session before the army split up. Only Master Kor was missing. He was isolated in his tent, tirelessly weaving the spells of forest shadow and firefly-light that shielded the host's cookfires, picket-lines, and en-campment bustle from discovery.

"What hours do they keep, Captain? By the sun, or by their own spans?"

"The Surin are closest to surface ways, but still Gryagi. They stir most from noon to midnight, getting half a human day that way if they've got any business to see to outside the holds."

"And how long did it take you to reach the hold's heart after you entered?"

"Two hours, going slow, but we went in by another adit."

"This one will be better," said Mrygo. "Shorter and wider, coming out nearer the main slave quarters for males and females."

"You never told me the Surin gave you the run of the hold, Mrygo," Iskander said.

"Not when I was first taken, but after they caught me tending to my kin who'd been wounded in the games; the Surin aren't famous for their healers. I did double duty, fighting my own folk one span, binding them up the next, and taking care of any Surin who fancied they wanted my skills." His face darkened. "I wish I could have taken care of them the way they deserved."

"So that's how you got to know their hold. Fine, you'll lead us," Dammon said.

"Help *you* lead us, I think my lord means?" Captain Iskander looked steadily at Dammon. "As the expedition was your idea . . ."

Dammon sensed the challenge. His jaw tightened in response. "That goes without saying. And you'll be in the van with us, at dawn, since you seem to know so much about the captives we'll be freeing."

"At dawn." Iskander's eyes slewed left, catching a signal from Beliza. "And when do the riders leave?"

"As soon as this meeting ends. Mar-Halira's several days' ride, and they've got to be there waiting for us."

"Several days' ride? How will we catch up, on foot, in time to reinforce them, my lord?"

It was Mrygo who answered for Dammon. "It's several days' ride on the surface, but the Surin have a shorter way. It'll be ours to use after we've done with them."

"If we win."

One corner of Mrygo's mouth twitched. "Then we'd better win, hadn't we? Don't worry, Iskander; war brings many surprises. For one, Master Kor's going to ride on with the horsemen, using his skills to breach any spell-wall Devra may have left behind covering her home fortress."

"How do we know she's not in Mar-Halira right now?" Captain Beliza demanded. "That seeing we had of her on her mountain, how old was it?"

"Not so old as you fear." Master Kor stepped into the firelight. He looked up, scanning an invisibly woven dome, and was satisfied. The translucent drop of gray stone twinkled on his palm. "I have searched for our queen. She is chained to Lar-Khana until it's finished. The three familiar spirits who serve her also guard her, force her to hurry the work to completion. She commands them, but their true masters have first claim to their services. Aglora, Avana, and Acova know where to give their real obedience. Devra won't leave the Silver Mountain until they let her. I found her at the moment the second terrace was finished." No one needed to ask what rite had marked that finish or why Master Kor looked so grim.

"How many? . . ."

"Seven. Five on the first terrace, seven on this, and more on the next. The work goes faster the higher they go and the narrower the mountain grows. The closer they come to the realm where the powers of air reign alone, the hungrier those powers become."

"And the more girls die." Captain Beliza jabbed at the fire with a stick. "*Why* do we wait? Why do we waste time? How many more terraces will she build while we—"

"That's enough, Captain Beliza. You're wasting time enough questioning my orders. Our course is settled, and it was settled well before this. The sooner you rally your troops and ride, the sooner we'll meet at the walls of Mar-Halira and the sooner we'll all destroy the Silver Mountain."

Dammon heard himself address the formidable cavalry-woman and marveled at his own force and bluntness. It had come to him naturally, and she retreated before his show of control, though not too graciously. She brushed soil from her trousers and bowed curtly to him before swinging away to give her riders the orders to pack and mount. Dammon saw Master Kor regarding him with a patron's benevolent approval.

He did not sleep when he retired to this own tent, although he had instructed the remaining foot soldiers to rest themselves well, with an eye on waking and mustering before dawn. Master Kor had ridden away with the horsemen. He was in sole command and would be until they met with the silver wizard again, at the other end of the Surin Gryagi territories.

"My lord, may I intrude?" Pryun's whine insinuated itself into Dammon's ear so gently that at first he thought he had dozed into a dream. When he realized he was awake, he sprang up from his blankets.

"How did you get in here? The guards—"

"—will be in with us and skewer me on their nasty spears if my lord doesn't lower his voice. Giving those lunks real weapons . . . tsk. I don't think they're ready for the responsibility, especially not your friend Turgan."

Dammon grasped the truth of what Pryun said. He lowered his voice accordingly. "How did you get past them?" he repeated. Decad Turgan himself and one other spearman stood on watch outside the prince's tent. If they learned that their guard had been breached, and by Pryun, they'd die of shame.

Pryun waved at the back wall of the tent. It was securely pegged to the ground, but in one place Dammon thought he saw a slip of outside light where the material had been stretched. "I'm good at worming my way in and around and under, my lord. The better to serve you, of course."

"Next time, come to see me directly."

Pryun waggled a finger at him. "Testy! Snappish! If I were to come in by the front way, news of my visit would be all over the camp in an hour. Some messages are better delivered privately."

"I'm waiting to hear what you've got to say that needs so much privacy."

"Treachery, my lord, is better kept a secret." Pryun smiled smugly at Dammon's startled look. "Does it surprise you, my lord? Who would betray a legend? But legends only grow so long as they're popular, and if you don't mind my saying so, you've made a very unpopular choice."

Dammon knew. "To free Mrygo's people."

"To waste the lives of surface folk freeing the Children of Stone. I was there when Mrygo first came to Khana, my lord. I heard what the survivors told their comrades about the thankless, useless task it was, and so many of their own lost! My lord..." Pryun spoke so quietly that Dammon had to lean near, whether he wanted to or not. "My lord, they will not make the same mistake again."

"Explain."

"Explain? So you are happy to have lost that wager, to have me for your faithful ear? Ha, but a prince needs eyes more: eyes to follow Captain Beliza once she's out of sight; eyes to keep on her lover, Captain Iskander, when you've got no silver wizards to back you with miracles."

"Iskander's loyalty—"

"My dearest lord, before you say that Iskander's loyalty is unquestionable, tell me: How long have you had it to question?"

Later, alone, Dammon stared at the back of his tent as if expecting Pryun to return and tell him that his earlier visit had been nothing more than the most elaborate of jests. Dammon's captains were faithful, their men eager to march wherever he directed, their hearts open to him as children's.

They were all he had now. He could not risk losing them. A prince without a realm or crown was nothing without the loyalty of his men. Without them, he would be less than a song, hummed in the byre and the field, its music soon garbled, its words sooner forgotten. The farmer's lout Ophar, with his hands on the plow and his ancient sword tucked away in the farmhouse rafters, would be worth more as a man than Lord Prince Dammon alone.

He would not lose them. He would change the orders, give them what they wanted most: revenge, taken directly against Devra. They would march on Lar-Khana, catching up with Beliza's cavalry on the way. They would conquer, destroy the crown jewel of Devra's reign, and take all.

Later there would be time for justice.

He could not sleep. He kicked his way out of the tousled blankets and burst from the tent, giving a brusque greeting to the guards on second watch. A film of green mist trailed through the silent forest encampment, the hem of a phantom lady's train. Dawn would follow the ebbing mist, and then he would assemble his men and announce the change.

There was the scent of water on the ground fog. Something unseen guided Dammon to the little stream that bubbled up out of the earth and trickled off to meet others of its kind until their many threads twined into the Great River, flowing out of the realm into the unknown southlands. Dammon knelt where small blue flowers grew and splashed cold water on his face and neck.

"Good morning." Mrygo's ashy face solidified out of the ripples. "Cold water's the next best thing to sleep, isn't it?"

Dammon pushed his dripping hair out of his eyes. "Do I look that bad?"

"I wouldn't send you to lead an aboveground charge with those bloodshot beauties, but the light below's soft enough to give you the advantage." The Gryagi sprawled on his stomach beside Dammon and dabbled his fingers in the stream. "I couldn't sleep either. I'm too—maybe excited's a poor word, but something's set a fire inside me about what we're going to do today."

Mrygo drew his hand from the water. The ripples smoothed, letting him see Dammon's reflection more clearly, and the strange expression on his face. It hadn't been a trick of light and water; it was there.

"What is it, Dammon?" Mrygo pushed himself up on his arms and looked directly at the prince. "Tell me."

"I think—I mean, we're marching after the cavalry today, bypassing Mar-Halira, and going directly on to the Silver Mountain. We'll enter the Surin holds later, once we've leveled Lar-Khana."

Mrygo stared incredulously. A spate of words spewed from Dammon's lips then: reasons, excuses, justifications cobbled up on the spot. "The Surin Gryagi are a minor threat. We'll rouse Devra's forces if even one of them escapes this attack and gets word to her. Every day we spend on skirmishes gives her another day to build the Silver Mountain higher. If she finishes it before we reach her, all of our little victories will be nothing. She'll have the full strength of the powers of air behind her. Do you think the people will join with us to help in the siege of Mar-

Halira if we don't rescue their daughters first? Devra kills more of them at every level of the mountain—"

He stopped. Mrygo was laughing.

It took the healer some time before he recovered enough to speak. "He does do effective work, doesn't he? I knew I should have let Turgan kill him, but I thought it would pain you. You wouldn't have understood. And he's such a sad creature." Mrygo rolled over and squatted on the tender grass, arms around his knees. "I'm talking about Pryun, my friend. We're not the sleepy fools he takes us for. I saw him slither around to the back of your tent and I tipped the word to Decad Turgan, but we let him alone. If he meant you harm, we knew you were quick enough with your sword to handle him. What we didn't count on was the harm that one can do without a blade."

"Pryun told me the truth." Dammon's mouth set into a stubborn line. "That's more than anyone's done for me since you dragged me away from Farmer Rycote's place without even an explanation!"

"Pryun told you the truth about Master Kor's child minstrels because it suited him. And that grand truth was one that Master Kor himself would have told you if you'd noticed the children gone and asked about them. It was no secret. Look, Dammon, when you buy beer in a tavern, the barkeep knows how it was brewed, but he doesn't ramble on about it unless you ask! He's got other things on his mind, and so do you."

The prince's mouth remained tight. "He told me the truth last night as well. The men don't want to march into the Surin holds to free your folk because they'll only try to die once they're freed. Why waste—"

"Dammon, I can tell you truths as well as Pryun. But mine— mine are blood truths. Will you want them?" A chill slid through Dammon's bones. Mrygo's voice was suddenly different. "Will you?" the healer insisted. The dark emptiness of the asking made the prince hesitate before bidding him to go on.

The Gryagi's face was unreadable. He spoke like a third-rate tale-teller—all rote recitation and no feeling. But as he spoke his blood truths, Dammon gave thanks that he hid his feelings so well. It was a telling that would have driven a weaker soul to self-destroying despair.

"When Captain Iskander's raid came, he freed only those

Gryagi waiting for the killing games next day. They were all males. The Surin keep our females elsewhere ... to breed. Oh yes! You look surprised, but I'm telling you the truth, the same as Pryun. It was like that from the first after they herded us into their holds. When you were our slave, we gave you back your strength, fed you, put you to work in the mines, but we never used you worse than our own criminals. Don't think our slavery with the Surin is like yours was with us.

"The males were forced into the killing games, as you know, and the females were forced to breed more fighters. In the beginning, they allowed couples to stay together, hoping to encourage breeding, but what parents will willingly engender young who'll only be raised to die for someone else's sport? The Surin soon grew wise. They drove the males apart and got their fresh crop of fighters regularly, siring them themselves. We Gryagi mature more rapidly than you surface folk, and our children don't wait so long to be born. Those of my tribeswomen who didn't die of hard handling or childbirth or sorrow by this time must have lived to bear at least seven children apiece; to see their sons taken from them to be trained for the fighting; to see their daughters tied down to the same beds where they were born, and raped as many times as their mothers."

There was no change in Mrygo's voice. He told the horrors casually, as a shepherd giving a tally of his flocks. The prince hid his face in his hands. He was Ophar again, watching the spirits of the Gryagi dead seep up out of the earth to haunt Larya's waking dreams. Terrible apparitions, but not half as terrible as the living nightmare of their surviving kin.

"When Iskander set us free, the Gryagi who ran back to attack the Surin were those whose wives and daughters were still captive," Mrygo went on. "They didn't think of what they were doing. They didn't even think to try to get hold of a weapon before throwing themselves at the Surin. They'd survived as long as they had because they *didn't* think. If they'd have thought about what was happening to their kin, they'd have gone mad that much sooner."

Mrygo followed the twirling wake of a leaf caught in the current of the stream. "When your people call mine the Children of Stone, you think that's what we're made of."

"They only went back to free their families..." Dammon

sat up. "Mrygo, the Gryagi who were freed with you—the ones who survived—do you know where they're posted in my ranks?" Mrygo nodded. "Find them and bring them to me now. Be sure no one follows you." The prince scooped up two fingers of mud from the streamside and squeezed much of the moisture from it. Flattening it in his palm, he pressed his seal ring into the wafer and studied the impression. He was making a second seal and a third as Mrygo ran to carry out the prince's order.

In the shadowed realm of the Surin Gryagi, the shaman's house stood directly under a pothole to the surface. Sunlight could bathe it, or rain, or any of the shifting sorts of surface weather. Inside, the shaman himself maintained an air of indifference to the elements; a calculated air meant to evoke awe among his tribesfolk.

Of course the shaman often dropped his stoic pose when he was alone and unobserved. His house was like all other Surin houses, having no paned windows and only a skin-hung doorway that let in all the worst of the weather. Other Surin could put up with this, since their homes were well sheltered by the caverns themselves. They had no need for proper doors and windows.

The shaman had not slept well. All his herbal brews were insufficient to banish the tenacious cold he'd caught as a result of his chosen manner of living. It had been a hard winter, made harder by demands from the surface-dwelling witch, who had called away nearly half the skilled metalworkers of the Surin hold to labor for her on a mysterious project. All of the shaman's attempts to pry into the witch's plans had met with failure, except for the last one. Then the scrying pool had only begun to yield a ghostly seeing when suddenly three green-eyed horrors had swooped down through that blasted pothole, in at the open window, and had proceeded to batter the shaman senseless. After that visitation, he left the witch's unseen, unguessed affairs well enough alone.

"Boy! Poke up the fire!" The shaman clutched a thick blanket around his shoulders and sneezed several times, making his chair rock. "Hurry, or I'll toss you back where you belong!"

"Do it. I don't care." The child was young and good-looking, but remarkably sullen. He ignored the shaman's furious gesturings meant to hasten him toward the hearth. He had not put on the wool tunic specially obtained for him by his master, but clung to the simple twist of loincloth that the other slaves wore.

"You'll care when they match you against an adult! They'd do it, too. They haven't forgotten how well you did in the last youth bouts. It wouldn't be sport to send you against your own age; it'd be murder."

The child said nothing, but poked up the fire as instructed. The shaman sneezed several times more, then cocked his head. "Did you hear something?" The boy gave no sign that he'd heard even the shaman's question. "Go to the door! Someone's there."

The boy pulled back the hides on their bronze rings. A creature barely taller than himself scuttled into the shaman's house.

"Who are you?" The shaman made a grab for the agate orb that was his mark of office. A dull orange light banded with shifting whorls of green emanated from the mottled stone. He raised it high to let its light spread. "You're Surin," the shaman said wonderingly. "But . . . I don't know you."

"My ancestors would be more familiar to you, master," said the visitor. "My grandfather was shaman here in his time. I am Pryun sed Byuric, son of Byuric sed Lyum. Do you know me now?"

"Byuric sed Lyum . . ." Nothing else Pryun had said captured the shaman's attention. "Not that Byuric who—"

"The traitor. But I come back to my home-hold, master, to destroy all the stains of treachery on my line and name. I return, seeking the healing that you can give, and the lifting of all curses on my bones."

"Curses? Healing? Ahum." The shaman lowered the agate orb and tried to understand what this odd specimen wanted of him, where it had sprung from, and how to send it on its way. Surely it couldn't mean—No, no, it might be ugly, but never mad enough to expect a Surin shaman, however powerful, to straighten the bones destined to grow that way. One could only heal the unintentional errors of nature; the simplest soul knew that!

Pryun tilted his head back to the limit, waiting for the miracle.

"O my true master, don't think I've come to ask for free forgiveness and healing. I've brought a price that will pay for everything—all insults, all betrayals of our Surin way that my cursed father made."

That fetched the shaman. It might be worth humoring the fool after all. "A price, you say?" He craned his wattled neck to see the size of the pouch this abominable creature might have at his belt. He saw nothing and scowled. "Where is it?"

Pryun's thin finger pointed at the hole in the shaman's roof, where the hearth smoke rose up and the rain could fall down. "Up there, my master. Up there a meager army marches against Queen Devra's strongest fortress. They will never take it— they'll die, and the Silver Mountain will drink their blood."

The shaman shuddered. He did not like to be reminded of the witch. He stole a glance at his personal slave and wondered if the boy would remain truculent if given the order to kill this warped interloper. He had killed his own kind readily enough in the ring.

"What do we have to do with the comings and goings of surface folk?" the shaman decreed pompously.

Pryun's brows came together in a frown. "Not much if they come and go on the surface. But, master, this army would have been marching down into your realm even now if not for me; marching, and setting your slaves free as they went. Freeing them, arming them, adding them to their ranks—and what do you think those slaves would do then?"

This time the shaman's shudder went deeper. He averted his eyes from the boy and fixed them on Pryun, trying not to imagine what the handsome child would do to him given the opportunity. Still, he was the shaman, and he had appearances to maintain. He rose from his chair, the blanket yet around his shoulders in the manner of royal robe, and looked down his nose at Pryun.

"I find it hard to believe that we owe salvation to such a . . . minor source. What's to stop any exile's whelp from slinking back into the hold and claiming he drove off a plague of dragons that *might* have been heading our way? I do not deal in possibilities."

"Send scouts to the surface, then!" Pryun snapped. "An army that size won't be hard to trace. And while you're at it, send a message to your queen. Tell her that her late brother sends his best regards. It is Dammon's army that's marching, you old fool! Lord Prince Dammon come again!"

The shaman observed Pryun's rage for a bit, then laughed until sneezes stopped him. Hawking and spitting, he managed to say, "That's even better than dragons! If you think I believe that—"

"I wouldn't," said a deep voice from the doorway.

"Not without proof," said a second.

The spear sang through the air, striking the shaman just below the breastbone, sending him tumbling. The agate orb rolled from his hands, and the slave flung himself out of its path into a raised and curtained cubby. The shaman's body sprawled on the stone floor, dead eyes striped with a trickle of dawn light from the upper world. Decad Turgan strolled into the house and wrenched his spear free of the corpse.

"Maybe now he'll believe you, blight." The spearpoint, still sticky with Surin blood, rounded on Pryun's hollow chest.

"Don't, Turgan." Dammon's sword was drawn, but his left hand stayed the spearman. "We'll judge him before all the troops and let him speak for himself."

"Him?" The big guard's laugh boomed in the small house. "He's got more wriggles than a worm, but this time the hook's fast enough—if you'll let me jab it in proper." He made a feint with the spear. Pryun jumped back involuntarily.

"I want him alive."

Decad Turgan shrugged, but eased the spear back a hair. Outside, the sounds of fighting—rout—penetrated the hide door and came readily through the open windows. Pryun looked from the guardsman to the prince wildly.

"Burning them out, the stinking slavers," said Turgan with deep satisfaction. "There wasn't that many Surin to deal with, for some reason. I was expecting more. Well, there were enough. I take back all I ever said against Mrygo's people—fought almost as good as spearmen once they knew we'd come to free them all. The Surin they don't kill will be driven into the deep tunnels, and the way blocked off. Bury your garbage deep, I always say. Come on, you." He twirled his spear fast enough to slap Pryun with the butt, then get the point back on him once he started moving.

"Wait a minute," said Dammon. He crossed to the cubbyhole and lifted the curtain. "Come out, please. There's nothing to be afraid of."

The boy emerged, showing no emotion. He skirted the fallen orb, but trod on the dead shaman's curling hand as if it were a carpet. Decad Turgan shouted at him to give an account of himself, but he ignored it, going to the hide-hung doorway and looking out first. What he saw pleased him, and he drank in the smells and sights and sounds of death for a long while before finally coming back and kneeling at Dammon's feet.

The prince raised him up. "You don't have to do that; you're free now, and the Gryagi aren't my subjects. If you'll come with us, we'll get you back to you kin. What's your name?"

"None."

"No name?" The old pain burned in Dammon's heart again; burned harder, because the pain was another's.

"No name and no kin." The young Gryagi behaved as if this were of no great moment. "My mother died having me, they said, and I was her first-born. They don't name us. What for, if we die? If you make it out of the youth bouts, you get a name. I was going to, but then that one took a fancy to me. He got me out of the games." The boy spat on the shaman's corpse, then touched his fighter's collar.

"We'll get that off you, lad," Decad Turgan said. "You just come with us, and we'll find you kin and a name, too."

The freed slave fell into step behind his liberators, but if they intended to take him to a new life or back to the killing games, it was all the same to him.

The heart of the Surin hold was a public square modeled after similar places on the surface. Here, Captain Iskander directed his men in the division of former slaves and former masters. A mass of Surin Gryagi females and children huddled together, taking up most of the plaza. The few Surin males left alive were cordoned off by a ring of soldiers.

Mrygo and the other Gryagi who had been rescued during Iskander's ill-starred raid moved among their people. They had been the ones to spread word through the troops that the orders to march off at dawn were false. They had been the runners sent bearing the prince's mud-pressed seal to give Lord Dammon's true orders—to enter the Surin holds as soon as Pryun turned up missing from camp and could no longer give his Surin kin any warning of their coming. The other troops now called them Prince Dammon's Voice, and were witnesses to how well Gryagi could fight.

Now the fighters of Prince Dammon's Voice were quiet. Very little was said. Touches, looks, tears told everything. Some of the older Gryagi were beginning to gather together and trade muffled questions. Decisions were made and passed on, reactions gathered and returned to the elders, all in a nearly imperceptible manner. Mostly, there were murmurs and silence.

The silence cracked into loud cheers when Dammon came into the square with Decad Turgan and his two charges. Turgan urged Pryun forward, and the cheers changed to shouted curses and cries for the traitor's death sentence. It took Dammon more than upraised hands to bring back the silence.

"My people!" He had to shout several times until they were still enough to hear him. "My people, you see the truth of what I told you!"

The crowd roared, but this time their acclaim was less than half the noise. Pryun trembled, hearing his name above every other sound; his name, and *death*! Even the recently freed Gryagi were quick to learn that there stood the one who would have turned their beloved Dammon aside, who would have led their blessed prince astray, who would have left them in their chains forever. They took the death cry for their own.

Dammon fought them back. "My people—my friends—don't ask me for this blood! For his father's sake—"

He heard a sound like the rushing of wind, an inhalation made of hundreds of breaths, a sigh. At first he thought it was all the wonder and reverence left behind by the memory of Byuric sed Lyum. He saw smiles spread across every free face in the crowd, but the pent Surin Gryagi paled, shook, and one female screamed the Surin word for blood.

Dammon turned. The nameless child-slave had lifted the clasp knife from Decad Turgan's belt without the big man feeling a thing and with a single slice had severed Pryun's head from his body. The wizened corpse fell, hardly more substantial than a dried puffball, and the boy was holding the jester's head aloft for all to see.

Mrygo yanked the hide curtain off its rings and tossed it out the door. "Stupid affectation," he said. "Why didn't they just build doors and be done with it, or keep an honest man's home open, the way it's supposed to be?" He came into what had been the shaman's house and squatted across the hearth from Dammon. It was suppertime, and throughout the captured Surin holds, Lord Prince Dammon's troops were billeted in the vacant houses. A pot of stew balanced on a tripod over the fire—Dammon's own cooking and kindling. The prince had refused the services of squire or page since the start of the great march from Khana.

"Where's the boy?"

Dammon indicated the cubbyhole, its curtains drawn. "What am I going to do with that one, Mrygo? A child! He killed Pryun just like *that*." He snapped his fingers. "Why? By the Seed, why?"

"He's a killer," Mrygo replied as if it were self-evident. "What else has he been all his life? No one's son, no one's brother, not even a name. . . . Well, he was the shaman's fancy for a while, but that's a distinction he'd prefer to forget. There's no better way to reclaim what you are than a grand public gesture. Lopping off Pryun's head with a clasp knife—and Turgan told me that blade wasn't worth much when an easy cut was wanted—now *that* was his way of telling us who he was." Mrygo raised his shoulders. "What else does he have?"

Dammon called over his shoulder at the cubby, "Come out!" The curtain stirred. The child perched on the edge, legs too short to touch the floor. "Come here . . . please." He obeyed, padding over to sit on the floor Surin-style, rather than squatting like Mrygo. His black eyes skimmed Dammon's face, then rested on the healer's.

Mrygo understood. "Yes," he said. "I'm one of your tribe."

"Slaves have no tribe."

"You're wrong," said Dammon. "A tribe—kin—friends—they're all bonds, and slaves know more of bonds than any other souls. I know. I was once a slave like you."

The boy sneered openly. "You're Lord Prince Dammon. You're—*everything*! When were you ever a slave?"

"Believe him," Mrygo said. "Our prince is a great believer in truth; he won't lie to you. He was a slave, child—ours."

The child's skeptical eyes grew wider as Mrygo and Dammon recounted the spans of Ophar's slavery. When they were done, he asked, "You didn't know who you really were? Honestly?" Dammon assured him of it. The boy became suspicious. "If you were our slave, why did you come to free us? If I knew the Surin were chained up somewhere, I'd only come to laugh."

"Your folk didn't take slaves as a rule, young one," said Dammon. "It was either punishment or . . . error. I saw how the Surin took their slaves and what they did with them. I might not have known my own name then, but I knew what was wrong."

"You had no name . . . no one . . . you didn't know . . ."

Children cry. Dammon remembered the many nights in the bad times when he'd heard the little ones up in Farmer Rycote's loft weeping. He remembered how he and Larya would climb up, find the sad ones, take them in their arms, speak comfort, and wipe away the tears. It had always hurt him to see children cry, but these tears—they were his as well.

He hugged the child close. "You have me, little brother. You have me now; don't cry. We're your kin—Mrygo and I— and . . . and we'll give you your name."

The boy lifted his chin. He tried to salvage his pride and act as if his cheeks and eyes were dry. "I won't have a Gryagi name," he declared. "No, even if I'm Gryagi—so are the Surin scum. If I'm your kin, my lord, I want a surface name."

Dammon grinned. "You'll have it: Frog." The boy looked puzzled.

"That's a surface creature that can't make up its mind," Mrygo explained good-naturedly. "Half in the water and half on the land; of two worlds."

"Frog," the Gryagi boy repeated. "Good."

"Glad you like it. Now go out and tell Decad Turgan that you're going to march with me." The boy raced from the hated house, leaving the two friends alone.

"Clever name you picked," said Mrygo. "It fits him."

"Does it?" Dammon stirred the stew. "You were the one

who explained my choice, but, Mrygo—you explained it to me as well. I just . . . lit on it as a name. I don't know why."

The healer's hand closed over Dammon's. His voice was rough. "Dammon . . . friend . . . today you set my people free. By the soul of the stones and the veins of the mountains, I swear that someday I will be the one to free you."

The army that had marched into the land of death emerged into dappled forest sunlight. The cold, musty smells of underground were banished by the sweet tang of crushed pine needles and the moist, living scents of the earth. The detachment of fighters detailed to mind the heavy supply wagons and the horses cheered madly and abandoned their posts when they caught sight of the first returnees. Tales of the battle mixed with laughter and the usual curses as the reunited foot soldiers shouldered their march-packs and got ready to move out.

Lord Prince Dammon wanted to keep out of sight, leaving it to Captain Iskander to organize the men for marching, but that was out of the question. He had to show himself to the soldiers at least a dozen times, had to receive their homage, had to visit the wounded, had to refuse full credit for the success of the attack on the Surin holds and pass some of the glory on to Iskander, Turgan, and Mrygo's Gryagi fighters. There had been no fatalities among his own fighters. He did not dare to dream that it would be always thus. Frog was at his side everywhere, and a bodyguard of Mrygo's newly freed kin who had chosen to join the cause of their liberator.

"Beliza would have a fit," Mrygo said to Captain Iskander. The redhead had to agree. Something about Graygi looks put off the cavalrywoman. "Maybe she'll soften to us more once she hears about Frog."

"How so?"

"The only thing our tolerant friend liked less than my looks was Pryun's. If she hears Frog's the one who rid us of him, she might come around."

Captain Iskander hauled himself onto his horse. "We'll see about that soon enough. Your folk mopped up the Surin right enough after we loosed them, making us a gift of time. We're afoot, but we should intercept Beliza's cavalry in a day or two at most. We won't even have to take that underground shortcut to reach them now. Thank the gods! I feel like a dead man every time I go into the Gryagi holds."

Iskander's words proved correct, with a slight difference. After two days' march they did intercept a company of riders. The riders were not Beliza's.

"You, there! You! Stop!"

The trees caught Decad Turgan's shout, but the thick fall of pine needles baffled the sound of running feet as the spearman and his decad gave chase to the figure they'd flushed out of hiding.

Riding at the head of the marchers, Lord Prince Dammon reined in his horse to turn back and see what the to-do was about. He saw his trusted guard lolloping through the woods like an angry farmer after a chicken thief. "Turgan!"

"It's a spy, my lord." A man from farther back in the ranks jogged up to grasp the prince's bridle and report. "Decad Turgan's spears spotted him."

"A spy?" One of the hunters threw his spear after the quarry. It missed the mark and buried itself in the bole of a tree. "By all the gods—Turgan, stop! Don't kill him!" Dammon jerked his bridle out of the soldier's hand and dug in his heels, pursuing the pursuers. Frog loped after, never far from Dammon's side.

"Turgan! Turgan!" The horse made poor time among the trees. Speed was sacrificed as the beast struggled to pick out a way for itself. Frog's small shadow slipped past the prince's steed and caught up with Turgan's men, then outpaced them. The Gryagi boy jagged right, angled in, and emerged ahead of the fleeing figure. When the man burst from between two trunks, Frog was waiting for him. He was going so fast that a flying tackle from even so small an opponent brought him down.

Frog and the fugitive were still struggling like bundled snakes when Turgan and his spears came upon them. The big guard raised his spear to strike, but reconsidered, not daring to risk a thrust that might harm Lord Dammon's charge. He sighed and ordered his men to separate the tusslers and hold the spy for Dammon's questioning.

"Thank all the powers!" gasped Dammon when he finally arrived. "Turgan, next time call *yourself* off."

"He's a spy," the spearman maintained, brows in that famous V again. "Or else why's he sneaking about in the forest?"

"Why are we?" Dammon replied. "Catch your suspects, don't kill them out of hand. The poor man may be a farmer put off his land, forced to live in the woods. I seem to remember a spearman who had that story to tell."

He alit from his horse and faced the prisoner. He was a tall man, face and body worn thin by care and hard living. His tunic was the rust-brown of ancient pine needles, much mended, but the hilt of the shortsword at his waist was set with a royal sapphire the size of a walnut. "Who are you?"

A strange thing happened. The man was bruised and dusty from his recent fall, surly and grim, but as he looked at Dammon, every vestige of anger melted away. Joy and wonder filled its place.

"Oh my lord!" He sagged between the guards who held him, going to his knees despite their best efforts to keep him standing. "Oh my dear lord!" His laughter could have been mistaken for madness. "My lord prince, you live! The songs were true! Praise the gods for it."

"The farmer seems to know you," muttered Turgan.

"Farmer?" The man's back stiffened where he knelt. "Be careful what you call me, lout. And speak up in the presence of your betters! I didn't get these at the plow!" He yanked his arms free of the guards' and tore open the front of his tunic. Old welts crosshatched skin the color of fine ivory—palace-pretty skin. Only where the sun had been able to touch him was he bronzed. Dammon saw one scar that was fairly fresh, a slash of pink through the thick, silvery hair on his chest. There were other souvenirs of the sword and dagger on the man's forearms, and a white mark along his jaw.

"My lord—" The warrior spoke only to Dammon. "My lord, I am surprised at your coldness. Has any liar come to you with false tales of me? If I did serve your cursed sister, it was only until I learned the true reason for your disappearance. Maldonar may be a fool and a laplick, but he's still got shame enough to regret what Devra's made of him. When he's in his cups, he talks. I fled Mar-Halira as soon as I knew what those two had done to you. I'm only sorry I wasn't able to make an end of Maldonar before I left."

Dammon felt a sourness in his throat. The man knew him—knew and loved him well, to judge from his words—and expected some sign of recognition in return. The black gap in the prince's brain had never yawned so wide or seemed so deep. Expectation ceded to hurt in the old warrior's eyes.

"My lord, my lord . . . how have I offended you that you turn from me now? Don't you believe me?"

"Of course he does, my lord Gerais," said Mrygo smoothly. He had come up behind Dammon and now stepped forward to bark at the guards: "Release him! This 'spy' you almost killed is Lord Gerais of Mar-Korhori—Lord Prince Dammon's tutor once, his most prized general . . . bah! Why do I waste my time speaking of generals to a pack of plow-drags?"

Dammon's look of gratitude was lost in the glares that Turgan's men shot at Mrygo. They released the general, who stood tall and ignored the filth of forest debris clinging to his knees. "How is it that a Gryagi knows who I am while my lord ignores me?"

Mrygo's smile never failed. "My lord Gerais, you can still see the mark of my collar if you care to. I am a survivor of Surin games. What else do fighters talk about but other fighters? Your name is only second to Lord Prince Dammon's in the songs, even in Hori-Halira. As for my lord the prince—"

"As for me, forgive me, old friend." Dammon gave his hands to the general. "Could I ever forget you? But if you see a lion come out of a badger's burrow—well, you wonder for a while if it's a lion or a trick of the eyes."

"That's apt enough." Lord Gerais spoke bitterly. "I've had to go to earth like a damn digger ever since I escaped your sister's rule. Praise the gods, I haven't been alone in my burrow." Seasoned eyes tallied the armed men ranged around the prince. "Are these all your troops?"

"The others are on the path—"

"Fetch them, and follow me." The general fell back into his ancient role of tutor, the firm hand that molded a spoiled princeling into an honest fighter. Dammon relayed the order and went on foot with Lord Gerais farther into the trees, keeping his horse on a lead. Frog clung to the stirrup just behind his adored prince.

They took what looked like random turnings in the unbroken

woodland. It was a wall-less maze reminiscent of the Gryagi tunnels, and it gave Dammon a prickling feeling in his legs. His one consolation was that once Mrygo had spoken Gerais's name, the memories had returned. He saw the old warrior blustering through the halls of Mar-Halira, dressing down the guardsmen, demanding better discipline all around, shouting in his face that if he didn't stop mooning after impossibilities, he'd never become . . .

Become what? That part eluded him. A good prince, probably—a good battle-chief, more likely. When he thought of Lord Gerais again, it was in battle, fighting for his prince better than many younger men. Dammon recalled holding the general's gray stallion while the older man held a council in his tent. The prince must have been very young then—his father still alive and at the council table—for him to be excluded from the meeting.

It was hard to tell in which direction Lord Gerais was taking them all. The leafy canopy fragmented the sunlight and deceived the eye. There was evidence of horses under foot— Turgan and his men were cursing loudly—but Beliza's troops couldn't have come this way. Then Lord Gerais made a doubling turn and the trees parted into a broad clearing. A line of tethered horses, specially bitted to keep them silent, stamped and shuffled while their human attendants saw to their needs.

Lord Gerais hailed his comrades. Dammon saw at least half a dozen palace-pretty faces among the rougher-cut soldiers in the clearing. One of these came at a trot to welcome the general back and to stare with unmasked hostility at the uninivited guests.

Lord Gerais slapped the young man on the back and used the friendly gesture as a cover. His true purpose was to seize the fellow's shoulder and force him to his knees. "My lord Fiel, I see you know enough to pay homage to your prince," he said.

The young man's frown changed swiftly to a gape of disbelief. Lord Gerais did not look pleased with such an open show of emotion. He had always said that good fighters were steel all the way through, and he seemed to have lived by his own words. Even his hair was the dull color of a battle-tried blade, and his eyes the sharp blue-gray of a new sword.

"Don't goggle like that, boy!" Lord Gerais smacked the back of the young lordling's head as if he'd been a scullion. "Say your piece the way you were trained. The gods know we've gone through it often enough, and never expecting to have the chance to use it!"

Lord Fiel rubbed his smarting scalp. Gerais had a heavy hand. He bowed his neck as he offered the prince his cupped hands. "My lord Prince Dammon," he began. The words came out half-choked. "I am Fiel, son of Lord Fergan. In the name of my father's loyalty, accept me as your man."

Lord Fergan ... a troop of the queen's men galloping past Farmer Rycote's lands, banners snapping ... tales told of the traitor lord who rebelled against his rightful queen, calling her foul names ... a severed head impaled over the gate of Lord Fergan's own castle. ... "I would be traitor to my rightful lord if I were not traitor to you, demon-lover!"; brave words spoken on the scaffold. ... The start of the bad times, when good folk everywhere were told that they must bear with it until their queen had wiped out all the wicked lords who might prove as treacherous as Lord Fergan ... the wanderers, the beggars, the burning lands, and a sick child dying in the night, in Larya's arms ...

Dammon remembered another lord kneeling with cupped hands upraised, giving himself and his men to his chosen sovereign. He had witnessed the ceremony many times: two cupped hands from below—the powers of water and earth; two cupped hands from above to complete the sphere—powers of fire and air.

The prince capped Fiels's hands with his own. "In the name of your father's true heart, I accept you."

"Cheer, you fools!" bellowed Lord Gerais, shaking his fist at the dumbstruck men. "This is our lord, our true prince, Lord Prince Dammon himself, damn you all! Do I have to beat homage into your hides? The songs are true, and I'm their witness! He's come back! He's come back to lead us, to aid us, to save us all!"

The sound was low at first, a rumble that began beyond the trees. It grew, and as it grew, the men came closer. There were more of them in plain sight now, and as the first came away from the picketed horses, others streamed out of the forest, and others after them.

From his side of the clearing, Dammon heard his own troops massing at his back. The pressure of all those souls around him frightened him, pressing in to crush him with the weight of all their dreams. He broke from Lord Fiel and leaped into his saddle, nearly kicking Frog in the face in his haste to put himself out of their reach. He held his mount on a tight rein, but as the clearing grew even more crowded, there was no need to restrain the horse, for there was nowhere for the animal to go.

Now the cheers were coming in waves of sound that buffeted him worse than a windstorm. Their faces were turned to him, their hands reaching, and in every face he read a different hope—a new demand.

The darkness inside him called seductively, beckoning with four curved claws. To be nameless again . . . to be nothing . . . to be free of all ties and desires but your own. . . . He gazed deep into the darkness and yearned to fall forever.

Green eyes swirled with fire leered up at him from the heart of the pit. His soul shriveled and scurried back from the edge, flying to the safety of a place in the world, and a name.

Lord Prince Dammon astride his steed raised his sword. *"Mar-Halira!"* Freed slaves and fugitives, exiled lords and farmers who had taken up the sword, all answered their lord's battle-cry.

"Mar-Halira!"

The shout still battered, but Dammon welcomed the pain.

Part VI

In Neb-Mar

Lord Maldonar stood on the castle battlements, his daughter by his side, and looked out across the grassland at the encampment of his enemies. There were many of them—many more than he had imagined possible. He wondered whether Devra had known she'd overlooked so many hate-filled souls when she ravaged her own kingdom.

And if she had known? Would she have burned the heart out of the land, killed everything human, and repopulated it at the pleasure of the powers of air? Lord Maldonar shook off the thought. It was too unsettling to dwell on what was very likely possible. There were no depths to Devra, as he knew better than most men.

Pretty Lilla looked up at her father. How serious he looked! How hard and dismal! She felt the soft, sucking mouth of her bat-winged pet against her cheek, but she had no wish to spend her attention elsewhere when she had her father near. Since the siege had begun, she had hardly seen him at all, and with Mama gone, she was frequently bored and lonesome.

She slapped at the nibbling creature on her shoulder. Gira flew up with a screech of anger, but it did not risk returning to its mistress quite yet. It knew her very well. Lilla sidled closer to Lord Maldonar and insinuated her tiny hand into his.

"Get away from me!" The queen's consort lurched aside, wrenching his hand from hers as if from a live coal. "Don't do that again! If you want to be allowed up here, you'd better keep your distance."

Lilla veiled her eyes—and where did a child of fair-eyed parents come by eyes so brown? Sometimes Lord Maldonar half believed that Lilla was not his daughter. That was a comforting thought. He would be more than willing to take the tag of cuckolded lover if it meant disowning that exquisite girl as his blood. No price would be too high to buy himself free of her and her accursed mother.

It was impossible. She was his. Devra herself had assured him of how hopeless it was to deny paternity. In the hidden room where she had finally taken him into the confidence of her deepest schemes, Devra had let him read the full riddle of Lilla. His blood was there, bound to Devra's until death.

Until death . . .

The child had forgotten him. Her attention span was short, and she was capricious. The spectacle of the besieging army on the plain had drawn her notice once more. The crenellated battlements came up to her chin at their low point, and she had to stand on tiptoe to get a really good view.

He might offer her his hand up onto the stone platform. He might lift her to stand on the jagged square teeth and then . . . she was very light, very small. He could pitch her headlong from the heights with the touch of a hand.

Cold breath was on his neck. He twitched around sharply, but saw nothing. Shadows lingered in the corner of his eye. Was it a true shape? Had something been there, something quick, something evil? He kept telling himself that *they* were with her now, with Devra. They would stay with her until the abominable thing was built, urging her to hasten the day of its completion. They couldn't be here as well as with her—not in two places at once.

Could they?

Lilla had scrambled atop the masonry by herself. Her bright red gown stretched into a bloody star as she pressed her hands against the gray stone merlons to either side of the gap. Red silk brought out the blue lights in her hair, which trailed down her back all the way to her knees. A wind came from the eastern woods and lifted the mantle of her hair, the hem of her gown. Lord Maldonar saw that her body already had the shape of womanhood, although she was only a child.

"What manner of things do you make in this world, Devra?" he murmured.

Lilla leaned into the wind, laughing. "Look! I see some of their men wearing Mama's colors. Isn't that funny? We wondered where they'd gone, Mama and I. I told her you were a passable soldier, but not much use at keeping tally of your men. So many seem to get away from you."

She didn't bother to look at him while she spoke. Lord Maldonar surveyed the foe and confirmed for himself that Lilla's eyes were keen. There were one-time queen's men camped with the besieging army, and he also saw the tattered colors of other noble houses—houses he'd thought safely extinct, their last heirs either exterminated or imprisoned. Was that Lord Gerais's device on that swallowtail banner? The colors were his, right enough, but anyone might have adopted that combination. At this distance it was difficult to read the blazon . . .

"So many fighters!" Lilla sounded delighted with the prospect. "I'll bet there are even more in the woods. We won't know how many there really are until they move against us. Do you think it's really true, what all the common folk have been saying? Is that really Lord Prince Dammon's army? Oh my! If it is, what are you going to do? Poor Father, you haven't a hope in the world! You wouldn't be much use against that many even if the songs were all lies, but if it's Lord Prince Dammon—"

He struck her between the shoulder blades with both fists. She shrieked and pitched into empty air, hair and gown twin comet tails streaking her flight. Lord Maldonar staggered to the parapet and looked over the edge. Between the curtain wall and the keep was a blot of red and black on the courtyard cobbles. An awful feeling of exultation swelled inside him. The unseen chains across his chest snapped, and he tasted free air.

Bat-wings scraped across his cheek, and a plangent pain. Lilla's familiar clawed and bit Lord Maldonar's face, its mouth no longer soft but bristling with razored fangs that carved flesh to the bone. His attempts to slap it away or seize it were futile. The creature darted in and out with an insect's quickness. All that his hands touched was his own blood. He gurgled with blind fear as the thing dove for his eyes.

"Stop it, Gira! Stop it!"

The assault cut off. Lord Maldonar leaned back against a merlon, wiping blood from his face with the edge of his cloak. The winged horror hung on the air like a dragonfly before returning to the outstretched wrist of its mistress. Lilla tittered at the stunned lord, then brushed the creature's belly with her lips.

"You see, Father? I love you very well, even if you don't love me half so sweetly." She gave her familiar another kiss. Its slash mouth opened and closed in pleasure.

"You—you fell. I saw you fall! I saw—"

"You pushed me. That wasn't loving. I don't think Mama would like to hear how wicked Father treats his little girl. What do you think I should do?" This to her tame nightmare. "Should I tell? You'd fly with the message, wouldn't you, my love? Should Mama know how well Lord Maldonar keeps her daughter and her castle?"

Lord Maldonar paled and felt the shock of nausea hit him in the pit of the belly. He fought to hide it from Lilla, but her eyes were sharp for seeing more things than distant liveries.

"Ah, don't shiver so, poor Father. It's cold out of Mama's bed, but you're no longer needed there. Don't I know how cold the nights can be, sleeping so all alone? Poor little Lilla." She tossed her creature into the sky and let it fly where it would. Unencumbered, she closed on Lord Maldonar, who still pressed himself against the square stone tooth and tried not to collapse.

"You're alive," was all that he could say to his daughter. "You're still alive." He made an old sign against evil, a sign that only made her wrinkle up her tiny nose in disgust.

"Save that for your bad dreams. I'm just as alive as you, and not come back from the dead, either!"

"You fell—"

"You *saw* me fall. You *see* an awful lot of funny things; don't you, Father? Is it your eyes? Such pretty eyes—so blue. They say that Lord Prince Dammon has blue eyes. But you're no prince; just a bedwarmer for a queen who may not need you anymore. . . . Did you see me fall, Father? Wasn't that something you'd wanted to see? I know it was, so I gave you what you wanted. Now . . . can't you do the same for me?"

She melted against him, laughing when he squirmed. Her soft hands closed the gashes that her familiar's teeth and claws had torn across Lord Maldonar's face. He moaned at her touch, skin gray and clammy. When the last cut was sealed she stepped back, an artist evaluating her handicraft.

"Now you're handsome again. But you don't look very well. Lilla will take care of you, Father, never fear. You must be at your best when the army comes. You have to hold this castle for Mama. Go now. Rest in your rooms. Eat and drink whatever you like. I'll see that they send up your favorites from the kitchen."

She took his hand just as if she were the most ordinary little girl in the world playing house with her father. "I'll take care of you."

The servants who saw their princess and her father come down from the battlements exchanged sideways glances. Rumors thrived in the shadows, and shadows themselves seemed to grow and spread a tapestry of whispers and conjectures through the darkened halls of Mar-Halira. The whispers were very low, most discreet. Servants learned discretion by example—the example made of their companions whose mutterings were a breath too loud and reached the ears of the queen. It was not a good place to be caught talking out of turn, Mar-Halira—Neb-Mar, now: Shadow Castle.

Lilla escorted her father to his suite and smiled sweetly at the pages who attended him. They smiled back stiffly. She read their fear and reveled in it. She was a very happy child. Down to the kitchens she tripped in little gold satin slippers. She paid the cook many delicate compliments, flattered him, cajoled him into preparing a service of all her father's favorite dishes.

Compliments, cajolery, flattery—all were unnecessary. The cook knew her nature as well as the page-boys, but he also knew it was unwise to balk at the game. Therefore he played the gruff, temperamental cook because that was what Lilla fancied today. He gave in to her requests only after a judicious amount of byplay, but once he had agreed to prepare the meal, he was not fool enough to dawdle over making it. The tray was ready shortly, and Lilla gave him her most charming smile.

"I'll take it to Father myself."

The cook breathed normally as soon as the slight figure bobbed out of sight up the castle stairs.

Lilla did not take the tray directly to her father's rooms. She paused twice en route: once to cut a rose from a courtyard garden and give a splash of color to the drab wood and metal serving dishes; once to steal into another garden—a smaller, darker garden—and cull a pinch of gray-green moss that fell to powder easily and blended well with Father's favorite wine.

It was not poison. Lilla knew there were more amusing things than murder, although the lesson had been learned at some cost. Mama had taught her the value of extending her pleasures. Lovely Mama! Some day Lilla dreamed of being so like her mother that Mama too would become as expendable as Lord Maldonar.

Lilla covered her giggles with her hands. She wondered what sort of visions this dose would bring. Her own death— that had been so funny! To stand safely away from the brink and see her father rush at phantoms, to watch his look of relief change to horrified surprise when he saw her still alive. . . . She added a second pinch of moss to the wine. It would make the illusions stronger if he drank it all, guarantee at least some amusement even if he only took a sip.

Singing, Lilla took the tray to Lord Maldonar. As she passed a western lancet window on the stairs, she glimpsed the flash of banners far across the plain. So that was Lord Prince Dammon's army? It didn't seem like much, no matter how she'd teased Father about their numbers. Her dabblings in the old history books had taught her that Mar-Halira had withstood more formidable sieges. Still, it might be entertaining to let them into Mar-Halira, if only for a little while. She had never had a prince to play with before. What a shame that they would never manage to take Mama's castle.

"So that's Mar-Halira." Dammon stood with hands on hips, Mrygo with him. The plains between the castle and the forest, where most of his forces were encamped, were stubbly after the winter's cold, but new green was beginning to stipple the gold of dead grasses. From the woods to the castle, the land sloped downward in a fine, graceful sweep. Beliza was already bubbling over with visions of magnificent cavalry charges, racing over the flatlands until she and her riders would skim the wind and sweep Devra from her stronghold in one stroke of the sword.

"How does it feel to come home?" the Gryagi asked his friend. "You had rooms in . . . *that* tower?"

Dammon chewed his lower lip. "No . . . no, I think the royal apartments were in the main body of the keep, just above the great hall and the bedrooms flanking the fireway from below. Or . . . maybe not. I remember being pretty cold in the winter."

"Well, you might have been practicing some kind of toughening exercise—sleeping on the floor, no blanket, pillowed on your sword, eating dirt . . ."

Dammon tried to stifle a laugh and wound up with it escaping through his nose. "Where did you get ideas like that, Mrygo?" he asked as he repaired the damage with his kerchief. "Eating dirt!"

"I was going to say eating nails. You were one of Lord Gerais's pupils, and that old man's got notions about hammering out soldiers on an anvil. Ever since we linked up with him and Lord Fiel's men, our Khana troopers have been getting tongue-lashings for breakfast, lunch, and dinner. We're *soft*, he says. Not like the fighters he was used to leading in his heyday—now *there* were *real* men. You can imagine how Captain Beliza and her shield-sisters enjoy hearing all that blather of *real men*. Can't you tie up your old hunting dog better, Dammon?"

"Lord Gerais is a good man and the best general in the realm. If we take Mar-Halira, it'll be thanks to him."

A rough young voice added, "He is a good fighter." Frog came out of the woods to be with Dammon. In the time since the prince had given him that oddly familiar name, anyone who wanted to find Dammon could do it by finding Frog, or else the other way around. He had made himself the prince's page despite Dammon's gentle objections—looking after his comforts, setting out his clothes, bringing him his meals. Decad

Turgan and Mrygo resigned themselves to the boy's omnipresent meddling and counseled Dammon to do the same.

"Besides, sir, it looks better," said Turgan. "More proper, you having an attendant. Lord Gerais's got one, and even young Lord Fiel, and them camping out in the woods all this time, living like foxes."

"I don't want a page." Dammon saw another young boy— human, not Gryagi—looking after his prince's wants, so happy to serve, so loyal, so brave...

Too brave. Prince Dammon had said that the child should remain behind while he and his squire descended into the caverns after the dragon, but the boy hadn't listened. His place was with his prince. Dammon had laughed and rumpled his hair, calling him sword-brother. How that little joke had made the boy's chest puff out with pride! He had gone under the earth with the prince he served, and he had never come back.

The memory made Dammon swear never again to bind any young soul so strongly to him. The loyalty of grown fighters was one thing, given for a myriad of selfish or selfless reasons, but always given after thought. Sometimes coin bought them, sometimes a dream, but the young gave their hearts too willingly, too blindly, and they dreamed too readily and too well. Sometimes they never awoke from serving another man's dream.

Frog came to stand between Dammon and Mrygo. The killing-games fighter's collar was still around his throat. He had refused all efforts to remove it as staunchly as he'd refused to give up his self-imposed post as Dammon's page. There was nothing anyone could do about it. Even direct orders failed— Frog simply feigned temporary deafness and long-range forgetfulness. ("Oh? I wasn't supposed to cook your dinner? Well, next time I won't ... but should I toss out this food now, my lord? That would be a waste. It's hot, and it isn't bad ...")

Dammon smiled and rested his hand on Frog's broad shoulder. He could be stubborn, too—hadn't he resisted Lord Gerais's notion of sending back the Gryagi fighters?—but Frog had him beaten. Like it or not, he had a page again.

"What is it, Frog?"

"My lord Gerais says you're wanted in his tent."

Dammon cast one last backward look at Mar-Halira. He had feared that when he saw it, there would be no spark of recognition, but the fear proved hollow. He knew his castle. One glance, and all the complexities of towers, battlements, halls, great chambers had come back to him. The memories were so lucid that he sometimes feared to trust them. Whatever else had been lost in the black places, Mar-Halira was still his.

It hadn't taken Lord Gerais long to resume the dignities of his lost office as the prince's right-hand man. His war tent was a huge affair, with inlaid poles, but collapsible to a pack that two good horses could carry. During the time of his self-imposed forest exile, he had kept this vestige of power tucked away. It was impractical to set up such a huge tent in the forest lair into which he'd stumbled, to the surprise of young Lord Fiel's band. But now—ah, now the wind was blowing from another quarter. The golden age was hurrying home, tracking its way by Lord Prince Dammon's footprints. It was time for men to recall who they were and live accordingly.

All of which high-flown talk simply meant that Lord Gerais felt justified in deploying his monstrous war tent again. The sectioned central pole with its inlays of precious woods had been nibbled by squirrels, and the edges of the close-woven silk were showing signs of mildew, but Lord Gerais demanded that it be erected for the siege, and no one had either the heart or the stomach to contradict the old man.

A pinecone plopped down onto the council table. Lord Gerais frowned up at the hole in the tent roof and cursed. He swatted the cone away and glared at the few fighters who dared smile. Dammon turned a snicker into a cough, doing it badly.

"You said something, my lord?" The general's question was a challenge.

"Not a thing, Gerais. Please continue. About the castle defenses?..."

"Hmph. Yes. As I was saying, there's the curtain wall to breech first, and afterwards, the barred gate of the keep. If we're lucky, Lord Maldonar won't have found out about the sluice-gate that can flood the space between keep and curtain from the great river, but I never trust to any luck but bad in war. Still, that sluice-gate was getting pretty rusty, and if Devra's felt too full of herself to see to repairing Mar-Halira's ordinary defenses—"

"She hasn't," put in Lord Fiel. "I know."

"Eh? How's that?"

"I know because I came from Mar-Halira." He held the old general's craggy look steadily. "I was there at the same time as you, only not so willingly."

"You never told us you were imprisoned in Mar-Halira, Lord Fiel," Captain Iskander said.

"I and my mother and my two sisters. Here." There was a well-drawn plan of the castle unrolled on the table for all to peruse. Lord Fiel's finger stabbed at the center of the great hall. "Right under there was the cell where she kept us. Sometimes our guards gossiped where we could hear them. One of them was angry that the queen was letting all the castle defenses go to seed; the other said that with her magic to protect them, who needed anything else?"

Dammon imagined the great hall as he remembered it. It was made for celebrations and solemn festivals, hung with the flags of all noble houses loyal to their prince. He saw himself seated on the dais, Devra beside him. It was Lord Prince Dammon's birthday, and one of the courtiers had made the age-old suggestion that since he ruled so well and wisely, why not call himself king and stop all this finickry?

Again he heard the words the prince had spoken: *If we rule you well, then what do names and titles matter? What we are and what we do names us better than any borrowed glory.* Devra hadn't liked that. She adored fine-sounding titles, the grander the better. He remembered seeing that killing look on her face when the courtier's idea was turned down. Soon after that, the dragon had come.

Lord Fiel was speaking, and his memories of Mar-Halira had nothing festive to them. "They killed my father and brought us to Queen Devra's court in chains. She looked at us curiously, trying to recall who we were and why we were taking up her valuable time. Lord Maldonar himself had led the raid that captured us as we fled from Father's burning keep. He looked mighty annoyed when she accepted his war-prize so casually."

Lord Gerais scratched his head. "Annoyed? I'm surprised he dared to show her anything but a smile. She's yanked his teeth and torn his talons. He was once a good soldier, was Lord Maldonar." It was the general's highest compliment.

Lord Fiel continued, speaking with the numb, uninflected

voice of a man who does not want to hear the story he tells
others. If he let the words become more than words, they would
kill him. "She turned us over to her guards and told them to
handle the situation any way they liked. We were all locked
in the same cell, under the great hall. I ought to be glad that
Devra was so bored to receive us or she might have done worse
with me, being my father's heir. As it was..."

"You don't have to tell us," Dammon said. Young Lord Fiel
might have been any age from seventeen to twenty-seven, but
his eyes were a hundred years old.

"What does it matter? They're all dead by now." Lord Fiel's
finger caressed the smooth parchment on the table. "The guards
enjoyed their work. They used my mother and sisters shame-
fully, even though Fleya was still a child. She died first, thanks
to them, and my mother never said another word or took another morsel of food after that. It didn't bother the guards. A
mute madwoman was still good enough for them."

Sir Raimon got up from the council table and left the tent.
Master Kor went after him.

"Was he one of the guards?" Captain Beliza asked. "He
used to be a queen's man, you know."

Lord Fiel shook his head.

"A man can feel shame for a crime that was never his,"
said Dammon.

"Ah, gods! What's become of our land? All that's left is
shame." The horsewoman's sigh came from the heart.

Frog crept up to Lord Fiel's chair. One face cavern-gray,
the other sun-browned, there was a common bond of loss
between them. "How did you escape, my lord?"

"My mother was dying. My older sister, Bienfer, and I were
with her. Mostly, I recall the smell of that cell, the reek of our
own filth made worse by the damp that came in and through
the bars on the only window. While we waited for Mother to
die, Bienfer showed me the knife. It was very small, but it
had a good edge. How did she get it? She told me that one
night while I slept and Mother sat gaping, understanding nothing of what she saw, Bienfer had seduced the kitchen-lad who
brought us our meals. She stole it from his belt while he had
her. The look I must have given her! Bienfer said that it meant
nothing. She had nothing, she was nothing, the guards had

reduced us all to nothing, but she was going to pay them back and give me a chance to save myself. The next time the guards came in—to have her, to take away Mother's corpse, whatever—she would attack them with the kitchen-boy's knife, kill as many as she could before they killed her, and if I didn't have the strength or slyness to escape while she gave her life for a diversion..."

Lord Fiel said no more.

What's become of our land? All that's left is shame.

"My lord Maldonar, let me send a message to the queen!"

Lord Maldonar rounded on the young sprig who had been pressing that suggestion on him every time chance threw the two of them together. He was a low-ranked officer, a stripling with the long bones and fine features Devra fancied. It wouldn't surprise Lord Maldonar to learn that the queen had taken him to her bed more than a few times. He was young to have earned even such a minor position of authority except through the queen's favor. She might have given him a score of nights, but she had given the keeping of Mar-Halira to Lord Maldonar, and this pup should be reminded of it.

"Again a message? What happened to the ones you've already sent—the ones you didn't bother asking me for permission to send, eh?"

The young man flushed. Lord Maldonar gripped the arms of his chair, satisfied at how well his bluff had drawn blood. There was a shocked murmur from the other officers present in the great hall. "Go on, tell me. You look like you're going to wet yourself. We're not speaking of the penalties for disobedience... yet."

"I—I got no answer."

Stupid! Lord Maldonar thought fiercely. *One bluff may be countered by another, but now you've written your own death. Admit nothing! You don't deserve to live.*

"No answer?" he repeated aloud. "And why not? I'd expect our lady to drop everything and come rushing right home at a word from you. Now, why do you suppose—"

"Oh, do stop it, Father." Sitting on the steps below her father's chair of judgment, Lilla was dressing her favorite doll. She held it up and adjusted the drape of its gown. "You're too rough to toy with someone properly. Just tell him why we can't call Mama and do what you want with him."

Lord Maldonar's knucklebones showed white. Everyone in the great hall fell silent whenever Lilla spoke. Her mother might have given Mar-Halira into Lord Maldonar's keeping but no one had to ask who held the consort's chain.

"There is a wizard with the traitors," he said slowly. "Not just a market-day juggler, but a silver wizard, one of the last. How did you try to contact the queen, boy? A scrap of paper tied to a pigeon's leg? A bribe to a nimble-footed kitchen-boy? Don't tell me you dabbled in the sorcerous arts and tried sending her word that way? You might as well have stuck to pigeons."

"There's a shielding spell set up around the castle," Lilla remarked cheerfully. "That's just like a big old basket turned upside down over a mouse. Only with this spell, you can't even hear the poor little mousie squeak. Poor mousie."

"Take him away." A brace of Maldonar's guardsmen answered his command at once. They pinioned the youth's arms behind his back.

"What shall we do with him, my lord?"

"What do you do with traitors?" Lord Maldonar's hand swept the air, sweeping the young man out of mind and existence with a single gesture. "The rest of you, attend them! I want you to witness this and remember."

Obediently, all the people filed out of the great hall. Only Lord Maldonar and his daughter remained. She had bundled her doll up in a blanket and was singing it a lullaby.

"Aren't you going with them, Lilla?"

"I've seen a hanging before, Father." The lullaby resumed, too sweet to be real.

"I thought you were your mother's child. Never enough, never enough of anything. Always she wants more." Lord Maldonar slumped in his chair. "Let them hang him on the western battlements! Let the traitor army see what's waiting for them!"

Lilla tittered. "Silly Father! Hang them one by one, and you'll run out of nooses before you're out of necks. Did you see how huge their forces are? And a silver wizard with them! They have horses too, many horses, and queen's men riding with them. Such a shame that Mama took the few loyal queen's men with her to Lar-Khana. Your best troops here aren't any match for queen's men."

"Renegades! Turncoats!" Lord Maldonar's fists struck the arms of his chair. Lilla's small pink mouth turned up at the corners.

"If wars were won by losing your temper, we'd have them in chains by now. Talk and talk, shout and shout, but in the end you'll lock the gates and wait behind stone walls for Mama to return and save you. Don't worry, Father, she'll come home in time to rescue you!"

There was a fluttering sound. Lilla's familiar zipped into the great hall through a high window and plunged to buffet its mistress's ears with its wings. The voracious red maw gabbled a confusion of squeals, coughs, and harsh twitters, but Lilla understood.

"Oh." She nodded with a little girl's wise look before shooing it away. It climbed to perch on the back of Lord Maldonar's chair. Its cold, pungent musk made him dizzy and ill. "Why, Father, what do you think? It truly is Lord Prince Dammon's army after all. Gira saw the prince himself and Lord Gerais and the silver wizard and—oh, so *many* others! But do you know what else Gira saw? Tell Father, Gira."

The black thing sidestepped along Maldonar's chair and leaned its mouth against his ear. He was unable to move away. The familiar's voice rasped his nerves, and he could make no sense of it. "Did you hear, Father? Did you hear?" Lilla bounced on her knees eagerly. He could just manage to shake his head no.

The hot, wet breath withdrew. The sourness subsided in Lord Maldonar's throat. Lilla was put out with him, calling him stupid, dull, good for nothing but warming her precious Mama's bed and sometimes not even good for that, but he didn't care. He had heard those same insults many times.

"Gryagi!" Lilla shouted. "There are Gryagi with the army, too!" His indifference piqued her. "Not *our* Gryagi; others. Burrowers, tunnelers, miners . . . don't you *see*? They won't have to besiege us if they've got half a brain among them! They'll send the Gryagi to undermine the walls. Do something, damn you! Do something, or I swear I won't wait for Mama to come home before I kill you!"

The sickness was gone. A terrible clarity took its place. Very calmly, Lord Maldonar got to his feet. Lilla was up, her doll forgotten, dancing with rage and fear before him. He hadn't realized his daughter was so small. Why did he let her speak to him like that? Her mother had spoiled the child; she needed discipline. He would have to teach her better manners.

Entirely composed and aware, Lord Maldonar slapped his daughter's face. The green-eyed familiar leaped from its perch, shrieking, until he drew his sword and showed it he meant business if not left alone. Gira uttered a last yowl before flying out through the same window by which it had come in. In complete possession of himself, Lord Maldonar left the hall. Lilla cradled her smarting check and cursed him.

A moment later, she was cursing herself. The pitcher of wine beside her father's chair was empty. He had drained it in the course of this short session with his men—something he'd never done before. At most he'd swallow a cupful, just to keep his throat wet. Lilla knew this, and Lilla had been tired of playing with her other dolls; accordingly, she had dosed this measure of wine with enough of the dream-spinning moss powder to guarantee some good sport even if Lord Maldonar only moistened his lips.

But she hadn't been paying attention, and he had drunk it all.

He was Lord Maldonar, and he was invincible. He was no woman's laplick, no brat's toy. He was afraid of no one, of nothing. He would line the battlements of Mar-Halira with the heads of his enemies. He roused the castle barracks, shouting for his men to arm themselves. He hurried the dawdlers along with the flat of his sword. He'd teach them all a lesson. He knew how they whispered about him and the queen—that he was nothing without her but a shell. Now they would see. Devra was gone, but he would save her castle, defeat her enemies, and all without a scrap of help from her and her pet monsters.

He brandished his blade and promised terrible punishments for any man who was not ready to ride within the hour. Even the foot soldiers were to have horses for this attack—a charge that would trample the foe into bloody dust. The common troopers stared at each other, overcome by the presence of the lord of Mar-Halira himself in their squalid dormitory, giving orders he usually delegated to their commanders. He had to threaten them all with imprisonment, mutilation, and death before they roused out of shock enough to obey him. Most of them were hastily arming themselves by the time Lilla had raced up to the battlements and summoned the officers away from one poor soul's final dance on air.

Lord Maldonar's mouth smiled, but his eyes were sober. "There you are. If this is the discipline you've been keeping among your men, my friends, we shall have to speak about it at length afterwards. See if you can get this rabble battle ready. Now!"

"My lord—a battle?" Only one of the officers found his voice to ask the question for them all. The rest were as stunned as their men. "But—but I thought we'd agreed to let the enemy waste their strength in a siege, buying us time—"

"—so that Queen Devra can return? We make a sortie." Lord Maldonar's false smile was gone. His brow wore a storm. "They expect us to tuck up like hedgehogs, but if we attack, we have the advantage of surprise. Surprise has turned many an uneven battle into a rout."

"My lord, there are so many of them—"

"—the silver wizard—"

"—think it is really Lord Prince—?"

"—what would the queen—?"

"*Silence!*" Lord Maldonar's roar filled the long barracks hall. Even the scuffle of pages' feet and the chink of men donning mail ceased. There was a special demon in the consort's blood, and the men who served in Neb-Mar had grown used to recognizing demons.

"You will obey me." He left them to do so.

Lilla poised herself at a window on a stairwell overlooking the stables and dug her fingernails into her palms, but even the pain would not pay for her folly. The troops were armed and the horsemen were mounting up. They would ride against

Lord Prince Dammon's army; no stopping her vision-maddened father now.

Unless someone killed him.

But who would do it? Who would dare? In her mind's eye, Lilla saw her mama preparing for the great journey south, setting Mar-Halira in order against her eventual return. She had summoned the officers who would remain behind and given them Lord Maldonar as their commander. Noting the looks of open envy, hearing the whispers of dissatisfaction—*stud-horse ... bed-toy ... no soldier left in him ... plaything*—Devra had smiled and addressed her men:

And because of the love I know you bear Lord Maldonar, I have placed a special mark of favor on him. If any traitor should succeed in harming him in my absence, his spirit will home to me and tell me who has dared to destroy the one I love.

They had watched her place a glow over Lord Maldonar's heart. It burned with all the colors of the setting sun. Then she chose a man at random from the crowd and placed a similar spell on him before ordering five of his comrades to take him into the cells below the castle and kill him—only one of them to do it, and by clever means. Shortly thereafter, a thread of cold air whipped through the great hall, a wraith of darkness riding it. The black shred of breath that had once been a man's life flew to Devra's ear and revealed who had killed him and how. When the five returned, their oaths confirmed it. The queen complimented the murderer on his imagination. The one who had done the deed smiled until Devra used his life to show what she would do to any who touched Lord Maldonar. Her own imagination remained unrivaled.

But if I killed him? wondered Lilla. *Surely Mama didn't mean me.* She watched helplessly as the mounted men rode out of the stableyard two abreast to mass in ranks behind Lord Maldonar in the main courtyard. She could kill him easily. She could send Gira after him to frighten his horse, to tear his throat, to claw away his eyes—

Surely Mama didn't mean me. Ah, but that was the thing ... even Lilla was never sure of Devra's heart. The serving women who went up and down the winding, windowed stair where she stood saw only a little girl hugging her favorite doll, worrying about her brave father who was riding off to battle.

"They're coming!" It was one of Lord Fiel's band who burst into the council tent with the news. Lord Gerais snapped erect, smelling battle. "The castle gates have opened, and they're riding across the plains!"

"The fools." The old general shoved the scrolled plan of Mar-Halira to the ground. "Walls that thick, plenty of water, the storeholds packed . . . and they come streaming out to fight when they could wait us out two years if they had to? Idiots!"

"Maybe they thought that since we were expecting to dig in for a siege, they'd do something unexpected like this and throw us off," suggested Mrygo.

Gerais snorted. "Stick to your herb pots. There is no such thing as the unexpected in this war." His gnarled fingers fondled the sapphire hilt of his sword. "At least we'll whet our appetites on an easy victory in this skirmish. We'll drive 'em back into the castle before the last of them clears the gate. To your posts!"

"Wait, my lord." Dammon stayed his general. "Hear me out."

"We don't have time—"

"I said *listen*." His grip on the general's arm tightened and what burned in Dammon's eyes was enough to make Lord Gerais remember who was in command. Mrygo and Frog sat back to admire while their friend taught the old battlehorse that there could still be a few surprises left on the field of war.

Lord Maldonar charged into the heart of Dammon's camp. All went just as well as he had dreamed—better! The ill-prepared enemy troops scattered like rabbits flushed from their burrows. At this range, he saw that the mighty host was really little more than a rabble of unlanded farmers. The only sign of anything vaguely royal in the whole camp was one fine tent, and it soon went down under the hooves of his riders' mounts.

"Ride them down!" Don't let them get away!" He reined in his horse until the beast reared and curvetted. Exaltation and bloodthirst gave him new life. This was where he belonged— here, with sword in hand, leading his men to one conquest after another. Not in the perfumed darkness of Devra's bed, not in the drafty hollow of the great hall, playing the stud or the steward at a woman's whim, but *here*. "Cut them off from the woods, or we'll lose them! Let's wipe them out once and for all!"

He spurred his horse so that the great beast plunged into the forest. His men caught the battle hunger and followed his example. They swung their swords like scythes to cut down the fleeing enemy, but they were mostly displaced foot soldiers. They lacked a cavalryman's experience for fighting on horseback, showing more enthusiasm than skill against their quarry. Many escaped between the trees. The riders dug in their heels and gave the shouts of a royal hunting party in full pursuit of any easy kill.

The dark green hand of the forest closed suddenly over them. Hunting calls rose into shrieks and death cries. Horses stumbled and fell, their flanks bristling with arrows. Their riders were already down, fletched shafts protruding from their chests. Lord Maldonar wheeled his mount to see the slaughter. Armed shapes were dropping like deadly fruit from the trees. Maldonar's men raised their swords to fend off the attack from above only to stare into the pure black eyes and the seamed gray faces of Prince Dammon's Voice. In the moment of astonishment, the Gryagi killed them almost too easily.

"Retreat! Retreat!" Lord Maldonar wasn't the only one to give that command. His men were streaming out of the forest faster than they'd charged in. He lashed out with his sword and split a grinning gray face. The blood that spattered his silks was red as his own. Blood streamed from the gashes of spurs in his horse's sides, but he managed to be among the first to regain the enemy encampment.

"For Dammon! For Dammon!"

Where had they come from, those mounted demons? They galloped in on his forces from both sides at once, a pincer charge that filled the air with dust and tumult. Eyes rolling, Lord Maldonar saw that the two wings of cavalry were small, but their size had permitted them to hide in the sparse groves of trees to either side of the encampment. Blinded by visions of swift victory over a flying foe, Lord Maldonar had overlooked them.

Now they paid back the oversight.

The foot soldiers who had thought it very grand to ride into battle like knights paid the greatest part of the score. Riding in the hunt was different sport from riding to battle. Their horses felt their fear, added it to their own, and bolted. Beliza's riders could pick and choose their targets at leisure, lifting them from the saddle with blade or arrow, while the men struggled to regain control of their steeds.

Yellow braid whipping the wind, Captain Beliza herself used nothing more than a coil of rope to drag down her kills. Her teeth were set in a wolf's grin, and she scorned the child's play of killing from the safe distance of a bowshot or even the length of a sword. She rode unshielded into the thickest part of the fight and cast her rope around any man she fancied, unhorsing him, leaping to earth to meet him, and ending his life with her dagger before vaulting onto her horse's back again. If the man untangled himself from the slack noose, he could put up a good fight—sword against dagger—but that was what made Captain Beliza's grin show all the wider when her blade went home.

She killed seven men before her final match got in the way of Lord Maldonar's retreat. She never saw the sword that lashed down on her skull from behind. Maldonar spurred his horse over her body and broke free of the milling combat.

He rode his horse at a foaming gallop over the grassland until the blood-streaked stallion faltered and refused to go on. The great sides heaved between his legs. A lesser beast would have burst its heart. Throwing the sweat of fear out of his eyes, Lord Maldonar spared a look back to see riderless mounts racing off in all directions from the center of the ambush. Only a handful of his trained cavalrymen were managing to hold their own against the mounted foe, and now spearmen were coming up to aid the horse troops. Huge battle steeds screamed and threw their riders as the spears plunged into their bellies. Forgetting his horse's exhaustion, Lord Maldonar uttered a groan of despair and jabbed his spurs harder, forcing the animal back to a run for the shelter of Mar-Halira.

Three-quarters of the way home, the horse keeled over and died, sending Lord Maldonar teeth first into the ground. He lay without moving, too stunned to feel the pain yet. An urgent hand on his shoulder finally compelled him to raise himself.

"My lord! My lord!" It was one of his officers, a man of his own age. Maldonar thought he knew him as a friend from the days before Devra's spells and his ambitions had singled him out and cut him off from any friendship. "My lord, lean on me."

Maldonar hauled himself up with the fellow's help. He cursed loudly when he saw the body of his horse. "Worthless beast." Blood flowed from his mouth, making him spit several times before he could ask, "What's happened?"

"My lord, the few of us who could escape did so. Come, mount up behind me quickly. We have to make the castle before Dammon's army comes after us!"

Lord Maldonar ignored the man's entreaties. His head hurt and he felt strangely slow, as if he were waking from a deep sleep. To either side he saw men wearing Devra's colors go galloping past, flying for the castle gate. His rescuer's horse snorted and skittered, only its tight-held bridle keeping it from joining the stampede. Maldonar added his grip to the reins and asked, "Dammon . . . have you laid eyes on Dammon himself?"

"No, my lord."

"Ah! But would you know him if you saw him? There's the question . . ."

"My lord, I beg you—"

"Because I do know him, my friend. I know him better than any soul alive. I killed him—does it shock you? I sent him to Hori-Halira in body and spirit. Yet he's come back. No man returns from the land of death, they say, but Dammon has. Black hair, blue eyes, and too handsome to be so powerful a warrior. And yet he is; he is . . . an impossibility . . . a hero. . . . Can anyone kill a hero?"

"My lord!" The officer was at his wits' end. Lord Maldonar was maundering like a madman. When he tried to shove him toward the saddle, he resisted strongly.

"Let me be! I can mount on my own!" He straddled the horse so unexpectedly that its master nearly lost his hold on the bridle. From the saddle, Lord Maldonar said, "I tell you, there is no Prince Dammon! All this is an evil joke against me, but I'll laugh last. Hero or not, ghost or flesh, whoever leads this upstart army will never take Mar-Halira once we've barred—what's that?"

It sounded like thunder, but the sky was clear. It came from the direction of the castle. As Lord Maldonar watched, he saw the great curtain wall shudder and hump like a serpent's back before tumbling down in a slide of rubble and dust. Gray forms emerged from the ruins, waving their arms to signal success. They cut wild capers around the mouth of the mine they'd dug under the wall's foundations. Mrygo's people had repaid their freedom debt to Lord Prince Dammon. The few men Lord Maldonar had left behind to garrison the castle were helpless to halt the Gryagi mole-work.

Three horsemen rode into sight through the settling dust to congratulate the gray-faced diggers. One Lord Maldonar recognized immediately as Lord Gerais. The second was a younger man dressed in Lord Fergan's colors.

Then he saw the third.

The last sound Lord Maldonar's unlucky rescuer ever heard was that awful cry of fear and disbelief—a hoarse, inhuman sound wrenched from Lord Maldonar's soul. The man's hand tightened involuntarily on his horse's tether, afraid that it would bolt with Lord Maldonar on its back. He could not know that Maldonar himself was desperate to be gone.

The faithful officer held fast when Devra's consort jerked at the lines. Lord Maldonar lost his head and drew his sword, slashing down wildly. He only meant to free the reins, but the cut went deeper and a corpse fell, cleaved neck to breastbone. Maldonar was already galloping away to the south. He did not turn back once, not even to see the broad gate of Mar-Halira's keep open to welcome back the prince he knew was a dead man.

Lilla gazed with mild interest at the changes already effected in the great hall. The rich tapestry that had hung behind the royal dais was gone. In its place a worn silk banner dangled limply in back of the throne. Lord Maldonar's lesser chair of judgment likewise had been removed, but the ponderous throne would have to wait. It was too huge and heavy to be easily displaced. In the meantime, no one came near it and no one touched it. It was clear that these strange invaders despised the empty seat because it had been her mama's, and they acted as if the very touch of it would contaminate them.

Or were they just afraid?

How funny! It was exactly as if Mama had never gone away. Her spirit hovered over the throne and still cast its spell of fear. Lilla bowed her head so that her guards would not see her satisfied smile. She knew what was expected of a good prisoner.

"Lord prince, this is the child."

"You're certain?"

Lord prince? Lilla dared a clandestine peek at one so addressed by the guardsman. So that was Mama's brother! He reminded her of Lord Maldonar, although not half so haggard and witch-ridden. He was a very handsome man, and she heard nothing in his voice to make her fear him. What Lilla didn't fear, she also could not respect. She raised her head and gazed boldly at the prince, but his attention was elsewhere.

"She must be the child, my lord. The only other young ones are all servants, and most of those are boys."

"I guarantee that this is the child, Dammon." There were two Gryagi standing with the prince on the steps below Mama's throne—two Gryagi and horrid Lord Gerais and a dark man in robes that blazed white and silver and gold. Lilla didn't like any of them, but especially not the Gryagi who spoke now and looked at her with such a dry, hard smile. "Look closely at her and you'll recall her, too—though not with quite the same force as my memories."

The prince was looking at her now. She let her eyes widen and her lip tremble, but these small ploys had no effect on him. Still, his face showed everything he thought, and there was only sorrow and sternness there when he regarded her; nothing to fear.

"Yes," he said. "Yes, I know you."

Lilla curtseyed gracefully. "My lord Prince Dammon, I swear that this is the first time I ever saw you."

"With this face, perhaps." He turned away, leaving her puzzled. What could he mean? Lilla only liked mysteries of her own making. She searched the older Gryagi's face for the key. As she did so, a flurry of wings overhead announced that Gira had returned.

Lilla's familiar darted in and out among the heraldic banners of the great hall. It dove for Dammon's hanging, claws bared for tearing, but the smaller Gryagi was quick on his feet and very accurate with the child-size sword he carried. Gira screeched and shot out of range, but on the sword's edge Lilla saw the faint stain of its thin blood.

Dammon followed Gira's flight. "Oh yes," he said again. "Yes, how could I ever forget a child like this?"

Everything came back to Devra's daughter. But oh, how lucky she was to connect that Gryagi standing there with the victim of a childish escapade enjoyed so long past! Now she remembered: She had crept into Mama's chambers and with Gira's aid had stolen a measure of magic to give her body the substance of shadow. (How angry Mama had been when she discovered the theft! She had cut Lilla off from access to all such spells since.)

Lilla recalled how she had stolen from the castle then, prowled the night, spied the lone campfire in the midst of the forest. How rare a joy it had been to see the solitary Gryagi's face when he witnessed her appear out of nothingness—how much sweeter the pleasure of tearing his throat to reward Gira, and to share that hotly pulsing stream.

Why was he still alive? Lilla held back her consternation. There would be time enough for answers to that question later; or else no need for answers. The taste of Mrygo's blood had been very good. She wouldn't mind repeating the experience, and this time doing it right.

She was back in the forest, leaning over Mrygo's body, when she sensed someone else approaching. What a lark to put on her victim's hooded robe and push his body out of sight, waiting to see what might happen. But the man who had come into the firelight hadn't been this prince. Dammon was so handsome, and the other—

Lilla burst into tears. She was furious with herself for all the errors of that vanished night: for having angered Mama; for not having finished her victim; for having met Dammon disguised and not reading past his ugly scar-faced mask; for not having killed him as well—oh, if only she'd known! If only she'd seen through that thin disguise and killed him . . .

All that Dammon saw was a weeping child.

Gira spiraled down to light on Lilla's shoulder. The guards flanking her would have plucked away the small monster, but

Dammon indicated that they were to step back. Gira gave a warning growl when the prince came near its mistress until Lilla reached up and grabbed it, pressing the black thing to her breast.

"Your name is Lilla," Dammon said gently. "You told me that when I first saw you and said I could kiss your hand. You're Devra's daughter. Naughty Lilla, you called yourself, but what you did to Mrygo . . ."

"I didn't! I didn't!" Dammon's clear blue eyes were filled with pity. Lilla saw how loath he was to believe her truly capable of such cruelty. Wasn't she his blood? Wasn't she beautiful? She would take advantage of blood and beauty. He'd be more than willing to believe her—the fool!—if she could lay the blame elsewhere. This was the moment to save herself—now, while her tears had softened him even more.

"It wasn't my fault!" Deliberately, she strangled the words with sobs and thrust Gira from her, almost straight into Dammon's face, stretching the batwings wide until her pampered pet writhed spreadeagled in pain. "Gira made me go there! Gira—and my mother's command! She's a witch, a monster, a worse thing than *this*!" Lilla yanked Gira's wings apart roughly, and the familiar screamed. With a sudden shift, Lilla's right hand released one wing and clamped down over the creature's face. There was an awful snapping sound.

Lilla dropped the crumpled black body, its green eyes glazing over. Softly, very softly, she asked, "What choice have I ever had, lord prince? I am Devra's daughter, but I am also Devra's slave. Even when she went away, she left me in Lord Maldonar's keeping. My mother wanted me to be like her . . . and what can I do against her will? Now I'm free of her at last, only—only you don't believe me, do you?" Her small body sagged in misery. "What's the use? If you don't believe me, I'm still her captive. You might as well kill me, too." She spread her hands, damp with Gira's blood, and waited.

He climbed the dais again, turning his back on her, but Lilla wasn't worried. When he ordered his men to escort her back to her rooms, she knew she had won. Her familiar's life was a negligible price to pay for the favorable effect she'd created by killing it before them all. Secretly, Lilla smiled. Her uncle's court was all as readily beguiled as Dammon himself, and she'd wager than even the fearsome silver wizard would have some doubts about her now.

Mama had barred her from the greater magics—too young and irresponsible, she'd said!—but Lilla had her ways. Sow confusion, plant doubts, nibble away at all their fine convictions until right and wrong melted into a vile gray moil and no man could separate them. Lilla did not need the great spells or the great swords to work her will.

As she left the hall, she paused before the improvised bier that the invaders had set up on one of the feasting tables. They had covered it with Mama's tapestry and laid out a woman's body on top of it. The lady's face and head were swathed with many layers of white cloth, her body unmarked. There was no need to wonder how she'd died. A long blonde braid trailed out of the snowy wrappings and lashed a yew bow firmly in the woman's hands. Even lifeless, they held strength.

A red-haired man was crying on the far side of the bier. Red hair, like Prince Dammon had had when he'd tricked her that night in the forest. Lilla was glad to see this man suffer, but she showed nothing but sympathy. A golden sunburst pin fastened her mantle to her pale azure gown. She took it off and laid it on the dead woman's breast.

"May the great river bear her gently on." That made the mourner look up. She gave him a melancholy smile before continuing to her rooms. She could feel all of them looking after her, a most delicious sensation. Whispers reached her: *So young, yet so feeling!; Can she really be that monster's child?; Did you hear how kindly she spoke to Captain Iskander?; It was Master Kor insisted we unearth her, but she seems so harmless! Greater mistakes have been made . . .*

Devra's daughter shivered with delight. Oh yes, naughty Lilla would have many new and better playthings now that Lord Prince Dammon had returned.

"How many times must I tell you, Mrygo? I don't give a damn what Lord Gerais says! Now go to sleep!" Dammon yanked his bed-hangings shut and drove his face into the pillows, exactly like a sulky boy.

Mrygo would not be put off. He opened the curtains and sat tailor-wise at the foot of the cavernous bed. "We both know you're lying. You need Lord Gerais, especially now that Iskander's little use to you."

Dammon rolled onto his back and threw one arm over his eyes. "Poor Iskander. I never knew how much he loved Beliza. They never acted like lovers."

"No, sharing a bed every chance they got is hardly an indication."

Dammon groaned. "Would you spare me your wit? You know what I mean."

"That they did not go around a-sighing for each other whenever they were parted? That Iskander did not send Beliza bad verses and Beliza did not try to kill any of her shield-sisters caught chatting with Iskander?" Mrygo chuckled. "If that's the only way you recognize love, you've led a very limited life. I thought there were more faces to love in a royal court than anywhere else."

"Maybe that's something else I've forgotten. I don't remember any lady in my life, and none of the songs of Dammon speak of him as a lover—only as warrior and prince. If I had a sweetheart and she's still alive, here in Mar-Halira, she'd better be the one to speak first if she recognizes me." He sighed. "I remember rooms and the faces of soldiers and sometimes I remember feeling lost in the heart of a crowd. . . . I don't remember love."

The two of them were silent for a time. Mrygo broke it by saying, "But you remember loving Larya." Dammon did not answer. "Dammon . . . I spoke to Master Kor today. I asked him for a seeing."

"A seeing?" Dammon's ears perked. "Like the one he gave us all of Lar-Khana?"

"He could only show us the outside of the Silver Mountain, remember. The inside . . . that eludes him."

"Why?"

"The inner chambers of the mountain must also have a silver skin. That's what Master Kor surmises, anyway. Devra's enchantments repulse all searchings. Only a mage who also serves the powers of air can enter her new stronghold with searching spells, and then only with her consent. The metal that cuts off the life of the powers of earth makes Devra's spells all the stronger."

Dammon sat up in bed and hugged his knees. The lights in his bedchamber had been extinguished and the only illumination was a muted glow from the clay lamp beside Frog's alcove. The Gryagi boy slept there now, after many arguments with Dammon in which he insisted on sleeping at the foot of his prince's bed to guard him through the night. For once, Dammon had won the argument.

"You asked Master Kor for the seeing because you wanted news of Larya?"

Mrygo nodded. "You're not the only one who still thinks of her, my friend. I will love her no matter where she gives her heart, but at least I've learned better than to hate the man lucky enough to have it. That's unworthy of her. She holds the powers of earth cupped in her hands, the ever-changing bonds of life. Hate and jealousy—they destroy us with chains that are immutable. For Larya's sake, I've forsworn them." The healer's hand formed the half cup of a man swearing service to his lord. "I've made my choice."

"For Larya's sake . . ." Dammon rested his chin on his knees. "But there's no way of knowing whether Larya's alive or dead."

Mrygo's eyes were black as a well. In the dark, they shimmered with flecks of silvery light. Dammon could see them blink once, then look away.

"There is no way for Master Kor to know. But there may be a way for someone else."

"Who?" Dammon groped frantically for Mrygo's arm. "Is there a more powerful seer than Master Kor in the castle? One of Devra's relics? I don't care! Send for him, pay him what he asks, give him—"

Mrygo's fingers were dry on Dammon's lips. "Hush. You'll have poor little Frog on us with a dagger in his teeth. It's only me."

"You? You're no seer! You're a healer."

"And a damn fine one. No, forgive me my vanity. Dammon, the time that I spent in Khana was not all given to brooding over my people's fate. Khana is as it ever was, a place of learning . . . and I learned. From books, from talk, from observation, from all these I gathered knowledge. There was talk of making me Master Byruic sed Lyum's pupil."

"You might have become a silver wizard." Dammon was

impressed. "Now *there's* something to throw in Lord Gerais's face the next time he objects to you sharing my apartments!"

His laughter was short and hard. When he'd been Ophar, he'd imagined the life a hero must lead, in full command of his own life and others' besides. Orders to be given, not taken! No one to dare tell him what he ought to do!

Not one of his daydreams revealed the truth—that the greater Dammon's victories, the more voices came to shout in his ears that he must do this and he must not do that; the more people looked to him for orders, the more advisers clustered around him to dictate what those orders should be. Things had come to a head when the prince announced that he wanted his two Gryagi attendants to lodge with him. He longed for the scant moments of honest talk that came only from Mrygo, and there was no way he could see Frog accepting a bed anywhere distant from him.

Lord Gerais had exploded. Let the prince choose his attendants from the correct sources—high-born, decorative youths to wait on him during court ceremonies and honest, hardworking peasant lads to do the real work of a fighter's page and squire. But Gryagi? It wasn't done.

"Now it is," Dammon had said. Lord Gerais had spluttered and turned red, but that hadn't ended it. The old warrior merely fell back to rearm and renew the offensive every chance he got. He would not be satisfied or be silenced until his lord prince came to heel. It was growing tiresome, like most sieges.

Only now Dammon perceived that Mrygo had a superior weapon to use in the ongoing debate. Not even Lord Gerais could object to Mrygo's attendance on the prince once he knew the full story. Good enough to be trained as a silver wizard yet not good enough to wait on Lord Prince Dammon? Gerais was not a fool.

The one thing wrong with this happy scene was that Mrygo refused to play.

"I won't be a silver wizard, Dammon. I've learned that you can love knowledge and serve the harmony of the powers in your heart as well as on a mountaintop. I do have some skill in the minor magics, and my own talent with herbs doesn't hurt. There are as many ways of conjuring visions as there are feathers on a birra's wing, and all answer to different laws. I'm going to try to find the one that can pierce Devra's silver

shell without her knowing. But to do this, I'll have to give
Lord Gerais the satisfaction of having me out of your rooms.
I'll want privacy, and I'll want to sleep close to Devra's own
apartments. There's one room she's got full of the most fascinating collection of scrolls and—"

"Oh, go. Even aboveground you manage to lock yourself into
a cave." Dammon stretched out in the bed again. He felt the mattress shift as the Gryagi slid to the floor, then heard Mrygo's quiet
departing tread, and the door closing behind him.

Dammon rolled onto his right side and peeled back the edge
of his bed-hangings. The glow of light from Frog's alcove was
still there. It calmed his heart to know that even with one true
friend gone, he was still not alone.

So many folk to press their words and worship on him, yet
where were they now? Old fears came home after dark. A
nameless man wandered through a labyrinth of caverns without
even self for company. A hungry heart was a worse terror than
any dragon.

Just before he fell asleep, Dammon wondered whether the
child Lilla was also afraid of the dark.

No one was more surprised than Lilla when the summons
from Lord Prince Dammon came. She had expected the man
to have more sense, and felt somewhat cheated. She'd been
looking forward to the challenge of working her way back into
her uncle's full favor. Already she had begun the groundwork.
When the time came, she intended to have more than one
friendly voice ready to whisper forgiveness into the prince's
ear.

Now this. In a way, she was glad. Her game would have
been longer and therefore more savory, but once in the prince's
presence, she would find amusement enough. She would also
be of help to her mother, and that was worth something. Devra
would be grateful to her clever daughter. Mama had other things
to do at Lar-Khana than fight off an attacking horde.

A horde was what Lord Prince Dammon's raggle-taggle
army was fast growing to be. Word of the fall of Mar-Halira
and the slaughter of Devra's garrison had spread quickly through
the land. Already, Master Kor had sent the child minstrels
dreams of a new song—"Bloodwood"—and they awoke to

sing the news of Dammon's triumph throughout the land. Fighters were coming out of their burrows to join their longed-for lord; swordsmen and spearmen who had gone to earth in the bad times, mask-wearers who had paid lip service to Devra's rule and waited, farmer's sons who had great dreams . . . so many. Incredible how Dammon's lieutenants managed to absorb so many into orderly ranks that only waited for the command to march on to Lar-Khana.

Common folk were beginning to come too—on foot, on horseback, in rickety old wains, any way they could get from there to here. Already the market towns nearest the castle were swollen with pilgrims, and more came daily.

Yes, pilgrims. She had seen the holy look in their eyes when they gazed in the direction of Mar-Halira when she conjured the visions. Lilla might have slain Gira out of hand, but that did not mean she'd cut herself off from all knowledge of what was happening in the great world. A pity that her faithful little familiar had had to die, but the gesture had done its work. Now she relied on less accurate, more mechanical means of learning how things went in the world beyond Mar-Halira. Mama had not cut her off from all magics, or else how would she have allowed her to keep Gira? Visions and illusions, most evanescent of all magics, were still hers, and the full range of herbery.

Lilla's rose lips curved into dimples at the corners. Who cared whether the entire realm rallied to Dammon's banner? What of that? It never mattered how big or small the serpent was that menaced you. All you needed to do was cut off its head.

She dressed herself with care when the page came to tell her she was wanted in her uncle's chamber. The pages and the other servants no longer spoke to her with that agreeable note of fear in their voices. Lord Prince Dammon's coming had put bones back into them. Lilla shrugged. This too would not bother her, provided it did not endure too long. She would see to restoring everything as it should be when she had played out this move of the game.

She followed the insolent page to Dammon's suite. Her dark hair was pulled back from her face with a golden fillet, and her honey-colored gown put a special glow in her eyes. It was her least favorite gown, cut too childishly for Lilla's tastes. For this interview, however, it was perfect. It suited her purposes to appear as a real child. The page did not even bow to her when he opened the door and announced her arrival.

The door closed behind her, leaving her in a reception room that appeared to be deserted. The hearth was dead, swept clean of every trace of ash. A heavy table with fruit and wine stood under a row of mullioned windows, and there were wooden panels carved with hunt scenes on the walls instead of tapestries. The floor was bare: the two empty chairs near the hearth were of the starkest design. Here was none of Mama's endless taste for luxury.

There was another door set in the wall opposite the hearth, probably leading to the sleeping room. As Lilla watched, this opened and a being scarcely her own height came out. He was the small Gryagi, the one never seen long apart from Lord Prince Dammon. Servants whispered that he dressed like a slave but carried himself like a soldier. Lilla rejoiced to have this chance to study him at close range.

"Hello," she said. The young Gryagi did not seem to hear her. He had a heavy tray in his hands loaded with steaming hot rolls, iced butter, crystal bowls of fruit conserves, and a platter of sweetmeats, the sticky kind that ordinary children adore. She greeted him again, but he didn't respond until he'd seen his burden safely to rest on the table. That done, he turned his attention to his master's guest.

"Good day, Lady Lilla," he said, all clipped formality. "My lord Prince Dammon will be happy to see you've been able to come."

Lilla forced a laugh into a discreet cough. Happy to see her after he'd ordered her here? Either the man was the thinnest of diplomats or incredibly soft-headed. She hoped it was the latter.

"No happier than I am to be here," she said. "I haven't had the chance to thank my uncle properly for setting me free."

"Free?" The Gryagi boy looked dubious. "You were no one's prisoner, my lady. This was your mother's castle."

"Don't call her my mother!" Lilla thought her fierce outburst very finely done. It made the hard-faced creature jump nearly out of his breechclout. "I hate her! I despise her! Oh gods, do

you think every prison is made of bars and stones?" Tears
showed in her eyes. She groped for one of the chairs and hid
her face behind the thick back-rest, sobbing.

That was how Lord Prince Dammon found them, poor little
Lilla in tears and Frog standing there like a speechless idiot.
Here was one question that couldn't be answered with a sword,
and he didn't know what to do. His eyes rolled from Dammon
to Lilla, silently pleading for his beloved lord not to think that
any of this was his fault.

Dammon strode past Frog, ignoring him. He placed his
battle-roughened hands on Lilla's silken shoulders and gently
coaxed the child away from the chair. When she lowered her
hands and looked at him, he was awed by the beauty of her
face, even reddened and streaked with tears. A soft memory
stole into his mind, a vision of Devra seen very long ago. She
and her ladies had been in the castle gardens and he recalled
a glimpse of her, bending over a bank of tasseled cornflowers
less blue than her eyes. So much beauty...

So much, that he heard his then-self ask, *How can anyone
that lovely be as evil as they say*?

"Please don't cry, Lilla. What's hurt you?"

"I didn't—I didn't do anything to hurt her, my lord!"
squeaked Frog. Desperately, he tried to make Dammon believe
him. "I only brought up the food you wanted from the kitchen,
and she was here, and—and—"

"He didn't do anything," Lilla confirmed, her voice husky.
The look of grateful relief on Frog's gray face would be turned
to coin later on. Devra's child knew the value of debts. "That
is... we were talking, and he spoke of my mother... that's
what made me cry."

"Why, child?"

Lilla only shook her head. "Please, my lord. Please don't
ask me. The shame... I wish I could die rather than have
people know whose daughter I am. I wish I had no family, no
name, nothing but myself, instead of being pointed out as
Devra's daughter."

Dammon knelt and took the girl's hands in a courtier's
gesture. "No one blames you for your mother's doings."

The tears were gone, burned away by the bright look of
accusation that pierced him to the heart of that lie. "No one,

my lord?" His cheeks colored with embarrassment. The child
was young, but she was just as wise as the castle rumors said.
As for what else the whispers told of Lilla . . . Dammon had a
natural reluctance to believe such horrors of a child.

Rising to his feet, he changed the subject. "Come and sit
with me, Lilla. I'd like to talk with you."

"As my lord wishes."

"No, Lilla. There's no need for formalities between us. I'm
your uncle, so call me that."

Her face shone with joy. "Can I?"

"Of course you can. Now sit and eat something. You too,
Frog. Fetch yourself a chair from the bedchamber."

Lilla cursed inwardly as the Grygai ran to do as his master
requested. She would have preferred to be alone with Dammon.
The game would have to be played with more care in Frog's
presence. Still, this was only the opening move.

She spent all that first meeting on charming her newfound
uncle and his bizarre page. She made it plain that they were
both the best things in her new life, that she regarded her years
before Dammon's return as lost and wasted, that she rejected
everything to do with her mother and Lord Maldonar. Hints—
carefully worded, more carefully insinuated into the conversation—let her victims know that any evils she might have
done before were all her mother's idea, carried out under threat.
By the time she left, all memory of that first encounter between
Ophar and Lilla in the woods seemed to have the quality of a
bad dream best forgotten.

Dammon was lord, and Dammon favored Lilla. Many
tongues did not know what to make of this turn. Lord Gerais
and Master Kor were the only ones placed high enough to
speak out against the situation, but there were others equally
as high who took the child's part. Captain Iskander argued for
her, thinking of the time he'd surprised the child laying flowers
on the newly turned earth where his Beliza slept. Sir Raimon
added his voice, pointing out that many had served Devra's
wicked purposes unwittingly or unwillingly, himself and all
his renegade troop of queen's men included.

Lord Fiel sided with Gerais and Kor, but in the shadow of
his former prison, he had grown pale and sullen. Many said

he was haunted by the spirits of his family, thirsty ghosts who clamored for a more satisfying vengeance than the taking of Mar-Halira. Ill at ease, ringed by insistent phantoms, Lord Fiel seldom spoke, but made his opinion of Lilla known by angry glares and half-uttered maledictions whenever they happened to meet. Lilla's partisans claimed that Fiel would accuse the innocent girl of any crime if it meant appeasing his personal demons.

For the rest of Dammon's force, their lord's will was their own, and so Lilla found herself gaining more supporters than she'd dreamed. Only the old staff of Mar-Halira still looked at her askance, knowing what they knew, but they did not speak of it or carry tales to Prince Dammon. Long service under Devra had taught them that palace folk were capricious and that the silent led healthier lives.

So Lilla had the freedom of the castle again, and what with all the new recruits swarming in to serve their promised prince, her opponents had other things to keep them busy. No one had time for nagging Dammon to be careful how far he trusted his dear little niece. Councils met several times a day, demanding the presence of every officer to discuss the march to Lar-Khana, and Lilla was left alone.

It was the perfect time for her to return to a much-neglected private garden. As she scraped at mold and moss, she promised herself that she had learned her lesson. She would not make the same mistakes as she had with Lord Maldonar. A pinch would suffice—enough to weaken, not madden—and her words would do the rest. This time she would be far more careful of how she dispensed her harvest.

"My lord, you don't look well," Master Kor said as Dammon came to take his seat at the most recent council meeting.

"It's nothing. The cooks here in Mar-Halira serve richer fare than I'm used to, that's all." He waved away the silver wizard's concern and took his place at the head of the table. "I'll be fine."

"I'd like to examine you later, my lord. Just to be certain . . ."

"Master Kor, that's all we'd need! A rumor that I'm ill will soon grow into news that I'm on my deathbed. You should know how easily these things get noised around." Dammon chuckled, but his skin had an unhealthy flat look to it, a sallow cast under the sun-browned surface.

"Could be that'd be a good rumor to use," Decad Turgan put in. He had been promoted to the company of the council on the prince's suggestion, and he occupied his place as proudly as if it were the throne of the realm.

Master Kor raised one brow. "How is that, Decad?"

"Why, to put off Devra's spies is how, Master Kor. If she knows her brother's strong and ready to march against her, she'll be building up defenses, now won't she? But if she hears he's ailing and not likely to raise a finger, less an army, she'll get too confident for her own good, put off her defenses, and then—"

"You see, Master Kor? My men think of everything." Dammon forced a smile, although the griping in his belly made it difficult. "Every disadvantage hides a point in our favor. Forget about my health, and let's hear those reports on the new fighters. Have they fit into the official ranks well?"

"Well as can be expected, given the short time we've got," said Lord Gerais. "They'll do in a tight spot."

"They'll *die* in a tight spot," Lord Fiel amended. "But not so many of them as I thought at first."

"What do you mean, they'll die?" Dammon frowned.

"They don't have enough training time to bring them up to the level of your original troops, that's all. On their own, taken as individuals, they're passable fighters, but they've never fought as part of a team. I can't promise you how they'll answer to a sudden change of orders issued in the field. They'll straggle or panic or stand and fight when the command for retreat comes, just because they're still thinking of themselves as single combatants—each one Lord Prince Dammon's faithful man, pledged to the death. Unless you can be everywhere at once in a battle, assuring them that you won't think they're cowards if they obey orders and *run*, they'll die for your name. Won't do anyone a bit of good, either."

Lord Gerais compressed his thin lips. "That's it. You've got more men now, but still the same number that belong to a workable *army*. We'll have to talk two strategies if we include them in our plans—one for the fighters who'll heed the captains, one for those who'll only obey you."

Dammon tried to think over what his comrades told him, but his stomach gave another lurch that made him sweat. Frog came into the council chamber, ready to take his wonted place at Dammon's right hand. He'd brought a bottle of chilled helgras wine from the cellars—oh, how commonplace the taste of helgras wine had become for Dammon now! The prince took the golden cup his page offered, sipped, and felt better.

"We should train the new recruits to fit in with the rest," Captain Iskander was saying.

"Train them? Just like that? We don't have time."

"We could leave them behind..."

"... insult them, and there's many of 'em come from the families of lords whose help our prince will need."

"If they join up now, they'll be killed."

"... waste them in a diversionary charge on Lar-Khana when we get..."

"... no time to waste on training fools! Every day Devra's killing more innocents."

The pain in his belly retreated, only to strike back with the force of a double-fisted blow. Dammon stood up, swayed, clung to the table. Master Kor tried to approach him, but he stiff-armed the silver wizard off. Decad Turgan too attempted to give him some support. The pain angered Dammon and made his growl a curse at the well-meaning spearman.

"Let—me—be! It's a bellyache, damnit. Any baby gets it. By the Seed, I'm sick of all of you hovering over me as if I were an invalid! I'm going to my rooms. This will pass by tomorrow. We'll meet then, and I'll have my orders ready. Frog—" The Gryagi boy seized his master's arm and escorted him gently from the council chamber.

In spite of himself, Dammon leaned more and more of his weight on Frog as they passed through the castle halls. The corridors seemed endless, stretching themselves out like ribbons of melted sugar, bending into atrocious curves that made his eyes blink and his head dizzy. When at last they reached the prince's rooms, he was nearly a dead weight across the young Gryagi's shoulders.

Frog helped him into bed. "My lord, I'm going to bring

Mrygo." Dammon opened his mouth to protest, but his tongue was swollen and dry. There would be no arguing with the boy either when it came to matters of his health. Frog had added a hundred meanings to *stubborn*. The sound of the door slamming made Dammon wince, his skull rocked by the intensity of its echoes.

He lay under the embroidered canopy and closed his eyes, letting silence seep over him. His belly still hurt, but not so badly. Something soft and cool, wonderfully comforting, caressed his brow. The cold metal lip of a goblet slid between his own and he drank a warm liquid tasting faintly of spice.

"There, dear uncle. That will make you better."

He opened his eyes. The pain was gone. Lilla gave him a knowing smile and stroked his brow again. "How did you get in here?" he asked.

"I saw Frog in the corridor. He told me you were ill and said I could go in if I like. Frog is so good to me. I suppose it's because he knows how dearly I love you."

Dammon sat up, expecting the pain to come back, or at least give him an aftertouch, but it was as if he'd never had it. "By the Seed, Lilla, where did you pick up such skills? You could give Mrygo lessons. When this is over, perhaps you ought to study the healing arts with him or with Master Kor."

To Dammon's surprise, the child scowled at his jest. "Please, don't speak of my becoming a healer. My dearest dream ... and it's empty; useless."

"Why, Lilla." She came to his arms readily, but she was not crying. "If you want to become a healer—"

Lilla laughed bitterly. "If *I* want? I don't dare to want anything. Master Kor hates me, Mrygo hates me, so many others..."

"But, Lilla. Given time, they'll understand that your mother's doings don't touch you anymore."

He meant that. She could see his sincerity came from the heart. He held no more doubts against her, no matter what the others might say. Now was the time. This was the moment, the move that would win her the greatest of games.

Bending her head, she whispered so that her breath made the small hairs on his neck tingle, "One thing my mother did that will touch me forever." She looked up, directly into Dammon's eyes, so that his blood burned with the power of her gaze. "And this thing—this crime—was never all my mother's doing."

Only a child's words, yet the prince shivered. Somewhere deep in his mind he stood on the threshold of the dragon's lair once more. Endless dark, endless horror called to him, and he chose to answer. A hero never turned aside. "A crime," he repeated. "What crime do you mean?"

Lilla shook her head violently. "Oh, no, no, it's enough that I know—and now Mrygo knows the truth as well. Be careful of Mrygo, my lord. Never offend him. He's still your man, and he'll keep the secret while it suits him. But you—you must be very sure to keep his goodwill if it buys his silence. As for me . . . he hates me and has never forgiven me for what my mother forced me to do to him that night. He can't pay me back the way he'd like to—not while you protect me— but there are other ways . . ."

"Lilla, what are you talking about? What does Mrygo have to do with—"

She broke from his arms and stared at him with wonder. "Dear powers . . . you don't know. You really don't know . . . You've forgotten." She twisted the bright rings on her earth-stained fingers and spoke low. "Maybe it's better."

"Don't know *what*?" Impatience seized him. Here was another mystery, another loss where the shadow of the dragon had passed. He grabbed her hands. "Tell me, Lilla! I command you, tell me!"

Her mouth worked a protest that was never uttered. She made a small sign of resignation. "I must obey you. Come."

She conducted him from his rooms to her own. Lilla's suite was a miniature version of her mother's apartments, although in preparation for this awaited visit, she had muted the decor to seem more modest, less indulgent to the senses. The scent of fresh-cut rushes and sweet grass replaced heavier perfumes, and many a bare spot on the walls had once displayed jeweled hangings. Most of the furniture had been swept into storage, leaving behind only a single clothes chest, a bed, a chair, and a low bronze stand that held a black glass bowl.

The bowl was filled to the rim with water so clear that it leached blackness from its container. Dammon looked for his reflection in vain. Sunlight from Lilla's wide windows fell into the dark and was swallowed completely. The unrippled surface gave back only cold.

"This is no witchcraft," said Lilla, her tone soft and insinuating. Dammon's bones felt weak—the aftermath of recent pain, he thought—and all Lilla's words cut deeply into his mind. "No evil is in reading visions. Even Master Kor does it, and who would accuse a silver wizard of wickedness?"

The child's hand passed over the surface of the water. A leaf of light trailed after it. "I have been very lonely here. No one speaks to me if they don't have to, except you and Frog, and since you've spent so much time with your councils, I have been alone even more."

"I'm sorry, Lilla, I didn't realize."

She went on as if she were speaking to herself. "I wanted everyone to believe what you believed—that my mother's sorceries have nothing to do with me. I wanted the others to like me. I hoped—I hoped that if I could find Mrygo again and explain to him, I'd be able to make him understand and pardon me. So I looked for him, but Frog told me he was gone."

"Locked himself up in your mother's rooms, studying her books."

Lilla's eyes were limpid and guileless. "I know. Frog told me that, too. That was why I set up my gaze-bowl. I hoped that I could reach him. I knew it would be hard—only the best seers can touch the future, the lesser ones can bridge the present, and the lowest of all can read the past. I'd conjured up scenes of forgotten things easily, and I believed I had the skill to try reaching Mrygo in the present." She touched the water with a fingertip. "The powers punished my pride."

Dammon could not take his eyes from the black bowl. "Show me," he rasped, fascinated. The midnight eye held him and would not let him go. "Call it back again, that vision. Show me what you saw."

Lilla's eyes slanted upwards. "As you like, my lord."

Pale hands floated over the black surface, tracing arcs of air. The water rose in the bowl, trickled like tears over the lip to puddle in a silver ring at its base.

A gray shape drifted up to the surface of the bowl, a gray shape bent above a bowl of fire. The scarlet flames rusted all they touched with the hue of blood. Then Dammon saw that there was blood in Mrygo's bowl—for Mrygo was the one who hunched on the floor of a strange chamber, greedily seeking a vision. The golden bodies of birras lay strewn around the floor, their limp wings draggled, their small throats cut.

The vision of bowl-within-bowl lapped outward until both rims entwined—blood-vision, water-vision—into one. In Lilla's gaze-bowl Dammon might learn what Mrygo had summoned into his own. The prince leaned nearer to see, and his eyes met what he first thought was their own reflection.

The face was his, but younger, harder. It drew back from the rim of the weeping bowl and retreated into the depths so that the gaze-bowl held a small circle of the past and not just a single face.

He recognized the room where his younger self stood, fists on hips, face contorted with what looked like anger. It was not his place, but his sister Devra's apartments. She was there as well, wearing the gown of his garden memories, blue eyes above a bank of cornflowers. Devra looked angry too, but also ... afraid. What could put that look of fear on Devra's features? He could not remember ever having seen her without full self-command. He tried to hear what she and his then-self were saying, but no words reached his ears. Brother and sister were engrossed in a violent argument whose sounds had been lost beyond hope of recovery in the past. She raised her hands, showing that she wanted him gone. He struck them aside and seized her by the shoulders. There was more than anger in his face now, and only fear in hers.

Dammon saw himself, and if there had been any way for him to look away, he would have done so. The taut look of desire was worse than any rage, the awful parody of tenderness as he pressed himself against his sister's body. She struggled, but he was the stronger. Gentleness had no place in that rough wooing. He was impatient again—the same impatience he had shown so often. He bore her down onto the bed and soon she had no further cause to struggle. It was done. A whirlpool of cackling shadows swept away the seeing.

The sole sound that eddied up out of the spinning darkness in the bowl was an infant's cry.

Lilla's hands fluttered before his eyes, scattering the last of the vision. He gaped at her, dumbly begging her to tell him that it was only a dream, a joke, anything but true.

Devra's daughter kissed him on the lips, a kiss to seal him fast inside a nightmare. Devra's daughter . . . and his.

Frog was worried. He, who had lived all his life answering masters he hated . . . and one he loved . . . was now at total liberty. Freedom was frightening to a child who had never known how to use it. Miserable, abandoned, he sat on one of the cold benches in the great hall of Mar-Halira and drummed his heels.

Many men came and went in the hall, but no one noticed him. There was too much afoot, too many matters of import to be discussed and argued over. The castle was a nest of confusion. The council meetings never lasted long enough for any of the senior members to salvage some sort of order out of the madness engulfing them all.

The name Frog heard in every breath was always the same: *Dammon*. Some spoke it with pity, some with fierce resentment, some with the anger that springs out of helplessness. He was sick, he was crazy, he was betwitched, he was in league with his witchy sister.

He was doomed, taken with the madness that only seizes the dying.

With each new theory concerning what ailed the prince, Frog's anxiety grew. He felt panic claw its way up out of his belly, making his muscles shake. Not even the fear he'd known the first time he entered the killing games could equal this. The strain of sitting still, doing nothing, became too much to bear. He slid from the bench and hurried off to find his master, even if it meant being driven away again.

The prince was in his apartments. The two guards recognized Frog at once and let him pass, though he caught their sorrowful whispers as he entered. His devotion to his lord was no secret. Even Lord Gerais had come to accept Frog's unswerving service as something admirable. There had been talk that the old warrior intended to grant the Gryagi youth formal investiture as the prince's page, an unheard-of honor.

That dream too had ended.

The scene had come in council the day after the prince was

seized with that awful pain. He appeared dressed in the same clothes he had worn the previous day, his hair matted and his eyes a blur.

No one could know that he had been missing from his rooms for nearly a full circle of the hours. The last time Frog had seen him was when the prince dispatched him to fetch Mrygo, but when the two Gryagi returned, the prince's rooms were empty. Mrygo made a joke of it, saying how it was plain that Dammon had recovered enough to go elsewhere. The older Gryagi went back to his studies in Devra's rooms—making it clear that he was not to be bothered for nothing again—but Frog remained to wait for his lord's return.

That return had not been soon, even though the boy kept vigil through the night. When the milky light of dawn filtered through the high windows, Dammon had come back. His clothing was rumpled and stained with smears of forest green, smelling of the earth more strongly than a dead man. He collapsed across his bed, ignoring Frog's cries and questions. All the boy could do was pluck withered leaves from his lord's hair and try to rub away the worst of the dirt from Dammon's ravaged face.

Dammon slept for an hour, then awoke with a terrible shout. He thrust himself up on his arms and darted desperate glances all around, like a cornered beast. Then the dream-grim left him. He rolled onto his back and lay staring up at the bed's canopy until a messenger rapped at the door to summon him to that day's council.

He called for wine at the council table and cursed the attendants when they did not run to bring it. When Master Kor and Lord Gerais asked him for his promised decision, he snarled at them to stop pressing him. They'd have it after he drank, not before.

The wine came, but not in the hands of the servants who'd been sent after it. Lady Lilla smiled as she entered, showing a grace beyond her years as she poured a cup for her prince.

Master Kor ordered her out of the room. Lord Gerais seconded his words, and even Lilla's partisans saw the wisdom in not trusting Devra's daughter so close to their councils. All submission, Lilla curtseyed and would have gone, but Dammon held her back.

Who are you to give orders in my house?

He made the child stand beside him and commanded that the discussion of battle plans go on.

Who are you to accuse her for another's crimes?

No one spoke. He called them all fools, and worse. Lilla made the soft suggestion that she had better go, but he wouldn't hear of that. The air in the council chamber carried the heaviness of an unbroken summer storm as the silence swelled to fill all the empty places.

Frog had been the one to break it. He came to his lord and tried to get him to come away, to bathe, to sleep, to have Mrygo look at him and charm away whatever demon made Dammon's eyes shine with so much fever-light.

Mrygo! Keep him away from me, if you love me. Stone-faced liar! Calling himself my friend when he still hates me for taking Larya from him . . .

Sir Raimon's face went pale when he heard the prince speak that name.

Now he has his dagger—Dammon went on—*a cunning dagger, easily concealed.* His hand flashed, and a real dagger lay on the council table. *Mine is more honest. Tell him that if he ever comes offering to tell you secrets . . .*

Frog saw the looks, heard the murmurs. He was overwhelmed with shame for his lord's sake. They must not think him mad! He was only ill. The Gryagi boy tugged at Dammon's arm, tried to make him come away.

Don't touch me! Dammon's arm lashed across Frog's face in a crushing backhanded blow. The boy had taken worse hits in the arena without losing his footing, but the surprise of his loved lord's attack made him stagger back. *You and Mrygo, you're the same damn breed! You're in league with each other— my enemies! Get out of my sight! Get all of your rock-scrapers out of my realm too! Bury yourselves in the tombs where you belong, where you held my Larya for so long—*

His voice broke into a sob. His hand shook with an old man's palsy as he sought Lilla's. *Take me away, child. Take me away . . .*

No one present had given Frog a more sympathetic look than Lilla as she led Dammon from the council room.

He had accepted the banishment for a week, learning how

Dammon fared by secondhand gleanings of gossip. He was unable to accept it any longer. He knew he was daring his lord's wrath by coming back like this, but he couldn't do otherwise. Mrygo was locked into his studies, answering no knocks on his door. Master Kor had taken himself off somewhere in the castle—no one knew where or why—and besides, the silver wizard was a bit too imposing a presence for the young Gryagi to approach directly.

As he loved his lord, Frog would have to approach him alone.

No one besides Dammon was in the prince's outer room. Dammon sat in one of the heavy chairs beside the fireplace. At least he had finally exchanged his earth-stained clothes for a fresh, loose robe—no one had seen the prince change garb all that week—but his hair was still a filthy tangle and his eyes were underscored with dark pouches, rimmed with red.

"My lord?"

The prince did not answer. For Frog, that was a hopeful sign, better than if he'd flown into another rage and ordered the boy away again. Timidly, Frog came to crouch at his lord's feet. "My lord?"

"He's sleeping," said a crisp, commanding voice. Frog whirled into a fighter's stance. His sharp reaction made Lilla laugh where she stood in the doorway to Dammon's inner chamber.

For some reason, her laughter raked over him like broken glass. "How can you say he's sleeping? His eyes are open," Frog said irritably.

"And yet he sleeps. You ought to be glad of it. If he were awake, he'd throw you out. He might even do it literally, through the window." The thought sent Lilla into renewed peals of laughter.

Frog knelt before Dammon again, his sword-hardened fingers gentle as a lady's when they reached up to push back the elflocks from the prince's worn face. "He's sick. He's terribly sick. I don't care what he said. I'm going to get Mrygo here to cure him if I have to chop down that door with my sword!" He straightened up and was on the point of acting on his words when Lilla spoke.

"Bring Mrygo, and you'll find a corpse waiting for you."

He looked at her as if he hadn't heard correctly. Lilla soon cured his doubts. There was a measure of wine in her left hand, and cupped in the palm of her right he saw a minuscule pinch of gray-green dust. She held this level with the lip of the cup and blew it in.

"Your lord is mine, Frog. Do you understand how it is?" Lilla's eyes were alight, relishing every emotion she saw cross Frog's face. "Don't think I've ensnared him only with my herbery—that would be too simple. Besides, I've learned that a tolerance for this powder soon grows, until I must guess how much of it to use in order to get the results I want. Sometimes I guess badly. I don't want to chance that with your master." She giggled.

"If you haven't drugged him—" Frog was at a loss to explain Dammon's wide-eyed trance. Lilla read his thoughts.

"Oh, now he's under the influence of a root I know, but I won't use it on him again. I just wanted to keep him quiet until you would come here looking for him. I knew you couldn't stay away." She swayed as she approached him, the wine cup held in both hands. She set it down on the small table beside Dammon's chair. "That will rouse him when I want. It's fun to play with a prince, but more . . . challenging to do it without my garden lore. I could poison him like that, but where would that leave me?"

In all the times he had faced death in the games, in all the nights he'd lain awake in the shaman's house, waiting and hoping that the old one would go to sleep and let him be, Frog had never been so scared. "Why . . . why are you telling this to me?"

She tilted her head slightly, a flirtatious mannerism. "Why, because I like you, Frog. You're . . . different. I've heard all about you from the others. I've heard about what you were when Prince Dammon found you. We are alike in that way. Everyone counts our years and thinks we're children, but we know better, you and I."

She was so close to him, so close that he could smell the rank scent of a serpent clinging to her, the ancient reek of magic turned away from serving the powers, bound only to serve the self. Her kiss was warm, her caresses subtly stirring, and yet he felt himself curling up into a tiny ball of ice inside.

"I could poison him so easily," she was whispering in his ear. "And I will if I must. But if you love him . . . love me. Love me, and I swear that I won't let him drink another cup of wine unless wine is *all* it holds. Do you trust my oath, sweet Frog? Sweet, strong, death-pawn fighter? I swear by the powers of air, and that oath will bind even me."

She kissed him again and fell back to offer him the drugged cup. "You may drink this if you like. It will make it easier for you . . . the first time."

Frog's eyes flew from her mocking smile to his lord's sightless stare and back. He was empty of any hope.

"Swear you will tell no one, my Frog," she said, holding the goblet high. "Swear by your lord's life."

He gave one last, lingering look to Dammon. Then he swore, and drank down the cup, and lost himself in the hold of Lilla's brew.

Mrygo bit his thumb thoughtfully and skimmed the scroll for the fifth time. It was a dry accounting of the staff serving Prince Dammon's private household—the names, parentage, origins, and qualifications of the many souls who attended the prince to greater or lesser degree. It was a document for the most crabbed, nitpicking scribe to find fascinating—the same sort of fellow who got pleasure out of seeing how many measures of grain were put aside this year as compared to last.

A strange shape for a seed to have, that scroll. Stranger still the ideas that sprouted from it, the other clues it had revealed to Mrygo's eyes. He had spent most of his time in isolation tracking them all down, one by one—passing unseen through the castle halls to the archives and back to Devra's rooms like a nightpad—until he returned to the original scroll once more.

It was pure luck that this same scroll had interested the Princess Devra because of what it told of Lord Maldonar. The fading script was underlined in fresher ink, a few comments made in the margin in Devra's own hand. Devra had wanted to be sure that her chosen consort had no living relatives, no close ties that might jerk him back before she had time to make him her creature. The scroll confirmed what she had hoped, and she had not thought to return it to the musty archives where it belonged.

It did not belong here, in Devra's hidden room of wonders. All the other manuscripts here were bound into book form— all indexed, making their contents more available to an impatient sorceress. The very fact that this lone scroll lay among so many books had attracted Mrygo's curiosity. What he found within was far more fascinating than any description of sacrifice or summoning.

He had taken the seed from that scroll and watered it with a quick gaze-bowl vision. What he saw after he forced his spell to pull aside the webwork of protective illusions shielding the truth confirmed his suspicions.

"Now what?" he had murmured aloud when he looked up from the circle of water. "Do I tell the truth first, or first confront the liar?" His back was kinked with long days of study and research. An extended stretch was a luxury he reveled in now.

"Ah, that feels good," he said, then smirked. "Talking to myself. I've been locked up here alone too long, and thanks to that damn, that wonderful scroll, I *still* haven't pierced the Silver Mountain's metal hide." A deep sigh filled his chest. "Larya, my dear . . . why do I think you'd be the only one to forgive me that?"

He tucked the scroll into his sleeve and secured Devra's rooms after him. A cool breeze, damp with the breath of the great river, refreshed him as he passed through a multi-windowed passageway. It bore the scent of rushes, and he lingered at one unglazed arch to watch the winding stream. There were no boats on it—there never were. The great river flowed out of the realm into unknown lands, and no one cared to follow where it led. The only craft that ever rode the water were the rafts that the marsh dwellers made.

"And it doesn't do to be caught out in the open too much these days, does it?" Mrygo asked the invisible folk whose living was the fish they caught and the rushes they harvested, both for the queen's feasting hall. "It must have been very different, then." The Gryagi was unsmiling as he continued on his way.

It didn't take him long to find one of his old council-mates. Young Lord Fiel, still withdrawn and word-spare, lounged on a bench in the great hall and stared at the dais as if seeing

Queen Devra enthroned there. Mrygo noted an air of negligence about the man's posture and dress. When he stopped to think it over, he'd seen similar laxness in every soul he'd passed on his way from Devra's chambers. Foot soldier, spearman, officer, or any of the multitude of camp followers serving Dammon's army—it made no difference. The crisp, trim sharpness of stance and attitude had disappeared. It was like seeing a famed warrior gone to flab, only the sorry dissipation was repeated dozens of times over.

And where were his own folk? Where were the Khana-trained Gryagi who had fought so well? Where were those newly freed slaves who had risked so much, starting to undermine Devra's outer walls out in the open, when there was always the chance that Lord Maldonar's forces might have turned, seen them, and destroyed them? They'd be needed when the army approached the Silver Mountain, that was sure. Where were they?

"So there you are," Fiel said when he saw the healer. "I thought you'd taken off with the others."

"Taken off? Where have they gone? Why?"

Lord Fiel laughed, then cast guilty eyes into the far corners of the hall, fearing to wake ghosts. "Where?" he repeated. "Some have gone home, for all I know . . . wherever home is for your tribe. That's mostly the Surin slaves we loosed, and I can't say I blame them. They've got plenty of rebuilding to do, and they've more than paid off their debt to our high lord prince." He toyed with a bloodstone ring, one of many Mrygo hadn't seen on Fiel's hands before this. "Some of them—Iskander says they're the batch you belong to—only went as far as the woods. They might be there yet, waiting for a word of change. How long they'll wait before giving up . . ." He shrugged. "As for *why* . . . Dammon."

Mrygo's finger touched the bloodstone ring. "That is a handsome stone, my lord. These others aren't bad either. How did you come by them?"

"Oh, we've opened the royal treasury." Fiel replied as if this were the most everyday sort of transaction. "Lord Gerais argued about it for a night and a day with Master Kor. Finally he said that the silver wizard could pack up his share of the fighters and go back to Khana if he didn't like it, but damned if he'd see his men go a day more without some reward. He said he'd set aside enough to befit the prince, if Dammon ever came back—"

"What?" Mrygo stiffened. "Lord Dammon's gone, and your pack of outlaws loiters here, stealing from his treasury? This, with Lord Gerais's consent? I can't believe it!"

Fiel gave the healer a wry sideways smile. "Don't. That's not how it is at all. Your friend's here in body, but not much more. While you've been playing scholar, the rest of us have been watching this castle crumble from the inside out. Poor old Lord Gerais is only trying to salvage something from the wreckage, keep something back from Devra when she returns and blasts us out of here. If any of us survives that, Gerais wants us to have a measure of Devra's wealth to start new lives with, if she lets us go to ground in peace and doesn't root us out."

"Where is Dammon? What's happened to him?"

"He's in his chambers, but I wouldn't go there if I were you. You'll get a sword through your gullet if he's not in the mood to receive guests. No, come to think of it, you'll be killed no matter what mood he's in. You've been declared outlaw, my friend; outlaw by word and writ, all sealed by the prince's own hand." Lord Fiel held the bloodstone ring to the light so that it gleamed. "Lucky for you no one takes his orders seriously, or you'd have been arrested as soon as you stuck your nose out of wherever you've been hidden all this time."

Mrygo could not answer. Something was desperately wrong, and the intriguing little scrap of information he'd gleaned from his concealed scroll suddenly didn't seem so wonderful or important. He bid Fiel a curt farewell and ran through the castle halls to Dammon's rooms.

There were no guards posted, although there was ready evidence that the men assigned to this post had come, loitered, then wandered off. They might return when their shift came to an end—witness the heavy, ceremonial spears left tilted against the door—but until then they would suit themselves. No one seemed likely to check up on them or to care.

Mrygo helped himself to one of the spears. The point was dull when he tested it on his thumb, but the tasseled shaft itself might serve as a formidable weapon. The Gryagi's ears had been formed in the vast silences of the caverns. He could sift through the babble of aboveground noises and find a trail of sound as skillfully as the best trackers followed a path of footfalls over sheer rock. Even through the thick door, Mrygo listened for how many breaths—and whose—were on the other side.

He heard only one, and that one young and strong. By its frequency, he marked it for Gryagi. There was only one of his race who would be in Dammon's rooms. The door was unlatched and swung back freely when he gave it a firm shove and went in.

Frog crouched by the fireplace, staring into the flames. A pile of wood high enough to warm a family for a month blazed up the chimney, the blast of its heat powerful enough to make Mrygo hang back, clinging to the door he shut behind him. Frog remained where he was, inches from the fire, and clasped his arms around himself like one who can't get warm.

"Frog?" The boy did not answer or act as if he'd heard. Mrygo shed his robe and lay the scroll carefully among the folds. He balanced the spear against the wall. In a Gryagi loinwrap like Frog's own, he crept closer and touched the youth gently on the shoulder. "Frog?"

"Late." The sound of the word was hollow and old. Mrygo felt gray skin crawl under his touch. Frog shuddered and twitched away from Mrygo's hand. "Too late."

"Too late? Too late for what?" All Mrygo got from Frog was a sigh and a shrug. With a rough curse in his own tongue, he hauled the boy to his feet, dragged him away from the infernal fire, and shook him. "What's bitten you, blast it?" he shouted in Frog's impassive face. "Where's Dammon? Is he alive or dead? You little idiot! Hadn't you sense enough to fetch me if there was a *real* need? Couldn't Master Kor—?"

A cold sharpness pricked Mrygo's arm. His head jerked around to see where a sword's edge had drawn a line of blood already trickling down to his elbow.

"Let the boy go, Mrygo," Dammon said dully. The Gryagi had seen more life in a slab of stone. "Now, or I'll give you some fresh blood for your gaze-bowl."

Mrygo relaxed his hold on Frog. Release appeared to mean nothing to the boy. Prince and page, both were wrapped in a frightening listlessness. The healer felt its presence among them all as if it were a living thing with form and a name. Dammon wore a robe that must have been fine once, when it was cleaner. It hung opened, unbelted. The prince's naked skin beneath had an unhealthy luminescence. The threaded dragon's claws looked like festering black crescent scars against his chest. His grip was steady as he kept the sword up, the point now higher, on a level with Mrygo's eyes. He could lower it with care or slash it down to kill. The worst of it was, he didn't seem to care which.

Frog slumped and began sidling back toward the fireplace. "He'll burn himself," Mrygo said. His own throat was already dried out from the heat in the room. "Something's the matter with him—with both of you. Dammon, let me help."

"How? You can't heal everything with herbs and strips of cloth. I've heard that sometimes healers must take their knives and cut away the sick parts of a patient's body. Some diseases can only be cured by cutting them out." The prince lowered his sword. For the first time, Mrygo thought he saw some waking spark in Dammon's filmy gaze.

"I—I won't know how to heal him until I learn what's ailing him. Have I—your permission to examine Frog?"

"Have you his? Or did you have mine when you went prying into past things, all alone up there in my dear sister's rooms?" The hopeful spark changed to a weird, morbid burning. Dammon leaned his face in toward Mrygo's so that the Gryagi smelled the sourness of stale wine on the prince's breath. "Tell me, Mrygo, my friend . . . if you call yourself my friend, tell me what you saw in the birras' blood. Speak the truth and swear not to tell it to another soul. Do that, and I might let you walk out of this room alive. You know me. I am capable of anything. Nothing is forbidden to Lord Prince Dammon, is it? That's why they made a hero of me, because I recognize no limits. Recite my crimes for me now—no. Not crimes. I am not like ordinary men. We must find a new name for the things I've done."

Frog moaned softly and rocked on his heels. He was back in the same spot where Mrygo had discovered him. He teetered dangerously close to the blaze and nearly toppled in. Mrygo uttered an unintelligible cry and lurched away from Dammon to grab the boy back by the hair. Frog sprawled on his back and stared spiritlessly up at the ceiling.

Suddenly, Mrygo no longer cared about the sword. "Are you really insane?" he bawled. "Babbling away about crimes and blood and—and—" He cut the air with a gesture of disgust. "Meantime, Frog nearly roasts himself whole, like a spitted pig. You can stay here and talk yourself into your grave, Dammon, but you're not taking Frog along!" Mrygo knelt to gather the boy up in his arms. Frog let himself be lifted, as uncomplaining and limp as a rag doll.

"You don't leave this room." Dammon put himself between Mrygo and the door. "You don't leave until you've sworn me an oath that no one—no one!—will know what you learned in Devra's chambers."

Mrygo's brows came together. "No one knows anything about it. I was going to tell you first, and then perhaps Master Kor, but—"

"Don't you tell him a thing!" Mrygo retreated a step, taken aback by the vehemence of Dammon's command. "He's—he's got his own idea of what I am. Let him keep it, even if it is only a dream. The gods know, I cherished dreams of myself for a long time. If they're gone now . . ." The fire in him faded and the deadly apathy returned. "Our war is over. I'll do what I can for Master Kor and the rest—Devra shan't touch them. I'll make us all as good a peace as I can, once I've spoken to my sister. I—understand her better now. There won't be any need to fight her. And after we've made an end to the fighting, I'll go away; I swear it."

Tenderly, Mrygo set down his burden. Frog balled himself up in the puddle of Mrygo's discarded robe and shook like a man with marsh-fever. The healer saw none of this. He could not take his eyes from Dammon.

"Peace with Devra? Oh, my poor friend . . ." He would have clasped Dammon's hands, but the sword came up abruptly, a short, definite barrier. The prince was skittish, deep fear and shame in every thread of his being. Mrygo spoke softly, as he would to a child. "My friend, I don't know what evil sorcery has touched you since I went into Devra's apartments, but it's nothing that can't be set right."

"You can say that when you saw . . . you saw what I did to

her? To my own sister! Ah gods, gods, none of us can blame
Lilla for being what she is. A monstrous birth, a birth that
never should have been, a crime . . . and mine alone. Mine."

The sword clashed as it fell to the stones. Dammon's dagger
was in his hands, turned against himself, aimed just below the
breastbone's base. Mrygo sprang to grapple for the weapon,
the bulbous sore of his captive's collar pulsing red with heart's
blood. Twice the blade cut him. Once it almost found its mark,
but in the end, the healer had it and dealt Dammon a smack
across the face that stunned him into momentary stillness.

"Now, you listen to me," the Gryagi panted. "I don't know
what kind of poisons have been getting into your brain, but
I've got a good idea of who's been doling them out. You haven't
done anything wrong. Whatever this crime is you're raving
about, you didn't commit it. I have proof of that."

The prince pressed one hand to his throbbing cheek. "This
. . . isn't what she said you'd do. Mrygo, you really are my
friend after all, but—friends lie. I saw a vision, a gaze-bowl
vision—"

"Illusions can also be conjured into the bowl."

"Then . . . how will I know your proof won't also be an
illusion, made to spare me? If the truth's cruel enough, Lilla
would show it to me, and what she showed me was cruel
beyond anything you could imagine."

Mrygo tossed the dagger aside. His face was full of weary
compassion. This time when he reached for his friend's hands,
the human did not pull away. "There we agree on Lilla. She
showed you how Lord Prince Dammon, the hero, committed
a crime that was unspeakable. Am I near the mark?" Dammon
nodded. "Then I don't even have to ask you what that crime
was to disprove your guilt. No matter how true or false the
vision of Dammon's sin, you are innocent."

"I—"

"You are not Dammon. Dammon is dead."

Mrygo's hands slipped up his friend's arms to steady him.
Solicitously, he helped him to a chair before speaking on. "Your
name is Heron. You were Lord Prince Dammon's squire, and
your younger brother served him also as page. Both of you
came from marsh folk, but you fit into the workings of Mar-
Halira quickly. There are many mentions of you two in the

household records, many commendations, some in Lord Prince Dammon's own hand.

"I found your name in a scroll in Devra's chambers, and with it a description of your appearance. You had taken a wound that left a bad scar across the face in a recent mock battle between squires. Do you remember the mark on Ophar's face?"

"Ophar—Heron—was my squire. But he died in the dragon's cave, and Master Byuric changed our faces..."

"Changed your faces." Mrygo's own hard features softened. "Oh, my good friend, every magic has its limits, didn't you know that? If it weren't so, Devra would have no need to erect her monstrous mountain. The powers could all criss-cross into each other's realms and the world would be chaos. Illusion is the most fragile of enchantments. It can only be maintained when the creator of the illusion is near—that much I learned in the days when they thought to make me into a silver wizard. All those spans you lingered under the earth in my land, no illusion could have lasted. The silver wizards were nowhere near—by the heart of the mountains, they didn't even know where to look for you until you came aboveground and into range of their searchings spells again! The face you wore when you were Ophar was your own. This one"—he touched Dammon's smarting cheek, and most of the pain ebbed away—"is a mask of Master Kor's making."

Mrygo sounded almost like one bringing news of death as he added, "They needed a hero. Only a hero could stand tall enough to bring down Devra's evil. Evil itself looms larger than any good in the mind of most men. What was Lord Prince Dammon? Only a man. Heron wasn't his equal in birth, but he had some skill with the sword and a good, quick mind for strategy, as you showed us all by your words in council, your plan for taking Mar-Halira. Heron could have led the army just as well—or Ophar, if that's the name you'd rather carry—but men follow names, songs, dreams, legends bigger than life. They wouldn't take risks or dare death so readily for anyone but their Lord Prince Dammon, who came back the way the stories promised. So there had to be a Dammon for the silver wizards to use against Devra—do you see? They made you a mask, tied it on, set you on a dead dragon's back, and there!

You were Dammon. You had to be Dammon, because they had to have a hero."

He had been nameless, then named himself, then been given a hero's name to bear. Now it was taken from him and in his heart he was nameless again. The crackling of the enormous fire was the only sound in that room for a time.

"So Lord Prince Dammon will never come again," he said finally. "The dragon killed him, and . . . did I kill the dragon?"

"I called up that scene, Heron," Mrygo replied. "Though I had to fight my way through Master Kor's false overvision to see what really happened. Lord Maldonar attacked Prince Dammon in the midst of his battle with the monster, and between the two of them he died. All the same, you fought the dragon side by side with your lord and it's past my ability to say whose sword gave it the deathblow. I hope it was yours. If it was, you avenged your brother's blood that day."

"My brother . . ."

"Lord Prince Dammon's page. The silver wizards can mold many things, but they can't cut away all of your past life. It clings, like a spider's web. His name was Frog, Heron. Your little brother's name was Frog."

"Yes. Now I remember. That was our way, in the marshes. I used to be ashamed of such a name when I was still a page in the royal service. The other boys teased me—until I taught them better manners." Heron smiled. "Frog did the same when he came into service. My little Frog . . ." Tears touched the corners of that smile.

"Well, now you know the truth of things. What will you do?"

Behind Dammon's mask, Heron stared out at the Gryagi. "Do?" he echoed.

"Yes, you heard me. What will you do? Tell Master Kor you've cut through his lies? Speak to Lord Gerais first and let him in on the truth? Summon your council? I'd recommend taking our small friend Lilla into custody first, before she finds out she's lost her hold on you, but after you've taken care of that, what?"

Heron retreated into his own thoughts. Mrygo took the other chair and waited for an answer. No creatures in all the realm could wait half so patiently as the Children of Stone, who were born with the ageless endurance of rock. When Heron's answer did come, it was hardly one Mrygo would have guessed.

"I am Lord Prince Dammon."

"You—"

"Hush, Mrygo. For you, for me, we know who I am. So does Master Kor. But for the others—the army from Khana, Lord Fiel's band, old Lord Gerais, your own people, the new recruits . . . even for Devra—I am Dammon. I must be Dammon. You said it yourself. I'm what they need to march behind. I'm what they need to make Devra afraid. Don't you see? If we tell them the truth now, we'll steal their spirits. They'll do more in the field if they can believe they're fighting for a prince who's part of all those songs and tales. What would they be able to do if they learned they were fighting for a marsh-brat squire?" He gave a half grin. "An ugly one, at that."

Mrygo was bemused. "You'd do that . . . go on with the masquerade . . . willingly? After all the lies that Master Kor and Master Byuric—"

"I'm not doing it for them," Dammon snapped. More calmly, he said, "I'm doing it for the others."

Mrygo didn't have to ask what others Heron meant. There were too many of them to be named and numbered individually. Some the Gryagi knew well. Some he had never met, would probably never meet. Some, like the first Frog, were dead. The illusion that was Lord Prince Dammon was a weaving of countless threads, all making up the wonder and the dream that were the promised hero. Touch one, remove it, and the whole would come undone.

The Gryagi were sparing when it came to physical contact. Their young ones received few embraces but much love. Nevertheless, Mrygo now left his chair and embraced Heron the way surface-born brothers might welcome each other home.

Heron laughed aloud for the first time in days. "You see, Frog, I'm cured! Mrygo's a fine healer, and if you'll tell him what's been gnawing away at you these past few days—"

He turned toward the open door. Mrygo's robe and the scroll lay where they had before. Frog was gone. From out in the hall came the sound of hard arguing.

Four guardsmen dropped their voices when their prince emerged from his rooms but kept up their dispute all the same.

If they reckoned that Dammon would ignore this slight mark of disrespect, as he'd been ignoring everything lately, they reckoned wrongly. An angry look flashed from the prince's eyes, harsh words were spoken, and to their amazement, the four bickering guards found themselves delighted to be put on report by Dammon himself.

"Now tell me, before I summon up your commanders: What were you yapping over like a bunch of old market women?"

"My lord prince," said one of the four. "Stevil and I are just coming on guard duty. We're supposed to carry special spears to show we're warding your rooms. Well, these two had the watch before us and they're supposed to turn the spears over to us, but they won't."

"Not *won't*; *can't*!" one of the accused growled. He sounded bearish enough to be Decad Turgan's own son. Lowering his head, he mumbled, "We—uh—I—lost it."

Mrygo chuckled. "Cheer up, fellow. You lost nothing. You were robbed." To his friend, he said, "I thought I might need some formidable weapon when I came into your rooms, and the spears in question were just . . . lying there, so I helped myself. No doubt these worthy guards were both seized with urgent natural calls at the same time, which accounts for their absence."

"No doubt," Dammon said, just as mock-serious as Mrygo.

"We can't really accuse them of abandoning their weapons. I tried the edge, and spears with points that dull aren't even good for spades. However . . ." He scratched his head and looked puzzled. "However, it seems that if anyone lost a spear, it's me."

"Well, never mind that. We've more important matters. Have any of you seen my page?"

The four guards eyed one another. All drew blanks. Just then, one of them darted a look down the hall and exclaimed, "Isn't that him? The young Gryagi?"

"Aye, that's him, and he's got my spear with him!" cried the bearish one, pointing.

It was so. The long, thick haft dragged on the floor behind Frog as he staggered slowly toward his master. The spearpoint, clean and bright as ever, mirrored a flash of light as he knelt before his lord.

"Frog, are you all right? Where have you been?" Heron asked with real concern, though as he looked more closely at his page, he saw that full life had returned to Frog just as it had to him.

"I'm fine." The boy's voice was husky. He took the spear in both hands and raised it in the ceremonial offering of weapons that ended every round of the killing games. "We are all free."

There was neither smear nor stain on the dull, useless blade of that spear. But the butt-end of heavy wood was bloody and laced with a strand of blue-black hair.

PART VII

Lar-Khana

As twilight fell, three mounted figures emerged from the father forest and saw how the dying light blazed to day's full brightness against the slopes of the Silver Mountain.

"So here we are," said Heron, who sat his mount between Master Kor and Mrygo. "Somehow I thought it would look more fearsome seen like this than in your visions, Master Kor."

The dark-skinned wizard answered, "Use your warrior's eyes before you say there's nothing to fear here, my lord."

Heron stiffened. "I'm not your lord. I thought I told you not to call me that when we're alone. Let's try for some honesty between us now, at least."

Master Kor's eyes were shadowed by the up-drawn cowl of his cloak. "Until you can be as sure as I of our privacy, don't take offense so quickly. A day hasn't gone by since we left Mar-Halira that you haven't found some way to remind me of how ill I've used you. Ill-use, to make you a prince! It grows tiresome. I was able to do much with the legend of Lord Prince Dammon before it was necessary to make him appear in the flesh. I can do it again if you're as tired of the masquerade as you pretend to be."

"Try it and see how long the army—"

"My friends, please." Mrygo's calm, measured words cut

the growing hostility. "As you said, Master Kor, this near Lar-Khana, who knows when we are truly alone? No bickering. And you, my lord prince"—he stressed the royal title ever so subtly—"you should know that the creditor soonest repaid is the one who doesn't harp on his debt constantly." A sharp smile flashed in the dusk. "Our Master Kor is human and not above the sweetness of malice."

"Malice?" The silver wizard scowled.

"What gives a man more delight—malicious delight—than owing a debt and refusing to act indebted?"

The wrinkles smoothed from Master Kor's brow. He sat less straight in the saddle. "You are right, Mrygo." He turned toward Heron. "Master Byuric sed Lyum and I have done much with you—and to you—but thanking you never played a part in it. We were doing what we thought was necessary and best for the freeing of this realm. We thought that the final prize would be thanks enough for you—a prince's identity, borrowed glory, all that went with it. . . . We presumed much; too much." He sighed and slumped down further, wearily. "I ask you to forgive us now; to accept our thanks as well, but mostly to forgive us."

Heron felt the burdens on the lone remaining silver wizard's spirit. He reached across to clasp the gnarled hands on the bridle. "Accepted. Now I promise, no more recriminations out of me."

"No quibbles about what I call you?" A trace of humor brightened the silver wizard's face. Heron's smile answered it.

"Within reason. Come, let's ride back to camp. You were right about looking with a warrior's eye. No guards! Not even the traces of a patrol. Devra grows careless."

Master Kor was thoughtful. "Careless? Not she. Look up there, both of you." His dark hand rose toward the distant summit of the metal-sheathed mountain. A jag of bare rock jutted up blackly into the sky. "Her work is almost finished, and her powers grow in proportion as she draws nearer the end. So does her confidence. She no longer needs her soldiers to protect her mountain against interlopers." The corner of his mouth twitched up to one side. "Now it's the trespassers who'd best protect themselves."

Back in camp, in the royal tent, Heron called council and

reported on what he had seen. "No guards or patrols, but that doesn't mean no danger. We don't know what sort of eyes Devra's using these days."

"She might not be using eyes at all," Captain Iskander suggested. "If she's as smug as you think, she wouldn't expend herself on watching for trouble."

"Aye, that sounds like her, my lord," old Lord Gerais averred. "Full of herself, and seldom without a good reason. We'd best go cautiously."

Heron chuckled. "I hadn't planned on riding up to the mountain and issuing a challenge for hand-to-hand combat with my sister. I've got the soul of an eel, when all's said, and I'd rather slip through by stealth instead of charging head on."

"Slip through . . . a mountainside?" The idea was a bit much for Decad Turgan. His beetling brows were in their V again. "My lord prince, are you a sorcerer too?"

Heron's chuckle became a full-fledged laugh. He clapped his loyal spearman on the back and said, "The powers keep all that from me. A sword's enough trouble to wield, most of the time, without bringing magic into it. Think, my friend. The walls of Mar-Halira were more porous but no less solid than the flanks of this mountain, yet we managed to breach them."

Realization hit. "The Children of Stone!" Decad Turgan snapped his thick fingers. "The Gryagi!"

There was a murmur of discussion around the table that soon turned to mutual agreement. Besides Mrygo and Frog, there were two Gryagi present—one trained with Mrygo from the days in Khana, one from the Surin slave-holds—and they exchanged looks of pride to be called back into the prince's service a second time.

"No patrols in the woods?" Captain Iskander asked, wanting to be sure.

"None, not even on the cleared land going up to the skirts of the mountain," Heron replied. "It's an incredible peak; you'll see for yourself tomorrow. It seems to stand alone, rising up apart from the girdling range behind it. The view from the summit must stretch far into the outer lands . . ." His voice grew vague with dreams, speculations, and unspoken desires.

"Then we're agreed," Master Kor said. "The Gryagi will

commence a tunnel on the northwest flank of the mountain tomorrow, before dawn. There's some brush cover there—no sense in us getting overconfident too."

"That's wise," growled Lord Gerais. "Might be the one hour and the one place she decides to spy on before she finishes her damn mountain. Is the cover sufficient?"

It was enough to hide the mouth of a wide tunnel, and then some. The brush Master Kor spoke of would have counted for a substantial thicket of young trees elsewhere, but so near the huge forests, it dwindled by comparison. The Gryagi diggers didn't wait for dawn to begin. Midnight saw them already stealing out of camp to start their task.

By morning's light, Heron, Mrygo, and Frog went out to see how things progressed. A grinning Gryagi wearing Dammon's device on his uniform popped out of the ground like a woodchuck and told them to hurry back to camp and have the troops ready themselves for battle. The tunnel would dip beneath the mountain's edge and come up under its root before the day ended.

High good spirits seized the entire encampment when the three brought back that news. Whetstones sang along the lengths of a forest of swords. Breastplates and helmets were cleaned, their leather fastenings inspected and oiled. Officers whose commands included heavy numbers of new recruits lectured long and loud on the need for discipline and obedience in battle. There would be victory but no heroes, they said.

The fighters, old and new, smiled. They knew that when the battle was done there would be, now as ever, one hero. All they asked was the chance to serve him best.

Heron lifted the flap of his tent and peered out at all the activity. "At least they're keeping the noise within reason. I never knew an army this size could make so little racket." He let the flap fall. "Have you seen Captain Iskander and Sir Raimon?"

Mrygo sat on a folding stool, his fingers swirling idly across the inner and outer surfaces of a red clay bowl. Four birras fluttered or clambered around him, their bright eyes ever critical and inquisitive. "Not I," he answered. "What about you, Frog? Have you seen them?"

"I know where Captain Iskander is." The young Gryagi

squatted on the cleared earth floor between his elders. Two more of the small golden winged creatures perched on his shoulders, running up and down his arms or tugging at his ears with prying paws when they felt like it. "He's back in the forest with Master Kor. He asked for a dead-call."

Heron felt his neck prickle. Frog spoke as if the red-haired captain's request were the most ordinary thing in the world, but death had been an ordinary companion for Frog from his earliest days. It wasn't so with other folk. Most dreaded of the earth-magic spells, the dead-call summoned up a spirit made palpable, a shadow of the dead that could touch the living.

"A dead-call . . . for Beliza?"

"I guess." Frog tickled the birra on his left shoulder. It gave a gurgling purr. Since the day he had presented the bloody spear to Heron, a week and more had passed without the boy uttering a sound or recognizing the presence of other people. His initial elation vanished abruptly, when he led them to the dark garden where he'd left Lilla's body. It was as if her spirit had bided there to spring out and bind him to her eternally with all the silences of death. Only when Mrygo and Master Kor together labored over him had he come out of inner exile. After that, it was Heron's gift of the two birras that had completed the healing—if it ever could be called complete.

"Iskander wants her to know of our victory—before the fact." Mrygo continued to stroke the glazed interior and raw-fired exterior of his favorite gaze-bowl. "He wants her spirit to know contentment—a hard enough thing for a warrior like Beliza to know when she was alive. As for Sir Raimon, if you want to know where he is, get me some water for this and we'll see."

"I'll get it." Frog got up and filled the gaze-bowl from a waterskin hanging on the central pole. The healer set it on the ground and knelt beside it, motioning the others to gather 'round. There was none of Lilla's dramatic pauses and flourishes, but a sure and simple calling up of power. The water quivered and opened into an image of Sir Raimon's face.

"He's alone," said Heron. "I'd've thought he'd be with his men. Why does he look so sad?"

"That's one answer you can't get from a gaze—"

The water rippled, then heaved upward with a roar, each

clear droplet turning to fire as it fell. The rain of flames peppered the tent's interior, most of the sparks falling to nothing on the moist ground, some catching on the walls, others flying into the faces of the three companions. They threw their hands up to shield their eyes.

Heron cried out in pain, batting at the line of fire that had latched onto his right-hand sleeve. Frog grabbed a folded blanket from the camp-bed and smothered it before much damage was done. With the same dogged efficiency, he saw to beating out the fiery flags waving from the walls of the tent. Small burn marks speckled his body. He still wore just a loinwrap, leaving him less vulnerable to the perils of clothing catching fire, but more readily scarred in the first spatterings of fire from Mrygo's gaze-spell gone wrong.

"Root and Seed, what happened?" Heron demanded. Mrygo shook his head, having no reply to give. The empty gaze-bowl shuddered and crackled, then flew apart to puffs of red clay dust. The Gryagi healer reached toward it, seeking an answer, but as his fingers grazed the powdery remains, the earth itself lurched under foot, throwing him backward into the tent-pole.

Heron fell flat on his face, red dust flying up his nose and choking him as he tried to find a fixed point to cling to in the midst of a world ariot. The ground bucked and screamed as narrow fissures opened, tearing the tent from its pegs and canting the central pole at a drunken angle. The birras took flight—Mrygo's as well as Frog's—swarming in panic around the younger Gryagi's head. The only one of the three still standing, riding the earthquake waves, Frog swatted at the meeping creatures and cried for help.

Where would help come from? The ground churned. From outside, the sounds of earnest battle preparations changed to shouts of soul-blinding terror. Hooves pounded through the encampment as horses tore loose from their pickets and stampeded, trampling anyone or anything in their way. Kettles upended themselves into cookfires, scalding those unlucky enough to be near. Blades fell, their sharpened edges turning against their masters, missing or wounding or even killing as havoc struck randomly throughout the ranks of Dammon's army.

Then it was over. Heron raised his face from the dirt and slowly released his hooked fingers. Still on his feet, Frog began to weep aloud, his sobs the one sound in the bizarre stillness of afterward. Mrygo sat up and felt the back of his head, wincing when he touched the spot where he'd hit the tent-pole.

Heron got up and went to comfort Frog. He and Mrygo led the boy outside, where they thought they saw the full effects of what had happened. They picked their way through a camp that looked as if it had been picked up and crumpled—tents, horses, soldiers and all—in a giant's hand. The eerie silence stunned them, yet what was more disquieting was the fact that not a leaf or twig of the encompassing forest had been ruffled by a quake that rightly should have uprooted whole stands of trees.

Master Kor came out of the forest, followed by Captain Iskander. The redhead gaped at what he saw. Master Kor was merely grim. Lord Fiel was nearby, kneeling over the body of old Lord Gerais. The faithful general had been killed trying to stem a wave of fear-maddened horses, flying hooves crushing his bones.

A score of wounded began to call for aid when they saw their prince and his two constant Gryagi companions. Mrygo had earned respect for his healing skills, and whispers told the tale of what Frog had done to free his lord from Devra's unnatural child. Mrygo motioned for Frog to come with him and give what help he could. Laudan, a human healer, materialized from a toppled tent to add his part to their efforts among the injured. Heron went with them, playing out his part as Lord Prince Dammon, speaking words that soothed his injured men almost as deeply as Mrygo's herbs or Laudan's bone-sets. Yet before they reached the first victim, something made Mrygo stop in his tracks and jerk to attention, listening.

"What's that?"

A faint noise came from the east, a rushing sound like water. They had left the great river far behind them, near the walls of Mar-Halira. Heron remembered how he had felt the pull of it when they'd forded over and wondered idly if there were powers of water that called to him that way, knowing his marsh-born blood. He felt no such sweet tugging now. No water made that sound.

The camp found its voice again. Questions and theories

about the disaster buzzed from lip to lip, most seeing only one possible explanation.

"Devra! She commands the Powers of Earth as well as the Powers of Air! We are lost!"

"Fools!" Master Kor's robes flashed through the tents, his anger and frustration making him sound fierce, impersonal. "Fools, what do you know of magic? You'll take the heart out of your fellow fighters with that gibberish and then Devra *will* be pleased. No one can serve more than one power fully unless he serves them all, in harmony."

"Worse, worse!" came a groan. "She has the skills of a silver wizard!"

Master Kor dignified that man with a worse title than fool. "Devra belongs to the Powers of Air, I tell you! They can't move the earth, no more than I could force such a quake myself."

"I thought the silver wizards could do anything," Decad Turgan whispered, within Heron's hearing. Shyly, he addressed the man he still thought was his prince, "Can't they?"

"Anything?" Heron repeated. "Yes, as long as it doesn't disturb any natural balance. I wouldn't call an earthquake harmonious, would you?"

"Well then, how did it happen? Never saw the like, not I. Here—you think that witch has got someone else up the mountain with her? One with the Powers of Earth eating out of his hand?"

Heron looked in the direction of Lar-Khana and shielded his eyes when a stab of silvered light from the mountain pierced the branches overhead. The possibility that Turgan suggested might be true. If it were . . . who but Larya had such mastery over the powers of earth? He had spent long days and longer nights waiting for Mrygo's spells to find a chink into the Silver Mountain just to find out whether she was still alive. Now, if she were and it turned out she'd bought her life by going over into Devra's service . . .

He shut off the thought. "We'll know that when we've taken the Silver Mountain and Devra with it; not before."

He was much mistaken. The answer came staggering out of the woods in twos and threes and stumbling lone figures. Patches of black skin peeled away from gray flesh, showing that the color of Gryagi blood was also red. The Children of Stone lurched back into camp to fall and writhe and mostly die at Heron's feet. The smell of burning wood in the near distance was not strong enough to cover the stench of seared limbs and scorched faces.

"The trees are burning! Turgan, bring men!" Master Kor gave his orders and ran. Mrygo and Laudan left off binding the wounds of the earthquake victims and tried to separate the dying Gryagi from the few with a chance to live.

Heron wanted to run with Mrygo, to fetch and carry anything the healers might need, to find some hope of life among so many deaths. He heard Mrygo calling for water and started after Frog, who was amassing skins from the wrecked encampment, but one of the few Gryagi who could stand gripped his wrist and held him back, moving cracked lips in agonizing speech.

"The . . . Silver Mountain . . . my lord prince."

"Don't talk now. Come with me. I'll get you water—"

The Gryagi's laughter wheezed. "Not . . . enough. My lord prince, we tunneled under Lar-Khana. We were . . . almost there. Then we touched the root." He closed his eyes. Flakes of char curled from the lids. "Silver. . . . It was silver too . . . all bottomed out in silver . . . and Surin bones. She killed them when they'd done their work. The last crag. Maybe she's got other servants to silver that. We touched the root . . . and a doom-wind blasted. It knocked over the lamps we'd used . . . spread fire . . . made the whole earth shake. . . . The silver gave back the flames like an oven . . ."

"No more." Heron couldn't even touch the Gryagi's body in sympathy or to offer comfort. The unburned places were too few. "Mrygo! Mrygo, here's a man to tend!"

The Gryagi healer came hurrying up, addressed the survivor in their common tongue, and led him away. The moans of the dying dwindled to whimpers or silence.

Master Kor was back. Heron told him what he'd learned of the underground disaster. "Devra's work after all," said the wizard. "Already the powers of air travel up and down the surface of the Silver Mountain with their strength unchanged and complete. When the final touch is put to it, there won't be a hope of stopping them or her."

"What can we do? We can't tunnel under."

"That we can't. What can we do? I wish I knew."

Heron's mouth tightened. "I'm calling council."

"We don't have time for council! Not after this. Even the most sensible of your staff will be mere babblers after what we've experienced. Ask for opinions now, and you'll be hearing them out until Devra comes riding in among us on a new doom-wind's back. They're afraid, Dammon. Your best and bravest fighters are afraid. The only one who might've regained his wits after that quake would be Lord Gerais, but we've lost him. If he still lived, he'd tell you the same as I: Now's the time your warriors need to be *told* what to do, not asked. Let them see that the one thing Devra's minions couldn't knock down and break is you, their leader. Give them strength, and courage will come back of its own accord after."

For once, Heron's eyes looked out of Dammon's face. It wasn't quite fear that Master Kor saw in them—not the coward's cold heart and deathgrip self-love—but still the wizard knew that Heron's blood trembled. "Master Kor . . . I can't. Not alone. If I can't call council, will you at least help me decide what to do? Please." He spread his hands helplessly. "There's too much at stake now for me to know what's best."

The silver wizard looked long at his handiwork. "I wonder if you'd say that if Mrygo hadn't told you . . . a certain secret? No. Knowing the truth wouldn't change what you are inside. There are a thousand masks in the world, ten thousand illusions between sun and moon, but the heart of things endures. No spell of seeming can change your soul."

"Then you'll help me?"

"I will meet with you in your tent when we've cared for our people."

"Yes, yes, of course. I'll see if Mrygo can use an extra pair of hands." Heron ran away as fast as if he could outrace the moment of decision in that manner.

Tragically, there was not much to be done for the Gryagi. They lived or died according to how much of their skin was left intact, and no amount of herbery or salves could change it. Most of them died. The victims of the quake were more fortunate—only eight dead—but many of the injured would not be raising a sword in Lord Prince Dammon's name until long after the decisive battle.

Late that night, Master Kor sat on a silk carpet spread on the floor of Heron's resurrected tent. He looked up when Mrygo dragged himself inside and threw himself down on uncovered ground. Little Frog held out his cupped hands where two birras had nestled to sleep and tossed them to his tribesman. They awoke in midflight and swooped to perch on Mrygo's shoulders, purring to ease his weariness.

"How does it go?" Heron asked from his fold-stool.

"It's done; done as best it can be. The hurt have been taken care of, and the dead have been buried." Mrygo's face showed no feeling. "Your troops aren't top-strength, but you should have enough to command for whatever you've got in mind."

"Did you find Sir Raimon?"

The Gryagi shook his head. "No one's seen him since before the earthquake. I've left word throughout the camp that you're looking for him. I mentioned a reward."

"That makes it seem like he's a fugitive." Heron didn't sound pleased.

"Most of your men were fugitives—outlaws of one sort or another. They know it's only a word, like reward."

Heron looked thoughtful. "I wonder. Decad Turgan said something to me after the quake. I didn't like to think of it, but he couldn't know. If he repeated his notion aloud, where Sir Raimon could hear . . . if Sir Raimon came back into camp after the quake and overheard Turgan say what he did, he might've gone off again."

"What are you mumbling about?" Master Kor snapped. Until Mrygo had come in, they'd been hashing over possible plans for taking Lar-Khana, not one of which sounded likely to succeed. Fruitless discussion had irritated the wizard.

"Decad Turgan said he wondered whether Devra had someone with her who could rule the powers of earth the way she did the powers of air."

"And you thought of Larya." Heron nodded. A half smile touched Master Kor's lips. "Your beautiful . . . sister; the one I helped to control her evil dreams while that old farmer raved at me and threw me out of his house. How did you come to think of her?"

Heron didn't smile. He clasped his hands before him and stared at them. "She was one of the maidens Devra had taken off to Lar-Khana—the ones she's been sacrificing on each completed terrace of the mountain. When Turgan spoke of the powers of earth, I thought she might be the one..."

"Not Larya!" Mrygo's exhaustion blinked away. Anger tore it from him. "No matter if she died for it, she'd never pact with Devra. You say you love her, but if you don't know that—!"

"I do know it; I do." Heron tried pacifying the Gryagi. "But even the unthinkable sometimes seems to...make sense for a moment. Now we all know that the quake was caused by Devra's creatures. Your folk touched the mountain's silvered root and the down-drawn powers of air attacked them. No earth-magic to it at all, but what if Sir Raimon only heard the first of it—Turgan's idea? What if he believed that Larya'd gone over to Devra? The despair he'd feel! He loved her too, you know. He was going to marry her."

"Why do you say I *loved* her, my prince? Is she dead, or am I?"

All eyes in the royal tent turned to see the former queen's man standing in the outer dark, the raised tent flap in his hand. His uniform was full of dirt and dead leaves, the stains of sleep taken on the forest floor. His soot-smeared face was harder than any dagger's edge, and his eyes glowed cold.

"I believe you were looking for me?" Sir Raimon let the flap fall behind him. It was pushed aside a second time by a scrawny youth, a farmer's brat who had run off to join the grand adventure of Lord Prince Dammon's army. His pocked face flushed red and white in the torchlight as he hovered uncomfortably half in and half out of the tent.

Mrygo gave the lad a coin and a word of praise, all the same dismissing him swiftly while Sir Raimon knelt at Heron's fold-stool. The Gryagi stuck his head out into the night to make sure no eavesdroppers lingered nearby before giving his attention to the fugitive returned.

"I said we needed guards," Master Kor rumbled, glaring at Sir Raimon's bent head.

The queen's man stood and smiled. "Why? Because I might have heard something I shouldn't? What? I'm only a traitor to my queen, not my prince; never my prince." His eyes rested on Heron. "To oppose Lord Prince Dammon would be like a mouse cursing the sun."

Heron ignored the remark, though the look in Sir Raimon's eye was too upsetting to be overlooked entirely. "Where were you, Sir Raimon? We were worried."

"Why, as my lord knows too well, I *loved* the maiden Larya. It was for her sake I joined your crusade, don't you recall that? When we made our camp here, I couldn't resist stealing off to see whether I'd any hope left of Larya still being alive. I crept away for a look at the Silver Mountain." He spoke with a deceptively cheerful tone. "Oh, how close to complete the mountain was! I lost hope then, my lord—all hope of Larya somehow having survived so many sacrifices. I wept—can you believe that, a grown man crying over his lost sweetheart?—and I couldn't go back to camp until I'd shed the last tear."

Heron answered quietly, "I believe you."

"I think I must've fallen asleep after. No wonder babies sleep so much, since they cry so much. The quake you spoke of woke me. I raced back to camp, saw what had happened, saw the Gryagi miners, saw many things . . . and wasn't seen myself." He plucked at the worst stains on his tunic and added, "Can you wonder? Hardly the expected turn-out for one of Lord Prince Dammon's chiefs. Since I was already filthy, I joined the brigade that Master Kor there rallied to put out the fire at the mouth of the ill-wished tunnel. How it burned, eh, Master Kor?"

"We were lucky that the stand was isolated, or the whole cursed forest would have gone up in flames too," the silver wizard said. He rose from the ground without the clumsy scrambling motions of ordinary men, apparently floating to his feet, and beckoned Sir Raimon. With a great show of mock obedience the one-time queen's man inclined his head for the wizard's inspection. A wide black smear ran slantways from the back of Sir Raimon's skull down across his right shoulder blade.

"Ah, sharp-eyed Master Kor! You've found the reason for my absence, I see. Yes, a falling branch knocked me senseless and I wasn't missed in all the uproar. Everyone thought I was still out of camp somewhere else. But then I got my wits back after nightfall and headed home. I had to be cautious; just as I was getting the branch off my back, I saw a slip of light against the mountain. Its flank opened a crack and five armed men came out single file."

"So she's got patrols going out after all," Master Kor reflected aloud.

"Poor ones. They passed near enough to hear my struggles with the fallen branch and never bothered investigating."

"Then they've grown as cocksure as their mistress. Good." The wizard looked well pleased. "You've brought us a prize, Sir Raimon."

"Oh, nothing compared to the gift you've given me, Master Kor. When I got back to camp, that earnest little man who brought me here was the first to recognize me. He jabbered at me to come with him at once, before I could even clean up or have Laudan look at my head." Sir Raimon folded his arms. "I should seek him out and give him a second reward. If not for his haste, I'd be a much more ignorant man."

"By the Seed, I'm sick of this!" Heron leaped from his stool and shouted his words full in Sir Raimon's face. "I'm sick of your twisted little knowing grin and the way you talk as if you're hoarding some wonderful secret! *What* do you know that makes you take that superior air? That I thought Larya'd done wrong? That I assumed you were hiding because you'd thought the same?"

Sir Raimon never lost that thin, aggravating smile. "Oh no, my lord Prince Dammon. None of that. Only that at last I see what a fool I've been to weep for Larya. Dead or living, she's lost to me, and freedom makes me smile."

"If she's alive—"

"Still lost. As good as dead, because so am I. How else could it be? When I was courting Larya—when I thought she was your sister—I always used to wonder about the way you glowered at me every time you thought I wasn't looking. I put it down to an overprotective brother who fancied no man good enough to wed his lovely sister. If I'd known then who you really were, and how you felt about her, there'd have been no mystery. You've gotten back your own face, my lord Prince Dammon. It's a handsome face, but it would still be a prince's face even if it were ugly as the one you used to wear. You can have any woman in the realm. If a lesser man stands between you and your desire, how easy to remove him—especially if he's in your army, yours to command, yours to send into the worst battles!"

Sir Raimon's voice rose. All of his affected calm was gone. "*That* is what I know, my lord prince! *That* is why I smile! Or will you take even that pleasure from me?"

Aghast at his accusations, Heron stammered, "Sir Raimon—Sir Raimon, even if I do love Larya, I would never—"

"Don't take me for a fool." The queen's man spat out his words. "Get that look off your face, my lord prince; I won't abandon your cause to save my own skin. I gave an oath of loyalty, and I'll keep it. But don't ask me to serve you in any way but my own." He whirled away before Heron could answer and dove through the tent-flap.

"Don't go after him," Master Kor said.

"I must! Did you hear what he thinks I'll do? Have him deliberately put in peril so I can have Larya—when neither of us even knows whether or not she's alive! It's madness."

"Just so. And it's unwise to follow a madman too closely. Let him go. He'll cool on his own, or else we can seek him out later and try to make him see reason."

"It's what he *doesn't* know that's making him mad," Mrygo put in. "Not what he thinks he does."

Somehow, Heron understood what the Gryagi meant. "If Larya lives . . ."

"He loves her. You and I know what that is. Uncertainty does awful things to a man. I wager that if I could open a way into Lar-Khana—a way of seeing—and I could tell him whether Larya's alive or not, he'd come back to himself right away. Even if she's dead."

"A seeing inside the Silver Mountain?" Master Kor clicked his tongue. "Impossible."

"For you, Master Kor. But you are bound by the fact that you serve all the powers. Some serve a single power, some are born with an affinity for one or the other. I am a Child of Stone, and the heart of Lar-Khana is stone beneath that silver skin. Stone can't keep its secrets from a Gryagi forever."

"You'd try that?" The Silver Wizard looked dubious. "I know what happened to your gaze-bowl before, when you sought Sir Raimon in it. That had no connection with the quake. Devra's got more patrols about than the human one Sir Raimon saw."

Mrygo was determined. "She sends her human patrol out at random. We saw no sign of them the other night, and there wasn't any evidence they'd been out for days before. She might be just as capricious about how she uses her other spies. I'll make my call alone, far from anyone else, far from camp."

"I don't like it. I feel the Powers of Air gathering in the skies above us, stooping like great birds of prey. They are wheeling in toward the Silver Mountain, pulled by the scent of blood, hungry, greedy, ready for more . . . the skies themselves grow heavy with so much magic. They'll break, and may all the other Powers save us from what they'll let loose on the land."

Master Kor raised his hand to touch the silk roof. It parted like a soap bubble's skin. The treetops overhead likewise bowed themselves out of the silver wizard's desired line of sight until Lar-Khana's peak, ghost-gray by moonlight, flickered into view. The black bit of uncovered rock still remaining stuck up into a sky where shreds of smoky cloud spiraled in toward it, draining the light from the stars.

Heron looked to Mrygo. The Gryagi did not seem to be afraid of what Master Kor showed or told him. Even if he had felt fear, it was his folk's way to keep it pent within. Master Kor too looked at Mrygo and sighed. He lowered his arm, and trees and tent-roof shreds wove themselves back into wholeness, undisturbed by the passing of a magic that never desired to disturb things as they were meant to be.

"Here." A cup of bright silver twinkled in his hand. "Use this for your spells if you're set on them."

Mrygo wouldn't take it. "Metal . . ."

"Metal may put her creatures off the scent of your magic, Mrygo, disguising it as something closer to their own. Try. It won't contaminate you."

Very reluctantly, the healer accepted Master Kor's gift. "I'll go back into the forest—"

"With me." Heron spoke up before his friend could protest.

"I was the first one who told you to seek Larya. If you run into trouble, I'm responsible. I must help."

"You're needed here."

"For what? Master Kor will tell my troops at sunrise that we're going to assault the Silver Mountain head-on." To the wizard he added, "Yes, that's right; head-on. If there's no stratagem sharp enough to get by Devra's eyes, maybe we should give her the one thing she won't expect: a straightforward attack on the mountain. We can't lie here doing nothing. We might not stop her, but we can distract her. If we're lucky, we'll buy time."

"Buy it with lives."

"Master Kor, that's all we've got to bargain with. If we don't harry her, she'll finish the peak and then we'll all die without having tried to fight back. I don't like this any more than you, but there aren't any further choices. I'm going with Mrygo now, to help with his seeking spells for Larya if I can. You once said you did well enough with Lord Prince Dammon's name before he came back in the flesh. If something goes awry, lead my men in his name again."

Outside, the night was bleeding away to slate and rose. Mrygo held the wizard's silver cup against his heart. "We don't have to go too far, my friend. Just far enough so that if Devra's minions are watching only the camp, they'll miss our seekings."

A wedge of light spilled onto the grass from behind them. Frog emerged from the tent and announced, "I'm coming too." Mrygo and Heron could just make out each other's faces in the ebbing blackness. Both expressions said, *I knew he'd come; I knew.*

They backtracked into the forest away from Lar-Khana until they reached a little clearing that Mrygo declared well-omened for his spells. A pool of crystal water bubbled up in an almost perfect circle of sandy bed, its sweet flow trapped in knots of stone, laced together with watercress and late violets. The Gryagi dipped the silver cup into the pool and set it down. The three friends knelt around it.

"Ophar, do you have your sword?"

Heron startled at the sound of his old name. He drew the weapon without a word.

"Lay it beside the cup." When that was done, Mrygo said, "Now reach into the pool and fill your hands with water, hold them above the hilt, and let it trickle down the blade."

"Into the cup?"

"The cup will be for my seeing, the sword for yours. I read many books in Khana, and one spoke of this means of summoning visions. You must try with me."

"I have no magic in me, Mrygo."

"So what? You don't need magic to see a summoning, just to make one. I don't trust a metal gaze-bowl, and we haven't time to find me another earthenware vessel that's glazed the proper way. Visions are like half-tamed birds that will come when you call, but only if the nest you've readied suits them. If what I call up won't come into my borrowed bowl, maybe it will find your sword a more hospitable perch. Frog will watch over both of us when I send out the spell. You watch the sword."

Heron felt foolish. A vision in a sword? The blade was narrower than the mouth of Mrygo's cup. What could he see in it? It was just a ploy to keep him out of the way or to keep him from bursting into howls of grief if Mrygo's vision showed Larya dead.

And if she were dead? He'd told himself many times that she was, but his heart refused to accept it. Dully, he scooped water into his hands and let the droplets fall onto steel. If the vision of death came, there could be no more room for lies.

The drips of moisture slid down the blade in threads of blue and white and sun. He watched their progress with a marsh brat's fascination for the fluid element bounding his birth and life. Light sifted through the leaves, a cool breeze blew, and the water drops seemed to respond and change under his eyes. They thickened as they fell, rippling into a strand of starry hair. Other strands twined with them, and others still, escaping the bridal combs that held them back from the face swimming up from the sword's blade—wisps and strands of Larya's iridescent hair ringing her face like a rain-fetch 'round the moon.

Larya's face . . . Heron's breath stopped as all of her came into the sword's sharp frame, and the smooth-walled prison cell where she and another girl stood speaking.

Soon it will be our turn.

The girl who spoke was older than Larya, or perhaps her flat, lifeless eyes made her look older. Her dress was torn open at the bodice and her bosom showed the marks of her own nails.

All of us, Kiara?

After so long, he had almost forgotten the sweetness of Larya's voice. It made him ache inside, yearning to thrust his hands into the heart of the vision and touch her. Already his fingers began to unclasp, letting the water flow more freely, but a hard pinch on his thigh made his grip tighten again. He tore his eyes from the seeing momentarily and saw Frog's severe look of reprimand. Unasked, the boy dipped more water from the stream and refilled Heron's dwindling supply while he looked back at the vision in steel.

Yes, Larya, all of us. When the next terrace is done, there will only be the pit of the summit to complete. That will be the end, and it will call for a grand slaughter. I just hope I'm one of those she kills for the terrace, not the top. The terrace sacrifices have always been clean kills.

But, Kiara . . . there are so many of us.

All the better for her. One or two killed at each terrace, sometimes more when she was eager to please those. I think she's saving the fairest of us for last. You'll be on the summit, then, but I'll be taken before.

You speak as if you don't care.

Kiara twisted the ring she wore on her betrothal finger and showed Larya its huge yellow stone. *Do you see this topaz? It was given to me by my lover—the handsomest lad in our village, and me so plain, the tavern-keeper's dowerless fifth daughter . . . it was the prettiest thing I'd ever seen and the finest. He said that's what I was for him: pretty, fine, precious . . . me!* She pulled the ring off and held it to the muted light of their prison. *When the queen's men came to take us, he tried to fight them for me, and he died with an axe in his skull. If I die too, it will only finish what began the moment they killed him.*

I know, said Larya sadly. *There was a farmer . . . a good, kind old man who was my foster father. When the queen's men came, he fought them, like your lover.* In a lower voice, she added, *And he, too, died.*

Kiara glanced at the ring once more, then let it fall. *Take it, Larya. You've made it easier for those of us Devra called away before this. I don't know how you did it, but I'd swear the touch of your hand made them—made them somehow sleep with their eyes open when they went to die. However she killed them, they never knew. Do the same for me when it's my turn. Take the ring. A friend-gift, for remembrance's sake. A short remembrance.*

Kiara, you shouldn't—let me give it back—Larya stooped for the ring. Her fingers touched the yellow stone, and all at once a shock ran through Heron's arms, a tingling awareness that made him gasp, seize his shimmering blade with dripping hands and raise it to his eyes.

"Too late. You've lost it," said Mrygo.

"Did you see the same in your cup?" Heron desperately wanted confirmation that it hadn't been a wish self-fulfilled, as in dreams.

"I got no seeing out of a silver vessel. I could've predicted it. That was why I put you to work and looked over your shoulder. Steel and water together—what better combination for you to use? You are Heron and Ophar, the water-bird and the Gryagi sword . . ." Mrygo gave a little smile. "You too have talents that might be worth training, my many-named friend."

"I—saw her. The vision was true."

"And grew truer. The girl with Larya didn't know one stone from another. It wasn't topaz in her troth-ring; it was amber."

Heron's brows went up, begging explanation.

"Amber. Once it oozed in golden drops from a pine's bark. It aged with time, like all living things, and became the yellow stone you saw. Larya knows what she has there. As soon as she knew, you felt it."

"What . . . did I feel?" Heron's arms were still prickling.

"The once-living drop of a dead tree's blood. A focus for earth-magic in the right hands . . . and inside Lar-Khana. Even if we don't find Sir Raimon and tell him that Larya's alive, we've still got good news to pass on. Let's go quickly. You were entranced by your vision longer than you know. The army's been rallying since daybreak."

Only half understanding, Heron accompanied Mrygo back to camp. There he found Master Kor already on horseback, aided by Lord Fiel and Captain Iskander, mobilizing the effective troops for action.

The men all cheered when they saw Lord Prince Dammon among them. Mrygo had no problem speaking privately to the silver wizard. No fighter had eyes for anyone but his prince. The prince himself noted how Master Kor's war-grim face softened after Mrygo whispered with him. He shouted for the army's attention.

"This is the battle that takes or loses all! Now is the moment that wins us back our prince's throne or leaves us broken under Devra's feet!"

"For Dammon! For Dammon!"

The battle cry went up, but not so loud or full of heart as before. Doubts had joined the prince's army since the day Lord Prince Dammon first came back to the slopes of Khana. Only some of the fighters now waiting to attack Lar-Khana had seen that wondrous return, but many more of the massed warriors had witnessed Dammon's mindless lethargy in Mar-Halira. There were others who had believed, like Decad Turgan, that a silver wizard with them meant some supernatural guarantee of safe passage. Then the quake had come and Master Kor had not been able to stop it. It was very hard to learn that great heroes and great magicians could be as human as the lowest cook's assistant in the baggage train; hard to learn, impossible to deny.

The diminished cheering died out more quickly, too. The prince's mount was brought and he rode up to join Master Kor at the head of the troops. "We ride!" he shouted, pulling back the reins to control the skittery animal. It was not his war-calm, familiar steed—that fine creature was dead. Many horses had been injured past the point of help in the stampedes, the prince's with them. Beliza's shield-sisters wept as they culled the lamed beasts from the herd and destroyed them.

"We ride!" Heron cried again. The clutch of dragon's claws clicked together on the silk noose around his neck. On impulse, he seized them and yanked so that the raveled cording snapped. He held the huge talons high, letting his army see them clearly against the fresh sky of morning.

"We ride as I once rode out to free this land of a monster! That monster was my sister's conjuring, but I slew it! The songs say I used an enchanted blade against the dragon, yet I tell you all that my own sword broke in that battle. It was my squire's blade that gave the killing blow! A common sword, and still it killed a dragon. *You* are my sword in this battle! And I swear to you all—I swear on the dragon's claws—that with such a sword to hand, there is no evil in this realm that we shall not destroy!"

This time the cheer went up again full of all its old belief and glory. Heron whirled the claws around his head and with a glad shout turned his horse's muzzle toward the Silver Mountain.

They rode out of the forest in processional formation. The wounded saw them off with hearty well-wishings and envious gibes because they were left behind. As soon as they could, on leaving the forest, they spread out into their separate divisions of foot soldiers, cavalry, archers, and spearmen, all going six abreast to meet whatever Devra might send out to meet them.

Nothing barred their way, either mortal or monstrous. The open space between the trees and Lar-Khana's silvered skirts could not hide any threats that men or Master Kor could sense. Scouts dispatched into the singed thicket where the Gryagi had begun their unhappy tunnel came back to report only one thing out of place.

"There's a dead man lying in the brush, my lord prince," the lead scout said.

"A Gryagi—"

"No." He shook his head emphatically. "Stark naked like that, there's no mistaking him for anything but human. And he wasn't in no cave-in nor fire. Throat's cut."

Heron dismounted. "Take me to him."

The dead man's skin was clean and smooth—another palace-pretty. He wasn't one of the men who'd gone with Master Kor and Decad Turgan to put out the small forest blaze, like Sir Raimon. He lay on his back with his head angled down like a snap-necked bird. The slash across his windpipe had been dealt by a master-fighter's hand, too quickly for much of a struggle.

Heron read the site for signs of what had happened. He spied a pile of rumpled cloth beside the corpse. Picking up the top piece and shaking it out, he said, "The tunic of a queen's man. No, not quite. The insignia's been torn off. This must belong to one of our own. Send for Sir Raimon."

A messenger came back, but with the second-in-command among the renegade queen's men. "Sir Raimon's not with us, my lord prince," the man said. He glanced at the body, then at the garment in Heron's hand. "That's not one of ours."

"This tunic—"

"The tunic's ours—cursed if we'll wear her emblem any more—but not the man." He looked back at the body, this time more carefully. "Huh. Guess I know him after all. We served in Mar-Halira together, but he was the queen's spitlick through and through."

Heron fingered the discarded bit of clothing and thanked the man before dismissing him. When he remounted, he said to Master Kor, "Mrygo told you about Larya?"

"If Devra hasn't noticed what the girl's got or what she's doing with it, Larya has a chance. Her gifts were great, although untrained."

Heron's mouth grew hard, remembering: children crying in the night, sweet songs of healing, and one child who never woke to cry again. "She got plenty of training during the bad times."

"For some things: healing, herbery, spells of growth, and lifesongs. The powers of earth are like their three brethren. They have their dark aspect, too. To their credit, I will say that most who master the nurturing ways of the earth-powers never explore beyond the light. Well, let's pray Larya finds a way to tap something more than a healing spell out of that ring. Who'd expect to find a focus for the powers of earth inside the fortress of the powers of air? Larya might be able to give Devra a nasty surprise—if she's got the time."

"Someone else is inside the mountain working for us too," said Heron. "Sir Raimon." He passed the discarded tunic to Master Kor. "He said he'd serve me in his own way. I saw signs that a patrol had come through the thicket recently. The man he killed must have been last in line, straggling."

"Killed him and took his place?" Master Kor pursed his lips thoughtfully. "Let's hope Sir Raimon entered Lar-Khana to serve you and not betray you, my lord."

Heron nodded soberly. "Let's hope so."

They rode on toward the Silver Mountain. Heron imagined that he would feel the evil centering there become more potent as he approached. The air might thicken, the ground under foot radiate invisible repulsion as the powers of air invaded the territory of the powers of earth. Instead, he felt only the normal sensations of a brisk ride across open country, and that was the most disturbing feeling of all.

The troops following him shared it. Lar-Khana's peak was imposing, its covering of silver marvelous to see, but there was no breath of magic about the place. The same natural freakishness that sets a priceless ruby to be found in a mud-wallow seemed to have been at work on this mountain, coating bare rock with precious metal on a whim, without the intervention of man. But malevolence? None. Just an all-pervading air of usualness that unhinged the nerves.

The closer they rode, the more this impression grew. Even when a scout holloed that the last naked jut of rock at the summit had also acquired a metallic skin, Heron felt no despair, could not feel that their rescue had come too late for Devra's fair prisoners. The malaise of false normalcy held him too tightly.

Lar-Khana's facade changed as the army approached. What seemed merely a long shadow down the unbroken metal-sheathed side became a black gap knifing into the mountain when the first riders came close enough to view it from a new perspective. Beliza's shield-sisters urged their horses to a gallop, riding past the prince and his vanguard, eager to confirm what their keen eyes told them.

"It's a way inside!" shouted the first to race back. "The mountain is open! The way is clear!"

That broke the tension. Heron loosed an unprincely whoop of joy and caracoled his horse before his warriors.

"My lord prince..." Master Kor's voice stilled the curvetting steed with eerie suddenness. "The way into the dragon's lair was also unguarded and free."

"And I came out that way again alive!" cried Heron. "Don't you think I know what it means for Devra to have left this gate unwatched? She's not afraid of us, and that's her mistake."

"With this mountain finished, she's got reason to be fear-less."

"Come, Master Kor, we only see one side of the Silver Mountain! If it were truly finished, would she bide inside? Not Devra! She's got a realm to retake from my people, a castle stronghold to recapture, vengeance to deal . . . she's not the kind to wait for her revenge."

"You may be right."

"Follow me, then, and see!" He spurred his horse ahead, and all the army raced after.

Up close, the crack in the mountainside proved too narrow for mounted fighters to enter. It looked like an irregular fissure in the rock—here broad, here narrow—meant to be wriggled through. Before Master Kor could call out the need for cau-tion—what a perfect place to station guards and pick off tres-passers one by one as they trickled in!—Heron had slipped through. Smiling, he popped his head out a moment later.

"I'll say it for you, Master Kor; I'm an idiot. I'd be a dead one now if not for Sir Raimon. This open gate's his doing, not Devra's; no ambush to fear. Come!"

The fighters poured through the fissure like a flood of sand. Their feet hit silver floors on the other side, slick beneath a film of grime. Twenty dead men in Devra's livery lay unmarked in the ample guardroom beyond the crack, their faces showing agony. Mrygo crouched to smell their breathless lips.

"Wine."

"Here's the pitcher," Captain Iskander said. His face looked back in reflection from the silvered walls, lit from behind by a row of torches burning low in their sockets. "My lord prince, would you come here and examine it?"

Heron wove a way between the corpses to the small alcove where Iskander warded his finds. "It's still got lees in it, but where are the goblets?"

Frog poked around amid the bodies, then announced, "There are some used goblets on the floor." He too sniffed for further explication, sticking his nose into the cup. "Smells like plain wine to me."

"A good poison wouldn't be so easily detected or who'd drink it, Frog?" Heron ruffled his page's hair. "Sir Raimon's been doing us all many favors. Let's not let him fight on alone much longer." He drew his sword and gestured for his people to come on.

One passage led from the corpse-strewn guardroom. It was broad but low-ceilinged, permitting the invading army to go four abreast and easing much of the congestion in the strait entryway. Dammon's fighters entered Lar-Khana one by one, each of them alone and secretly frightened. Once through the gap, after the sight of Devra's dead guardsmen struck their eyes, they banded together instinctively, relieved to be in the company of their shield-mates again.

The silver walls of that wide tunnel took all human noise and absorbed it like a tangle of rags. Then the passage ended, and even though each fighter felt his neighbor's shoulder against his own, he was once more alone.

Up and up soared the roof of the great chamber, up and up in a sweep of icy metal that still shone where it became only a hint of curve among the higher shadows.

Heron's chest knotted. He knew this place too well. He had awakened in a cavern much like this, under the dead weight of a slain monster, and believed himself dead. No torches burned, but a radiance throbbed out of the walls themselves to let men see and know how small they were, how insignificant each life. It was a cavern of the gray underworld, with the all-swallowing vastness of death, the adit to the land of shadows, Hori-Halira. It was done up in a festive wrap of silver, but the gift beneath was still a skull. The puny sparks of the vanguard's torches could do nothing to warm away the fact that every person saw his own face reflected as a ghost's in the encircling, pitiless metal mirrors.

Master Kor cupped his hands and blew into them. A fleecy rose-colored flame unfolded there, very small but very strong. Uncounted strands of it snaked out between his fingers and quested through the gloomy air until each touched one of Dammon's warriors. The fighters stood entranced, accepting the magic wires of flame, gossamer of an ancient silver spider's spinning. Airborne, made of fire, rippling like water, Master Kor's creation brought all the mothering warmth of earth in its touch—a magic kindling that united aspects of all the powers.

A thread of it touched Heron's chest, and the unnatural fears haunting Devra's silvered cavern fled. Lucid thoughts returned

and he shook off the slow, petrifying terror that otherwise would
have held him helpless in this huge chamber until it pleased
Devra to come after him. He looked to his right and saw Frog—
even Frog, who had grown up numb to common fears—wiping
cold sweat from his face.

"It's all right now," Heron said.

"But it wasn't," Frog replied.

A scout ran ahead into the darker recesses of the cavern,
something impossible a moment ago. He came back to inform
his prince that there were several branching tunnels at the far
end of the chamber and not a sign of life in any.

"She can't have sacrificed all her soldiers the way she did
the Surin Gryagi," Heron said, voicing his thoughts.

Coming up from the rear, Captain Iskander and Lord Fiel
agreed with him.

"How many tunnels?" the red-haired captain asked. The
scout held up four fingers.

Lord Fiel's face darkened. "And I'll be surprised if those
tunnels don't also split up into more, further on. What can we
do? If we split our forces now and split them again and again
as the tunnels divide..." Any man there with even a little
battle sense knew what Lord Fiel was thinking. Divide and
redivide even the greatest army, and it becomes no more than
single soldiers, easily picked off in whatever ambushes the end
of the tunnels held.

"No," said Heron. "Devra hasn't laid this labyrinth out to
kill us. Delay's more valuable to her now. She's trying to make
us afraid, to go cautiously through her burrows smelling an
ambush around every bend. For all we know, there's not a
single one of her men waiting for you, but the *possibility* is
going to slow you down until she's completed the mountain.
Then every surface of this maze will draw the powers of air,
and she won't need ambushes to kill us all, wherever we are."

"Then what should we—?"

"Run!" Heron commanded. "Run boldly through her tunnels, turn back if you meet a dead end, fight if you meet a
foe, but do it quickly! Cheat Devra of your fears, and you
cheat her of her most powerful weapon. Master Kor?"

"My lord?"

"Is there a spell you can work—like a seeing-spell, maybe—

that could unite us all inside this mountain even when we're separated?"

The silver wizard's eyes lit up. "A fine notion, my lord. And a possibility." He made a pass with his hands and a golden cloud splashed warmth through the cavern's cool, metallic light. It was a cloud of life, a cloud of birras that flew like wind-blown pollen to alight one by one on every fighter's shoulder.

"The first who finds Devra can dispatch his creature to bring the rest," Heron said, and it was as if the birras themselves relayed the message to the ranks of warriors who might not be within hearing range of their leader's words. Decad Turgan's spear blade and the swords of Dammon's other officers flashed to lead their separate troops into the mouths of the four passageways. Heron himself led the way into the leftmost tunnel.

As predicted, that tunnel soon branched off into three more, and the chosen passage of the three split into five. At each division, he lost men. Chambers of various sizes intervened along the way, every one filled with the same deathlight of silvered walls and floors and ceilings but otherwise empty. All the turnings he chose were likewise deserted. Heron ran on, not pausing to see how many still followed him, how many had gone off to seek the ends of other tunnels. He heard the echo of running feet behind him lessen as each branching claimed some of his party, but he never stopped to look back.

In that single-minded race, the old nightmare first lived in the Gryagi caverns returned. Once more he was the lost, nameless one who wanted escape almost as fiercely as he desired a name. Without thinking, his free hand drifted up to grasp the dragon's claw, their broken string retied around his neck. This time they brought back memories, not emptiness: A prince saying, *The monster's gone to ground in there. Will you follow me, Heron?*; a young boy's proud, *I'm coming with my brother. I'm not afraid, my lord prince*; a woman whose face had been aged by the hard life of the marshes, who did not know how soon that life would end, saying, *You may make a fine fortune for yourself in Mar-Halira, my son, but for me I only ask you have an eye on your little brother. Look after my Frog, Heron, and go blessed.*

Her face rose, and the way under foot rose too. Heron fought to find traction on the metal sheathing beneath his boots. Farther ahead, where the slope became still steeper, the light changed. The birra on his shoulder sensed this and flew toward it, chirring with excitement. It soared at a blur of bluer light that should have been a wall and plunged through.

Heron stopped dead, and the man behind ran into him.

"What's the matter? Why did you stop?" It was Mrygo.

"My birra—I think—" The small golden animal swooped in through the circle of blue again and fluttered to land on Heron's shoulder, filling his ear with urgent cries. A fresh, cold scent clung to its fur, a free scent that had nothing to do with dank, silvery caverns. "It's a way out, a way into the air."

The Gryagi's underground eyes measured the gap through which the birra had flown. "High up that wall. It must've been a natural part of this mountain, too out of the way to be worth sealing off."

"I can reach it . . . with your help."

The healer grinned. "So I'm a stepstool now? Fine." He knelt and offered his linked hands as a stirrup. Heron set his right foot lightly in the sling and leaped for the opening. His fingers clutched the lip of it, but there was no purchase to be had on the silver-coated stone. His hands slipped, and he fell back.

"Maybe I should give you a boost, Mrygo. You're smaller and lighter."

"We Gryagi go down easier than up, but we can try it." Mrygo's words proved themselves true as he too missed his grip on the silver-slick sill. He landed with an angry exclamation. "That does it. I'll send our birras back to bring others to help us."

"Help us to what, Mrygo? What if there's nothing beyond this hole? We might distract just the party of men who are following the true trail out of here. Link your hands, and I'll give it another try."

Mrygo sighed and looked very put upon. "If it is just a hole to nowhere, you'd better have a gentle tread."

"That's stupid." Frog came up out of the flickering shadows. A birra fluttered just ahead of him, an obvious guide.

Mrygo looked at Heron. "I should've known we couldn't

lose him." He rested one elbow on his knee and asked, "If our way's so stupid, I trust you've got a better one?"

For an answer, Frog drew his knife. It was a thick blade, not too sharp, good for hacking lumps off a loaf or sawing coarse bits of meat from a joint, though if the joint proved tough, teeth would do a better job. The young Gryagi held the haft in both hands high overhead—a rank amateur's style in a knife fight. But the seasoned arena fighter knew better than that when facing living opponents. His target was the cold, unliving wall beneath the day-lit hole.

Frog gave a wild battle yell and charged. Mrygo and Heron both dived in opposite directions, thinking he'd gone insane. The knife struck metal with a harsh scream. A shallow gash followed the blade's course without breaking the silver skin. Frog took a deep breath, yowled his battle cry again, and made a second gash running at right angles to the first. His knife broke where the two lines met, but the buckled silver made a small nodule protruding from the wall.

Frog rubbed it with his thumb and announced, "Toehold." Clearly, he thought it unworthy of further comment.

Heron picked himself off the floor and rounded angrily on the younger Gryagi. "Are you out of your mind? Don't you remember what happened to your kin when they touched the bottom of Lar-Khana?"

"You touched the walls when you went in," Frog replied with a shrug. "Nothing happened. And if something would've happened this time, it was only me touching the knife. You'd've been all right."

"Only you..." Heron stared at the boy a moment before wrapping him in a powerful embrace. "Brave Frog, brave little brother, don't let me lose you a second time to your stupid bravery!" Frog snorted and broke free, giving Heron an indignant look that made him laugh. "Sorry. You're a fighter, not a baby to be hugged like that, and you're a greater hero than I'll ever be. I won't do it again."

Frog lowered his head and mumbled, "I didn't mind... much."

Heron stepped back to view Frog's handiwork. He stood just under the hole and sprang for daylight. His leap was short but high enough for him to use Frog's toehold for the one extra boost needed to clear the sill. Clinging low to the ground, he pulled himself through and looked around, then stuck his head back into the hole.

"We're on the summit," he hissed. "There's a rill of rock just outside that we can hide behind and scout further." He extended a hand to help Frog and Mrygo join him. Only when the three were together did they creep for the small silver-covered crest and peer over.

"By the Seed . . ."

In times long lost, Lar-Khana had not been a quiet peak. The huge bowl that now caught the sun's fire in its blue-white surface had once held true earthfire of molten rock. Quakes had shaken the land around the mountain's flanks long before there was a Devra to call down the powers of air. All that was finished. Only the dead cone was left, extinct forever. It formed a natural amphitheater, and at the nadir of the bowl Heron saw a company of queen's men struggling to move a block of strangely pocked black stone into the position their commander indicated.

Their commander. . . . He held one arm above his eyes to shade them from the reflected sunlight. A cloud shifted, bringing shade, and he was able to lower his arm. His raven hair was streaked with gray and his face was haggard, but he still could bark orders imperiously. At first glance, nothing much seemed to have changed with Lord Maldonar.

There were seven arches ringing the silvery bowl where the queen's men labored. As Heron watched, he saw more soldiers issue from six of these. At Lord Maldonar's order, some of them added their strength to that of their fellows, laying their weapons and helmets aside to do so. A wide iron ring—cruder gray against all that silver—formed the platform that would hold the weird black stone.

"Scrape the mountain's skin, and you'll die for it!" Lord Maldonar bellowed as they pushed on the heavy boulder. The men paused, then arranged themselves differently and began trying to lift the stone free of the ground. It took the aid of still more queen's men, stripped and disarmed, to convey it that way, but at last it was accomplished.

"Good." Lord Maldonar looked as satisfied as if he'd done all the work. He turned toward the seventh archway, the one that lay almost directly across the bowl from Heron's hiding place. A solitary queen's man stood there, guarding a square of rock still uncovered with silver. The metal patch that would fit that empty space was held by a weeping young woman. Heron recognized her from his seeing of Larya: Kiara, still not dead.

"All's ready. Tell her!" The guard saluted and ducked into the tunnel. Heron did not wait for him to reappear.

"So many tunnels that lead to the top!" he whispered. He beckoned for his birra to come to his hand, praying that the bit of golden fluff in flight would not be noticed by any of the eyes below. "Bring the others," he breathed into its tiny ear. "Bring your kin, but tell them to fetch my men by the nearest way. Seven tunnels end here—they must all be near at least one of those. Go!" He blew the birra back into the mountain. "Mrygo—"

"I've already given mine the same message," the Gryagi said softly. "And Frog's birra was gone before I finished with mine. We'll have them here soon."

"If they didn't all get lost up too many dead ends," Frog said with his odd old-man's voice. "Or find any traps on their way."

"And in the meanwhile"—Heron touched his sword—"we are here."

The queen's man reappeared. A stately woman in midnight-blue and silver came after him, hair falling in waves of night down her back. She wore a crown that sparkled whiter than an ice storm and carried a short sword of mixed metals—black and gray and blue—in her hands.

Lord Maldonar lost all of his self-command. He hurried to greet her as obsequiously as the lowest door-porter. "Is it as you wanted it, my queen?" He gestured toward the iron-enthroned black rock.

Her blue eyes flicked over the exhausted men and the object of their efforts. "You had better hope it is," she said coolly.

"I tried to arrange it exactly as you said."

"If you'd honored my wishes half so carefully before this, my lands would all still be my own, foolish mice would not now be creeping to their deaths in my mountain, and my daughter—"

"I came to you as soon as the castle fell, my queen!" Lord Maldonar raised his hands before his face to ward off blows that did not come. "If you'd have given me the men to retake Mar-Halira then, I could have saved Lilla."

Not a line of emotion appeared to wrinkle the beauty of Devra's smooth face. "In the end it will not matter, Maldonar. I will have other children. Let us see how well you've seated my altar."

Bowing rapidly, looking much relieved, Lord Maldonar guided Devra across the basin to the black stone. She lay her sword down and ran her hands over its pitted surface lovingly.

"A pledge," she said. "A promise. This altar stone was a gift from the ones I serve—a sky-gift that fell to earth just as they will descend when my work is finished. An appropriate place of sacrifice . . . *if* it is correctly placed and secured." She gazed at Lord Maldonar meaningly.

"My queen, I assure you . . ."

"You shall. Aglora! Avana! Acova!"

Three black shapes took form from the air around Lord Maldonar. Slitted green eyes burned, fanged mouths gaped in greedy joy, claws sank into the proud man's flesh. He never had time to realize fully what was happening. The three took wing, yanking him up with them to hover just above the altar stone, then dropped him so that he fell bent backward over it. Devra had her sword, and cut deep. Lord Maldonar's blood puddled into the honeycombings of the rock.

"I shall have more children, Maldonar; I alone." She made a small sign to the three demons and they sprang eagerly to feed. The queen's men in attendance whitened and would have turned away, but Devra marked their squeamishness and would not allow it.

"You! All of you, attend! Schoolboys who run from their lessons are whipped, but I have worse in store for you than a whipping if you fail to learn from this. You are the last of my queen's men—the select, the chosen! I didn't choose you for weak stomachs and soft hearts. When I have secured my powers in fullness, you shall be the first messengers of it . . . the first *human* messengers." Her exquisite lips curved in a coy smile.

The queen's men who had moved the newly blooded altar stone were still exhausted from their work. Their limbs ached, their backs burned with strain, but they did as their queen commanded. They remained on their feet and watched as Aglora, Avana, and Acova devoured the last scrap and splinter of Lord Maldonar. It was not a tidy feast. When they were done, they took to the air again, casting oily shadows over the faces of the witnesses below.

"That was well done," said Devra to her men. "I am pleased that when I chose you to survive, I chose rightly."

One of the men swallowed hard and dared to ask, "My—my queen, we don't understand... when was there a choosing?"

Again that milkmaid's smile. "That answer waits for you in the guardroom, Hanos. That is where I sent your companions to... wait until the final summons is complete. Your fellow queen's men, you see, came to me in delegation after the latest thank-offering on the terrace below this and asked me whether I thought the Powers of Air might not be satisfied with fewer sacrifices. I have saved the most lovely of our captives for this moment, but those guards... they coveted the beauty I'd set aside for the great powers. They thought it a shame... a pity to waste such lovely flesh that way. They asked that rather than the rewards I've promised you all, I instead let them each select one of those last girls to wed and I could do as I liked with the leavings. Table scraps for the powers of air, as it were." The notion made her give a small, close-lipped laugh.

"They asked that... of you, my queen?"

"I see you are a sensible man. They were not so wise. I gave my consent and had them await their brides in the guardroom. I even asked our late Lord Maldonar to bring them all some cheering drink while they waited. They didn't care to witness what we shall do here. Wine improves courage."

The man's face slowly changed as he began to comprehend what sort of wine this dark queen of his had sent to her impudent servants. She enjoyed seeing how well he understood her without the need for more words, and simply nodded. "I promised to send them brides. If they wed them here or in Hori-Halira, what does it matter? Now let us proceed. It's impolite to keep such devoted bridegrooms waiting."

Behind the rill, Heron whispered, "*She* poisoned her own men?"

"She bottomed the Silver Mountain in Surin Gryagi bones," Mrygo hissed back. "Why not add a layer of her own race? I suspected something like this. Where would Sir Raimon have procured such a subtle poison as killed those men?"

"We didn't see their faces. Do you think that he too? . . ."

"No. He'd play the loyal queen's man here and offer Devra no chance for suspicion. Look; look carefully at the guards down there. See if you can't spy his features under one of those helmets."

Heron tried, but saw nothing. Sir Raimon was not one of the men who had wrestled with the altar stone, for they had laid off their helmets and for him to do that would have meant instant recognition and death. However, there were yet some helmed men in the basin, their faces blocked from sight.

As Heron searched for Sir Raimon, he saw the queen cross to where Kiara huddled, still hiding her eyes from the gruesome spectacle of Lord Maldonar's death.

"Get up girl. Give me that."

Kiara kept her head down, passed the thick silver plate to Devra without looking at her. The queen gave her a box on the ear that knocked her over.

"Stupid cow. Get up, or I'll use your blood to cement this last bit into place."

Kiara rose heavily to her feet. Devra patted her clasped hands in motherly fashion. "That's a good girl," she said. Then she struck the girl full on the right temple with the heavy square of silver. Kiara fell soundlessly, a flower of blood opening above her cheek. Devra laughed and set the last of Lar-Khana's silver skin.

"Bring the others," she said to the helmeted guard who waited beside the seventh tunnel.

It was not long before the queen's command was obeyed. The guard ducked into the passage and returned with four of his fellows. After them came the women, more than a score, attended by more queen's men spaced in ragtag fashion among them. Heron could not be bothered with counting how many queen's men came, how many were already in the summit's bowl. Among the throng of dark heads and fair and auburn there was only one whose hair was white as the northern star for which she was named. Larya was there, alive, walking between two other girls.

Alive? The living only walked like that in restless dreams. The girls on either side of her did more than accompany, they literally held her up and urged her forward. Every step Larya took was stiff and forced, her arms bent awkwardly at the elbows, her hands balled to unbreakable fists, and her eyes . . .

When her nightmares still ruled her and the ghosts of Gryagi dead came with the moon, that was the way her eyes had looked.

Devra's angry voice made the women bundle together like a flock of storm-frightened doves. "Carif!" A queen's man whose emblem bore an additional mark of office saluted his lady. "Carif, are these all the queens's men?"

"My queen, all but those you said were to wait . . ."

"There are more than *these*, surely?"

Carif took a gulp of air. "My queen . . . we are invaded."

"So?" Devra balanced her shortsword on the palms of both hands, looking as if she sought the same sort of vision Heron had found in his own steel. "The mice are bold. But my men will harry them as they climb. They will not be able to fend off what I call down, not with the best swords in the world." Her eyes sparkled. "Not even with my brother's sword beside them."

Her look passed once around the bowl, then drifted upward. Heron shuddered, certain that she saw him or sensed his presence. So that was Devra. He remembered her from his days as her brother's squire in Mar-Halira. She had always been beautiful, nothing like the grimy marsh-folk women, even outdoing her flowery attendants by comparison. With shame, he recalled how desperately the lowly squire had loved and worshiped Devra's beauty, never caring whether good or evil lay beneath its surface, scorning the plain-faced palace serving women because they could not equal the peerless Devra.

Bitterly, he admitted how just it was that Larya had chosen a handsome queen's man over the scarred and ugly one she knew as Ophar.

If Devra did know he was there, she did not show it. Her eyes completed their sweep of the bowl and came back to rest on her men. "Bring the first offering." Two of the armed guards stepped forward to cull a victim from the crowd of maidens. The girls pulled back, but it would only buy them a little time. One by one they would die, that was sure. Survival told them another story, however, and even if their retreat meant just a few minutes more of life, they would fight for that precious scrap of time.

Only Larya did not pull back. Only Larya stood there, apart, fists clenched, eyes seeing nothing. The guards gripped her arms and led her forward without a struggle. She walked in a trance and obeyed the slightest guiding touch. They made her stand before the queen, who looked beguiled by this apparently docile sacrifice.

"Who are you, pretty one?" No answer. Devra nodded. "Mindless, poor child. Fear snaps the ribbons tying mind to senses." She clicked her tongue in feigned pity. "You unhappy thing. I must heal you quickly. So lovely, and such magnificent hair!" She ran the star-white strands through the fingers of her left hand, her right holding the sword. "How they will thank me for a gift this rare and wonderful!"

At a gesture from the queen, her guards led Larya toward the stone. Heron's muscles tautened. He started up from his hiding place. Mrygo seized him, wanting to hold him back. He turned on the Gryagi, killing rage in his face. His sword caught sunlight, wanted blood, and would have severed his friend's hand if Mrygo had not released him.

But before he could go to Larya's aid, a shout rose from the basin below. A figure in a queen's man's uniform tore itself from the ranks, blade bared, and threw itself against the small mass of people by the altar stone.

"Larya! Larya!" Sir Raimon's voice was tight with despair, and desperation made him strong. He killed the guards who held her. Others leaped forward to the defense of their queen, but a sword stroke takes a moment. They would not reach the altar stone in time, not if Devra truly needed their protection.

Devra saw the sword raised against her and laughed. The basin of the Silver Mountain's summit caught the laughter and amplified it. It beat in waves of sound that rolled away and back again redoubled. The sword in Sir Raimon's hand began to vibrate with a metallic whining that mounted to a screech as spell-sound burst the blade to threads of steel. Unarmed now, Sir Raimon was still desperate. He launched himself barehanded against the ice-crowned queen.

Devra had a lady's hand, a small, white, soft, delicate thing. But when it closed around Sir Raimon's throat, he felt cold iron clutch his windpipe. Only a lady's hand, yet inexorably it choked breath from the body of a warrior. His sight grayed, darkened. Devra's figure swam with shadows over his eyes. She blurred and her image multiplied. When the moment of death came, it gave the knight one final vision: It was not Devra alone who killed him, but she and her three demonic minions all inhabiting one skin. Four pairs of eyes—three green, one blue—mocked him as he died.

The killing took less to do than to tell. Sir Raimon dropped when Devra released him. Larya had not moved. Two fresh guards came forward to replace their slain comrades and convey the girl to the altar. They gazed at their queen with renewed respect as they fulfilled her wishes.

"We begin," said Devra. Three black shapes took to the sky from her body. They circled high as she raised the shortsword and made her invocation. Heron still stood in plain sight on the ridge, but no one spared a glance anywhere away from Devra. Not even when a runner burst from the mouth of one of the tunnels and panted out the news that fighters were coming—almost upon them all!—did any witness to the sacrifice dare to stir.

Devra's chant ended with a hoarse cry, a summons that set the demons circling faster until they formed a ring of darkness with tendrils trailing up into the farther reaches of air. The darkness began to glow, to shine with doomlight, and thunder from an empty sky shook Lar-Khana.

The dragon's claws on Heron's chest rattled as Devra turned her sword's point to rest above Larya's heart.

A whir of golden specks exploded from four of the seven tunnels. Birras swooped and fluttered around the heads of the queen's men. They swatted at the little beasts, who dodged with ease. The birras were not fighters, but forerunners. Boots on silver floors boomed from the tunnel mouths. Lord Prince Dammon's troops had come.

Devra's concentration broke, but only for an instant. Her guards had broken from their places to draw steel and fight off the invaders. The fools! As if she were not about to call down things that could rend her enemies, body and spirit! She spared a moment to curse the guards' stupidity as they fought and died on the swords and spears of Dammon's army, then lifted her own blade high.

This time Mrygo did not hold Heron back. Mrygo himself, Frog with him, sprang from his perch and slid down into the basin behind his friend. Devra raised her eyes to see her brother's face descending.

"Aglora! Avana! Acova!" Fear and surprise made her command go shrill. The three circlers in the sky paused, then two maintained their swift whirl, calling in their masters. One of their number would be enough to deal with this. The demon plunged in a slash of fangs and talons.

Frog's sword rose to meet it, and Mrygo's, and Heron's with theirs. Iron forged to steel was always pure enough magic to cut the life out of shadows. The monster shrieked and tried to rise. Frog's sword, stuck in a wing's joining, was torn from his hands. The demon shook itself free before a skyward leap, but Frog leaped first, his dagger out, and knotted bare toes and fingers into the wires of spun blackness on its chest. A quick climb, a quicker thrust of steel into the demon's shining eye, and Avana perished.

A wailing fell from the two surviving spirits. Devra's face was bone. "You should have stayed dead, my brother," she hissed in Heron's face. He struck at her, but she parried his sword with a trained warrior's skill. The thick blade of her weird weapon cut a notch in his. "The Silver Mountain is done! The powers of air wait for my word." She caught every stroke he dealt coolly, never bothering to play more than a defensive game. Other duels clashed all around them. Her cold, perfect fighting style made him sweat just to see. He pressed his attack, which only made her fend it off without bothering to mount an attack of her own.

Only once, when his blade met hers and skidded down until hilt met hilt and breath met breath, did he see her eyes lose their calm. "You . . ." It came in an awed whisper. "You aren't Dammon . . ."

Abruptly, she bounded away, up onto the altar stone where

Larya lay, and flung her head back as a wild, final incantation to the waiting powers of air soared from her throat.

"Come! Come! Come, O my masters! And more blood than this will come to you in sacrifice!"

Her blade fell as Heron's rose to shield Larya. The two swords met, and in the instant of their crossing, Larya sat bolt upright, one fist now open and a golden light blazing from fingers that grasped the amber heart of earth-magic. The blaze engulfed them all just as a rolling wave of night more horrible than any cavern could hold descended on the Silver Mountain.

Gold erupted against black as in the birth and death of stars.

EPILOGUE

In Mar-Halira

Warm earth lay under her back, cool silk over her naked skin. Larya opened her eyes. Master Kor's serene dark face bent over her, smiling gently, haloed by a softly swaying crown of willow leaves. Other trees stood nearby, some still touched with gusts of blossom. She raised herself, eyes alight with the wonder of still being alive. More trees came into view, and stiffly orchestrated arrays of flowers, and the formal fences of clipped hedge that marked her bower for part of a man-made garden.

The silver wizard spoke before she could utter a word. "You've done better than I hoped, my dear child. I didn't look for your recovery for at least two more days. Mrygo's notion of having you rest here, no mattress between you and the earth, may take the credit for it. We'll see." He lifted her hand to his lips. "Welcome back, Mistress Larya, daughter of the earth-magic. In the name of the council, I welcome you to Mar-Halira."

"Master Kor, Mar-Halira you say? How did I come here? What happened?"

A brisk familiar voice—a voice Larya thought never to have heard again—cut off the wizard's explanations.

"Don't you dare start in spinning her long tales and tiring

her out, my poor babe!" Farmer Rycote's wife—now his widow—came to embrace Larya. Her hair was grayer and thinner, her face more seamed, but all of her glowed with contentment as she pressed her cheek to Larya's silver hair. "Just look at you!" She began fussing with the silk coverlet. "I call this disgraceful! A weedy rag like this for covers and not a bit of soft between you and the hard ground? Fine bunch of pennypinchers this council will be, and what do you need 'em for?" She snorted and took a pin from her own dress to turn Larya's scanty cover into a makeshift garment.

"That's better. Leastways it'll do until you get a proper dress at home." The old woman sat on her haunches, hands resting on her thighs, and studied Larya with head cocked to one side. "Praise all the powers, it won't be so long as I thought to make you fit again. Maybe even marriageable before the year's out or harvest's in. After all you've suffered, poor sweeting, a nice home of your own's what you need, and a man to keep you, and a gown pushing out with your first babe growing."

"My good woman!" Master Kor succeeded in getting in a word by shouting. "Where have you been keeping yourself? The songs of the Silver Mountain are already on the roads two weeks, and every soul with ears to hear knows what Larya did on that cursed mountaintop. Yet you go nittering at her as if she were a common rustic! She is a mistress of the earth-magic! Her presence on the governing council will be just as important as Lord Fiel's or Captain Iskander's or—"

"Or your own?" Rycote's widow had endured too much ever again to be the woman who had trembled when a silver wizard entered her humble home. "Piffle. She's my darling girl, and she's coming home with me. The Holy Ones bless our good lord Prince Dammon, she'll want for nothing. Five fine, strong farmhands he's sending to work poor Rycote's land for me, may he live eternally for his kindness. We'll prosper, and she can pick and choose her man from the best families."

"A mistress of earth-magic—"

"My girl, she is, and—"

The willow branches rustled. A hugely grinning gray face popped through. In his fresh white robes, Mrygo came to squat Gryagi-fashion between the bickering wizard and farmwife. Rycote's widow gave a little squeak of alarm to find herself so close to one of the fabled Children of Stone. It was clear she wanted to reach out and touch him, equally clear that she wanted to sidle away.

"What's all this? They can hear you all the way up in the council chamber." Real joy filled his voice as he added, "Larya, you're healed."

Larya clasped his hands. "Mrygo, please tell me what happened. Master Kor started to, but—"

"I'll do it. Master Kor wasn't even there."

"My party took the tunnel that was the longest route to the summit," the silver wizard said. "We were just emerging from its mouth when the fire fell."

"Fire . . ." Larya touched her brow. "I don't . . . I remember taking Kiara's amber ring and entering the trance state. I needed to read the earth's currents so that I could learn the spell to save us. It was very hard. There was so much silver all around, so much dead metal, and the amber was small, old. I had to trace its life back through all the ages until it became a drop of sap again, and the sap a part of the living tree. Only then the power came so fast! I didn't know if I could control it. I fled back up the paths of time, and the magic followed. I flew back inside my skin and felt it flood me . . . oh, what did I do with it? Mrygo, what did I do?"

"You killed that witch, that's what!" snapped Rycote's widow. "And too neat a death for her, I say!"

"I killed Devra?"

"No," Mrygo said quietly. "Not you alone."

Larya looked inside herself just as she had looked without eyes into Kiara's amber. "Ah," she said when remembrance came. "He killed her."

Rycote's widow began to nod. "That's right, he—"

"Ophar killed her."

"*Ophar?!*" It was a shriek that turned to sarcastic laughter. "You *have* been ill, sweet lamb. Ophar's been gone years. Where'd you scrape out such a notion? *Ophar!*"

Larya began to cry. The sight of her tears stilled the farmwoman's mirth.

"Sweeting, I know how you miss your brother, but you know he must be dead by this time. So many things have happened to our land since the night he ran off, and him no more than a farmer's lout, though if he'd stuck by us, he might've done some good for himself and my unhappy man."

Larya cried harder. Mrygo spoke in muted but authoritative tones to both Rycote's widow and Master Kor. "I think you had better go now. Master Kor, the council waits for you." To Rycote's widow, he said, "One of the farmhands who was to go with you has decided to try his luck in service here in Mar-Halira, but there are several others interested in the job. They are in the castle stillroom. Will it please you to speak with them now? You might as well. Larya and I shall require privacy. This is the first chance I've had to examine my patient since she's awakened."

He spoke so reasonably that there were no objections. As soon as the others had gone from the garden, Mrygo knelt to dry Larya's tears. "So you saw his true face," he said. "You are a mistress of the earth-magic—a great one—to pierce a silver wizard's illusion."

"Was it . . . Ophar?"

"His real name is Heron. He has his true self again. True as it can be, I suppose, after all the layers of spell and falsehood that've covered it." Briefly, he told her of the many illusions and deceptions the silver wizards had worked on the marsh-brat squire who had become the hero-prince of legend.

"He was there, with a sword in his hand, fighting Devra. I saw him through a blue light, a rippling blue and green brightness all around him. And there was blackness too, and then the blast—"

"All is balance in the world," said Mrygo. "All the powers are strong, but harmony is stronger. Sometimes one power is ascendant, sometimes another, but never for long. The balance endures."

"You speak like a silver wizard."

Mrygo held up a pinch of his white robes. "So I shall be . . . perhaps. There was only one hope that could have kept me from the halls of Khana once our war with Devra was won." He let the soft material fall back into its naturally elegant folds. "That hope ended one night soon after we brought you here. You talk in your sleep, did you know that?" This last was said with a grin that belied the sorrow in Mrygo's eyes.

"What did I say?"

"That you loved Ophar—Heron, now; and once upon a time, Prince Dammon."

"Go on, Mrygo. Tell me what happened on the Silver Mountain."

"Devra called down the powers of air and they came, more out of greed than obedience. For your part, Mistress Larya, the powers of earth surged up at your command. There should have been a long battle of your two sorceries then. The struggle between power and power, vessel and vessel, is always long and always tears apart the land that hosts it. Two powers can war for a long time without disturbing the balance."

"How long—how badly did we hurt the land?"

Mrygo dared to frame her face with his hands. She did not object, but he knew that there was only friendship to be had from her. There had never been anything more. The name she had uttered in her fever dreams was merely final confirmation of what he had suspected.

"The land is safe. The realm is untouched. There will be no more bad times, Larya. A third vessel was there, a child of the powers of water, which we so poorly understand. How can we, when running water has the strength of magic that still waters don't? There is only one mighty river in this realm, few streams; the rest of us drink from pools or wells. But the powers of water still abide and choose their own."

"Ophar." She could not think of him by another name yet. Mrygo nodded. "A vessel. But is he more?"

"That I don't know. At any rate, to be a vessel was enough. Three powers—earth, water, air—met in anger on Lar-Khana's summit and the balance was wrenched, the harmony destroyed. It could not be. The powers of fire felt the pull of their three brethren powers. They came. For that moment, all four powers clashed. Equals in might, they destroyed nothing but the spells that summoned them before subsiding into their assigned kingdoms again."

Larya asked, "Nothing more?"

Mrygo sighed. "The silver skin that made Lar-Khana has been burned away. Men who live near its slopes watch the skies, daily expecting them to rain silver."

"But Devra is dead."

"Yes." He shifted in his white robes as if still growing

accustomed to their weight on his body. "Devra is dead. Those of us on the summit when the powers fought were blinded, but Master Kor and his party were not. They disarmed Devra's troops and helped the rest of us keep calm until our sight returned. When it did, we all rushed to the altar stone. You and Heron lay to either side, unconscious, but Devra's body lay across the black stone." He stared hard at Larya and added, "Her head lay at its base. His sword was edged with blood."

"And . . . Heron? Where is he? Have you healed him too?"

"He recovered two days before this. As for where he is now . . ." Mrygo stood up wearily and offered her a hand. "I promised him I'd keep it secret until he was gone, and I would've done it if you'd delayed recovering an extra day. But I know your feelings, and I've never been able to deny you anything, Larya."

Very gently, she kissed his mouth. "I do love you, Mrygo."

"I know. Not as you love him, though."

"No. Not as I have always loved him."

Frog stood glaring at the red-haired stranger whose face was disfigured by a long white scar. The big man continued to make the last adjustments on the fisherman's raft of bundled reeds while the Gryagi boy growled warrior's curses under his breath. When the craft was done and pushed to ride at tether on the current of the great river, the man spoke.

"I can't take you with me, Frog. I don't even know where I'm going."

"Why go, then?" It sounded savage, but the terror of loss underlay Frog's question. "Stay here! Master Kor will give you back Lord Prince Dammon's face again and you can be king if you want!"

"I don't." He said that in such a way that there was no possibility of discussion. "The land is free, there's a council to rule it and laws made already to see that new councils will always govern the people justly. The holy places in the mountains can thrive, the gifted souls be taught by Master Kor and his apprentices. There will be more than one silver wizard to keep this realm safe in the future. There is harmony among the powers. Dammon did everything he came to do. Now he can disappear back into the songs and legends." He gazed at the beckoning raft. "They don't need him anymore."

"I need him." Frog's voice trembled. "I need you."

Heron gathered him into his arms and gave him a powerful hug. The young Gryagi scrubbed at his cheeks when his friend set him down again. Heron reached for the silk cord around his neck and lifted it over his head.

Four dragon's claws dangled and clacked together, but only one was black. Some separate magic had flowed through them when all the powers met atop Lar-Khana. Red as fire, blue as water, green as the sweet births of earth, the other three claws gleamed like small miracles in the misty light rising from the great river. Heron dropped the looped cord over Frog's head.

"Wear them for me, little brother. Keep them for me, if I should return. If not, be the hero if this land should ever need another hero. I haven't your bravery, little Frog—Frog the demon-killer! No true hero runs away."

Frog removed the last traces of tears. He held Heron's look resolutely. "I won't run away. Captain Iskander said he wants me to join the garrison at Mar-Halira, and Decad Turgan says that once he gets his land-grant from the council, he'll take a wife and I can live with them. And maybe I'll go with Mrygo to Khana! I can be a fighter and a farmer and a wizard and—and—whatever I decide!"

Heron chuckled. "Then fare well, little brother, and may all the gentlest aspects of the Powers guide you." The Gryagi youth simply bowed his head and gave the lie to the saying that no true hero runs away. Heron saw his racing figure out of sight before turning to the raft.

Someone was on it.

"What are you doing here?" He sounded angry, an anger born of guilt for the clandestine way in which he was stealing out of the land where he'd been born.

"I am coming with you, Heron." Larya folded her arms across her chest. She sat cross-legged on the bundled reeds, a sack of provisions and a second sack of borrowed boy's clothing beside her. Her tunic was wet from the underwater swim she'd made to gain the raft unseen, and her silver hair was a sheet of flat strands against her head, but she maintained her dignity. "Mrygo told me that Heron is your true name."

"Mrygo told you too damn much," Heron snarled.

"Don't be hard on him. I've given him an awful task. Since we are going away, he must explain my reasons to Farmer Rycote's widow. I wish him very well, and I hope he'll make her see that I had no choice in the matter."

"You've got no choice but to stay behind. Why should you come? I'm going where my name means nothing, where even Lord Prince Dammon's name means nothing! You have no place there."

"I have a place and a name wherever you go, Heron; Ophar; Dammon—a new name. I am Sirta now."

"Sirta . . ." He had not heard that word often when he toiled in the Gryagi mines. He had scarcely heard it at all during the spans he had passed among the children of stone, but he knew it. He had learned its sound and clung to its meaning as a talisman of something wonderful that might, through miracle, be his someday; someday when he was free.

It was the Gryagi word for love.

"You love me?"

"You refused to see it. I didn't know how to make you see. I agreed to marry Sir Raimon because I hoped the shock of it might make you open your eyes and give up your scheme to leave us." She dropped her voice. "You left me anyway."

"Not willingly. But—I was—I am—how can you love me?" he blurted. "You're so beautiful! More beautiful than anything I ever . . ."

"You are beautiful." She stood and with outstretched arms invited him to board the raft. "Believe me now or later. Love me as I love you or never love me at all. I will wait. The earth-magic is all change and waiting. And nothing you can do or say will make me leave you."

Half in doubt, half in fear of waking, he picked up the two saplings he'd cut to be the raft poles and handed one to her as he stepped aboard. They did not exchange another word until they were well into the center of the great river and the current began to draw them off toward the unknown lands.

The only witness to their departure was a little boy who lived in one of the marsh folk's wattle huts. His mother's despair, he was an indifferent fisherman and only cut reeds when he needed to replace the latest toy sword he'd made himself. As he paddled in the shallows, stabbing at invisible monsters, he saw the sun-brightened mists part as the raft sailed by. Babbling madly, he sprinted home and dragged his mother out to see it too.

"Mama! Mama! I never saw such a big 'un! What is it? Who'll it be?"

The marsh woman wiped her doughy hands on her apron and tried to make out the dwindling craft, but the sun was diffused by the mist, so her eyes were dazzled. She thought she saw a lady prettier than any other and a giant of a man, but their features and even the colors of their clothes and hair were muddled by the tricks of light.

Her boy was growing restless, tugging at her skirt, splashing water into her wooden clogs. "Mama! Mama! What can it be?"

"What can it be, my love? Why, that's our lord Prince Dammon sailing off. They're singing how his work's done here and sleep's what he wants most. Did you see the lady with him? Ha, you've got keen eyes, son, and you'll make a fine fisherman one day if you settle down. Well, that's Lord Dammon's lady, the lady he serves in the far lands where heroes sleep. She's come back for him now, but if we ever need him again, he'll return. He'll return and gather heroes to his horn."

The child looked at his mother in awe, then turned to watch the raft. Gilded to a royal barge by mist and sunlight, it slipped from view. The boy raised his reed sword and swore, "When he comes back, I'll serve him, Mama. I'll be a hero, too."

"Dreams." His mother laughed, and would have stroked his head, but a warning smell of flatbread burning on her hearthstone made her run back into their hut. Children must dream, but bread would never wait on dreams.

He did not see her go. With upraised sword, he stood in high salute until the mists that had taken the hero wreathed his blade with gold.